A Falling Friend

by Sue Featherstone and Susan Pape

LAKEWATER PRESS

About the Authors

Sue Featherstone and **Susan Pape** are both former newspaper journalists who between them have extensive experience of working in national and regional papers and magazines, and public relations.

More recently they have worked in higher education, teaching journalism to undergraduate and postgraduate students – Sue at Sheffield Hallam and Susan at Leeds Trinity.

The pair, who have been friends for twenty-five years, have already written two successful journalism text books together: *Newspaper Journalism: A Practical Introduction*; and *Feature Writing: A Practical Introduction*.

Sue, who is married with two grown-up daughters, loves reading, writing and exploring the cycle paths near her Yorkshire home. She blogs about books at http://www.pinkbicyclenooks.com

Susan is married and spends her spare time walking and cycling in the Yorkshire Dales and on the east coast, and playing the ukulele.

ISBN-13: 978-0-9944511-5-6

To Geoff and Kevin

'But we, poor souls to hope and fear,
Are never of our joys secure.'

<u>'The Fall' Lord Rochester</u>

Chapter One

Teri

It was thanks to Peter Heron's love of television that I met Dan Caine.

Peter, dean of the faculty of English and Media at this former polytechnic turned University of Central Yorkshire, is not just a corporate know-all, but a TV and radio tart too. Which means, as well as talking a lot of mumbo-jumbo business-speak about better empowering the core, he goes into orgiastic mode whenever there's any topic or issue on which he can spout in the media. He loves being on the radio and wakes at some unearthly hour on a Sunday morning to do the local station's 'What the Papers Say' slot. And he adores television and will do any interview about education and academia, anytime, anywhere. Come to think of it, he will do *any* interview. Full stop. And, after an appearance, he never washes off the studio make-up.

Somehow, Peter got to hear that Ridings Today, the regional teatime news programme, were considering a new Friday night book show, a late night, intellectual discussion featuring a group of hoity-toity types arguing in detail about the latest hardback releases. Peter nearly wet himself at the thought of it. He could just see himself as chairman: choosing books, directing debates and generally being erudite, witty and wise.

'Who else could do it?' he asked us in the senior common room. He could talk about nothing else. Oh, the books he would feature. The guests he would invite. Would Ridings Today's budget stretch to Salman Rushdie, he squealed. 'Really, Peter,' Lee said to him over coffee. 'It's Ridings Today. They're more interested in sixty-five-year-old grandmothers getting pregnant by IVF, water-skiing piglets and talking horses than intellectual discussion. The only books they'll ever feature are by footballers or Big

1

Brother contestants who happen to come from Yorkshire.'

But Peter wasn't to be put off and, shortly afterwards, all of us from the faculty were invited to his 'Widening Involvement and Networking in Industry' events. There would be red and white wine and nibbles and, surprise, surprise, a producer and several researchers from Ridings Today.

Chrissie, from admin, who'd had to issue invitations, informed us Peter had also invited some hack from the evening paper, the Evening Leader, and a spotty, bog-brush-haired youth from the radio station to make it look less telly-orientated and more wider-media-friendly.

Peter tried to tell us earlier the event was to 'cross the cultural divide between the televisual and the academic in the digital age', but no one was in any doubt as to the main aim: to see our Peter playfully quizzing Salman in front of a devoted Friday night audience of book lovers.

Peter commandeered the producer from the start leaving two researchers and the bog-brush-haired youth – all of them young, gawky and slightly embarrassed – standing together drinking. I went over to talk to them on the basis they looked about as young as my Level 1 students, and, therefore, I should be able to recognise some of the things they might say. But after a desultory stab at something to do with one of the latest up-and-coming bands and the lack of decent music venues in this part of Yorkshire, I could tell they were only there because their various bosses told them to come and, being young, trendy media types who had nothing in common with this crusty bunch of lecturers, might as well get as much of the university's cheap plonk down their necks as they could.

There were tight little knots of people dotted about the room, but, because I'd only recently joined the university and didn't know many of them, I didn't want to risk getting stuck in conversation with a load of boring idiots. I spotted Chrissie gazing up at a man who had his back to me. He had light-brown hair (not mousy), which was long and floppy and curled cutely over the top of the collar of his pale blue shirt. Broad shoulders, slim waist and a nice, tight bum in black jeans. Mmm. But I couldn't see his face, and it would be too obvious for me to go over to talk to them. Besides which, Chrissie looked enthralled. Huh, I thought, she'll be dragging him off to the admin office supplies room before the night is over.

I looked around for Lee. She was talking to two other lecturers – Stella

2

Lastings from History (what was she doing here?) and a tall, dark-haired man I vaguely recognised, presumably having seen him in the senior common room. I went over, and just as Lee was about to say something, I butted in and said conspiratorially to no one in particular, 'Isn't this a farce – having to entertain these media tarts just so our dear dean can sit in a studio reading autocue?' I noticed Stella's plump little face light up in delight at some secret joke, no doubt. Then I turned to the man and asked, 'Which department are you in?'

He looked at me with a slight smile. 'I'm not with the university.'

I suddenly felt very hot. Stella giggled, and Lee looked at me with an earnest expression.

He grinned. 'I'm with the media tarts.'

'Oh. What do you do?' I asked already knowing the answer.

'Oh, this and that,' he said. 'I'm Dan Caine, television presenter, but I mostly sit in the studio reading autocue.'

At least he had the grace to smile.

My embarrassment was plain; I was lost for words. Lee, bless her, stepped in.

'Oh, Teri,' she gasped. 'As usual – say what you think without thinking.'

Dan laughed. 'You know,' he said, 'it's amazing the number of people who believe that's all I do: turn up at six o'clock to look pretty in front of the cameras and read whatever's put in front of me. Of course, it's not as intellectually demanding as being an English tutor in a former poly.'

Ouch!

'Of course not,' Lee said, leaning towards him in mock conspiracy, her red wine sloshing in the glass. 'Anyone could write the sort of stuff you tell us about on the news: "One person was ever so slightly injured today when he was hit by a yodelling parrot riding a bicycle along the inner city ring road".'

'Well, at least we're on to the big stories,' laughed Dan, 'which we wouldn't be able to do if we worked your hours.'

'Our hours? What could you possibly mean?' Lee was getting into her pseudo-indignant stride and clearly loving every minute of it.

'Don't work Mondays as you're travelling to university from your bijou cottage in North Yorkshire,' Dan said. 'Do an hour's teaching on Tuesday;

read an improving book for the rest of the day. An hour's lecture on Wednesday and possibly a tutorial – although be careful, as you don't want too many students cluttering up your day. Hour's lecture on Thursday – perhaps – and then bugger off in the afternoon as you've got to get back to the bijou cottage and prepare for Friday's "research", which, if I'm not mistaken, is usually into some existential nonsense about "The Creativity of the Sense of Soul in Mankind and the Media: Representations of the Skateboarding Duck in an Enlightened Digital Age".'

'I'll have you know there's a lot of research to be done into skateboarding ducks,' Lee said.

I do believe the girl was flirting.

I looked from her to Dan and back again. I hadn't seen Lee quite so animated in a long time. She was rosy-faced and giggly, and enjoying every minute of this encounter with a famous star. They were clearly playing with each other. Would they make a good couple, I wondered; Lee in her black leggings and faux-denim smock top, clutching an orange straw shoulder bag that she'd bought at the Oxfam shop, her hair in need of a decent cut (again), and an expression of open, honest worship on her face. Dan, meanwhile, was smoothly good-looking, and wearing a light-wool Italian suit in a colour that can only be described as pale biscuit, a dark blue t-shirt and what looked like expensive Hudson antique-leather brogues. Not for him the comfy old slip-ons that Lee preferred. In fact, that was Lee: comfy. You could go to her with any problem and know the encounter would be comfy. There'd be wine supped while sitting on her comfy sofa in the comfy little house her dad built for her; there'd be a comforting ear and comfortable words of comfort spoken.

Examining the expression on her face (as she imagined herself in the arms – or bed – of Mr Dan Caine), could I see her living it up in the fast lane as a television wife? All those media parties, mixing with the celebrities, spending the vast fortune these telly types earn? Actually, no.

Growing up, her family and friends were either Irish or first-generation Irish-English and they seemed to move exclusively within an Irish-Catholic community that never went beyond their own 'little Ireland' in the middle of our northern city. 'We were so poor,' she used to tell me before going on about some Irish bus conductress who never took any money off her mammy for the fare. 'We Irish had to stick together.' What bollocks! I'll tell you something, I'd have sacked the bloody conductor for theft.

But that so-called 'poor' upbringing has rubbed off into adult life; she won't spend her cash on decent clothes, despite my attempts to persuade her. 'What's wrong with this?' she'll ask, smoothing down the floral A-line skirt she often wears, or pulling a long, white t-shirt over her black leggings. A row of beads and a hastily-tied silk-effect scarf round her neck and she's ready to meet her public.

She's not so much let herself go as never got hold of herself in the first place. She has chin-length, brown (mousy) hair, which she shoves behind her ears. She then dabs some hand lotion on her face telling herself it's as good as face cream, and that's the beauty routine done.

I've tried to educate her. I give her all the little sachets of lotions and potions that come free in whichever glossy mag I pick up, and I once gave her some vouchers for her birthday for Vanilla Pod, the beauty studio I use. She went and Sasha worked her magic – cut her hair, put some colour on it – and Lee came out looking fab. But she moaned she'd never be able to blow dry it the way Sasha did and, sure enough, next morning she was back to the sticking-it-behind-her-ears routine.

Of course, I am totally qualified to give Lee this beauty advice. People tell me I'm good-looking and have a good figure. They're always asking how I stay so slim. Well, you lumps, the trick is not to shove cream cakes down your face and to get off your backside every now and then. The number of people I see in the senior common room tucking into chocolate eclairs because it's so-and-so's birthday. They tell themselves that 'one little cake won't hurt', but I tell them it will be a couple of seconds in the mouth, three days in the stomach and forever on the backside.

Lee? I think she's living the 'I'm Irish and poor' dream. But she's clever and she's popular with the students. The rest of us lecturers know it, and as a second rate, former poly that's trying to be a grown-up uni, we're damn lucky to have her and, frankly, I don't know why she stays.

But no, she's not really media-wife material. I'm not saying she's not glamorous or anything, in fact she's quite pretty, but she's not exactly knock 'em dead gorgeous, which I suppose you have to be to be married to a well-known television presenter. Or am I being shallow in my thinking here?

5

And there we were: Lee flirting like crazy with the only half-decent looking man in the room, and the only half-decent looking man in the room thinking I'm a loud-mouthed idiot.

I peeled myself away from Dan and Lee to visit the loo and repair my lippy, and on returning to the dining room, I saw Lee talking to the floppy-haired guy in the tight black jeans at the other side of the room, and Dan now commandeered by Stella Lastings (what *was* a History bod doing here?). I tried to give Stella a wide berth, and not just because she was a size eighteen and needed wide berthing. I couldn't understand why someone who teaches History was so caught up in the present, as in staff room goings-on. There was no subject to do with anything or anyone in the university that she hadn't got some tale to add to the drama. If she couldn't find any fresh gossip, she'd make it up. She once started a rumour that Lee was having an affair with Mike Orme, Peter Heron's deputy, on the premise that the speed at which information flows accelerates in direct relation to the strength of the rumour; i.e. the more likely a piece of gossip, the faster it would spread through the faculty. And although nothing could be more unlikely than Lee having an affair with anyone, let alone someone who wore knitted tank tops, this particular rumour spread rapidly. Secretly, I think he'd been quite flattered so many people thought him capable of pulling Lee.

I was told the story by another lecturer shortly after joining the university and thought it odd Lee never mentioned it. When I tackled her, she became defensive. 'You shouldn't worry about petty gossip,' she said. 'It's all in the past; water under the bridge.' But I was so angry with Stella I determined to get revenge on Lee's behalf. The next day, I put it around to anyone who'd listen that Stella was having an affair with Frank, one of the porters. At lunchtime I gleefully told Lee, but her reaction was not as I expected.

'Oh, for God's sake, Teri,' she snapped. 'Don't be so malicious.'

'It's just a bit of fun,' I told her.

'For…just for once, Teri.' Then she stomped off.

She must be having her period, I thought.

Back in the Peter Heron soiree, Stella was doing her squirming act for Dan Caine. She was pretty with silly blonde curls, but large, and she squirmed in a girlish way when talking to men as though she were an insecure six-year-old. Having a visceral dislike for women like that, I couldn't bear to watch. I know that's judgmental of me, but why do girly women think squirmy/flirty is attractive? Men apparently fall for it.

The alternatives were to join Peter Heron and the Ridings Today producer, or barge in on Lee and the mystery man. Funnily enough, something about Lee's demeanour stopped me. She was having what looked like a really intense conversation with the guy. I'd question her about it later. I wandered over to the window thinking I'd stare out of it until a polite length of time elapsed and I could leave.

But then I became aware of Dan's reflection in the glass and of him standing behind me.

'You know, I really do more than just read autocue,' he said, adding, 'No, I spend a lot of time in make-up getting tarted up.' That glimmer of a smile. So smug yet so sexy.

'Look, I'm sorry about earlier,' I said.

'No problem. As I said, people are always making assumptions. It goes with the job. If my viewers see me on holiday or on a day off, they come up and say things like, "You're going to have to run if you're to read the news tonight." Ha ha.'

'It must be difficult.'

'Well, it makes shopping in Morrisons tricky. People look in my trolley and tell me I shouldn't buy so many biscuits as I'll get fat and then the telly won't want me. Or total strangers slap me on the back because they think they know me and they puzzle about how we know each other. And then they realise it's because they recognise me from the telly and get all embarrassed – and somehow it's my fault they're humiliated as though someone with a recognisable face shouldn't venture outdoors and put temptation in the way of the viewing public.'

'Do you get people squirming up to you because they want to be on telly themselves?' I asked, looking in the direction of Stella Lastings. Dan followed my gaze.

'Not a lot,' he said. 'But I do get propositioned by some women. They don't exactly throw their knickers at me – oh, how I wish – but as good as.'

'She didn't proposition you...?' I nodded towards Stella who was busy shovelling nibbles into her ruby red lips.

'Not exactly,' Dan said. 'But she asked me what my favourite position in

7

history was.'

'What did you say?'

'Right here and now,' he replied. 'But talking of that, I have to dash. I'm reading the late-night bulletin tonight. But, hey, why don't you and some of your colleagues come down to the studio in the next couple of weeks and see the programme go out live?' He grinned as though visiting the TV studios would be the highlight of my year. It would be for Lee and Stella, but the highlight for me would be seeing Dan again.

'That would be lovely,' I said.

'Just ring the studio and ask for Doreen at Ridings Today – she'll sort out the details,' he said, then drained the last of his red wine, put down the glass and strode off, waving goodbye to his producer and anyone else watching him go.

Spotting Lee still in conversation with the mystery man, I stepped in her direction only to find Mike Orme barring my path.

'Ah, Teri,' he slurred. Oh, God. He'd had too much of the free booze. 'Glad I caught you,' he said, reaching out a hand to place on my arm but, in doing so, slopped some red wine down the front of his blue tank top. I couldn't help noticing the jumper was pilling quite badly. 'I just wanted to make sure you're okay with the new university initiative...? "Your Success Starts Here".' He grinned triumphantly.

I wanted to ask which numbcluck came up with that one but decided it was likely him and probably diplomatic to just smile sweetly.

'Very good, Mike,' I said. 'I'll try and work it into one of my Rochester lectures.'

'Oh yes...Rochester,' he said. 'Er, I notice you're planning on keeping Rochester in for all levels of students? Do you...er...feel he's still appropriate for...?'

'Sorry, Mike. Got to go. Can we talk about this later?'

I dashed out to my car, found my mobile, looked up the Ridings Today number, rang and asked for Doreen.

And that's how I found myself two nights later sitting in the gallery of Studio One watching the live transmission of Ridings Today, with Dan Caine coolly and smoothly – having been made up like a media tart – reading the news from the autocue. I'd asked him to make some sign on camera to acknowledge my presence.

'Use your right arm to scratch your left ear,' I said, 'then I'll know you're thinking of me.'

'I think I'll just gaze at you via the camera, if that's all right,' he said.

Chapter Two

Lee

Here's a sight as rare as hen's teeth: Teri making a complete and utter fool of herself with a bloke, Mr Dan Caine, no less, chief autocue-reading media tart at Ridings Today – her description, not mine.

He took it very well – clearly not cut from the same up-his-own-backside cloth as the other luvvies who'd graced Peter Heron's previous social gatherings. Peter is ever so slightly star-struck and, despite all the evidence to the contrary, remains convinced that anyone who's appeared on TV or – at a pinch – radio, or who simply writes for the local press, is a cut above the rest of us. His little drinks parties are supposed to raise the university's profile within the local community, but I'm not convinced. They're lacklustre affairs – an astonishing number of these demi-gods seem surprisingly ordinary, even dull, out of the media spotlight. The only exception, if I'm honest, and it almost kills me to admit this, is Declan O'Brien, news editor of the local newspaper. He must've been born kissing the Blarney stone because he has more charm in his little finger than most of Peter's guests have in their entire bodies.

If you detect a note of cynicism here, you're absolutely dead right. After a long day of teaching and marking, with a bit of admin problem-solving thrown in, who in their right mind wants to spend a couple of hours clutching a glass of cheap plonk and making polite conversation with people only marginally less interested in you than you are in them?

Tonight I was ravenously hungry as well. And, no offence to the university's catering staff, but their canapés barely lined the bottom of my stomach. God! I could've eaten a scabby donkey – and still asked for more, please.

Teri, bless her, provided a welcome diversion from my aching feet and rumbling tum. Not to mention Stella Lastings, who was fishing for information. Dan Caine, standing next to us, was trying to look interested – and failing miserably.

'I suppose you and Mike work very closely together since your promotion?' Stella asked.

Daft question. Of course we did.

'Very closely,' she added with undue emphasis.

Good heavens. What was she insinuating?

'Is there anything you can tell us about your latest project?' She leaned forward conspiratorially.

Yes, lots, but I wasn't telling. Not the right time – she'd have to wait, just like everyone else.

'I wouldn't tell a soul,' she promised.

Hah, I thought.

Dan was clearly not enjoying the conversation and turned with relief as Teri joined our little group, jumping straight in with her tactless witticism about media tarts and autocue. She realised her mistake as soon as the words escaped her mouth and blushed scarlet – which was a departure from her usual nonchalant insouciance. Normally, she'd have just laughed it off. But tonight she seemed tongue-tied. I glanced from her to Dan and back again. And then again at Dan. Was there something I'd missed? He looked – sorry, Dan – an ordinary enough sort of bloke. More my type than hers. In fact, I'd have expected her to make a beeline for Declan, who was the only halfway attractive bloke in the room, and was currently listening intently to something Chrissie was whispering in his ear. Not like Teri to resist a challenge – she'd have taken great pleasure in snaffling Declan from right under Chrissie's nose. But, no. Tonight she was squirming with embarrassment. If I'd have been Dan, I'd have been charmed.

In retrospect, it would've saved all of us a lot of heartache if I hadn't come to her rescue with a light-hearted quip about skateboarding ducks. But

I did, and Dan, to his credit, responded in kind. I suddenly realised Dan had forgotten about Teri and was flirting with me. Flirting with me? I'd have been chuffed to bits if it wasn't for the little matter of the previous evening's positive pregnancy test. That had been a bit of a bombshell. Me? Pregnant? I was pretty surprised myself. And pleased...I think...I must've been feeling a little reckless – that's the effect pregnancy had on me, and I leaned flirtatiously towards Dan and whispered something in his ear. He roared with laughter, and Teri – ungrateful creature – stomped off in the direction of the loo.

It was the highpoint of the evening – and, yes, it wasn't much of an evening. Once I'd disentangled myself from Dan, I headed off for a quiet word with Mike. It was early days, but I thought the sooner I told him the 'good news' the better. Fat chance. Every time I headed in his direction, I got waylaid by someone else. First Stella, complaining about the inappropriately tight-fitting dress Teri was sporting; then Chrissie, drooling over Declan, who'd charmed the literal and metaphorical pants off her; and, finally, Declan himself, who tipped his champagne flute amiably in my direction.

'Hey, Lee. Long time no see.'

Yes, thank God.

'You've cut your hair – the fringe suits you. New colour too – makes you look pale and interesting.'

Dear God, was he flirting with me? The bastard just can't help himself. 'Yes, I've cut my hair – the pigtails went when I hit puberty.'

'Highlights?' he asked.

Bah! They were supposed to be a subtle hint of colour. Even Teri hadn't noticed. How come he had?

'I'm a connoisseur,' he said modestly.

Tell me something I don't know. But he lost interest and returned to the subject of the pigtails.

'Ding-dong. Next stop.' He mimed the action of pulling a bell rope. And grinned. For a brief moment I relived the rush of fury my seven-year-old-self had felt every time he surreptitiously tugged my plaits and whispered provocatively as we knelt, heads bowed in prayer, in school assembly. It didn't matter how carefully I edged myself at opposite ends of the line-up, he always inched himself into position behind me and, at regular intervals, gave a little tweak of my hair ribbons. I hated him with the sort of passion supposed to be reserved for the devil and all his works. I begged Mammy to let me cut my hair, but she wouldn't hear of it. 'Long hair is a woman's crowning glory.' God knows where she got that from, probably St Paul – he has a lot to answer for where Catholic women are concerned. Even sweeping my hair into a more fashionable ponytail didn't make a difference. If anything, it was worse. There was better purchase on the long flowing tail. 'Ding-dong. Next stop.'

If I'd had brothers I might've been more used to boys and their almost pathological inability to resist teasing such a ready-made target. Certainly, it was fortunate Declan was the only one who 'got' the bell-stop joke. And that he confined the ding-dong to assembly. He sat behind me in class too so could've made life a misery if he'd really tried.

'Oh, Lee,' he laughed. 'You were always so predictable. And those plaits were such an open invitation.'

Dear me. If I hadn't spent practically every waking minute of my primary school years praying he'd one day rot in hell, such candour might've been attractive.

'Which it would've done your soul good to have resisted,' I observed.

'But I did,' he protested. 'Never more than half-a-dozen pulls in any one assembly.' I couldn't help myself and laughed with him. 'Now Lee, tell me, who's the glamour puss talking to St Michael.' He inclined his head in the direction of Teri, who was clearly distracted from something more important by Mike Orme. Bet he was telling her about his latest initiative. I didn't need to see her face to know she thought he was talking a pile of bollocks. She was probably right.

'St Michael?'

'He's dressed head-to-toe in M&S own brands – or have they dropped the St Michael label?'

'Never you mind!' I had no intention of facilitating a romance with my friend – even if she was more Versace than Per Una.

'How's Marnie?' I asked. 'And the kids?'

He waved airily. 'She's fine. The kids too – we've got another little one on the way.'

13

'So your interest in Teri…'

'…is purely professional.'

Oh, yeah. Tell that to the fairies.

'I'll give you a call,' he said and walked away.

He was back a few minutes later. 'I don't suppose you have your friend's number?' he asked.

Now that's a daft question. 'I do, but I'm not giving it to you.'

'Why not?' He seemed genuinely puzzled.

'Because…' I spluttered.

'Oh,' he said, comprehending, 'because I'm married?'

That might have something to do with it.

'Don't let it worry you.'

I opened my mouth and closed it again, lost for words.

'And don't keep opening and closing your mouth like that,' he chided. 'You look like a demented goldfish.'

And, with that, he tipped his champagne flute in my direction again and walked away. He was back two minutes later. No peace for the wicked, I thought.

'By the way –' he said.

'What now?' I interjected.

'I forgot to say I was sorry to hear about your Grand-daddy. He was a nice chap. You must miss him very much.'

Yes, he was. And I did.

Declan gently touched my arm. 'It was a good send off,' he said.

Yes, it had been. The church was packed. Tears filled my eyes. Grand-daddy had been a loving, lovely man. 'You were there?'

'Of course,' he said. 'I wrote the obituary.'

Oh. It had been a generous eulogy, paying tribute to a hard-working Galway-man who'd come to England as a penniless immigrant and started a one-man odd-job-building business, which Daddy, his son-in-law, joined and helped turn into the thriving Harper Homes it is today. Both Grand-daddy and Daddy became leading lights in the city's business community and, more importantly as far as they were concerned, prominent members of the diocesan Catenian circle.

'I didn't know,' I said. 'Thank you.'

14

'No worries,' he said and tipped the champagne flute again. 'I really must go and get a refill.'

I blinked away the tears, remembering the funeral and later the wake at the Irish Club in the city centre. Mike had been there representing the university. I was grateful to him for taking the trouble.

'I'd say it was my pleasure,' he said, 'but I wish it hadn't been necessary. These events are never pleasant.'

Empty platitudes. But just what I needed to hear. Daddy was comforting Mammy, and Fliss had her husband Charles. I had no one and had never felt more vulnerable.

And that, in a nutshell, is how I ended up in bed with Mike.

Chapter Three

Teri

Lee doesn't think much of my academic achievements and, compared to hers, they are lacking in certain areas.

When we first met at sixth-form college, she was a quiet thing and a bit plump and mousy. But I encouraged her to cut her hair, buy some new clothes and come out with me looking for boys (shame it doesn't work as well now we're older). But then, hey, we were seventeen, and the world was waiting for us.

We had fun, but there was always something holding Lee back; as if she was ever-so-slightly disapproving. For instance, when I managed to get off with the good-looking bloke and left her with his friend, she was annoyed. 'You just grab whatever you want and leave everyone else behind, don't you?' she used to say. 'You don't care what happens as long as you're okay.'

Her Catholic upbringing, I suppose.

Although her dad is the Harper of Harper's Homes property development and her parents have this fabulous five-bedroom place in the Alderwood area with a couple of Mercs outside, Lee's never really shed her Irish-Catholic mentality; that chip on her shoulder about being an 'outsider'.

After A levels, Lee and I went our separate ways. I didn't quite scrape the grades I needed to go to our first choice university, but Lee did – and she went. I didn't quite scrape the grades to go to my second choice university either and ended up at a teacher training college, an old-fashioned, backward-looking establishment on the northern edge of town. A large, rambling Victorian creation, squatting on the edge of open moorland, the college was a throwback to an age when 'nice young gels' took their training to be primary teachers ever so seriously.

While Lee sailed through university getting a First, I struggled. I didn't settle to studying, but did meet Jazz, the lead singer in a local rock band, who was a wild, rebellious layabout and the perfect antidote to life as a primary school teacher. But I grew bored of Jazz and the college and left at the end of the first year to go travelling. When that palled, I did a short catering course and had a succession of cheffing jobs.

Returning to my old hometown, I noticed my old college hadn't managed the transition to the twenty-first century. The grim, old building had been demolished to make way for a massive new Harper Homes development of luxury four- and five-bedroom executive homes.

Bumping into Lee, the brainy bugger had completed an MA and was now installed as a senior and well-respected lecturer at the University of Central Yorkshire.

'You should go back to studying,' she said, dismissing all my adventures, 'and get a proper job.'

I wasn't so sure. I didn't think any university would take me. In my thirties, I was older than your average student, and my A-level qualifications were not what you would call A star, rather, lowly Cs and Ds. But the University of West Riding uttered a lot of guff about allowing applicants of all backgrounds and persuasions to join an 'inspiring and vibrant community' where individuals could enjoy a 'liberating and exhilarating' experience, so I enrolled and found myself as a student again.

It was one morning literature session that changed my life. The lecturer, Vic Brennan, burst in, did a theatrical wave of his arms and declaimed, 'Restless he rolls about from whore to whore...' That was one way of getting the attention of sixty-or-so Level 1 English Language and Literature students who'd congregated to hear about the doings of John Wilmot, the 2nd Earl of Rochester, and probably the most controversial poet within the restored court of Charles II.

I was hooked. I love things to excess and Rochester, the Restoration

17

libertine, was excess all access points. He abducted a wealthy heiress, had more than several mistresses and spent much of his time roistering and boasting about it. He gambled. He drank. And he wrote the most deliciously satirical and obscene poetry; some of it about the king of whom the accusation about rolling from whore to whore was directed.

Fabulous stuff.

When I graduated with a decent enough 2:2, I went on to do an MA – on Rochester and the complex emotional and sexual nature of the man and his work, of course – and then spent the next couple of years doing half-hearted supply teaching at various schools before getting bored and jacking it in.

I was out of work and, although my allowance was still coming through from Dad by way of the family steel mill, which kept us afloat financially, it wasn't as regular or reliable as it could be and even I recognised I'd have to get a job.

I spotted a notice about the Association of English Educators announcing an AEE bursary for a research project – thirty thousand pounds was up for grabs for a researcher, working in higher education, to produce an academic volume of up to eighty thousand words on a character of their choice from the Renaissance period. There was some small print about why that period had been chosen – something to do with a bequest from an authority on the 1500 to 1700s who died tragically in a car crash, and even more waffle about why it was being left up to the applicant as to whether they elected to concentrate on a writer, poet, sculptor, painter or musician. Right up my street, I thought, downloading the application form. And I could do with the dosh.

I filled the application form's question about 'Why this particular character?' with a treatise about Rochester raising interesting points about the circulation of literature in that historical period and whether what he was circulating was poetry or doggerel, paying particular attention to the elements involving sodomy, buggery and incest, believing I could put some intellectual gloss on Rochester's putting flesh on, into and through flesh. I find people aren't so shocked by these things if they're done in the name of art.

The only problem with the application was I wasn't working in higher education, so I left the 'current academic employment' question blank and thought that, by the time they called me for an interview, I'd be in work and hey ho.

I wasn't entirely convinced the lecturer's job I eventually got teaching Victorian Values in Manuscript at the second rate Mid-Wharfevale College was what the bursary minders at the AEE had in mind. But three months after applying for the bursary and not hearing a thing from them, they emailed me to ask not 'if' but 'where' I was working. So I told them, quite honestly, Mid-Wharfevale College, in the certain expectation they'd never have heard of it but nevertheless deem it suitable enough as a place of academic learning on which to place their precious cash.

Confident I would soon be thirty thousand pounds richer and the bursary would allow me to give up Mid-Wharfevale and its Victorian Values and spend a year simply researching and writing (and shopping), I rang Lee and offered to buy her a drink to tell her about it.

She said, 'What a coincidence. I was just about to ring you because I have something important to tell you, but didn't want to discuss it over the phone.'

Someone might think I was intrigued, but, honestly, I don't get too excited when Lee has something important to tell. It could be she was about to say she'd met a new man and it was mad, passionate sex all night long, but this is Lee we're talking about.

'Don't tell a single soul,' she said over the latte I bought her. 'But there's a vacancy coming up at our place. One of the English lecturers is leaving, but it's all very hush-hush because the job's not been advertised yet. I thought if you got in touch with the dean of our faculty, Peter Heron, and had a quiet word, you'd be top of the list when the advert goes in. What do you think?'

I told her about the research bursary, and she did her famous slightly-doubtful-but-concerned-and-caring face and said, 'Well, you could mention that you're working on a major research project, which presumably you'd continue with even if you didn't get the bursary? Our research quota is a bit low, so they'll do anything to up it a bit.'

'Oh, thanks,' I said, laughing. 'You mean I'd get the job because I'm the only one around doing any research?'

'Something like that,' she said.

The interview at the University of Central Yorkshire for the position of Senior Lecturer in the Department of English, within the Faculty of English and Media, went smoothly. In fact it was a foregone conclusion I'd get it. When I looked round at the other candidates sitting nervously on sofas in the carpeted corridor outside Peter Heron's office clutching their folders full of CVs, lecture plans and notes, anyone could see I was the best person for the job: cool, confident and better looking than any of them.

I'd done as Lee suggested and contacted Peter Heron who, surprisingly, didn't ask me to 'pop in' and see him for an informal chat as I'd offered but said there were protocols and procedures which had to be followed, and he would facilitate a response once I'd applied in the usual manner following the guidelines as stipulated in the advertisement for the position. All very formal.

On the day of the interview, we applicants were ushered one by one, by admin girl Chrissie, into Peter Heron's office where he sat at the head of a large, rectangular boardroom table in a single-breasted, three-buttoned, dark grey jacket and slim-fit trousers, which I thought a tad sombre and formal for a uni boss. On his right was Mike Orme, for whom sombre and formal were not part of the sartorial lexicon. He wore what I soon discovered to be his usual attire of smooth-knit tank top over a white shirt and dark blue trousers. There was also a bod from Human Resources who I later found out was called Tim and the only man working in a personnel department full of girls. Although he was sitting when I came into the room, he stood to lean across the desk to shake my hand and say 'Welcome Miss Meyer' after both Peter Heron and Mike Orme had done the same. I considered Tim: tall, with smooth, blond hair. Reasonably good-looking. Mmm, I thought. He could be interesting, but left it there for the time being.

Lee also sat in on my interview along with Stella Lastings. Apparently they like their interviews to be done on an inter-departmental level to broaden the 'spectrum of knowledges' and Stella, from History, fitted the bill.

Lee raised the question about research, fully knowing what the answer would be, and I waxed lyrically about my pet Rochester project and, surprisingly, fatty Lastings leaned forward, pursing her ruby, heart-shaped lips and said, 'Ah, how interesting.' What could Miss Ruby Lips possibly know about John Wilmot, I asked myself, but I supposed she was a closet *Fifty Shades* reader and I smiled as graciously as I could.

And I got the job. But, then, was it ever in doubt? Problem was I didn't get the bursary. After another three months had gone by and I hadn't heard anything, I rang the AEE only to be told the money had been awarded to someone else two months previously and had I not been told? The stupid pricks apparently missed my email telling them I'd transferred to the University of Central Yorkshire and had written to me at Wharfevale instead. I was sure I'd emailed them when I changed jobs. Ah well. But how to break this to Peter Heron and Co? Best to leave it for now, I thought, besides which, there was bound to be another bursary somewhere along the way.

Chapter Four

Lee

I know Teri thinks I'm a bit of a goody-two-shoes but, perish the thought, she'd have been the same with a mother like mine. Mammy's girls were 'properly brought up' with due regard for the Church and the laws of God. And, without quite buying into the whole hellfire and damnation shtick, I never quite dared to do anything very wicked – just in case. In fact, as a kid, probably the worst thing I ever did was nick an exercise book from the school stationery cupboard. It was an impulse theft. I was in my going-to-be-a-famous-author-when-I-grow-up phase and needed somewhere to scribble my stories, but I suffered agonies of guilt afterwards. Though, when I finally went to confession and admitted everything, Father Johnson roared with laughter and said not to worry. 'Everyone steps out of line sometimes, Lee.'

True, but in being deliberately misleading about the outcome of her Rochester research grant application, Teri had done a bit more than step out of line. She'd taken a great big running jump across it and compromised the integrity of herself and a number of other people too. Me, for instance, and I was hopping mad. She had absolutely no concept of how far I'd gone out on a limb to get her, first, an interview, and then a post at what she dismissively refers to as our 'little' university. Good heavens, if I'd gone out any further, the limb would've snapped in half. Peter Heron, for one, had taken a hell of a lot of convincing. 'A very poor 2:2,' he said studying the CV I'd placed in front of him.

'But, a very good second degree,' I pointed out. In fact, Teri had been disappointed she'd 'only' got a merit for her MA, and I'd had to explain that distinctions were as rare as daffodils in August and a merit was damn near brilliant.

Pity Peter hadn't been party to that conversation. 'A distinction would have been better,' he said.

Miserable bastard.

'Nor,' he said, turning over the page, 'does she have much relevant experience.'

Okay – the work she was doing at Wharfevale was a far cry from what we'd expect. But how often did we employ someone who was able to hit the ground running? New recruits were always cut a bit of slack while they bedded in.

'Vic Brennan speaks very highly of her – and he wouldn't do that without good reason.'

Peter harrumphed. 'Vic Brennan. Man's a charlatan.'

Too late, I remembered that Vic, who taught at the neighbouring University of the West Riding, had beaten Peter in recent elections for the chair of the Association of English Educators. Perhaps not the best choice of referee. But, it was a tipping point of sorts – because Vic's academic reputation couldn't be denied – and Peter agreed to put Teri on the shortlist.

Not that Teri ever acknowledged – or even recognised – the length of the leg up necessary to secure her appointment.

Nor did the ungrateful cow appreciate her indebtedness to Stella Lastings; she'd have been dead in the water, despite all my best endeavours, if Stella, rather surprisingly, hadn't thrown her weight behind Teri's candidature. And, in the end, it was the guarantee of the research bursary that did the trick. In fact, Peter almost salivated when she told the interview panel, with an airy wave of a hand, that she was expecting confirmation of the bursary 'any day now'.

I'd been surprised; when we'd discussed it, her application had been at the 'I'm very hopeful of getting the dosh' stage rather than a done deal.

And now, many, many months down the line, here she was sipping an Americano in the coffee lounge of the Majestic Hotel on Waterloo Street, telling me the bursary had gone for a Burton. And she'd known for months. Months! Ye Gods! Did she know nothing?

Of course, I didn't let on to Teri that I wanted to shake the brains out of her beautifully coiffeured head. First, because going off on one with Teri doesn't work. She just has a mega-strop, blames everyone in sight – apart from herself, of course – and sulks for England. Which is fine; it's no skin off my nose if she wants to behave like a toddler suffering from a severe dose of the terrible twos, but it doesn't achieve anything purposeful. And, second, Teri, as always, chose a public place in which to break bad news, knowing I'd therefore be constrained in my response.

Mind you, she must've been a little bit nervous because she began by admitting, hesitantly, that her cherished Rochester project had hit a brick wall.

'A brick wall?' This didn't sound good.

She was sorry, she said, but the Association of English Educators bursary on which she'd depended had inexplicably been awarded to another candidate.

'Inexplicably?'

'Well, who wants to read about northern heroines in the novels of Mrs Gaskell?'

'Might be interesting. She's a bit more mainstream than Rochester – who reads him these days?'

'Lots of people read Rochester.'

'Only the ones who sign up for your Renaissance literature classes.' Which wasn't many. Teri might live and breathe John Wilmot, 2nd Earl of Rochester, but, with the exception of Stella, his modern-day fans were few and far between – an exclusive group that certainly didn't include significant numbers of the English and Media students from the University of Central Yorkshire.

Teri, herself, was surprisingly sanguine about the low numbers. 'More time for my research,' she said. Except, of course, as she admitted over coffee at the Majestic, there wasn't any research and nor was there likely to be.

And that's another thing – over coffee. I've lost count of the number of times I've told her I don't drink coffee, milky or otherwise.

'You find a seat,' Teri said. 'I'll get the drinks.'

Find a seat? I was spoiled for choice – apart from the ageing barista behind the bar and a couple of slick-suited businessmen, we were the only people in the room. 'Weak Earl Grey for me,' I said. 'And could you ask for some extra hot water?'

Well, no doubt she could've asked for extra hot water – and for a weak Earl Grey too – but she didn't. Why was I surprised?

'I got you a latte,' she said sitting down. Why? Why? Why?

And, of course, she made her usual silly comment about my latte moustache. How could I have froth on my top lip when every time I raised the cup to my mouth I put it down again without taking a sip? The sickly sweet smell made me retch. Not that she ever noticed.

'Okay,' I said, poking at the latte with a spoon. As if that would make it taste any better. 'The research bursary has gone somewhere else, what's your backup plan?'

'Backup plan?'

Clearly, she didn't realise the seriousness of this.

'It was a condition of your employment,' I reminded her. 'Peter Heron was very specific – a two-year temporary contract that would be consolidated on publication of your research, for which, you assured us, you had funding.'

'I don't remember him saying any such thing,' she argued, completely ignoring the implication she'd been a little cavalier about the veracity of her research funding.

I did. 'Read your contract of employment. It's there in black and white.'

'Oh dear,' she said.

Indeed.

But, if this was a knock-down, it certainly wasn't a knockout. At least, not in Teri's eyes. 'But we're only a former poly,' she said. 'Teaching's our forte, not research.'

She really didn't get it. Like so many of the other new post-1992 universities, we were re-positioning ourselves as research-driven centres of teaching and learning, and her inability to lift her research profile from the tail end of the university's Z-list was likely to be a major disadvantage if she wanted to secure her tenure at the University of Central Yorkshire.

But did she want tenure? Her father, probably one of the wealthiest men in the county, had always bankrolled Teri and her brother and, though she might assert that she liked to maintain her independence, I'd always been under the impression she didn't really need to work. And, it was pretty clear that a modern university wasn't her natural environment. Oh, yes, she was engaged and engaging with the students – teaching is often a bit of a performance and Teri put on a good show – but her frankly dismissive attitude towards university conventions and procedures meant she was upsetting lecturers and admin staff left, right and centre. The academics resented her cavalier attitude towards academia, in general, and university rules and regulations, in particular, while the administrators found her patronising and arrogant. Teri might think they were just there to do our dirty work – 'deadline obsessed pen pushers,' she called them – but they played a pivotal role in student support which undoubtedly helped boost our score in the National Union of Student Satisfaction rankings.

Ah, yes, the annual NUS student satisfaction survey, an increasingly important barometer separating so-called 'good' universities from bad ones. Every university in the country was on a mission to improve their NUS polling and we were no different. Somewhat belatedly, the university's senior management group had caught on to the fact that students had swapped texting for tweeting and preferred 'liking' someone on Facebook to liking them in the flesh. And, that if we wanted them to like us better, we needed to get on their wavelength. Accordingly, I'd been tasked with researching and 'facilitating the early adoption of a social media student engagement programme'. Sorry, about the jargon. It's hard sometimes not to slip into university-speak.

I'd been thinking for a while that I could do with someone to do the nuts and bolts donkey work, and, though it wasn't as 'sexy' as Teri's Rochester stuff, it was a lot more useful. Perhaps it wasn't such a bad thing that Teri's project had fallen at the first hurdle. However, having previously dismissed tweets as the twitterings of the semi-literate and YouTube as background wallpaper for sofa surfers, she couldn't jump onboard without a modicum of prevarication. 'Oh no,' she said. 'I've no intention of ditching Rochester. The AEE bursary is just a minor setback.'

No, it isn't – it's a bloody car crash.

26

'I'll get the money from somewhere else,' she said.

No you won't. 'The AEE is practically the only funding body that sets aside grants for first-time researchers,' I pointed out.

'I'd hardly class myself as a first-time researcher,' she said.

You might not, but I would – and so would any other academic worth their salt.

She continued to filibuster for several more minutes. But, my comment about her contract of employment had clearly rattled her. For reasons, which I didn't completely understand – she must know by now that she wasn't totally suited to the life of an academic – she *really* wanted to keep this job. And, for all her grandiose posturing, she knew, and I knew, and, more importantly, she knew I knew, she was pretty desperate.

And Teri, who frankly didn't know her research arse from her elbow, could do a lot worse than chuck in her research towel with me.

'Oh,' she said as we got up to leave, 'you've let your latte go cold.'

Chapter Five

Lee

Persuading Teri to help and then getting her up to speed was an uphill task. She says she has a lot of respect for my intelligence and learning, but *saying* is one thing and *showing* is another. I think she found the shift in the balance of our relationship hard to handle. Until this point she'd been the star of our show, and I was the assistant stage manager, facilitating her performance and orchestrating her curtain calls.

Now, for the first time, she was dancing to my tune and she didn't like it – and she wasn't much good at it either. If I really had been an ASM, she'd have been in the back line of the chorus – if she'd been lucky enough to make it onstage in the first place. She didn't take direction very well.

Partly, it was because she had a misplaced confidence in her own research experience – she didn't seem to appreciate there was a world of difference between an MA dissertation and doctoral-level research. And she didn't take it kindly when I pulled her up a couple of times. We had a number of what can best be described as full and frank discussions, which I think surprised her. She's often chided me with being a bit laid back and easy going. 'You let people walk all over you, Lee. You've got to stand up to them. Be firm,' she'd encourage. But, she wasn't happy when I took her advice and told her where to get off a couple of times.

'You're turning into a horrible bossy boots,' she accused when I asked her to take a second look at some material from an author who'd been one of the first to critically examine the function and purpose of blogs. 'And a real slave driver too,' she added.

The other problem, of course, and this was something I'd never realised before, she was bone idle and completely lacking in even a smidgeon of a Protestant work ethic.

I shouldn't have been surprised. When I first mooted the idea to Mike that she might get involved in my social media research, his response was less than enthusiastic. 'She'll do the minimum of work for the maximum glory,' he warned. Even my mother, who, on the whole, liked her, reckoned she'd been born with a silver spoon in her mouth. 'And she has no intention of removing it from between her teeth to share a morsel with a starving man.'

Fliss, too, was equally sceptical. 'Fool. If you hadn't let her copy your homework, she'd never have scraped a pass in anything.' Actually, even copying my homework, she barely scraped a pass – she only ever copied as much as she needed to get by.

Well, there'd be no copying this time, though God knows I had to watch her like a hawk. For one thing, she didn't seem to have quite grasped the concept of plagiarism. 'Didn't anyone explain it to you at UWR?' I asked the first time I caught her out.

'UWR?'

'University of the West Riding – the place where you spent three years studying for an Honours degree.'

'Oh, there. I suppose they must've done. Everybody here seems to make such a big fuss about it, I guess they did too.'

'So, why the hell didn't you take any notice?'

'I did – I do.'

You do? I glared at her, lost for words.

'You're being awfully picky about this, Lee. It's not like you.'

Actually, she *did* understand the conventions of academic research and the importance of referencing sources, it's just that she liked to wind me up. It was her way of evening things out.

'Look,' I said another time, when she lifted huge chunks from a conference paper I'd co-authored, 'you've got to acknowledge your sources.'

'I have,' she said.

'Where?' I couldn't see any discernible references.

'Here,' she said, scrabbling around in the bottom of her handbag. 'I made a separate note of the sources.'

And she triumphantly produced a tattered list of a handful of unrelated dates and titles that looked more like an extract from a TV listings page than a properly referenced Harvard-style bibliography. I scanned the torn off sheet of paper. 'It's incomplete,' I said.

'Incomplete? No it isn't.' She was very indignant. 'You're very quick to criticise, Lee. I was very careful to make sure I wrote everything down correctly.'

'So, how come you've missed my name off the list?'

'Oh, it's there somewhere. I'm sure it is.'

No, it bloody well wasn't.

'Sorry,' she said, digging into her bag again. 'Wrong list. This is the one you want.' And, grinning, she produced a perfectly typed, correctly referenced bibliography. And stuck her tongue out.

However, mostly we worked well together – once we'd established the ground rules and she stopped teasing. Even Mike was pleased when our first research paper was published by the AEE and received some very positive peer feedback.

'We'll soon be known as one of the leaders in the field,' he said.

Teri was less pleased – largely because, though I'd listed her as co-author, my name came first.

'It's the convention,' I explained. 'I'm the lead researcher.'

'For now,' she said.

What did that mean? Maybe, she hadn't entirely given up on her own research ambitions? That was a good thing, wasn't it? Certainly she hadn't given up on her ambitions towards an office of her own. She thought it terribly unfair I had a large room all to myself while she, like all junior academics, shared an office with a couple of other lecturers. She was forever complaining about her colleagues. 'Silly little girls,' she said.

That was a bit unfair. Both were in their late twenties and both were on the verge of completing their doctoral theses.

'Always giggling about boys,' she said. 'I wouldn't put it past them to try it on with the students.'

That wasn't just unfair, it was dangerous talk.

'They wouldn't do anything so stupid.'

Teri snorted. 'Some of our undergraduates are very good-looking young men,' she said. 'Haven't you noticed?'

Of course I had. But it never occurred to me to see any of them in the light of a potential suitor.

'You're so innocent, Lee,' Teri said.

Sometimes, I was glad – it made life a lot easier.

Chapter Six

Teri

Peter Heron hadn't picked up positive vibes from the Ridings Today producer. 'I don't think he understood the concept of what I was suggesting, which was to negotiate the intellectual motif of the modern novel through the *salon* of the twenty-first century digital medium,' he told us the following Monday when Lee and I found him in the senior common room. 'He simply didn't understand the nature of the modern day academic logographer. He kept talking about reality television and Harry Potter,' Peter said. 'And have you heard of a footballer called Shayne Brickham? Plays for Wakefield, apparently, and he's the next best hope for English football and, he's written his autobiography. For goodness' sake! He's only eighteen. What the hell has he got to say?' He paused, then went on. 'However, all is not lost. The producer was just the monkey. I'm having lunch with the organ grinder next week; the MD of Ridings Today. Then we'll find out what's what – and it won't be Big Brother or silver balls Brickham.'

As Peter turned to go, Lee leaned over to me and whispered, 'Sounds like the producer spotted not so much a case of logography but logorrhoea. Anyway,' she added, 'how did you get on at Ridings Today – and with the gorgeous Dan Caine?'

Lee had taken it quite calmly when I told her about my invitation to watch Dan at work. True, he had said something about being welcome to visit the studio in the next couple of weeks and bring colleagues along, but

I'd taken it as an invitation that had to be followed through immediately and by me personally. Factual television would be lost on Stella Lastings, who was studying cliometrics rather than a period in which TV actually existed, and I couldn't trust Lee to behave herself with Dan, so I omitted to tell either of them of the invite.

I was met at the studio reception by a tarty, middle-aged woman of about fifty-five, with bright red hair piled high on her head and held in place by a large, black comb. She wore a tight, black skirt (cheap fabric) and a frothy, white blouse (nylon) that exposed an amount of suntanned but crepe-y cleavage. This, I assumed – correctly – was Doreen. I'd spoken to her on the phone to arrange my visit and guessed she and Dan were quite good mates so I decided to be nice to the old cow. She introduced herself as D'reen and led me to a long, narrow waiting room with the words 'Green Room' painted on the door. Once inside, she motioned for me to sit on a brown leather, two-seater sofa on one side of the room, the other one opposite having been taken up by a young man of about sixteen who was sprawled on it, legs wide open in that way men have when they're dominating space. D'reen tottered over to a small table at the top end of the room on which were squatting two large urns.

'Tea...coffee...if you want it.'

'I thought there'd be champagne at least,' I said, grinning at the sprawled young man.

'No, darling,' she said. 'This is Ridings Today not bloody Newsnight.' She screeched with laughter and teetered off.

Clutching my plastic container of what turned out to be disgusting coffee, I glanced across at the young man opposite now dangling perilously. He was lying back in the sofa with his bum hanging off the edge, his groin slightly uplifted in a table-top position and his legs spread wide exposing the bump of his willy against the cloth of his white tracksuit trousers. His feet, wide apart, were clad in box-new, white trainers.

'Are you just visiting to see how the programme works?' I asked, thinking he was probably on school work experience.

'Nah, I'm on it,' he said.

'Oh. Why?' I asked. 'Have you got a skateboarding duck?'

He looked at me oddly. 'Nah, luv. I'm a footballer.'

33

Something began to dawn.

'You're not...?' But before I had time to finish the question the Green Room door opened, and Dan Caine walked in. He saw me first and smiled.

'Agh. Don't drink the coffee. Great you could come...nice to see you. Are the others here too?'

And just as I was about to explain, he turned to the footballer. 'Ah. Hi Shayne. How are you?' And before Shayne had time to shuffle into a more upright position and respond, Dan added, 'We won't be long...they'll come and get you in about ten minutes, if that's okay. I'll ask you a couple of questions about how the season's going; any injures; latest girlfriend; and then a bit about the book. Okay? Great. Lovely. Well done.' And he was gone.

Dan explained later that what with research, rehearsals and checking the autocue for phrases he couldn't read or pronounce, there never was much time to have a pre-programme chat with guests. 'And anyway, with someone like Shayne, you're not going to get much by way of stimulating conversation. It's not as though I have to do deep research on an eighteen-year-old footballer who's got someone else to write his autobiography.'

'You mean he didn't...?'

'Heavens, no. The boy can't read let alone write his own name.' Dan laughed.

A bit like some of my students, then.

Eventually, in came a girl wearing headphones with a mic attached. She said they were ready for Shayne, and he dragged himself upright from the sofa, turned and said 'See ya' to me and lolloped off.

A few minutes later, D'reen poked her head round the door. 'D'you want to come into the gallery?'

I followed her into a long, thin, semi-dark area. To my right was a low mixing desk of switches, buttons and levers and, above, a bank of video monitors each showing a different aspect of the studio floor or a freeze frame of some video to be screened later. D'reen motioned for me to sit on a short row of seats on the left, and I lowered myself next to a plumply-faced man leaning forward to talk to the director seated behind the mixing console. The director had headphones hooked over the back of his head with one earpiece over his right ear and the other on his left cheek, the better, I

34

supposed, to be able to hear what was being said both in the gallery and on the studio floor.

The plumply-faced man glanced at me and smiled in welcome.

'Hello, I'm Richard Walker,' he said, offering his hand. It was gloomy and I couldn't see properly yet, but I made out his hair, which had been gelled into a little peak at the top of his forehead. Very boyish, but not a good look on a man his age.

'I'm Teri...' But I didn't have time to finish because the director, who'd obviously heard something through his headphones, shouted 'Aw...shit!' and Richard Walker smiled in apology and leapt up to move closer to him to see what the fuss was about. D'reen, who'd plonked herself down on my right, pointed out who everyone was: the director, the PA, the sound controller, the vision mixer and the autocue operator.

Then, suddenly, the director shouted to everyone and no one in particular 'We'll have to go without it' and I assumed some top-of-the-news report had failed to arrive, and they were going to have to lead on a skating-duck story.

The transmission went by in a mad confusion of shouted instructions.

'Roll ident...coming to camera one in thirty seconds; camera two ready with the close shot; fifteen seconds to the interview; take camera three; have we got the item...where's the fucking item? Ten seconds to caption...no, that isn't Chief Superintendant bloody Fisher, it's the bloody victim's mother. Where's the right caption? Aagh. Too late, she's gone...Next caption in five seconds. NO! That's the wrong fucking caption AGAIN. Camera three...camera three? What the fuck are you doing? I don't want a shot up his nostrils – back off...Ten seconds to the break...wind it up Dan...wind it up...'

Not entirely sure which of the monitors on the bank above the gallery desk to watch, I plumped for whichever featured Dan. He was hearing all the instructions, all the swearing, all the panic through his earpiece, but you wouldn't think it to see him at work. He was cool, only occasionally lifting his left hand to nudge his left ear – not as a sign to me – but to show the director he'd heard – or misheard – something.

'It must be so confusing,' I said when we met back in the Green Room after he'd washed the make-up off his face.

35

'It's all part of the job,' he said. 'Goes with reading the autocue.'

He had an after-programme post-mortem to attend that evening, but suggested we have a meal together at the end of the week and I could tell him what I thought of his performance. We agreed he'd pick me up on Friday.

'Anywhere you'd like to go?' he asked.

'Where do you telly types normally eat?'

'Well, I like L'homme-vert,' he said. 'Let's treat ourselves and go there. I'll book,' he added.

I wasn't sure if I should be treating myself at L'homme-vert, one of the priciest places in Yorkshire. I didn't mind spending, but my allowance from Dad was late arriving that month and I wasn't sure if my lecturer's salary would cover the cost. I looked around for Shayne, who likely earned more in a week than I earned in a year, wondering if he might sub me. Dan must have seen the look on my face.

'Don't worry,' he said. 'Look, it's my birthday on Friday, so it'll be my treat.'

Chapter Seven

Lee

Teri was unrepentant. 'It was just a bit of fun,' she said.

Fun? Fun for whom?

Not for Stella, who was mortified, and not for Frank either, who was thoroughly fed up with the endless teasing from his fellow porters. 'You've a funny idea of fun,' I told her. 'Especially as nobody really believes it – you do know Frank is gay, don't you?'

'Of course,' she said. 'That's what's so delicious. Nobody really believes it, but then they look at Frank and Stella and wonder, what if...? Perfect.'

There was no reasoning with her. The only saving grace in the whole sorry mess was that no one ever traced the rumour back to Teri, which, all things considered, was little short of a miracle because she made absolutely no attempt to hide her guilt.

It did make me wonder though whether it had been such a clever idea to help Teri secure a post at my university.

Things settled down eventually and people forgot what the fuss was all about – as they always do. You'd have thought I'd be happy? Not a bit of it, because the next thing that had tongues wagging was Mike's wife, Mrs Orme, erupting into the senior common room demanding to talk to the 'Harper hussy'!

Oh my God! I could've died. The morning had started so promisingly as well – it had taken a few days, but I no longer felt quite so shit-scared about the whole baby thing and, after a sleepless night, had decided whatever Mike said, I was going through with the pregnancy. I'd come into work feeling quite positive and almost bouncy.

Mike? Oh yes, I'd told Teri a little white lie when I dismissed the rumours about me and Mike. What do I mean? A little white lie? A bloody great whopper of a lie would be more accurate. True, things between us had begun to cool off – he was too scared of Peter Heron to really 'enjoy' an affair with someone at work, and I was too scared of Mammy to feel really comfortable being the 'other woman'. The thought of what she'd say if she ever found out brought me out in a cold sweat – hark at me. If she ever found out? How was I going to explain being pregnant? She might believe in the virgin birth of Christ but not in even my most optimistic moments could I think she'd swallow the notion I too had received a visit from the Angel Gabriel.

I said a quick Hail Mary. I'd been doing that a lot over the last few days. Kinship, I think. Me and the Virgin Mary had a lot in common – no husband and an unplanned pregnancy. At least Joseph made an honest woman of her. Would Mike do the same for me? Did I want him to do so? Hmm. Not sure. And the longer I dallied at the senior common room coffee bar while Mrs Mimms told me about her new grandson, the more unsure I felt. She was almost fizzing with joy as she pulled out her mobile phone and scrawled through a photo gallery of snapshots of little Sebastian. Honesty compels me to admit that, from pretty much every angle, he looked little more than a nondescript blob, but I made suitably admiring noises to his doting granny, who clearly thought he was perfection personified. I wanted some of her fizz though – would Mammy be so adoring of my little blob?

Slide show over, I took my drink and headed for my usual corner seat. The room was half empty; it was early afternoon and most people were either teaching or in meetings. Nevertheless, there must've been a good half dozen people who copped an eyeful when Mrs Orme charged through the door. Nothing new there. She'd been a former hospital sister – senior charge nurse, I suppose they call them nowadays – and always strode purposefully. I'd once accompanied her on a tour of the university's new George Gissing media centre and practically had to trot to keep up. Today, however, Chrissie from admin was flapping behind her.

'Judy,' Chrissie said, 'I really don't think this is a good idea.'

Heavens above. Nor did I. It didn't take much imagination to work out this wasn't a polite social call.

'Chrissie,' she said, 'just point her out.'

Dear God – why did she have to shout? Now the whole room was staring. I felt a little trickle of annoyance. What did she mean 'point her out'? We'd met umpteen times, both before and since our high-speed tour of the Gissing building. Didn't say much for me that she was clearly struggling to put a face to a name. Was I so nondescript? Teri often complained I was too inclined to disappear into the crowd. 'Stand tall,' she'd command, pulling my shoulders back. 'And you need a bit of colour,' she'd say, whipping out a lipstick. 'Pout,' she'd order, swiftly colouring my lips and dabbing at my face to accentuate my cheekbones. I'm not quite sure why she thought a smear of lipstick could be transformational but, after stepping back to admire her handiwork, she always nodded approvingly. 'You'll do,' she'd say, linking her arm through mine and dragging me in her wake.

I could've done with a bit of Teri's lipstick confidence now. 'Are you looking for me?'

I felt like a worm but Chrissie later said I'd been magnificent – calm and authoritative and completely believable. Let's just gloss over the implications of the 'believable' part of her comment but it's nice to know that, when push comes to shove, I can do calm and authoritative with the right amount of credibility.

'You're Lee Harper?' She eyed me uncertainly. 'You're not what I expected.'

Oh! Was that good, or bad?

Who knows? I'm not sure Mrs Orme did. I decided to play dumb. 'What was it you wanted to see me about?'

She hesitated, looking like a woman who'd had the stuffing knocked out of her. 'I'm not sure. The other women have always been...' she waved a hand vaguely and took a deep breath, '...more obviously attractive.'

Gee, thanks. And other women? What was she trying to say?

I sat down, suddenly feeling weary of the whole damn charade. Why didn't she just come out with it?

'You must understand,' she spoke quickly now as if she'd rehearsed this speech many times and wanted to get it all out in one piece before she forgot anything, 'I'm not accusing you of anything – wouldn't dream of accusing you...but you've got to admit that it's a little odd...'

For heaven's sake! Get to the bloody point!

'The fact is,' she said, 'Mike had been working late a lot, and your name seemed to crop up rather frequently. And when I peeked at his phone messages yesterday, there seemed to be a lot of text messages from someone called Lee.

'You?' she presumed. And when she'd mentioned it – 'just in passing to Chrissie' – she (Chrissie) confirmed that we (Mike and I) were 'extraordinarily close'. Chrissie's words, exactly – apparently. I gave Chrissie a filthy look. The muck-stirrer. And she'd just popped in to see Chrissie this morning 'for a little chat' when she decided it would be a good idea to 'have things out'. To speak her mind, so to speak.

But now she didn't know what to think because she 'knew from the moment she set eyes on me that I wasn't that sort of woman'. I never did find out precisely what sort of woman she thought I wasn't but, at least, I didn't need to deny anything or admit to anything either. Couldn't if I'd wanted – she barely gave me room to get a word in edgeways until, speech concluded, she sat down abruptly, like a pricked balloon, put her hands in her face and sobbed.

It was awful. I didn't know what to say and simply patted her back and scrambled in my bag for a clean tissue and couldn't find one, so offered her the serviette I'd picked up from the coffee bar counter instead, which quickly disintegrated into a myriad of crumply pieces as cheap serviettes always do under pressure. Eventually she quietened down a little and apologised for being such a nuisance.

'But you don't know how difficult Mike can be.'

Actually, I did know only too well; he could be a bloody irritating manager with his nit-picking little ways, and he wasn't exactly a hot-shot as a – what...boyfriend? lover? bit on the side?

She'd had a lot to put up with over the years, she said, and – here's the surprise, and something I didn't know – it wasn't the first time he'd had an affair.

'Even before we were married he had a bit of a wandering eye,' she confessed.

So, why the hell had she married him? Usual reason – she was pregnant. Oh, and she loved him. And still did. What? I almost shouted in disbelief.

He'd had how many affairs? At least four, possibly five, she said. Did I think he was having another affair now?

'Oh God,' I said, which could have meant anything.

For a long time neither of us said very much – she, because she didn't have anything more to say, and me, because I no longer knew what to say. Or, what to think either. Let's face it, I'd always thought of myself as a nice Catholic girl – but no two ways about it, nice Catholic girls don't have affairs with married men.

We sat, almost companionably, each lost in our thoughts. Chrissie coughed discreetly, motioning to the old-fashioned wall clock. She knew I had a class at 3pm, she said, and Judy had a hair appointment.

I had? She did?

'I'd completely forgotten,' Judy said, gathering up her handbag and rearranging a floral silk scarf around her neck. Oh, how Teri would've itched to fasten it into a fashionable knot rather than the loose cub-scout kerchief-style affected by Judy.

She held out her hand. 'Thank you,' she said. 'It's been lovely to talk to you.'

Had it? Wish I could say the same. It had been, I thought, a most unsettling conversation.

Chapter Eight

Teri

'Well, the programme was quite interesting…' I began.

'How many skateboarding ducks?' Lee asked, laughing.

'There weren't any of those, but there was a footballer – Shayne Brickham – all shiny white trainers and testosterone-fuelled track suit.'

I told her about D'reen, the tarty meeter and greeter with the crêpe-fuelled cleavage, the swearing director and Dan's professionalism and coolness on camera.

Lee looked at me closely; a look she gives me when she knows there's something more I'm not telling her. 'And you went out with him afterwards?'

'Er…not immediately that night,' I replied. 'But on Friday.'

'Ooh. You bugger,' she said. 'Why didn't you tell me?'

I could hardly tell her that a) I'd denied her the chance of going to watch the programme being made and, therefore, b) also denied her the chance of being asked out to dinner by Dan Caine, could I?

'How did it go?' She sounded less enthusiastic now. But still interested.

I built the story up: the invite to L'homme-vert; the little black dress; the doorbell going on the dot at 7.30pm.

'And then…?' she asked, impatient now.

The story crumbled, just as my night out with Dan had.

Before the doorbell rang on Friday, I'd rushed in from a late meeting at work, waxed, plucked, pedicured, manicured and dressed in a new little black number. The gin I'd had in the bath steadied my nerves. I was ready. And so was Dan, but not for L'homme-vert judging by the t-shirt, chinos and trainers he was wearing.

'Ah,' he said, eyeing me up and down. 'Fabulous. You look great…but…didn't you get my message?'

I looked at the hall table where I generally throw my keys and phone as I come in, and my mobile was showing a message. Must have got it while I was in the bath.

'Change of plan,' Dan said, 'we're going bowling.'

He half-turned and motioned to the silver-grey BMW parked on the kerb. In the front passenger seat sat a girl of about seventeen or eighteen with long blonde hair, staring straight ahead at the road. Even from this distance I could see she wasn't happy.

'My daughter…Victoria…wanted to help celebrate my birthday,' Dan said. 'But she doesn't like L'homme-vert…wanted to do something a bit more active. Hope you don't mind. Won't take you long to change, will it?'

I changed out of the little black number and into a clean pair of jeans and t-shirt and dashed out to the BMW where Dan had chosen to wait with his daughter.

Dozens of questions raced through my mind, not least, was he married? Did he have any more bloody children?

As I approached, I could see Dan motioning the daughter to get out of the front passenger seat and into the back. She didn't budge. Dan opened the driver's door and got out.

'It's okay,' I trilled. 'I'll get in the back.'

Dan pulled his seat forward so I could crawl onto the back seat. The girl didn't look round.

'This is Victoria,' Dan said, climbing back into the driver's seat.

'Oh. Hi, Toria,' I said, pulling myself into an upright sitting position by clutching the back of her headrest and heaving.

'It's VIC…toria,' she said, not turning round, but bouncing slightly with the force of my pull.

'Not Toria, Vicky or Vickers?'

She gave a theatrical shrug as though my pulling on her headrest had unsettled her entire equilibrium.

My attempt at conversation proceeded along these lines for the rest of the evening although, thankfully, the noise of the bowling alley – with the clattering of falling pins, the loudly-piped music and the cheering of teams when one of them made a strike – meant any meaningful conversation was difficult.

I'd had a go at ten-pin bowling once before, but thought it might be a good move to pretend I hadn't, which allowed Dan to help me.

'First you need a suitable ball,' he said, eyeing me up and down as though gauging my height and weight (5ft 8ins and 8.5 stone). 'They can weigh a tonne,' he said. 'Select the heaviest you can comfortably manage – that's right – and then try the finger holes. Put your thumb in the thumb hole – yes, there – you should be able to pull back out without catching it, then lay your hand across the ball, placing your middle fingers over the top of the finger holes. Here, let me help...'

Letting him help involved him moving up close behind and putting his arms around me so he could manoeuvre his hands over mine. I only had to lean back slightly to feel the strength in his chest as he braced himself to hold me. I glanced out of the corner of my eye to see Victoria gazing heavenwards.

I hoisted the ball into position and set off towards the lane.

'Aim just to the left or just to the right of the head pin,' Dan advised.

Above the din, I thought I heard Victoria mutter 'Oh, for God's sake', then I swung my arm back and then forwards, like a pendulum, dropping my right knee slightly to make sure the ball was not too high when I released it. It went spinning onto the lane where it bounced once and shot into the gutter.

'Oh. Bad luck!' Victoria said, looking as though she was enjoying herself for the first time.

My game didn't improve but I enjoyed Dan's personal coaching. When he disappeared off to the loo, play was temporarily suspended and I sat down beside Victoria.

'Have you got any brothers and sisters?' I asked.

'No.'

Phew.

'Do you like bowling?'

'It's something to do,' she said, shrugging dismissively.

'You don't mind if I want to spend time with your daddy, do you?' I was beginning to get a sense of something here.

'What on earth did you do?' Lee asked later.

I told her: over the course of the evening, I learned a little more about Dan Caine. He'd been married but divorced from his wife, Sara, two years ago when Victoria was thirteen. Since then, she'd lived with her mother and spent weekends, high days and holidays with her father.

'Tricky age,' Lee said.

'Any age is tricky where children are concerned,' I replied.

The truth is I've never liked children; never wanted any myself. I'm not one of those yummy mummies who feel the maternal pull to be surrounded by designer-clad brats. I think children get in the way of your career; they're selfish, costly and not worth the effort.

Lee laughed. 'Typical. A woman who hates kids ends up with a man who has a clingy, possessive teenager.'

'Excuse me. We've had one date – if you can call it a date. We're not exactly ending up together. Anyway, Dan tells me the brat'll be off to university soon so she'll be off his hands for good.'

Lee looked at me in that way she does when she knows what I'm saying is doubtful, but she hasn't the heart to point it out. 'You'd feel differently if you had children of your own. You'd understand,' she said.

I hadn't heard from Dan over the weekend, and although I'd texted him to thank him for a 'fabulous' evening's bowling, there'd been no reply. I didn't tell Lee that. I could see she was about to ask if I was going to see him again, so I made some excuse about a Level 1 module meeting with Mike Orme and rushed off.

Chapter Nine

Lee

Teri was incredulous when I told her about the encounter with Mrs Orme. And I was incredulous, first that she hadn't heard about it from someone else – clearly the SCR gossips were losing their touch – and, second, that she'd sneaked off to the Ridings Today studios without me.

'Why didn't you say anything?'

Didn't think it was your cup of tea, she said. Huh! You might have asked, I thought.

But I knew why she hadn't and, really, I didn't blame her – in similar circumstances I might've been tempted to do the same. Shame though, I would've loved to have been a fly on the wall when D'Reen left her in the waiting room with Shayne Brickham. I'd heard him interviewed on local radio once – his mumbling inarticulacy made it a painful listen. Bet he and Teri found a lot to talk about.

And talking of flies on walls, I'd have given my right arm to have had a ringside view when Dan turned up on Teri's doorstep with Victoria in the front passenger seat. She'd been lost for words, she said. Not for long, I thought. But no, she said, she'd been very friendly and made an effort to talk to 'the girl'. Bet 'the girl' responded in kind – I'd seen Teri make an effort with people before. It wasn't pleasant. And, I most definitely did not believe she was 'cool' about the ex-wife. Or 'the girl'.

Nor was she 'cool' about Dan. Lord! She was red hot for him. And full exposure to the media glamour of Ridings Today had confirmed she was ideally suited to life in the fast lane with one of the biggest stars on local TV.

'Arm candy?' I suggested.

'You're jealous,' she teased.

Of what?

'Media parties, mixing with celebrities, spending the vast fortune these telly types earn.'

What did she need with a vast fortune? She was doing her best to spend her daddy's vast fortune – wasn't that enough?

'Oh Daddy,' she pouted. 'He's becoming a real miser in his old age.'

Really. I looked pointedly at Teri's expensively clad feet, her designer work frock and her large, leather tote bag – at a guess, the entire ensemble had probably cost upwards of two thousand pounds. Possibly more.

'Sack cloth and ashes?'

She grinned and sashayed down an imaginary catwalk. 'Worth every penny,' she said. 'Knock 'em dead gorgeous, don't you think?'

Yes, I did. But wild horses wouldn't have got me to admit it. She was too bloody cocky, by half.

Still, it was good Peter's perfectly ghastly little shindig had ended so happily – for her at least. And, now, as I flipped through the satellite TV listings trying to find something – anything – worth watching, I was jerked out of my musings by the ear-splitting ring of my mobile from the bottom of my handbag. Cue a frantic scramble to get to it before it switched to voicemail.

'Hello?'

'Lee – great to talk to you the other night.'

Really? I didn't recognise the voice. And couldn't think of a single conversation that might merit the word 'great'.

'It's Declan.'

Declan? Funny, I hadn't seen hide nor hair of him in donkey's years – hadn't wanted to either – and suddenly I practically tripped over him every time I turned around.

'What do you want?' No point in beating around the bush, he wouldn't be ringing if he didn't want something.

'Now Lee, don't be so negative. It's just a courtesy call.'

Courtesy call? To me? Who was he trying to kid?

'Don't get on your high horse. It was nice to see you again – long time no see and all that. I thought it would be nice to catch up.'

Nice to catch up? Sorry about all these questions, but if you knew Declan – well, you wouldn't trust him with a barge pole either. Bet he was after Teri's phone number – I'd seen the way he was eyeing her up.

'Honestly, Lee. Scouts honour – no ulterior motive. Just thought dinner and a chat would be nice.'

It was the 'honestly' that did it.

'No thanks, Declan.' And I put down the phone.

It was only afterwards that I wondered – if he needed my help to get Teri's number, who helped him get mine?

Turned out it was Mammy who gave Declan my phone number. He spoke to his mother, chair of the local branch of the Union of Catholic Mothers, and she spoke to my mother, UCM treasurer.

'I didn't think you'd mind, Lee, you were always such good friends at school.'

Good friends? Where was she when I was growing up?

You'd have thought Declan might've taken the hint. Not a bit of it – he rang again the following day.

'Lee, since when did you become your brother's keeper?'

What the hell? 'I'm sorry, you've lost me.' I knew I shouldn't have answered the phone. What's the point in having call screening if I never use it?

'Teri – since when did you start vetting her phone calls?'

'She's not my brother.' Which was stating the obvious but two could play at being obtuse.

'But you do vet her callers?'

'Declan, get to the point. What do you want?'

'You know what I want.'

Aagh! 'You do realise she's seeing someone? And you're a married man.'

'Tell me something I don't know.'

This conversation was going nowhere fast.

'You don't think that as a married man,' I emphasised those last words, 'it's not perhaps very nice to be propositioning an attractive, single woman, who already has a boyfriend?'

'I'm not propositioning you. And you're not *that* attractive.' A miniscule pause. 'And you *have* a boyfriend?'

The note of surprise in his voice was distinctly uncomplimentary. And I didn't much like the rest of what he'd said either. 'I didn't mean me.'

'I'm not planning on propositioning Teri either. Although, she is attractive. Very attractive.' And again, he emphasised his last words.

'There's no need to rub salt in the wound.'

'Oh Lee,' he mocked, 'have you been nursing a secret passion all these years?'

'No, I haven't,' I snapped. I hadn't, had I? No, on reflection, definitely not. Although why not? He *was* very attractive. Perhaps, best not to go there.

'Why do you want Teri's phone number?'

'It's not really any of your business.' And he paused, waiting for me to jump in with an angry retort.

Bloody hell! He was winding me up, just as he'd done all those years ago at primary school. I breathed heavily. I really wished I'd ignored the phone in the first place. But if I gave in to my inclination to hang up, or to rise to his bait, I'd be letting him win, just as I had every time I'd overreacted to his ding dong bell on my pigtails as a freckle-faced kid.

So, with an almost supernatural effort, I said nothing.

After a moment, Declan continued. 'But if you must know, the Leader is producing an autumn business supplement and we're doing profiles of some of the county's most successful industrialists. I know her dad is more or less retired now, but he's still head of one of the biggest companies in the area.'

'And where does Teri come in?'

'The old man's living in France now, isn't he? And the guy who's taken over the day-to-day running of the business won't talk to us. So, I thought, maybe Teri could provide some insights, a few personal anecdotes...you know the sort of thing.'

God! The man was exasperating.

'Why couldn't you just have told me this in the first place?'

'You didn't give me a chance. You just jumped to conclusions.'

Hmm...I hate it when people like him are right.

'And why don't you want to interview me about Daddy? His business wasn't handed to him on a plate. He had to work hard with Grand-daddy to get the business where it is today. Teri's dad inherited everything from his dad.'

'I know – toffs who go back generations.'

'So...my dad?'

'His profile's already in the bag.' Declan laughed. 'But your filial loyalty does you credit.'

'I hope you haven't said anything horrible about him?'

'Wouldn't dare. The Catholic Mafia would be after me like a shot.'

So, since there didn't seem any good reason not to, I gave him Teri's phone number. And, being a good journalist, once he added her to his contacts list, he kept her on it.

Chapter Ten

Teri

What was there to understand? I know if I had kids, they wouldn't be as greedy and self-centred as Victoria. I thought if I was to have a relationship with Dan I would have a fight on my hands, imagining it was going to be like something out of a cheap movie: spoilt daughter sets about making misery for Daddy's new girlfriend because she wants her parents to get back together and play happy families again. I was going to have to watch this one carefully.

On the Monday morning after the bowling date and my unanswered text, Dan rang me at work, full of apologies. He'd lost his mobile in which he'd keyed my number. He'd had to look up the university and ring me at work; he hoped I didn't mind. Mind? I was absolutely delighted and suggested a drink after work, and we met in a local wine bar after he'd presented that evening's programme. We were just settling down with a nicely chilled bottle of French white when his mobile beeped with a text message.

'Oh,' I said, eyeing it suspiciously. 'You found your mobile?'

'Oh, yes,' Dan replied. 'Funny thing. It was right there on the coffee table where I usually leave it – under a pile of newspapers. I'd obviously not looked properly. How daft can you get?'

He looked at the text, smiled and started to text something back.

'Excuse me a second,' he said, tapping. 'It's Victoria. She wants to know what I'm doing this evening.' He tapped some more, reading out the words

51

as he keyed them in: 'Having. Drink. With. Gorgeous. Lady...x'

I liked the 'gorgeous' but I wasn't sure about Dan having to check in with his daughter. And I wasn't sure that mobile phones went missing on-their-own and then turned up in the same place you left them.

'Was Victoria staying with you this weekend?' I asked.

'Yes, she was. Took her shopping on Saturday and then to a movie she wanted to see. We spent yesterday chilling.'

Yes, all right. Enough about bloody father-daughter bonding, thank you.

The rest of the evening was fabulous – just Dan and me getting to know each other, and getting drunk. He called a taxi and came home with me.

The rest of the night should've been magical.

We got back to my flat and I opened a bottle of red. Dan sat on the sofa, and I set two glasses on the coffee table and flopped beside him. We joked about skateboarding ducks, and I punched him playfully on the arm and teased him about being a famous face off t'telly. We drank some more. He became serious and leaned towards me.

'I hope I'm getting the right impression here...' he said.

'You are,' I breathed.

'Because I don't want you to think I'm taking advantage.'

Oh, take advantage, I thought.

He pulled me to him and kissed me on the mouth, moving his lips slowly, carefully, pulling me in even more.

'Come with me,' I said, standing and holding out my hand.

We went into the bedroom and somehow became nervous with each other again. We did a bit of play-fighting while helping each other undress then we both fell onto the bed. Dan raised himself on to an elbow and leaned across and over me.

This is where the lights should have dimmed and soft music played. But Dan was unable to get an erection.

'I need a fluffer,' he joked.

'A what?'

'A woman who'll come and get things moving – a fluffer. They use fluffers for magazine shoots when they're taking pictures of naked men and they don't want a full erection, but need more than a damp squib.'

'Fetch me half a dozen fluffers,' I yelled. 'And why don't they want a full erection for the magazine shoots?' I asked once we'd stopped laughing.

'The newsagents won't allow it,' he said. 'You can't have pictures of fully erect, naked men in magazines that children might pick up.'

'Gosh, you know so much, don't you?' I said.

'It's amazing what you pick up, interviewing people on telly,' he replied.

We tried again, but to no effect. Dan tentatively suggested he'd had too much to drink and couldn't we just cuddle instead? So we did, and fell asleep in each other's arms.

In the morning, Dan awoke with a hard-on so we started to use it rather than lose it. But as he was getting into his stride, thrusting with determined firmness, small droplets of blood appeared on my naked breasts – one or two and then larger drops. I squirmed. Dan looked down and yelped when he saw the blood.

'Oh my God!' he cried, pulling back sharply and out from between my legs. He leapt backwards off the bed and rushed naked into the bathroom. 'Aagh. I'm bleeding…I'm bleeding.' He was almost hysterical.

I pulled on my dressing gown and stood in the doorway. 'It's only a nosebleed,' I tried to reassure him. 'Put your head back.'

He emerged with a torn twist of toilet paper jammed up each nostril, his face white and his eyes darting from side to side clearly considering whether I was the sort of person who'd call an ambulance or leave him to bleed to death on my bathroom floor. I took in the sight of a naked Dan Caine, head back with mouth open in a silent scream, nose jammed with tissue slowly becoming wet and red, his penis, not so much a damp squib as a limp squid, and looking as sorry and dejected as its owner looked pale and frightened. Get me a fluffer, I thought.

Dan was rather reticent about trying again.

'It must've been first night nerves,' he said. 'Never happened to me before.'

I wasn't sure if he meant the nosebleed or the no-show the night before.

For the next two nights we tried, and that which didn't happen didn't happen again; Dan couldn't get an erection.

On the third night, Dan pulled away from me and sat, head in hands on the edge of the bed.

'I'm sorry, Teri,' he said. 'I don't know what's wrong with me.'

53

Nor me, I thought. I'd never known a man with this problem: what's wrong with him? For a nanosecond, I wondered if there was something I was doing, or not doing that might be a cause. But I dismissed the thought almost instantly. Heavens, girl, I told myself, you've never had problems with men and sex. Why, you just have to click your fingers and they come running, trouser zips at the ready.

Dan didn't look any different in the men's department: not excessively big and not as big as Nigel, one of my earlier boyfriends, but then not excessively small and not as small as Al, one of my one-night stands. Boy, that Al was a bummer; looked absolutely gorgeous with his clothes on in the wine bar, but when we got home and he took them off, that was another matter entirely. Talk about expensive clothes making the man. He didn't get to first base – he did look stupid standing there buck naked with me telling him to get on his bike, or words to that effect.

'It's not physical,' Dan explained after taking himself off to the GP the next day to make sure he wasn't suffering from some incurable man-disease. 'The doc thinks it's psychological.'

'Psychological?' I repeated. 'What, you mean you're mentally scarred or something?'

'Well,' said Dan. 'Could be.'

'By me?'

He reached out. We were sitting on the sofa in my living room, a bottle of white wine on the coffee table in front of us and two filled glasses. But neither of us was drinking. He reached out and put his hand on my arm.

'Not you, Teri. My ex.'

The delightful, maintenance-spending Sara, who'd spawned the wretched, interfering little bitch-child, Victoria.

In a way, I was pleased to hear the ex-wife was the cause of concern. Another big cross against Dan Caine's former family.

In another way, I wondered if I had time and patience for all this – this being a situation which was going to need careful handling and what would probably turn out to be expensive sex therapy. And I decided I wasn't going into any sessions in the sex department as I definitely didn't need them.

Dan hadn't told me much about Sara – and now it poured out. She was a class model: a blonde-haired secretary to one of the managing directors of a local radio station where Dan had started out as a reporter. The poor sap had fallen for her charms, which involved large tits, shapely legs and few brain cells, and she'd fallen pregnant with the devil child, so they'd married in haste and Dan repented at leisure.

Sara urged Dan to leave the poxy little radio station and try his hand at TV because she fancied the bright lights and bigger pay packet that telly journalists could provide. She also wanted to pack in her own job and become a woman who lunched.

She turned out to be a grasping, pushy wife and mother who constantly found new ways to spend money: bigger house, softer furnishings, riding lessons and then a pony for Victoria, far-flung exotic holidays, and the designer wardrobe to meet all occasions for both her and her blasted daughter.

Now, while I don't object to anyone wanting the finer things in life – hell, I demand them myself – I didn't like the sound of the manipulation being played out by the Mrs and Miss Caines.

Dan didn't put it all quite like that; he's far too nice and loyal. But I read between the lines, and out of the gaps popped a nasty, grasping wife who dominated her husband, laughed at his mistakes, pointed out his weaknesses and assumed credit for his successes.

Worse, she used sex as her bean counter right from the start of their marriage. They only had it if she was in the mood (which had to be good, and her good moods were linked to being able to look forward to something luxurious and expensive). When Victoria was about ten, they palmed her off on Sara's mother for the night and went off to stay in one of the Denbyside Hotel's most expensive suites to celebrate their anniversary. Dan hadn't seen the point of going to stay in a hotel just a few miles from the house they lived in, but Sara had insisted and he didn't like to argue as the thought of all that pampering put her in a good mood – and good mood spelt sex. Sara fell pregnant with what was to be a little brother or sister for Victoria. But then she lost the baby at eight weeks and refused to have sex again.

'So you've not had sex for...' I was about to say but thought better of doing the maths as the poor love'd had enough humiliation to last him a lifetime.

'Oh you poor darling,' I crooned, pulling his head down onto my shoulder. He leaned against me, nuzzling my neck. I kissed the top of his head, and he moved closer, pressing himself against me. I slid sideways back into the sofa pulling Dan with me. He kissed me, tentatively at first, and then in a sudden burst of passion he seemed to come alive and kissed me so fiercely and passionately I knew we might not need those therapy sessions.

Sure enough, and urgently, he started clawing at my shirt, managing to dislodge two buttons and thrusting his hand inside to fondle my left breast while I reached between his legs.

Okay, I thought, feeling the confidence stirring inside Dan's trousers, cancel the fluffer.

Chapter Eleven

Lee

I really wish Teri hadn't felt it necessary to tell me about the fluffer, or the nose bleed, or, and most especially, Dan's failure to get an erection, again and again and again. I know it's a big deal, I know it's not that common and I know it never happened to her before – but TOO MUCH information!

Of course, I'm glad they worked through their problems – but, again, I really didn't need to hear ALL about it, especially as I don't think I'll ever be able to look Dan straight in the face again. Or watch him on TV – I can't square the serious, authoritative, polished news presenter with the mental image of a naked bloke, chest streaked with blood and two plugs of toilet tissue wedged up his nostrils. Shame really, Ridings Today had been a good watch until then.

But, apart from anything else, I found it hard to work up any enthusiasm for Teri and her doings when I was struggling to sort out the stuff messing up my own head. I'd never thought of myself as particularly maternal so the protective rush of affection I felt for the little blob had been an unexpected whammy. I even found myself toying with baby names – I quite liked Stella for a girl and, perhaps, Henry for a boy. Or maybe something more Irish? Aileen? Or Conor?

I was badly in need of a dose of Teri's brisk common sense, and I tried several times to chat to her about it, but it was difficult to get a word in edgeways. 'Dan this' and 'Dan that' and 'Dan the bleeding other'. She was like a broken record. At any other time, I might've tried to get her to put the brakes on. It was all very well being totally wrapped up in her darling Dan, but she was forgetting he came as part of a package that included a demanding ex-wife, an unhappy teen and a whopping great mortgage. She could kiss goodbye to spending this telly type's vast fortune – plenty of other people had got there first.

But she was too loved up – sex three times a night and twice in the morning. Surprised she could bloody walk; I'd have been on my knees long before that first week was out.

Good God – had it only been a week? It felt much, much longer. Sod Teri, let her deal with her own problems. I'd got more than enough on my plate. Mike was proving every bit the rat his wife said he was – why was I surprised? If he could cheat on his wife why should *I* expect unswerving loyalty and support? But, I certainly didn't expect the relentless pressure to get rid of the baby. Oh, he didn't put it quite so bluntly, but he made it perfectly clear if I went ahead with the pregnancy it would be a one-woman show. And, he hinted about forthcoming cutbacks at work and possible redundancies. There were no threats, not even a hint or an insinuation, but I got the distinct impression I'd be first in the firing line. I didn't know which way to turn. I'd never felt more in need of a friend.

Chapter Twelve

Teri

After our romantic tangle on the sofa, I was confident things could only get better between Dan and me. I realised, talking to Lee later, that Dan had a lot of baggage, but now it was out in the open, the air had been cleared and we could move forward (talk about mixing clichés).

Lee nodded understandingly – as she does, bless her – as I told her the sorry tale of life with the ex-wife.

Perhaps I was a little graphic telling her how Dan and I then made love on the sofa, in the hallway and on the kitchen table. 'Enough information,' she said, laughing. But I could tell the poor girl was imagining herself in my place and dreaming of one day meeting someone as fabulous as Dan and having glorious sex with him. I often wondered about Lee. How did she manage not having any – sex, I mean? She'd not had a relationship for years. Use it or lose it, kid, I'd tell her, and she'd give me one of her funny looks.

After what I came to think of as the confessional therapy session (I could've charged Dan for curing him), he and I spent the next couple of nights together 'just to cement progress' as Dan put it. Having found a new spring in his step, he didn't want anything to trip him up. He was on a roll, and I was rolling with him.

I should've been more alert. Things had been quiet on the Victoria front. I was basking in a highly-charged and passionate relationship with a handsome man but had forgotten to listen to that quiet little voice at the back of my brain saying 'Where's the kid gone?'

We'd been seeing each other for exactly a fortnight, and I decided to celebrate – not with an expensive meal at a high-end restaurant (I'm aware that's what the delightful Sara would've done) – but by cooking Dan a meal, lighting the candles, lowering the lights and letting nature take its course.

All was going well. Dan arrived straight from the programme. He still had traces of make-up on his face.

'What is that colour?' I asked, poking at his cheek.

'It's Sienna No 5,' he said, reaching into his man-bag and pulling out a powder compact. 'This is what I use whenever I'm in front of camera.'

Now, I've known a lot of men (Lee would say far too many), but I've never known one to carry his make-up around with him. Oh, hang on. Jazz, the singer in the rock band used eyeliner and, anyway, more and more men are using moisturiser, aren't they?

The meal went well. The candles burned softly. We took our brandies to the sofa and settled back. Then Dan's mobile rang. I murmured for him to leave it, but he said it might be important and moved perhaps a little too swiftly to answer it.

'Ah, hello, darling. You're back,' he said.

Darling? Back?

'What? Tonight?' he continued. 'Well…well, yes, Okay then. I'm with Teri at the moment, but I'm sure she won't mind.'

Turns out Victoria had been to a health spa with Mummy and they'd just got back, and Victoria was missing Daddy and would Daddy pop round to see her and say 'nighty night'.

'You don't mind, do you?' he asked.

'What on earth did you say?' Lee asked the next day.

'Well, I could hardly say I did mind,' I told her. 'I couldn't stop him going to see his kid.'

'There's going to have to be some big compromises if you're going to keep seeing Dan,' Lee said, looking at me in that concerned way she has.

'I can do compromise,' I said. 'And I'll win – watch me.'

But Victoria and Dan didn't do compromise, and by the time I realised that, it was too late. I'd fallen for Dan and convinced myself I could wean him away from the clingy kid. But as Lee so often pointed out, I didn't have kids so didn't understand the pull of the little beggars. And nor did I appreciate that, as well as loving his kid, Dan loved his work.

It was two against one.

But then I'm nothing if not up for a fight. I was determined; Dan and I were going to be an exclusive item.

When he invited me to the Royal Television Society annual awards dinner, I knew I'd cracked it. He wouldn't take someone to a work's bash he wasn't serious about.

Chapter Thirteen

Teri

I took the day off to get myself ready. I should've been running Level 1 tutorials to go through some work I'd left them the week before. I call it homework, but that academic arse Peter Heron calls it 'ongoing lecture-orientated discussion'. However, half the little beggars didn't turn up for tutorials, and those that did arrived with none of the prepared work and couldn't take part in a 'lecture-orientated discussion' if it lay on the floor in front of them and shouted 'take me'.

So what was a girl to do? Sit in her office all day with sweaty Level 1s or pop down to Vanilla Pod and get ready for a big night?

I chose the latter. I have relatively little to do with my hair, which is blonde at the moment, but the wonderful Sasha put in a few highlights. She does eyebrow threading, so I had my brows trimmed and tinted at the same time.

I come out of Vanilla Pod looking the million dollars I so obviously am. If you've got it, shout about it, I say. Why some women can't look after their looks and make the best of themselves, I shall never know. It's something I'm forever telling Lee.

Dan and I looked the couple: him in his tux, me in a long, shimmering evening dress and the highest heels I dared wear.

We arrived at the Denbyshire Hotel and the doorman said, 'Evening Mr Caine,' giving ever such a slight bow. 'Enjoyed your show last night.'

'Thank you,' Dan said and strode further into the foyer. 'It's not a *show*,' he hissed to me. 'It's a bloody *news programme*.'

'Dan!' some screechy female yelled from the opposite end of the foyer – a girl of about twenty-three, in the shortest, tightest, yellow freak of a frock. She tottered over, her arms outstretched to embrace Dan in a bright yellow cloud hug. 'Who are you with?' she asked him, not even looking at me. I suppose the dazzle from all that yellow had made her have some sort of retinal explosion, and she couldn't see me behind the glare.

'Er, this is...' Dan began to introduce me but screechy female wasn't interested. She undid the hug and hooked her arm in his, dragging him to the heavily carpeted flight of steps leading up from the foyer into the ballroom.

'Just got to tell you...' I heard her say, confiding in a loud stage whisper, before the two of them, leaning closely into each other, climbed the stairs. Dan didn't even look behind him to see where I was. Screechy was obviously giving him some good gossip because he threw back his head and laughed. I followed at a sedate pace.

And so it was for the rest of the evening: lots of producers, directors, autocue cuties and gallery assistants pouting and parading, guffawing at the in-telly jokes and congratulating each other on whichever little programme they'd just made. Dan was so busy talking skateboarding ducks he hardly said a word to me all night.

Throughout the meal, people would come over and put their arm round his shoulder or kiss him and shriek about something that had happened in telly-land that week or something they were setting up for next week's programme. At one stage, between the strangely coloured, shrimpy-looking starter and the barely cooked, rubbery duck, I jokingly asked if telly was always like this, and Dan looked at me quizzically and asked, 'What do you mean'?

'Well, all this kissing and shrieking and patting yourselves on the back,' I said.

He looked hurt and was just about to say something when the yellow frock suddenly appeared and screeched, 'Dan, darling. Do us a big favour, will you? Can you present the Sports Programme of the Year award?'

'Why? Who's supposed to be doing it?'

'That prick footballer, Shayne Brickham, but he's not turned up.'

Ooh, my friend Shayne.

'That's a shame,' I said, interrupting screecher in full flow. 'I like him.'

They both looked at me in puzzlement. Screecher swept her hand between us to dismiss me and said, 'Anyways…' and turned back to Dan. She didn't need to encourage him any further. He was on his feet and pushing his chair back.

'Hey, you're not going to leave me?' I asked, but he didn't hear. Screecher grabbed his arm (again) and tugged him away, presumably to read up on sports because, as far as I know, the only athletic thing Dan knew anything about was ten-pin bowling because he'd never shown an ounce of interest in anything else that involved movement and sweat (apart from sex, but that's hardly an Olympic sport, is it?).

So I was left alone to tackle the rubbery duck in front of me and the boring businessman on my left who'd only been invited because he was sponsoring one of the awards – Most Boring Business Programme, no doubt.

There was an appreciative roar from the audience when Dan appeared on stage to present the award to some boys and girls who worked on the sports desk of Ridings Today and, to be honest, he did it very smoothly; but then he's a television professional so should be able to perform on demand. There was much obligatory back slapping between Dan and the boys, and kissing between Dan and the girls, and then kissing between the boys and the girls. The photographer got them all to line up with Dan in the middle handing over a garish little glass sliver, which I suppose was meant to be the award. Then there was more shrieking and kissing, and Dan stepped off the stage where screecher was waiting, ablaze in yellow, to lead him away to another table full of scantily-clad screechers.

Mr Boring on my left had given up on me and turned to the person on his other side, no doubt to have an intelligent chat about upward, inward and sideways investment entrepreneurs and Industry of Directorial Time-Wasting. I stared gloomily into my glass of what was now slightly warmish white wine. I knocked it back and reached for the bottle standing in its little glass cooler in the middle of the table.

'Here, let me help,' a man standing behind me said. He leaned over, forcing me gently but ungainly forwards into the table as he reached for the bottle, grabbed it by the neck, slipped into Dan's vacant seat and started pouring wine into my glass. I was about to say 'What the hell...?' when some instinct stopped me and I looked closer. I vaguely recognised him from somewhere. He was a plumply-faced man with dark hair gelled into a little duck's arse on the top of his head, which, frankly, is a ridiculous look on any man over the age of twenty-five, and even more odd-looking on someone in his late forties.

Hot breath, sticky with stale, red wine wafted over me as he said, 'You're with Dan, aren't you?' And before I could reply he went on. 'You're Teri from the university?'

'Yes, how did you...?'

He introduced himself as Richard Walker, managing director of Ridings Today – and Dan's boss. Thank God for that instinct of mine. Yes, Mr Walker had been in the studios that night I went to watch the programme go out. Mr Boss Man was not my type. I don't go for duck-arsed plump guys, so I was hoping this one wasn't going to give the old come-on. And, in fact, he wasn't.

'I'm glad I've caught you,' he said. 'You'll know Peter Heron...?'

'Oh yes,' I replied, wondering what was coming next. 'He's dean of my faculty – English and Media.'

'Ah, yes. So he probably knows his stuff,' Duck's Arse said. Something stirred in my memory banks. 'You probably know he's being considered to present our new Friday night book programme?'

Ah, that was it! Peter Heron the would-be television literary star.

'Oh, I knew he was angling, but I didn't know he was seriously being considered,' I said. Duck's Arse looked closely at me.

'You don't think he should be seriously considered?' he asked. 'You seem doubtful.'

Now, I must confess, it was the wine; it was Dan leaving me on my own; it was the screechy female in the yellow frock; it was the arrogant, back-slapping television types; it was the boring businessman; it was this plump man with the ridiculous hair. But, most of all, it was the thought of Peter Heron, made up and coiffed, talking the late-night talk with amateur authors, boring bloggers and bloody book club members that conspired to make me say what I said next.

'Between you and me,' I said, leaning towards that slightly reddening plump face and trying to avoid looking at the sticky little tuft of gelled hair, 'I wouldn't touch the old imposter with a bargepole let alone a bookmark. He's never read anything in his life apart from post-it note-sized psychology sound-bites on delivering best bloody practice in the corporate environment.'

At that moment Dan reappeared at the table. He and Duck's Arse did a bit of hand shaking and back slapping, and Mr Boss Man said something about having had a 'very interesting' chat with me and then he excused himself and went off, presumably to reapply some gel (I tried not to imagine how his pillow must look in the morning).

The dinner was well into the pudding stage – a sort of creamy mush with speckles of chocolate on it. Dan was looking delighted with himself.

'Well done,' I said.

'Oh, it was nothing,' he said, preening with self-importance.

'You're quiet,' he said in the taxi going home.

'Just a bit of a headache,' I lied and didn't invite him in.

Chapter Fourteen

Teri

I hate Christmas. As a child, my jolly Xmases had usually been spent on my own playing with my expensive toys – a new doll's house, a pink-painted bike or whatever. Charlie would be in his room reading the manuals he'd asked for: Animal Husbandry for the Amateur, Allotment Management for the Self-Starter and, oddly, Fashion through the Ages. Strange lad, Charlie, but I suppose it hinted at what was to come. Dad usually took himself off for a walk and, when we resisted his invitations to join him, ended up in the pub, only to come home to the delights of my mother's burnt offerings; she having spent too much time on the cooking sherry and not enough time tending the turkey. They would row, Dad would head off back to the pub, Mum would burst into tears and, pausing only to pick up a bottle of brandy, would rush to her bedroom, slam the door and lay, sobbing quietly on the bed until falling into an alcoholic stupor. I did go up once and rub her back, telling her to 'shush, it'll be all right', but she simply buried her head deeper into her pillow and ignored me. I remember taking the bottle of brandy back downstairs and emptying the rest of the contents down the sink but then got a massive telling off from her the next day for wasting expensive drink. So I decided leaving her to her own devices was probably for the best. Charlie and I would later sit together on the sofa watching the festive telly programmes while stuffing ourselves with cold, burnt turkey sandwiches.

But this Christmas was going to be different. I had Dan in my life, and I would be spending the holiday with him. I started Googling exotic festive breaks and eventually narrowed the choice down to either a Caribbean cruise or a trip on the Eastern and Oriental Express.

Lee was impressed but concerned (her default position, generally). 'Won't it cost a fortune?' she asked.

'Well, yes,' I said. 'But I'll give Dad a ring and get him to send me a bit extra this month – tell him it's his Christmas present to me. Anyway, it's my first Christmas with Dan, and I want it to be special.'

The trouble was, although Dan wanted Christmas to be special, he wanted it to be special for his daughter as well. When I broached the subject of going away together, he loved the idea.

'Oh, that'll be great. We'll be together like a real family,' he said.

'A real family?'

'Yes. You, me and Victoria.'

'Oh. I wasn't thinking of taking Victoria.' I tried not to sound horrified. 'It will be just you and me. Think how lovely and romantic it will be.'

'Oh, but it's my turn to have Victoria for Christmas. She was with her mother last year.'

I tried to persuade him; I even suggested he gave the devil-child some money so she could go off for the holidays with some little playmate of hers, but Dan was having none of it; he was spending Christmas with the fruit of his loins.

So we rowed about it, and I told him to do what he liked. We made it up later, but I couldn't change his mind and so we agreed we'd do our own thing for the festivities.

Chapter Fifteen

Lee

Christmas was a compromise. Teri wanted, indeed expected, to spend the holiday somewhere sunny and exotic in new-love bliss with Dan, and I'd expected, if not wanted, to spend the day with the ghost of Grand-daddy hovering over Mammy and Daddy's dinner table. Instead we ended up together at my place.

Dan had been much taken with Teri's idea of a romantic getaway – as long as they brought Victoria along too. It was his turn to spend Christmas with his daughter, and he thought it would be a lovely idea if the three of them could have some 'family' time together. The poor sap. I bet he really did think a 'little holiday' would help cement the relationship between 'his two girls'. Fat chance. He'd have been lucky to come home in one piece and Victoria lucky to come home at all.

My own somewhat half-hearted arrangements were also scuppered. Seems Mammy and Daddy shared my apprehension about the ghosts of Christmas past and booked themselves onto a festive Caribbean cruise. They invited me to join them, but I refused – too much dressing up for dinner and too much sea-sicky boat. And I also turned down an invite from Fliss to join her and Charles and the children for turkey sandwiches and trifle at tea time. I just couldn't face it. So, I made my excuses, putting the blame on Teri, who was, I said, going through a rough patch.

Fliss had been rather rude. 'Her idea of a rough patch is most people's idea of a walk in the park.' In other words, she thought Teri was being her usual spoilt self – which, to some extent, she was. Whatever she might say, and she said a lot, believe me, it *wasn't* unreasonable of Dan to want to spend Christmas with his only child. And, nor, however much she might wish for it, was Dan ever going to divorce his daughter.

'I get that,' she said. 'But they're not joined at the bloody hip.'

Not physically, perhaps, but emotionally, yes. Fliss and I both adored Daddy, who spoiled us rotten – but, not in the sense that he showered us with money and gifts and material comforts. Instead, he gave us his time, which was far more valuable. Before we moved to the Alderwood area, he played cricket with us in the back garden every Sunday after we came back from Mass – pretty much his only completely free afternoon. He taught us to catch and to hit a six in the direction of the back fence, and he'd laugh with us when one of us bowled what he called a 'dolly mixture'. Not a term that forms part of the official MCC lingo, but in our house it meant a ball that dribbled from the bowler's hand in the vague direction of the batsman. To be honest there were a lot of Sunday afternoon 'dolly mixtures'.

Once we moved to the Alderwood area, the park was almost literally across the road so, in summer, we went there almost every evening. As soon as Daddy came home from work he'd shower and change his clothes, and we'd skip off together for an hour of running and catching and playing before tea. By then, Grand-daddy had moved in with us and he often came too. We were very lucky, Fliss and I, that the two most important men in our lives made time to play with us, and this at a time when the idea of men playing an equal parental role was still far from the norm.

If Teri'd had a daddy like my daddy she wouldn't have been surprised that Dan made time for his little girl.

But she didn't. Instead, and I'm being charitable here, her father was a miserable money-bags, who cared far more for the pound in his pocket than he did for either of his children. Little wonder really that Teri had a skewed idea about how a father should behave towards his kid. Mothers too. As kids, Fliss and I had often been irked by Mammy's insistence on homework before tea-time and early-to-bed on school nights, but we both knew darned well that we owed our good jobs and rewarding careers to her belief in the importance of education. Teri's mother, on the other hand, was a stuck-up lush, who didn't care a fig whether her daughter went to school with or without clean pants and socks so long as she could meet her posh cronies for a booze-fuelled lunch that almost always segued into an evening of drinking, gambling and extramarital sex. As a role model, she sucked. And Teri's dad wasn't much of an example either.

All things considered, it's a wonder Teri has turned out as well as she has, although there was no convincing her Dan's desire to spend Christmas with his daughter was either normal or understandable. And his insistence on 'dragging' her overseas with them effectively put the scuds on her plans for a romantic getaway. No way, Teri said, was she forking out a fortune to take the 'devil child' on a holiday she didn't deserve. So, Dan, forced to choose between Christmas without his daughter or Christmas without Teri, made the only possible choice and left Teri to enjoy – if that's the right word – the festive season chez Harper. Lucky me.

Chapter Sixteen

Lee

Teri rang the front door bell mid-afternoon, just as the Festival of Kings on Radio 4 was drawing to a close on Christmas Eve. She dumped her overnight bags – yes, bags! She doesn't travel light, even for an overnight stop – in the spare room and immediately opened a bottle of wine.

'Isn't it a bit early?' I asked.

'No,' she said, pouring us each a large glass of Chilean red. I sipped cautiously, shuddered and put the glass to one side. Teri is forever trying to educate my wine palate – red, she says, is richer and more flavoursome, but, so far, despite her very best endeavours, I seem to have hung on to my penchant for a dry, white wine.

'Lightweight,' she mocked, pouring my discarded glassful into her glass, which she emptied in a single, purposeful glug.

'Come on,' she said. 'I've brought some box sets. We're going to have some girly time.'

Actually, that seemed a very nice way to spend what remained of the day. So we curled up on my settee – or, sofa, as Teri calls it – and watched endless re-runs of various comedy classics. It didn't take long for Teri to get sozzled – not enough though to completely blunt her powers of observation.

'Lee,' she said, as she poured herself another drink, 'is there something you're not telling me?'

Pardon?

She held up her glass, leaned across me and picked the empty wine bottle from the living room waste basket. Sorry – that should've been lounge not living room.

'This bottle,' she said, taking a hearty slug of wine, 'is empty. My glass has been filled and emptied several times. Yours has not.'

I knew what she was trying to say, but I still didn't feel ready to confide in her – largely because any support she might provide would be more than offset by the obligation to defend Mike from the inevitable torrent of abuse. He might deserve it – okay, he *did* deserve it – but I couldn't be bothered.

'I'm off the booze at the moment.'

'You? Off booze?'

Hell's teeth. Don't sound so surprised. I'm not a bloody alcoholic.

'It's Christmas Eve. We should be having a drink. I'm having a drink – you are *not* having a drink?'

Talk about stating the obvious.

'Why?' she asked.

'I don't like red wine,' I said.

'That won't wash,' she said. 'I brought white wine with me as well as red – you saw me put it in the fridge – you could've opened it. Why haven't you?'

She leaned back, drained her glass, stared at it for a moment and said, 'What gave Mrs O the idea that you and Mike might be an item?'

Oh God! She was getting close.

'Stella effing fat cow Lastings!' she said. 'Now,' and she looked at me, 'what does she know that I don't?'

As it happens, nothing, I thought. In fact, if anyone had alerted Mrs Orme to her husband's latest fling, it was probably Chrissie. She was Mike's de facto personal assistant, and he confided in her a lot. 'She's a good sounding board,' he'd told me once. 'Very trustworthy.' Depends what you call trustworthy, I suppose – most of us academics thought Chrissie was about as reliable as a leaky ship. She was forever tittle-tattling to Mike about senior common room spats and slip-ups. I could well believe if she got wind of an affair she'd blab.

'I know.' Teri was on a roll here, and, leaping to her feet, pointed a finger and wagged it. 'The rumour's true, isn't it?'

What to say? I didn't want to lie.

'And,' she said, 'what's more, you're pregnant!'

Bloody hell. The woman was omniscient. Was there anything she didn't know? 'That's why you're not drinking.'

She looked at me, and I stared at the floor.

'But you're not going to keep the baby, are you?'

I didn't answer.

'Lee,' she said. 'Be realistic. You can't raise a child on your own.'

She was right – although, even in my miserableness, I noticed that she rightly assumed Mike would not be part of the picture.

'No,' I said. And then I told her everything about the half-hearted relationship, the very much unplanned pregnancy and the pressure from Mike to get rid of the baby. 'I can't afford to support another child,' he'd said. 'And I don't know what to do,' I wailed.

Teri did. She went into the kitchen, poured a large glass of dry, white wine and ordered me to drink it. 'Every last bloody drop.'

#

Teri and I both agreed that Christmas hadn't been the best ever, but it wasn't the worst either. We both ended up drunk, but, were nowhere near as hung over as we deserved the next morning. I woke about seven thirty and stumbled downstairs to get a glass of water and a dry cream cracker. Sometimes, if I was quick enough, I could avert the inevitable sick-fest. Too late. Teri came into the kitchen a few minutes later and found me being sick into the washing-up bowl.

'Lord,' she said. 'I didn't think you'd had that much to drink.'

'I didn't,' I said in between bouts of retching. 'Well, I did but it's not the booze. I'm like this every morning.'

She considered me. 'Wouldn't it be less messy to just hang your head over the toilet?'

Of course it would! But I wouldn't have made it back up the stairs in time.

'The downstairs loo?' she enquired.

'Was occupied,' I snapped.

'Oops,' she said.

Oops indeed!

I heaved and retched for several more minutes before finally daring to lift my head. Teri tore off a piece of kitchen roll.

'Wipe your face,' she ordered. She looked at the bowl and its foul-smelling contents with dislike. 'What are you going to do with that?'

Save it for posterity? 'I'll sort it out in a minute.' I felt exhausted and the day had barely begun. I waited a couple of minutes just to be sure my stomach had settled down.

'You look terrible,' Teri said.

You don't look so brilliant yourself, I thought, eyeing her panda eyes and streaky face. Clearly, her normally extensive bedtime beauty regime had slipped a bit last night. She peered at her reflection in the copper kettle on the stove and pouted.

'I look a bit rough myself,' she admitted. 'But nothing that can't be cured with a couple of paracetemol and a hot shower.'

If only.

I carried the disgusting bowl across the hallway. Teri kindly held open the lavatory door. 'Don't splash,' she warned.

As if I needed telling – it wasn't the first time I'd had to perform this operation. And probably wouldn't be the last. Teri watched as I poured the horrible mess down the toilet pan and handed me some more kitchen roll to wipe round the rim afterwards.

'What you need,' she said, 'is a nice cup of milky coffee.'

Coffee! I felt my stomach heave again. 'No!'

'Only trying to help,' she said, turning away and shrugging.

I sighed. 'Trust me. A dry cream cracker and a glass of water is all I need right now.'

She looked sceptical. 'If you say so.'

I would've loved to go back to bed and let the day wash over me, but Teri, who didn't go to church from one Christmas to the next, insisted on accompanying me to the 11am Mass.

'I've never been to a Catholic "do" before,' she said. 'It'll be an experience.'

'You won't enjoy it,' I warned. 'There'll be a lot of ghastly singing,

75

never-ending prayers and the sermon will go on forever and ever.'

'Bring it on,' she said.

It wasn't quite as bad as I predicted, primarily because Teri was fascinated by the candles, the incense and the rituals.

'Teach me how to curtsey,' she whispered as she followed me into our pew.

'It's not a curtsey,' I said.

'It looks like one,' she replied.

'It's called genuflecting.'

'Genuflecting.' She rolled the word around her tongue. 'Teach me how to do it.'

'Hush,' I whispered. 'You're in church – say a prayer.'

'Later,' she said, looking around wide-eyed. 'I didn't know Catholic churches were so pretty.'

I pressed a finger to my lips. 'Keep your bloody voice down.'

But she wouldn't be silenced. 'What's that thing they're doing with their hands,' she asked as a family of five genuflected and crossed themselves before piling into the pew in front.

'What thing with their hands?'

'This,' she said, waving her left hand in front of her face and across her shoulders.

'No, this,' I said, showing her how to do it correctly with her right hand, tapping her forehead, lips and left shoulder, then the right one. She copied me – and grinned.

'This is fun.'

The matriarch of the family in front turned and said 'Happy Christmas'. It was Mrs O'Brien. 'Have you heard from your mammy,' she asked.

'Yes,' I said. 'She phoned yesterday. They're having a lovely time – she's a cruise convert.' Mrs O'Brien smiled at the little joke. Don't mock – it was very appropriate for the venue.

Before she could reply, the choir and orchestra, led by Mrs O'Brien's husband, Rory, launched into the opening verse of 'Adeste Fideles', we stood and, fumbling to find the right page in the hymn book, joined in as the priest swept up the central aisle, splashing holy water on the assembled congregation as he progressed.

'Hell's bells,' Teri squealed, wiping her eyes. 'What in God's name was that?'

Declan, who was standing next to his mother, turned and raised a quizzical eyebrow. I shook my head and frowned at him. Teri stifled a giggle – but at least she took the hint and stopped broadcasting every thought that came into her head to the entire gathering. But she also raised a quizzical eyebrow in Declan's direction. 'Who?' she mouthed.

'Hands off,' I mouthed back. 'He's married.'

So what, she smirked.

'And,' I added, 'you're supposed to be in love with another man.'

'What's that got to do with anything?' she whispered in my ear. 'A girl can look, can't she?'

So long as that's all she does.

But she was very well behaved – until we came to the kiss of peace. She was a little bit too enthusiastic there, pecking at my cheek and the cheeks of both the lady on her other side and her husband too. Mrs O'Brien turned and offered us each a handshake. (She doesn't believe in kisses of peace.) Declan followed suit and offered me his hand, then with a wicked wink, brushed his lips against Teri's cheek.

'Happy Christmas,' he said, 'and a Happy New Year.' The bastard.

Mass finally over, we declined an invitation from Mrs O'Brien to join the family for a cup of tea in the parish centre. Teri caught Declan's eye and she hesitated, briefly tempted, but then changed her mind.

'Come on,' she said, grabbing my elbow. 'I need a proper drink.'

Back home, she opened a bottle of bubbly and poured us each a glass. 'Cheers,' she said, 'and Happy Christmas.'

I raised my glass to my lips. 'I shouldn't really be drinking.'

'Why?'

'Because...' Words failed me.

'Lee,' she said, 'are you really going to have this baby?'

'No,' I said. 'No.' And I drained the glass. 'I can't do it.'

Perhaps if Mike... But that wasn't going to happen.

And, besides, I was sick of feeling sick. 'I suppose I need to go and see someone as soon as the holiday is over,' I said and held out my glass for a refill.

Chapter Seventeen

Teri

Okay, so I'd rather have spent Christmas with Dan, walking hand-in-hand along a white sandy beach and making love on warm, star-filled nights, but Lee and I made the best of it and I think it did her good having me there.

I'd sort of guessed there was something up; Lee had been 'off' for a while, and I thought she was still upset about the rumour of her and tank-top Orme. I could even believe the daft mare had been having it off with him. But when I realised she hadn't touched a drop of her drink, it dawned on me there was something more going on. A lot more. Lee had been putting on weight recently; she looked pale; she wasn't drinking. 'You're pregnant,' I declared.

I was right. I tried my best to put on a sympathetic face as she told me about the affair with Mike, the shock and then the hopes she had when she found she was pregnant, and the pressure she was under from Mr Misery to get rid of the thing.

'I think Mike's right,' I said, resting my hand on her arm. 'You can't keep it. Be realistic. You can't raise a child on your own.'

I'm not sure the mummy manuals allow for the amount of wine we drank, but in the morning I found poor old Lee chucking up in the kitchen. It was disgusting, but I sorted her out. I made her shower, put on clean clothes, and eat some unbuttered toast. Don't ask me why, but unbuttered toast is the best thing for a hangover, so I assumed it would be okay for morning sickness too.

She was feeling better by the time we'd settled ourselves in front of the little Christmas tree in her lounge. It was a real one – complete with pine needles. I never bothered with real trees at Christmas; couldn't see the point – they make such a mess. I always make do with a little fibre-optic thing. But Lee is a traditional girl and had decorated hers with silver and red baubles. It looked quite tasteful – for her.

She plucked a present from under the tree and handed it to me saying, 'Here you are. I hope you like it. I've got the receipt so you can change it if you want to…but I thought it was your colour.' People are generally nervous about buying me things because I have such specific taste. When I moved into my flat, Lee bought me a set of tea towels (tea towels!) decorated with Yorkshire sayings, like 'See nowt, say nowt, spend nowt'. Well, you can imagine what happened to them.

More in hope than expectation, I ripped open the Christmas present. My heart sank even as I pulled at a pseudo-silk scarf decorated in a swirly pattern in shades of orange and gold. Orange and gold! For me! I sometimes wonder whether Lee knows me at all. That was heading straight for the charity shop. I reached under the tree and pulled out a box, beautifully wrapped in red tissue paper. Lee opened it nervously. I'd bought her some expensive truffle serum in the hope she'd use it rather than that cheap hand cream she slathers everywhere.

'Oh,' she said, her expression doubtful. 'I'll keep it for best.'

'Put some on now,' I insisted, taking the bottle from her and undoing the top 'and then, let's do the Christmas thing and go to church.'

I thought it would help Lee to spend a bit of time thinking good Catholic thoughts – and coming to her senses about this wretched pregnancy.

It was all rather nice – candles, gentle music, soft intonations. I didn't understand the ritual of it all, but it felt peaceful and welcoming. Most of the congregation was made up of older folk and small knots of families. One such family group shuffled into the pew in front of us. I took no notice of the two women and kids, but there was something very familiar about the bloke: light brown, floppy hair that curled cutely over the top of his collar, and a neat, tight bum from what I could see. When he turned round to wink at Lee (wink at Lee!) it dawned. He was the good-looking chap from Peter

Heron's soiree who was all but having it off with Chrissie. I nudged Lee to intimate 'Look who's here – and who the hell is he?', when she hissed, 'Hands off. He's married.' Cheeky cow – that hadn't stopped her having it off with Orme-features.

When it came to the kiss of peace, I made sure I kissed everyone – including the chap in front – and I was pleased to note he made a special beeline for me to brush his lips against my cheek.

After the service, everyone was heading for tea in the vestry, but I'd left a bottle of Prosecco in Lee's fridge, and I was determined that girl was going to drink it, and then we could talk seriously about what was going to happen about this baby of hers.

Chapter Eighteen

Teri

I'm not a monster, really I'm not. But the truth is I don't like children; never have done. I can't bear the sight of pregnant women flaunting their enormous bellies and then, later, flaunting their tedious little offspring. You can hardly go into a coffee shop, library or gallery without there being a tribe of mumsies with their four-by-four chariots and assorted children taking up space, making too much noise and leaving a sticky mess.

But that wasn't the reason I was so against Lee having this kid of hers. I didn't believe that gormless Orme would do the right thing, leave his wife and support Lee in playing happy families. Nor did I think Lee would cope bringing up a kid on her own. Let's face it, her good Catholic mammy would excommunicate her for having a child out of wedlock and Daddy Harper would probably disown her and kick her out of the house he built for her. But the real reason was that Lee would be throwing away so much of what she'd worked for. Even I could appreciate how much she'd been through to get to where she was professionally. Once she'd taken the maternity leave of however many years women get nowadays, she'd want to come back part-time and we all know women have to be full-time and full-on to get anywhere, even in our poxy university.

On top of all this, I wasn't convinced Lee really did want this child. She dithered one way and then the other. So, without telling her, I went to see my GP and asked how you went about getting an abortion, assuring her, of course, that it was for a friend and not for me.

She went through the ghastly options. I thought the best solution was to book Lee into a private clinic so she wouldn't need to go to her own GP (probably a good Catholic doctor who'd looked after the Harpers since they first came to live here and might take a judgmental approach toward Lee's predicament).

Lee objected when I told her I'd been to the clinic and given it my approval, but when I told her I'd also booked her first appointment, she seemed relieved. 'Don't worry,' I told her. 'It's all paid for. Daddy has sent me a bit extra this month.' This was a lie. Daddy hadn't even sent my usual monthly allowance, but I put the clinic's bill on my credit card and hoped for the best.

After her first appointment, it was recommended she have a vacuum aspiration because she was more than a few weeks' pregnant. 'I don't want to know the details,' I told her, but I drove her in and sat with her until they took her to theatre. She was having a general anaesthetic and staying in for the night – might as well make the most of the clinic's facilities. I waited until she'd come round and was tucked up in bed and promised to be back in the morning to take her home. She looked as if she was about to cry, so I plonked some glossy mags on her bed and told her I'd see her later.

I picked her up the next day, drove her home and insisted on staying with her for a couple of days. I didn't tell Dan about the abortion. I simply said I was having some girly time, and he smiled and said how nice it was that we were such good friends. 'But I miss you,' he said when I phoned him from Lee's.

'I miss you too,' I told him and I realised it was true. I was getting used to having him around.

I stayed at Lee's for almost a week. She was on sick with an official note. She'd told Chrissie in admin she had a tummy bug, which is pretty close to the truth. I pulled a sickie to look after her. 'You got a tummy bug too?' Chrissie asked.

Lee was very quiet most of the time; no fun at all. But, given the circumstances, I suppose she wouldn't want to be cracking jokes. Gormless Orme-features rang a couple of times. I managed to get to the phone the first time and told the spineless bastard she didn't want to speak to him. But Lee managed to get to it the second time, and she took the phone into her room so I couldn't hear what went on.

I went back to my flat at the weekend and found on the doorstep the biggest bouquet of flowers. 'Miss you, need you, love you' was all the card said. Dan! I rang him straight away and told him I was home. No doubt whatever he had planned for the rest of the weekend had involved spending money on his only child, but, to his credit, he cancelled all arrangements and devoted himself to me.

And he did devoting in the most amazing way. On Monday morning as he was dressing to go to the Ridings Today studios and I was getting ready for uni, he said, 'You know, Teri. I hate having to leave you.'

'Well, you don't have to,' I said.

'No, I mean…this,' he said. 'Leaving you here in your flat, while I go back to mine.'

'What are you suggesting?' I asked.

'Let's get married.'

Chapter Nineteen

Lee

Teri was a godsend in those awful days in January. She arranged everything – found a private clinic, booked appointments, accompanied me through seemingly endless interviews with business-like nurses and medics, held my hand when I needed it and, afterwards, hugged me and wiped away my tears. And she never uttered a single word of criticism or condemnation – just offered a loving, efficient practicality that was surprisingly soothing. She was a star and, if she wasn't there in the middle of the night when I woke and sobbed myself back to sleep, it was hardly her fault.

Mercifully, work intervened in the shape of a long-planned trip to India in February, organised by the university's international office to meet with officials from our recruitment partners in New Delhi and Mumbai. We were attracting an increasing number of applications from the subcontinent and my job was to ensure the applications were being processed correctly – and to do a little schmoozing with the agents in order to keep the wheels well oiled. So the days were spent visiting their offices and meeting their staff, and the evenings on wining and dining the managers and their spouses along with the team from our newly-opened New Delhi and Mumbai offices. Busy, but not particularly demanding work. It was a relief though most nights when I was finally able to hole up in my hotel room, kick off my shoes and call for room service to deliver a bottle of wine. Good job it was on expenses – a very decent New Zealand Sauvignon Blanc that costs six quid at my local supermarket was billed at £60 on the hotel wine list. I balked at the price tag on the first evening – expenses or no – but after day two, I decided sod it, I was worth it!

Best of all, there was precious little time for introspection. It wasn't until I was on the flight home I started thinking about the future – and more pertinently whether there was any future for me and Mike. Technically we were still a 'couple' – or as much as a couple as we'd ever been. Mike had been sweetness and light ever since the abortion, hinting that we might put our relationship on a more formal footing. Teri thought I should tell him outright to sling his hook – she put it more elegantly – but I'd hesitated. Why? God knows? I sure as hell didn't. Whatever affection I'd felt for him had evaporated ten minutes after I told him I was pregnant and he started extolling the virtues of an early termination. True, he didn't exactly frogmarch me to the abortion clinic – strictly speaking that role fell to Teri – or hold a gun to my head until I agreed to go through with it. But he made it very clear that parenthood would be a single-person enterprise and this was my problem – not his. None of which should have mattered – after all, I was a professional woman with a decent income. I could afford to raise a child on my own. But, it did matter – just as it mattered that both Mammy and Daddy would be disappointed I was having a child out of wedlock, with a married man too.

And, without making excuses, the morning sickness was very, very debilitating; morning after morning, I hugged the toilet, retching and vomiting until I longed for death. In retrospect, I should've just stuck it out – nothing awful ever lasts forever – but, God forgive me, I'd come to resent the poisonous little interloper who'd invaded my body and I just wanted rid of it. That's not nice – and I'm not proud of it. But, true, nevertheless. Perhaps, it would've been different if there'd been a nice man wiping my brow and making appropriately sympathetic noises. I wish...

But, as the aircraft taking me home chugged across the Indian subcontinent towards UK airspace, I decided I rather liked the idea of a nice man of my own – as opposed to a not-so-nice man who belonged to someone else. And, perhaps, even, one day, I might get another shot at being a mother.

One thing was clear though – Mike didn't fit the bill. Shame really because before I'd left for India he'd offered the ultimate reward for doing as I'd been told: a firm promise to come clean about the affair and leave his wife.

Hope he'd held his tongue.

Chapter Twenty

Teri

Dan's proposal took me completely by surprise. Yes, I thought we might move in together eventually. But marriage? After his Monday morning proposal, I told Dan I'd need to think about it. Oddly, for someone like me who'd always loved 'em and left 'em, the idea of having Dan as a permanent fixture in my life grew on me. Rapidly. By the end of the day, I'd made up my mind. Dan was kind, generous and patient and, best of all, he loved me. And, let's face it, who else would take me on?

I told him yes, but under the condition we got married as soon as possible as I didn't want time to change my mind.

I'd had visions of a tropical beach wedding: just Dan and me and a couple of stranger witnesses. Me in a floaty outfit and bare feet, Dan in one of his classic pale suits. Both of us watching the sun set over a pale turquoise sea. No family, no guests, no cake, no fuss and definitely no Victoria.

Dan agreed – to the tropical beach wedding – but when he heard of my suggested guest list (or lack of it) said, 'But I couldn't get married without my little girl being there.'

And as I hadn't wanted to give his little girl the satisfaction of a two-week tropical beach holiday (with the minor matter of our wedding tucked in the middle of it), I suggested we have a register office wedding at which she could be present and then Dan and I would leave for a tropical beach honeymoon. He'd bought the idea, although it took some persuading not to invite his work colleagues. 'They'll all be expecting a big party,' he reasoned. But I didn't want a load of screechy, flashy television types whooping it up and drinking themselves stupid at my expense. I persuaded Dan I wanted it to be just the two of us, intimate and private; in fact, I managed a little tear as I told him the thought of a 'big bash' actually frightened me, and he stroked my face and kissed my cheek by way of reassurance. 'It's your day,' he said, 'and you must have what you want.'

What I did want was life to be about just Dan and me. I'd finally found someone I loved, and who genuinely loved me, and I didn't want anyone coming along and ruining it.

Lee asked later whether I wanted any of my family at the wedding. Hardly. My father had all but given up on the factory, leaving it in the hands of Edward Pranks and communicating only by email from his cottage in rural France, and from which he never stirred himself. It wasn't even worth the effort of phoning him.

I didn't really understand the arrangements with the factory. Good old Edward started out as Dad's driver, became his personal assistant, then became manager at the mill – and now runs the whole caboodle. Don't ask me about the financial side. All I know is Dad takes money out of the business to keep him in red wine and gourmet cheeses while sending me (and Charlie) the odd cheque when he remembers. My mother, who was always very fond of the cooking sherry but not to living permanently in France, turned to drink in a more determined way once Dad was out of the way and no longer there to check the bottles outside the scullery door, and was now boozing it up in a one-bedroom apartment amongst a pile of ex-pats in Lanzarote. I rang to tell her I was getting married and she – dramatically effusive – said, 'That's wonderful, darling. But I can't possibly come. I couldn't stand the airport...the flight...and where would I stay? Oh no, it's all too much.'

I didn't push it.

She arranged for a bunch of pink carnations to be delivered. If there is one flower I hate it's a carnation – cheap and scraggy. I put the bunch straight in the bin.

Charlie was supposed to take over the steel business when Dad left, but he'd a run in with Frank and took himself off to run a smallholding in Suffolk from where I received the occasional Christmas card from him and his partner, Denis, but little else in terms of sibling support. I rang him too, to tell him about the wedding, and he made some excuse about how he and Denis couldn't get away as they'd just bought four new goats and didn't want to leave them until they'd settled in.

'Goats? I queried.

'Make lovely cheese, sweetie,' Charlie said.

I told Lee she'd have to be mother of the bride, matron of honour and chief bridesmaid.

'Wouldn't you want Victoria as bridesmaid?' she asked.

'Bugger that,' I replied; wouldn't want to give her the satisfaction.

On being told her father was to marry again, Victoria had gone out and got thoroughly blathered.

'She's so pleased for the old man,' Dan said, recounting how he'd gone to pick her up from a nightclub in town, where she'd told him she was celebrating his news, and found her sobbing outside having drunk her way through the best part of far too many vodkas (or whatever these young idiots drink nowadays).

More likely drowning her sorrows.

There'd been much hushed talk between Victoria and a gormless-looking school friend one evening when we were all round at Dan's flat. Odd phrases poked to the surface such as 'gold digger' and 'sugar daddy' but not said in any meaningful context one could respond to.

'What was that?' I asked.

'Oh, nothing,' Victoria said and she and her daft little friend giggled.

That girl had her act down to a fine art, and her father didn't suspect a thing.

'I think we should give Victoria a wedding present,' Dan announced as the date came closer.

'But it's *our* wedding,' I explained.

'I know. But in a spirit of the occasion,' he replied, 'I'd like to give her some money.'

He was *always* giving her money: for nightclubs, for clothes, for drinks, for day's out, for holidays. For simply being. I pointed out he was generous enough already.

'Oh the odd ten quid here and there.' He smiled in agreement. 'No, I was thinking of something a bit more; an amount she could use to buy something really nice so she feels part of the celebrations.'

'But you've already given her money to buy an outfit and, by the way, a new dress does not have to cost £650. Not from Topshop.'

I could hardly contain my anger when I later told Lee. He'd given her five thousand pounds.

'She behaves so badly – and he gives her money,' I cried.

'But she is his daughter, and he feels bad about divorcing her mother and leaving her.'

'He's hardly left her,' I said. 'She's with him every bloody weekend.'

'I know,' Lee said. But even she couldn't think of anything more comforting to say.

Chapter Twenty-One

Lee

I might as well be honest, I was disappointed with Teri's choice of wedding venue. Okay, I understood she didn't get her first choice – but swapping a tropical beach ceremony for a utilitarian service in a dingy register office smacked of a rather Pyrrhic victory. Especially as there were plenty of alternative venues nearby. The Civic Hall just round the corner, for instance, did a lovely line in bespoke wedding deals and the Mayor's handsome Georgian parlour was a much more attractive setting. It didn't cost an arm and a leg either – not that Teri's excuse of saving money to spend on the honeymoon rang true. When had she ever bothered about saving money?

The other bonus, she said, was that the register office was available at short notice. Why the rush? The daft beggars had the rest of their lives to plan the perfect wedding. It just felt too soon, and I certainly didn't buy Teri's 'we're so in love, we can't wait' claptrap. She'd been quite sharp with me when I said as much.

She'd whipped her hands onto her hips and jutted her chin. 'You're jealous,' she said.

'Jealous of what?'

'Of me and Dan – our happiness.'

But, I wasn't – truly, I wasn't – because, unfortunately, I didn't really think they were happy. Or, perhaps Dan was – he *seemed* thoroughly smitten – but I didn't think Teri was. Not really. For one thing, she spent far too much time moaning about Victoria, and, for another, she never seemed to stop finding fault with Dan. Or detailing his foibles at length whenever we met. And, though, I'm no relationship expert, even I knew enough to know the scales shouldn't have fallen from her eyes quite this early.

Granted, some of the things she told me about Dan would've irritated me too – his trick with the shower, for instance. Apparently, he'd read somewhere that a thirty second blast of ice cold water before getting out of the shower would set his senses tingling and invigorate him for the rest of the day. So that's what he did: every morning after he'd soaped and washed his hair, he adjusted the shower thermostat and rinsed for thirty seconds under a freezing cold jet of water. Exactly thirty seconds too – he counted, Teri said: one elephant, two elephant, three elephant, four elephant... Personally, I thought it sounded like madness – but, what the hell? It didn't harm anyone – apart from himself, of course.

Teri, though, used to get apoplectic – largely because Dan never switched the thermostat back to the scalding high temperature at which she showered and, because she always forgot to do so, her day also began with an Arctic shower. Very annoying, I agreed. But it was hardly the end of the world.

'And,' I told her when she appealed for sympathy, 'if it happens every morning, get into the habit of adjusting the thermostat before you turn on the tap.'

But, no, that wasn't Teri's way.

Partly, I think she just wasn't used to sharing; even as a kid she'd had an ensuite bathroom, and the family home was so large she'd once told me she sometimes went for days without seeing either her mother or father.

'Saw the housekeeper more often than I saw either of them,' she said, without a trace of self-pity. I thought it was horrible, but she said it was normal. 'Better really – parents can be a bit of a nuisance.'

Good God! It's a parent's job to be a nuisance and keep their kids on the straight and narrow. Teri's parents were little more than nodding acquaintances who flitted in and out of her life and didn't much care if they saw her from one week's end to the next. She'd have hated it if she knew how much I pitied her, but I thought I'd snaffled a bargain in the parent stakes and she'd been sold a pup.

But, it wasn't just that she didn't know about families, I had a niggling suspicion Teri's constant carping was an indication she really wasn't quite ready to settle down. Or at any rate to settle down with someone like Dan. Despite his glamorous job and celebrity friends, he was basically a very down-to-earth, ordinary sort of chap. Teri made a big deal about the sexual sparks between them but, from little things she said, it was clear she sometimes found him a bit clingy and needy. Dan was an affectionate, touchy-feely sort of guy – he always greeted me with a peck on the cheek and a swift hug, for instance. It was the 'lovey' in him, I suppose, but Teri found it intensely irritating. She preferred a more hands-off approach.

'Just once,' she said, 'just once, I'd like to sit down and watch a film without Dan feeling the need to cuddle up. And he doesn't need to pucker up for a kiss every time he enters or leaves a room either,' she added.

Sometimes, I wondered if those sexual sparks were quite as bright as she made out. It seemed a bit soon for her to be feeling annoyed that he couldn't keep his hands off her.

And, I wondered too about Dan's constant need for reassurance. Did he suspect Teri's feelings were only skin deep? And did he really love her? Or was he just grateful she'd ended his sexual desert.

I tried airing some of these concerns with Teri.

'You're paranoid,' she said.

And, that, in itself was worrying, because Teri only becomes intransigent when she suspects she's in the wrong. It's a defence mechanism – if she doesn't listen, she doesn't need to face her fears.

'I'm sorry,' she said. 'You've been through a difficult time lately. It's only natural for you to be cautious.'

Perhaps – but I didn't think so.

In the end, I gave up trying to persuade her otherwise and simply went with the flow. We had a lovely day in London choosing her wedding dress – a most untraditional red chiffon little number from an up-and-coming young designer who'd grabbed media headlines when she made her Paris debut last year. It was beautiful – and Teri looked stunning.

Dan suggested Victoria should join us – he's a nice man, but goodness, how tactless. Teri's face was a picture. Fortunately, I was having dinner with them. 'No,' I said as she opened her mouth to speak. 'It's probably the last time Teri and I will be able to have a proper girly time together, so nice as it would be to include Victoria, I'm going to be really selfish and say I want Teri to myself.' And Dan – idiot! – bought it.

So, we had a Victoria-free day – until we boarded the train home when, apropos of nothing in particular, Teri started a rant. We'd been adding up how much we'd each spent – a horrifying amount but peanuts, apparently, in comparison to the wedding gift Dan had given Victoria.

'Wedding gift?' It was the first time I'd heard of the groom buying anything other than small tokens for the bridesmaids – an honour Teri had been at great pains not to confer on Victoria. (And which had been the subject of a big argument – but that's another story.)

Without wanting to stoke the flames of Teri's fury, I had to agree that five thousand pounds seemed a tad excessive. 'I suppose he wants to make sure she has something nice to wear,' I suggested uncertainly.

No – Victoria was a spoilt brat who could twist her father around her little finger.

'She's his daughter – and he feels bad about the divorce.'

'Feels bad? Do you know how much he pays his ex-wife in maintenance? Money-grabbing trollop!'

'Well, he does have a responsibility…'

'Maintenance? I don't know what she does with the money – certainly doesn't go on the bloody daughter who's always coming to him for money. New clothes and school trips and pocket money. I thought maintenance was supposed to maintain the kid, not the bloody mother.'

'I expect he likes to treat Victoria now and again.'

'Now and again. I wish – it's all the blasted time.'

I tried again. 'I expect he feels bad about leaving Victoria behind.'

'He's hardly left her,' she said. 'She's with us every bloody weekend.'

I'm afraid this was the point at which I mentally switched off and focused on the view outside the train window. Not that there was much to see – dusk was already falling. But it was more diverting than the alternative.

'You're not listening to a word I'm saying,' Teri accused suddenly.

No, I thought, but if you listened to yourself sometimes, you'd realise how much you and Victoria have in common.

Chapter Twenty-Two

Teri

The Town Hall is a giant Victorian edifice that dominates Market Row, the main road that sweeps through the centre of the city. The exterior of the building is in need of a sand-blast, dark and dirty as it is from the constant traffic grinding past the monumental flight of steps that lead up to the ten-column Corinthian colonnade through which visitors move to reach the building's heavy wooden doors. The entrance opens into a domed vestibule where, by crossing the Minton encaustic tiles laid in a geometric pattern on the foyer floor, access can be gained to the eight-thousand-seat concert hall, the council chamber, the magistrates' court, the ladies' and gents' lavatories (tiled in elaborately bright red and lit by miniature 'Odeon' fittings), and the register office.

Lee and I – late, having had a last-minute gin to steady our nerves – dashed in. But we needn't have rushed. Dan wasn't there. 'Hah. We should have driven round the block,' Lee said, trying to cover her nervousness.

'Where is he?' I hissed. Then suddenly, he too ran in panting for breath.

'Sorry…sorry,' he said. 'Victoria…'

He didn't need to explain. Behind him, hardly rushing, was the sullen little cow sporting a look of indifference. Clearly she'd decided to change the colour of her lip gloss before venturing out for the occasion of her father's wedding, her make-up being of more importance than her father's nuptials.

Chapter Twenty-Three

Lee

I didn't for one moment believe Victoria was quite the complete devil child Teri made her out to be, but it was definitely unfortunate, to say the least, that she was responsible for making Dan late for his wedding. 'Poor girl,' gasped Dan. She'd been feeling poorly and almost fainted just before they left the house. They'd had to wait twenty minutes until she felt a little better.

Teri was frankly disbelieving and looked as if she'd like to throttle the child. But the registrar didn't give her time. Instead, she said, now everyone had arrived we might as well get on with things. Which we did, and Dan Caine and Teri Meyer duly became husband and wife. It was telling, though, that Teri and I arrived only a matter of minutes before Dan and Victoria. Teri had downed a couple of stiff gins straight after breakfast and a couple more as she dressed and did her hair and make-up. And another one before getting into the taxi.

'Just to steady my nerves,' she said.

Steady her nerves? She didn't have a nervous bone in her body.

Chapter Twenty-Four

Teri

Because Dan had moved out of the marital des res and into a rented flat when his marriage broke up, it seemed sensible he should give that up and move in with me until we could buy something expensive and luxurious together; something that reflected his status as a highly-paid television presenter. But when I showed him brochures for beautiful five-bedroom executive homes on landscaped and gated estates that Lee's dad, Mr Harper Homes, had produced, he said he couldn't afford that sort of thing.

'Why ever not?' I demanded. 'I'm on a decent enough salary at the university – and I have my allowance when Dad remembers to send it – and you're on megabucks.'

He shook his head. 'Don't forget, I'm still paying the mortgage on my old house – and maintenance for Sara and Victoria.'

'But why should you be paying for Sara? And why can't she pay her own mortgage?'

'You know she doesn't work, Teri,' Dan said.

It was true: he'd told me that after losing the baby, Sara had become not just frigid, but depressed; claimed it was something like ME. But whatever it was, the former secretary lost the will to work. Tapping away on a computer spreadsheet in a nice little office in town had been too much for the fragrant Sara to contemplate. Better accept as much cash as possible from her ex and take herself off for nice, restful spa breaks.

'You should tell your bloody ex-wife to get off her lazy backside and get a job. She's bleeding you dry,' I said.

'Ah, if only I could,' replied Dan. 'But don't forget, Victoria still lives at the house.'

Ah yes. Victoria. She liked to spend weekends with her daddy, and if her daddy was living with me, how would that work?

When I got the job at the university, I'd bought my two-bedroom duplex; or rather Edward Pranks had supplied enough dosh for the deposit, and my allowance helped pay the mortgage on what wasn't exactly a vast expanse but was a carefully decorated and expensively furnished cream and vanilla bachelor girl pad.

'But what about Victoria?' had been Dan's first question when we contemplated his moving in.

'What about her?' I asked.

'Well, she likes to spend weekends with me, so she'll need a bedroom for when she stays.'

How did I feel about having the devil child staying in my flat? I'd rather pull my glossily painted toenails out. 'But won't she want to spend weekends with her chums? And anyway, you said she'd be off to university soon.'

And somehow the conversation teetered out with no real conclusion, and Dan gave up his flat and moved in with me on the understanding we'd start looking for a house together big enough for us and for Victoria when she came to stay (but even then my thought had been: over my dead body).

Chapter Twenty-Five

Teri

'Are you listening to me?' I asked, knowing full well he wasn't. He'd rushed in from work and pecked me on the cheek, but his eyes were on the pile of envelopes on the kitchen table.

He was always distracted when he came home at night. He claimed it was the adrenalin from that night's programme; he was still on a high from the effects of live television and couldn't sit down until he'd sorted out his brain. He couldn't concentrate on anything until everything was in order, and the only way to get things in order was to go through his evening ritual. Until that was complete, he couldn't allow himself to relax.

We'd only been married a few weeks, and I was already getting a tad irritated by this. Even though I usually uncorked a bottle of wine and placed two glasses on the kitchen table (ostentatiously pouring wine into mine to make the point I wasn't going to wait for him), Dan would first have a soft drink – to line his stomach, he said – before drinking alcohol. Lime juice was the flavour of the moment, and he'd reach into the fridge for the bottle of cordial, unscrew the top, place the top on the counter near the fridge, move over to the opposite side of the kitchen and the cupboard where the tumblers were kept, get himself one, pour the juice into the glass, put the bottle down on the counter, move to the sink to top the cordial up with water (splashing the work surfaces on either side, which I then had to mop up), take a big slug and go 'Aah, that's better'. Every evening! Always the same.

I'd stopped trying to tell him to pick up the bottle, walk across to get the top, screw the top back on and put the bloody thing back in the fridge, because he would say 'Yes, okay' in a distracted way but never did as I asked. He'd be too busy glugging back the juice – and making something of a noise while doing it too, which, frankly, I found a bit off-putting. But, all the while, his eyes would be on the pile of post on the table, which he'd have to read before anything else. I then had to go over, get the bottle of juice from the counter, walk over to where the top had been abandoned, screw it back on and put the bottle back in the fridge, shutting the door with a heavier force than was entirely necessary but with which I hoped to make a point. 'It's okay,' I would say. 'I'll clear up.'

'Mmm?' he queried as he examined the first envelope.

He never opened his post straight away. No ripping of the envelope for him; he liked to savour the process, especially if a particular letter was handwritten, and he received a fair few handwritten missives addressed to him care of the Ridings Today studio and either left for him in his pigeonhole or redirected here. Most of these delicately scrawled notelets were from middle-aged, menopausal, empty nesters who had nothing better to do with their sad little lives than voluntary good deeds at the local church and fantasising about the chances of a good-looking television presenter falling for them once they'd written to him telling him how much they liked the suit he was wearing on Monday night's programme and how well the purple tie went with the lilac and white-striped shirt. Some of them enclosed little presents: a scarf he might like, a silk hanky embroidered with his initials to wear in his top jacket pocket, some ginger biscuits they'd made themselves, or worst of all, pictures of themselves in natty little bikinis 'having fun in the surf'. I made that last one up.

He loved those handwritten letters. He really did. He'd look at the writing on the envelope, trying to work out who it might be from, then he'd turn the thing this way and that as though the process would shed some light on proceedings. If he was in a particularly self-tantalising mood, he'd put the envelope back on the table, unopened, while he looked through the rest of the post, saving the cream until last, as it were. Each letter got its own due veneration; even a gas bill was examined in detail even though we paid by direct debit. He would put all his concentration into whatever missive he held in his hand.

'Anything interesting?' I'd asked.

'Mmm?' he'd replied.

That 'Mmm?' was so irritating; it drove me up the wall. He would be reading the paper, for instance, and I would say something and, without looking up, he would say 'Mmm?' and carry on reading!

'Are you listening to me?' I would say, raising my voice. He'd lower the paper and give me a distracted look.

'Er, what?'

'Oh, go back to your paper,' I'd say – and so he would! And when he'd finished reading the paper, he'd simply lay it down on the coffee table in front of him, generally open – open! – but certainly out of page order so when I came to read it the sport section was somehow at the front while the interesting lifestyle bits were at the back. Why?

And books. He couldn't put his books back neatly on the bedside table. Oh no. He had to leave them open but facedown on the floor next to the chair in which he'd been sitting reading. He wouldn't even put a bookmark in. 'You'll break the spine,' I told him when he pushed the book down to better flatten it against the pale oak floorboards.

'Books are meant to be read and used,' he laughed. 'You're so anal, Teri.'

'I'm not anal,' I said. 'I just like things to be nice.'

'Well, everything in this flat is very nice,' he said. 'And you're nice too. Come here and let me show you how nice I think you are…'

I was tempted. It would be so easy to slip into his lap and feel his arms wrap around my waist. But I was irritated. I can't relax when the flat is a mess and things are out of order.

'I haven't got time,' I said. 'I must clean this place up.'

If anyone was anal, it was him and his lime juice and letter-opening ritual. Once the envelopes had been opened and contents read, they were left in no particular order, in an untidy pile on the table, which I'd just laid for our meal. Why couldn't he put the envelopes in the green bin for recycling? Why couldn't he chuck away the circulars and the charity begging letters? Left to his own devices, he'd leave piles of correspondence on the table to grow – torn envelopes and inconsequential letters, discarded now he knew they didn't carry the promise he'd earlier thought they contained, whatever promise that might be.

He went through the letter opening ritual while I watched with mounting impatience; his annoying little habits were beginning to get to me. I leaned against the edge of the kitchen unit, a tea towel slung over my arm midway between drying up that morning's breakfast dishes, left to drain, and moving over to the oven to take out whatever it was I'd been cooking.

Next, he will ask me if there are any messages.

'Any messages?' he asked, looking at me for perhaps the first time that night and obviously believing it was my role as an unpaid secretary to check the answerphone, even though, since he moved in, most of the calls on the landline were for him. It would be the Claxton Women's WI, or a local Rotary Club wanting him to give a talk – Life as a Famous Television Presenter – or it would be a local library group or animal rescue sanctuary wanting him to become their president. The glamorous life of a celebrity.

When these blessed organisations rang and I answered, I said Dan wasn't available and they should ring the studio to talk to Doreen. But invariably it had been Doreen who'd given them this number, and anyway, they said they didn't want to disturb him while he was busy at work, so could I take a message? So, I'm not busy, then?

Why they bothered ringing the landline anyway, when Dan gave his mobile number to anyone, willy nilly, I just don't know. And why he gave his mobile number out, I don't know either. He hated to miss a call, I suppose. Even when the phone rang and there was no one there when we answered, it clearly being a try-on by some call centre in Delhi, Dan would press 1471 to get the number and ring it back.

'Don't do that, you idiot,' I yelled at him.

'But it might be something important,' he replied.

'Yes, the call centre cashing in on you ringing a premium number.'

So, you'll understand when I say how annoying it was while we were out together, Dan would be constantly checking his mobile.

'Sorry about this,' he said, having answered his phone as we walked around the local lake, hand in hand, on a rare day off together.

He'd turn away to concentrate more closely on the call eventually flicking his hand in my direction in the hope I'd interpret it as a sign to get a pen and paper out of my bag so he could make a note. It was always either the studio – could he do a last-minute interview, now, this afternoon? – or some do-good organisation wanting his services. And he always said 'Yes' whatever the request, even if it meant leaving me on our day off to dash into the studios and record some inane, fatuous interview with someone like Shayne Brickham.

Chapter Twenty-Six

Lee

Frankly, I was an emotional mess for a long time after the abortion. It's funny – well, actually, it isn't funny at all – but, however much intellectually I believed in a woman's right to choose, emotionally I couldn't get my head round it at all. And, typically Catholic, I thought being miserable served me damn well right. I tried, once or twice, to share my misery with Teri, but she was too wrapped up in her own troubles to care about mine. She was finding married life difficult. The humdrum reality of domestic bliss seemed to have bypassed her. Instead she was mired in an almost continuous frenzy of irritation. She was irritated with Dan because he was untidy; she was irritated with Victoria, principally because she was alive; and she was irritated with herself for being irritated with everybody else.

To be fair, I had some sympathy with her. Whilst no one would ever call me house proud, I could understand why she wanted to kill Dan over his inability to PUT THINGS BACK!

A couple of years ago I went home for a few days to look after Daddy and Grand-Daddy while Mammy joined other members of the UCM on a pilgrimage to Lourdes, a Catholic shrine in the Midi-Pyrenees where the Virgin Mary revealed herself to St Bernadette. Are you familiar with the story? Briefly, Bernadette, a poor village girl, had around eighteen visitations from our Lady, who told her the water that had miraculously sprung from the mud on which Bernadette was kneeling could cure the sick and dying. It's not something I've ever fancied, but something like five million Catholics take the water every year. Mammy had wanted to make the pilgrimage for years, but it wasn't really Daddy's sort of thing, so when the UCM put a Lourdes package together she jumped at the chance to join them.

Her only reservations concerned Daddy and Grand-daddy. Could they be trusted to cope on their own? Probably, although God knows what sort of mess she'd have found when she got back home. Her solution was to rope me in to cook and clean for the pair of them. They nearly drove me round the bend. The kettle seemed to be permanently on the boil – one or other of them was always making a cup of tea, and neither of them ever returned the tea caddy to its rightful place on the shelf next to the sugar and coffee jars. They were also incapable of rinsing out and re-using the mug, which they'd been drinking from just five minutes earlier. Instead, they used a clean one, discarding the empty wherever they happened to be when they remembered it was still in their hands. I found them on the coffee table in the living room, on the dining room bookcase, the utility room windowsill – anywhere but back in the kitchen. Nor did they return the milk carton to the fridge, leaving it instead on the kitchen table where it invariably dripped and stained the tablecloth, which had been clean on that morning. And don't get me started on the mess left behind when they made themselves a sandwich – breadcrumbs and congealed pickle everywhere.

I had a new respect for Mammy – if I'd been there longer than a week I would've killed the pair of them.

So, I understood where Teri was coming from – but, on the other hand, I thought a more laissez-faire approach might be more effective.

'You don't want to seem like a tiresome nag,' I said. But, no, turning a blind eye was not an option – even when I told her it worked a treat with Daddy and Grand-Daddy. When they eventually ran out of mugs, they collected them up from the four corners of the house and one of them washed while the other dried.

'No,' she said. Her home, her rules.

I thought she could learn a lesson or two from my naughty Daddy. He and his brother Patrick were the only boys in a family of girls and, whenever their sisters annoyed them, which was often, the boys would 'punish' them by stealing items of clothing and hiding them. Sometimes, they'd take a single black stocking from the washing line or, perhaps, a lacy underslip or camisole. Or a precious pair of earrings would mysteriously disappear from the dresser. The missing stuff would always turn up – eventually – behind the back of a headboard, stuffed down the side of the settee or under a chair cushion, but the boys would watch with glee as the sisters searched high and low. Mean little sods.

As children, Fliss and I used to love hearing these tales of bygone days although neither of us had a clue what Daddy meant when he said he and Uncle Pat were delivering 'just desserts'. We thought it was Irish slang for being naughty.

Perhaps Victoria, I suggested to Teri, was also trying to redress the balance – did she ever wonder, for instance, why her mobile sometimes went missing?

'Pah,' she said. 'Victoria hasn't the brains to think of something so fiendish.'

I wasn't so sure. If Daddy and Uncle Pat could do it...

But before I could say more, Teri was off again about Dan and his bloody letters. He had, apparently, spent ten minutes puzzling over an envelope that morning that first, turned out to be addressed to Teri anyway – 'so none of his damn business' – and, second, had the logo of a Parisian perfume house plastered in large letters across the front. 'So, who the bloody hell did he think had sent it?'

Fair point – though the picture of Dan working himself into a frenzy of excitement over someone else's mail made me chuckle.

Bet Teri tossed it into the bin without opening it too.

Her grumbles about his mobile phone habit though – talk about the pot calling the kettle black. I know she didn't come out of the womb with the thing glued to her ear, but she'll certainly go to the grave begging for the chance to make one last call or send one more quick text.

'You should lighten up,' I said. Why fight a battle she was doomed to lose, I asked? Stupid question – Teri had never been a pushover in all her life, and she wasn't about to start now. Why not? Another stupid question, which elicited a long and detailed answer that involved several references to

106

that 'fucking devil child' and her 'anally doting dad'.

Okay. I tried another tack. Victoria and Dan had been an 'item' for many years – yes, an unfortunate choice of phrase – while Teri and Dan had been an item for little more than half a year. I deserved the outburst that followed.

She apologised afterwards though.

'I shouldn't take things out on you,' she said. 'Not when you've had such a hard time yourself.'

That was Teri all over – one minute she was an unreasonable termagant and the next she was as thoughtful and considerate a person as you could wish to find. Ever since January, she'd been endlessly supportive and kind and, if sometimes she was a little wrapped up in her own affairs – wedding, wicked step-daughter and clearly wonky marriage – who could blame her? Not me. I was unendingly grateful for her brisk, no-nonsense approach to Mike, who she thought deserved 'to eat dirt and die', and her equally shrewd observation that he wasn't giving me a hard time at work because 'he's scared witless that you'll blab to his wife or Peter Heron or both'. Huh! It was uncharacteristically charitable of Teri to credit Mike with even a smidgeon of concern for his wife – more likely he was worried about crossing Peter, whose first wife had left him for a married colleague at the hospital where she worked, and whose views on philandering spouses were well known. I don't suppose I'd have emerged with my reputation intact either, so I said a silent prayer and kept my fingers crossed Mike would continue to tiptoe around what could've been an awkward situation.

But, for all Teri's sympathy and well-intentioned efforts to cheer me up, it was my sister Felicity who saved me: she persuaded (bullied?) me into joining a two-week family trip to the Île de Ré off the French Vendee coast. I'm cutting a long story short here, but basically our conversation boiled down to me protesting 'I can't, I'll spoil your holiday', and her replying 'I'm not taking no for an answer. You're coming and that's that'. She was always a bossy cow.

So, I crammed into the back seat of the car, uncomfortably wedged between baby Fiona's child seat and seven-year-old Ritchie's booster seat, and endured a 796 mile drive, enlivened by little Fee's attempts to break my nose with her rattle and Ritchie's endless games of 'I spy...' and 'alphabet car number plates'. Just what the doctor ordered.

Chapter Twenty-Seven

Lee

There were many, many times during the almost interminable drive between Yorkshire and Dover when I thought I must've been more than several sandwiches short of a picnic to have agreed to tag along with Fliss and co. We were barely south of Sheffield when Ritchie asked, for the first time, if we were nearly there. No, we bloody well weren't. And not likely to be there any time soon since both the M1 and M25 seemed to be little more than an endless succession of slow-moving road works – and toilet stops. Either Ritchie needed the loo or Fee's nappy needed changing. Lord! Who would've thought such a small creature could produce such an overpowering stench?

The ferry crossing provided some relief. Ritchie and I went on deck and counted how many boats we passed on the way – sadly, I got bored and lost count even before we hit double figures. Still, it kept him amused. Despite a lazy sea breeze that went through, rather than round, it was a good crossing. Fliss and Charles entertained Fee in the kid's room – a horrible den, full of squabbling brats and their obnoxious, loud parents (Fliss, Charles and Fee excepted, of course).

On balance, I got the better deal.

Once on land we headed for Évreux, just south of Paris, where we were booked overnight into a hotel. Felicity was map reading – badly. In fairness, the map, which Charles had downloaded from the internet when he made the booking, was a poor one that seemed to bear little relation to the physical geography of the outskirts of the town centre where we got helplessly lost – several times. In the end, I was deputised to ask for directions – which was less a vote of confidence in my ability to communicate effectively in French than a recognition that my schoolgirl Français was better than anyone else's. Eventually, after squeezing past Fee's baby seat three times and getting three conflicting sets of directions we, more by luck than good judgment, found the hotel – just before eight o'clock, close to two hours after we first hit the town.

The accommodation was pretty basic, but we had a decent meal in the restaurant, shared a couple of bottles of rosé and retired to our rooms in a much better frame of mind than when we arrived.

The weather, and our moods, improved as we drove further south, getting snarled up in traffic through Rouen and circumnavigating Poitiers on the A10 and eventually to La Rochelle where we drove across the bridge connecting mainland and island – to Ritchie's tuneless rendition of 'Sur La Pont d'Avignon'.

It was like driving into a different world. The approach road into La Rochelle was busy – signposts to the airport, the shipping port and a hypermarket whizzed past. But, as we accelerated across the downside of the bridge, the sunny metropolis abruptly turned into sleepy Rivedoux-Plage where stereotypical beret-clad fishermen tended their rods and bosomy grandmothers pedalled their sit-up-and-beg bikes down the middle of the road. It was enchanting.

For a while we followed the coast road before cutting across the island to our campsite. Across the hedgerows, the heads of cyclists crisscrossing the island's cycle paths bobbed up and down. They seemed so alive. Oh, I thought, I want to be one of them. So did Ritchie.

'Mum, Mum.' He bounced up and down. 'Can I get a bike? Mum, Mum, can I?'

Fliss hedged her bets.

'We'll see, darling. They might be too expensive.'

Ritchie grimaced. He'd heard that line before.

I nudged him gently and, mouthing 'yes', put a finger to my lips and nodded meaningfully towards the front seats. He grinned and nodded back.

Chapter Twenty-Eight

Teri

One thing that was really getting to me was the fact Victoria was in almost constant touch with Dan. But the devious little sod never rang the landline at my flat; she preferred to ring her daddy on his mobile or text him.

We'd be enjoying a meal at a local restaurant or a weekend away and 'beep' his mobile would announce a new text. He'd reach into his jacket pocket and retrieve the mobile, look at the message and smile. I'd never know what it said unless I asked.

'What is it?'

'Oh, just my little girl,' he said.

'Well, what does she want?' I said, cross at the intrusion.

'Oh, nothing…just hoping we're having a nice meal.'

'How does she know we're out having a meal?'

Dan looked at me incredulously. 'Because I told her earlier.'

'When, earlier?' I demanded.

'She popped in to the studios for lunch,' he said.

'Well, you never said,' I said.

'There was nothing to tell,' he replied. 'She pops in from time to time if she hasn't got any lessons. It's a nice thing to do.'

'You never invite me for lunch at the studios,' I accused.

'Well,' Dan said, with more impatience in his voice than I thought necessary, 'you don't have a very high opinion of the people I work with.

You're always saying how screechy and needy they are – your words, not mine. So I just thought you wouldn't want to come to the studios to have lunch with me – or them.'

True, I'd told him often enough I thought the telly types he worked with were a bunch of drama queens, and he was a fool for dropping everything when they rang to ask him to go rushing down to the studios to host some last-minute televised debate or stand in for another presenter who was away. 'Teri,' Dan would say, 'it's my job...And I happen to really like all the people that you call "drama queens". They're my friends as well as colleagues.'

Then it dawned on me Victoria was clearly included in the jolly TV crowd.

'Oh, so she gets invited to telly lunches with you and the team – but I don't?'

'Oh...Teri...' Dan sounded exasperated now.

I desperately needed to talk to Lee. But, of course, she was on holiday, and her mobile was going straight to voicemail. I needed to tell her how the Victoria situation was getting out of hand. It wasn't so much the intrusion but that most of the time when Victoria contacted her father it was in some way to butter him up for something she wanted. There would be one or two calls and one or two texts and then a clincher. 'Victoria wants...' Dan would tell me as a precursor to whatever it was she'd demanded: new clothes, driving lessons, a holiday. I told him he was being too generous, but he just smiled and said how he liked to indulge her. 'She's had a tough time, poor kid,' he said, 'what with the divorce and everything.' She'd had a tough time? My God, she should try stepping out of the cotton wool blanket her parents wrapped her up in and see what the real world was all about.

Chapter Twenty-Nine

Lee

So, Ritchie and I hired a couple of bikes and every day for two weeks, we set off mid-morning and cycled around the island. We had ice creams in Saint-Martin-de-Ré, pizza in La Flotte and climbed the lighthouse tower at Saint-Clément-des-Baleines. We explored the different beaches, and concluded that the one on our own doorstep was the best, and, once, most memorably, tried our hands at catching frogs. We were lounging in the grass by a large pond, digesting our baguettes, when a tubby Frenchman arrived with a rod and line to collect his evening meal. But there was no poisson on his menu – instead he'd come to catch frogs to make the local delicacy of Cuisse de grenouilles and, to Ritchie's delight, invited him to have a go.

It looked easy – M'sieu gently tapped the surface of the water with the end of his line – a nylon string with a knot at the end, supposedly to trick the frogs into thinking it was a particularly appetising fly. The greedy frogs raced to gobble it up and the winner, or rather the loser, found its teeth caught on the knot. With a deft flick of the wrist, M'sieu had the helpless creature in his hessian sack before you could say Jacques Cousteau.

Sadly, it wasn't as easy as it looked. Ritchie proved adept at enticing the frogs to nibble his line, but his wrist flicking left a lot to be desired. There was a knack to it because unless you flicked the frog quickly into the sack, it wriggled free – and Ritchie had a lot of wrigglers before he finally flicked a winner. The Frenchman was patient though and, since his English was as good as my French, used a combination of mime and monosyllables to instruct him: 'Comme ça' and 'Non' and 'Ici', all accompanied by extravagant hand gestures that were, frankly, almost as confusing as they were instructive. Eventually, though, M'sieu captured the forty-or-so critters he needed for dinner and offered us his surplus – a kind act, which we politely, and, at least on Ritchie's part, regretfully declined.

It was a perfect afternoon and a glorious holiday. I wouldn't have believed a small boy could be such a good companion.

I came home pounds lighter – all that cycling had taken its toll on my waistline – and felt and looked better than I had in a very long time. Ritchie's simple pleasure in my company had salved the open wound that had been eating away at me. And I loved that my clothes felt looser. My asthma was easier too and, in a rash of enthusiasm and determination to build on the good work of the holiday, I signed up at the local gym. No doubt, my resolution would've faltered sooner rather than later if it hadn't been for Gorgeous David Greenspan. He was one of half-a-dozen-or-so freelance trainers who worked out of the club. Like me, he was fairly new and, unlike me, touting for business. He approached one afternoon as I pedalled away on one of the static bikes – nowhere near as much fun as cycling on the Île de Ré but a necessary evil if I was to achieve my goal to drop two dress sizes before Christmas.

I can't precisely recall the exact nature of his chat-up line but it was very effective – I agreed to a taster training session, and, subsequently, signed up as a regular. Initially, I'd thought it would be enough to have a guided session once a month, or, maybe, at a stretch, once a fortnight, but I very quickly became addicted to the rush of endorphins that followed a demanding training session and, more importantly, to David himself.

Chapter Thirty

Teri

When Lee finally came back from her holiday, I recounted the latest row with Dan and told her about Victoria and the intrusive texts.

'Why does she need to do that?' I asked when we got together for coffee in the senior common room. 'Why does she feel she has to hope we have a nice meal...a good weekend? And why do she and Dan meet up so often without telling me?'

'Well, ringing to hope you're having a nice time is a kind thing to do,' Lee said. 'And maybe Dan is a little sensitive to how you feel about Victoria so he feels awkward about mentioning her. He realises you're jealous.'

'I'm not jealous,' I exploded. 'No, she does it because she wants to interfere and be involved in everything we do.'

'Isn't that a good thing?'

'No. I want there to be things that just Dan and I do; things that just Dan and I know about. Why can't we go out for a meal or go away for a weekend without him having to tell her?'

'He's her father, Teri. He wants her to feel involved.'

'Well, I wish he didn't. I'd like a private life – one which doesn't involve a selfish brat of a daughter.'

Chapter Thirty-One

Lee

Initially the gym was a means to an end – I'd lost some weight and I wanted to lose more and preferably whilst still indulging in the occasional dry white wine. (Occasional? Who am I kidding?) Be that as it may, it proved addictive in more ways than one. For starters, it soon became clear it was the centre of a fascinating sub-culture of exercise junkies, yummy mummies and ladies who lunch. Not to mention the insomniac geriatrics who every morning between half six and seven turned the pool into a heaving maelstrom, and the lazy treadmill plodders on the other end of the spectrum who never broke into a sweat.

The changing room conversations were corkers and, because of the hum of the hairdryers and the boom-boom from the spinning and step classes overhead, were always conducted at top pitch. Impossible not to listen as one woman detailed every gory cough and spit of her recent colonoscopy; or to chip in when the middle-class, time rich, common-sense poor mother of a teenage son wondered aloud why he didn't dump the girlfriend whom he clearly despised.

'Are they sleeping together?'

Ping! The penny dropped.

'The little so-and-so…' I'm not sure his mother didn't think it was half admirable to keep shagging the poor girl until something better came along.

The staff were an interesting bunch too. Hayley, the receptionist, who was saving up for a tummy tuck – a surgical fix that was surely contrary to the whole exercise ethos promoted by the trainers – and Colin, the assistant manager, who was accused by a furious husband – who burst into a Thighs, Tums and Bums class – of having an affair with his wife (he wasn't – he was seeing Natalie, the membership secretary, whose partner was oblivious to the liaison); and, of course, pregnant Glynis, who ran the beauty salon, and whose boyfriend was in prison for GBH. You think I'm making this up, don't you? Honestly, I couldn't. I don't have enough imagination.

It was a people watcher's paradise – which was just as well, since the gossip and the goings on proved a welcome distraction from the tedium of the cross-trainer and the rowing machine. At least, that is, until Gorgeous David Greenspan came along, and my whole attitude to exercise changed.

Our first training session was a killer – the good intentions with which I'd originally joined the gym had long since slipped into lethargic antipathy. David blew away the cobwebs: he kept me pounding on the bloody treadmill until I'd lost almost half my body weight in sweat – a slight exaggeration, but only a slight one. He gave me a minute to recover while I poured half a gallon of water down my neck and then moved into the weight room. Forty-five minutes later I ached in places I didn't even know had muscles.

That was Friday. Next morning I got up at seven, foregoing my usual Saturday lie-in because I was so stiff and sore I couldn't get comfortable enough to drowse any longer. Instead, I went to the gym, figuring I needed to up my fitness levels if I was to have a hope in hell of surviving another session with David. And so a pattern was established – no two training sessions were ever the same, but, once a week, twice, if I could, I trained for sixty minutes with David and then spent the next seven days, striving to repeat everything we'd done in the previous workout. Partly, as I said, it was self-preservation – he worked me so hard I couldn't afford to coast along as I had before. And, partly, I wanted to please him – he was so encouraging and so thrilled when I executed a perfect squat or lifted an extra five pounds on the bench press, that I kept pushing myself a little bit harder.

I can't say I actually *enjoyed* any of these work-outs – personally, I think people who claim to enjoy training are a shade touched in the head.

Every training session began with a grinding ten-minute cardio workout, sometimes on the treadmill (hate running!), sometimes on the bike (can't stand cycling!) and sometimes on the rowing machine (loathe rowing!). And I didn't keep my opinion to myself. 'Stop grumbling,' David would order, and I'd swear rudely. Sometimes under my breath – mostly not. 'Potty mouth,' he'd tease. 'F*** off!' I'd reply.

And, while the weight didn't exactly melt away, gradually I lost my saddle thighs and gained muscle definition in my legs and arms; and then, though the bikini stomach proved elusive for a very long time, the ripples of flesh became noticeably tighter and more taut. I tightened the notch on my belt, first, by one buckle hole, then two, and, finally three. Goal!

In the meantime, I also developed a little crush – which is something that happens, I suspect, to all women of a certain age who place their bodies and their well-being into the hands of a fit twenty-something, with an endearing grin, floppy hair and a sweet smile. For at least sixty minutes every week I had his undivided attention, and the fact I paid him thirty-six pounds a time didn't detract from the niceness of being the focus of so much interest from a good-looking bloke. Hard not to fall just the teeniest, tiniest bit in love.

Oh, and by the way, those of you who think thirty-six pounds was a snip: a) this was a couple of years ago, prices have gone up since; and b) this is Yorkshire, no fancy London prices here.

Of course, I wasn't daft enough to think the crush was reciprocated, but we developed an easy-going banter and we even once shared a bed – I know what you're thinking, but it wasn't like that. And, no, I'm not going into details – at least, not right now.

We worked out together but I never told a single soul I was seeing him. Obviously, people at the gym knew I was one of David's clients, but gym and home and work were separate (until, of course, David developed ambitions – but more of that later) and I never even breathed a word about him to Teri (even after David's ambitions came to fruition – stop being impatient, more of that later too). I don't know why; Teri would've enjoyed hearing about my gym travails. Perhaps I might've told her if she'd even once commented on my weight loss and my new, more svelte figure, but the change occurred so gradually she simply didn't notice that Miss Plump and Mousey had become Miss Jenny Wren. And, of course, she was so wrapped up in her own doings that, admittedly, were pretty time-consuming, there was no space for added distractions.

Mind you, it was a bit mean of me not to tell her about David Greenspan – she'd have been extremely interested in him. And she'd have been especially interested in the developments that ensued when he first confided his preference for older women. Initially, I didn't pay much attention – I was on the eighth of ten push-ups and not really in the mood for banter so, apart from a quizzical look, I ignored him and focused on the last couple of punishing lifts. Tell me, honestly, in a similar position, would you have spotted this was a chat-up line? And then, as I lay spread-eagled on the gym mat, gasping for breath, he repeated his earlier assertion.

'Older women, like you, Lee, are so much more attractive than younger ones.'

His words took a moment to sink in. I remember thinking: why are you telling me this? I wondered briefly if he'd been drinking – beer goggles might just about account for such a ridiculous assertion. But, no, he was standing still, upright and sober.

'Really?' I asked.

Yes, really. And me, in particular.

I struggled to a sitting position, not quite sure how to respond. Good God, the age gap between me and David was almost the same as the age gap between Mammy and Daddy, only their gap was the right way round. And it was one thing for me to fantasise about David – let's be honest, I'd been fancying the pants off him ever since we started training together – but quite another to think the fantasy might be reciprocated. It wasn't...well, seemly is the word that most immediately springs to mind.

However, I'm nothing if not persuadable, and stifling the little voice that told me bluntly not to be so damn stupid, I accepted his shy invitation to meet him for a drink in town.

You could've knocked me down with a feather when, as he sipped tonic water, and I slugged something considerably stronger, he confessed he'd had a crush on me for months. A crush on me? Blow me – there's a first time for everything.

'I've always had a thing for older women,' he said.

Steady on, mate. Be careful who you're calling old.

'Younger women can be very shallow,' he said.

Older ones can be too, I thought, admiring his well-toned pecs.

'And they've got nothing interesting to say.'

Takes two to make a conversation though. Hell's bells. Why was I mentally contradicting everything he said? Stop looking a gift horse in the mouth.

Chapter Thirty-Two

Lee

Be careful what you wish for: once I'd thought it would be rather pleasant – rather pleasant, who am I kidding? – to share a bed with Gorgeous Greenspan. But the fantasy was as short-lived as it was fantastical. Exposing my lumps and bumps to someone like Mike, who was also age-appropriately lumpy and bumpy, was one thing, but I couldn't quite bring myself to undress in front of David. And, if a relationship is to advance beyond hand-holding and chaste kisses, then clothes need to be removed at some point.

David was kind and understanding. 'We'll take it at your pace, Lee,' he said.

That's good – because, after Mike, I had no intention of rushing into anything.

'I'm happy to wait until you're ready,' he said.

Just as well, I thought, because it will take a hell of a lot more gym time before I'm svelte enough to feel comfortable slipping between the sheets next to you.

'I know you've been hurt and you need time to recover,' he added.

The patronising git!

Chapter Thirty-Three

Teri

My hope that the Victoria situation would fade when Dan moved into my duplex was not to be. There was something masochistic about the way she delighted in turning up at my door on a Friday night. She deliberately dropped her bag in the hallway instead of putting it in the spare room as I asked. She never used the drink coasters, instead plonking her coffee mug directly on my polished, white-oak side tables where it left round, brown stains. She helped herself to my magazines, which I kept in date order in the wicker magazine basket by the wood burning stove, and, having half-read them, left them splayed open on the sofa.

'Can you not do that?' I asked, snatching up the mags, closing them and piling them neatly on the coffee table. 'The newsprint rubs off on the cushions.'

Whenever I tried to explain how leaving her school books on the floor by her chair was making the place look untidy, she forced herself to say sorry, shrug and slouch out of the room.

She enjoyed the misery she caused. The only time she was happy was when nestling on the sofa (MY sofa) with Dan (MY husband). They'd either be swapping humorous comments about some crappy TV talent contest they were watching or they'd be talking about something from their previous life – BT (Before Teri). Oh God, how that annoyed me.

'Do you remember that time we went to Marbella and Mummy tripped over that Spanish waiter and fell in the pool?' the child asked.

'Oh, yes,' Dan said. 'She was fully dressed as well…but she kept hold of her wine glass…'

The two of them nearly wet themselves laughing.

I'd already decided even though the thought of staying in my flat and spending time with me was probably anathema to the teenage-hell child, the need to keep close to her father was stronger. She needed to because she couldn't exist financially without him.

One spectacular crisis nearly brought Dan to his senses. Victoria and her mother had taken a two-week holiday in Antigua (and how was that paid for, might one ask?) The girl had taken her mobile phone to keep up-to-date with her pals on Facebook and, on arrival home, found a bill for the roaming charges had clocked up nine thousand pounds. Dan was furious, and I delighted in the way he yelled at her about how irresponsible she was. But once he'd argued with the mobile phone company and got the bill down by half, he told the precious one to take more care in future.

Chapter Thirty-Four

Teri

What really annoyed me about the Victoria situation was that I didn't get any support from Dan.

'Will you talk to her?' I asked him one Saturday evening when I'd been hoping for a lovely, expensive meal out somewhere alone with my husband but which turned into a quiet night in with the two of them, a Chinese takeaway and a boring card game they played at the kitchen table. 'Come and join us,' Dan said as the wretched child dealt them each a hand. 'We're playing for money,' he added, laughing.

'Your money, I suppose,' I said, staring at him meaningfully and ignoring his grin.

'Oh, it's only ten pence pieces.'

I looked around at what should have been my spotless vanilla cream kitchen. Crumpled cartons of discarded takeaway on two of the counters, chopsticks sticking out of a half-filled washing up bowl of greasy water, my lovely little Cantonese bowls, still sticky with leftover food and piled precariously at the edge of the table. And just as I reached to rescue them, Victoria saw what I was doing, reached out in front of me and knocked all three bowls onto the floor where they smashed.

'Oh, God. I'm so sorry,' she wailed. For a moment I almost thought she was genuinely mortified. She leapt to her feet, flapping about and trying to pick up the pieces.

'Oh, leave it,' I said. 'The damage is done.'

Victoria looked at her father in appeal. 'I really am sorry,' she said. 'I was trying to move them.' She even let herself go red and tears appeared in her eyes. Hah! Don't pull that trick on me, I thought.

'This flat is getting wrecked,' I muttered, now on my hands and knees picking up the broken shards. When I looked up, Victoria had left the room, and Dan was glaring at me as though it was me who'd done something wrong.

I threw my hands in the air. 'Will you talk to her?'

'What about, Teri?' he said.

'The way she behaves,' I said. 'The way she tries to ruin everything.'

'Teri, she doesn't try to ruin everything. She's a normal kid and she's doing the best she can but, if I may say so, you don't make it easy for her.'

I stiffened. 'What do you mean by that?'

'Well, you're always on her back – don't do this; don't put that there; pick that up. The poor girl's being nagged to death.'

'Oh you would take her side,' I said. 'She can't do anything wrong, can she, your precious, fucking daughter.'

Dan's look was cold and hard. I made a big thing of clearing up the rest of the mess and went to bed early feeling sorry for myself and wondering why it was always me who was treated like this: side-lined, left out and misunderstood.

Was it unreasonable or irrational of me to be so upset? No, of course it wasn't. I was his wife, for goodness' sake, and he should pay me more respect. He spent half his time with those up-their-own-arses television people and the rest with a whining, needy seventeen-year-old.

Chapter Thirty-Five

Lee

David was still being patient about my inability to consummate. Which was to his credit, I suppose, but, irritatingly, I thought he was being a bit wet. If he'd got annoyed and told me to stop being so bloody stupid and that he loved me, warts and all, I'm sure I would've succumbed immediately. (Not that I have any warts, I hasten to point out.) But he didn't, instead he reiterated his willingness to take things slowly and to let things happen naturally. I began to wonder if he might be gay.

In the meantime, we continued to see each other at the gym and to meet two or three evenings a week, either for a meal or a drink. Not that we ate much – the list of things he didn't eat was extensive, and it's hard to enjoy dinner when your partner is picking at a wholefood salad – and he was a kill-joy where alcohol was concerned. 'Another glass of wine? You've had two already.' Yes, and I'm having a third – and probably a fourth and fifth as well.

It seemed sometimes as if he was on a one-man mission to educate me about the importance of good nutrition. 'We are what we consume, Lee.' Which perhaps explained why he had a six-pack and I didn't. He eschewed alcohol, chocolate, sweets, crisps and biscuits; ate hardly any carbohydrates or red meat; and filled up on good proteins – beans and pulses mostly. And eggs. He was passionate about them: breakfast was half a dozen egg yolks – or was it whites? – plus a vegetable smoothie. I'm not much of a breakfast person myself, but I'd have lost the will to live if my day began with such a depressing feast. And what did he do with the spare egg whites – or yolks? Seemed a waste.

I also learned about his early life – his dad's death when he was eight; his mother's remarriage; his much younger step-brother and step-sister; his first job as a brickie's labourer; and the bank loan he'd taken out to cover the cost of studying for a personal training qualification.

And he shared his views on politicians – 'waste of space' – and immigrants –'dragging the country down' – and his plans to sort out career criminals – 'lock 'em up and throw away the key'. You couldn't call David a bleeding heart liberal.

We also discussed his plans for the future because training was proving less rewarding than he'd expected.

'Too many ladies who lunch, Lee,' he said.

Possibly, but without those ladies he wouldn't be able to afford lunch himself. He agreed.

'But I just can't see myself still doing this for another ten, twenty, thirty years...'

No – helping middle-aged women get their figures back wouldn't get me out of bed either.

As relationships went, it was all a bit dull really.

I did, though, get a great deal of pleasure from being seen out with David; he was, in the nicest possible way, good arm-candy. I noticed several envious stares – and some frankly incredulous ones – when we walked into a bar together and, it seems a pity, in retrospect, that I never flaunted him in front of Teri. She'd have been gob-smacked and, hopefully, insanely jealous.

Chapter Thirty-Six

Teri

If Dan wasn't going to sort his bloody daughter out, I would have to. A couple of weeks after the idiotic child smashed my Cantonese dishes, I decided to have a girly chat with her. I decided the theme should be how she felt about me and her father getting together. I didn't really want to know about her precious feelings, but felt it would be a good place to start.

Dan was out for the evening. He didn't normally work on a Friday night, but the late evening news presenter had fallen sick so the studio had asked Dan to stay on that night to read the 10.30pm bulletin.

'You should've said no,' I told him when he rang to say he'd be home late. 'You do have a life outside Ridings Today.' But he said they needed him, and he couldn't let them down. Too nice, he was; too kind; too considerate.

So I was left with the spaghetti Bolognese I'd prepared – and Victoria.

'Is this okay for you?' I asked as she pushed the food backwards and forwards across the blue and white patterned Tuscan pasta bowl, showing every sign she was not prepared to eat this muck and if she did, it would choke her.

'Yeah, okay,' she muttered.

'I hope you're all right in that spare room – it is quite small.' I thought pretending to be considerate and kind might do the trick.

'It's fine,' she said, all mock graciousness.

'It's only until we get a house, and then you can have a much bigger bedroom.'

'It's okay, I said,' she said, looking up from her plate with a resigned expression on her face as though she was talking to an irritating aged aunt who was trying – needlessly – to teach her the facts of life.

'I just wondered…you sometimes seem dismissive about me…er…about my marrying your father.'

'What do you mean, dismissive?' she asked, a defensive but hard note coming into her tone.

'Well, unfriendly…'

'You think I'm the one who's unfriendly?' she said, looking directly at me.

'Yes, I do…sometimes. You seem to resent me, and I don't like the way you …' I wasn't sure exactly what I was going to say, to be honest, but I didn't get a chance to finish the sentence because, suddenly, in one violent movement, Victoria pushed the pasta bowl away, shoved her chair back and stood up.

'If you don't like the way things are, you shouldn't have married my father,' she spat. Then she stormed out.

She came back later – with Dan. She'd called a taxi to take her into town to the studios, watched him do the late bulletin and then came back with him in his BMW. God knows what she told him, but by the time they got back to the flat, I was in bed asleep. The next morning Victoria gave me a wide berth and disappeared to a yoga class, and Dan tiptoed round me as if walking on broken glass because he was obviously too scared to raise the subject and launch into another discussion about his daughter.

So, it was going to turn into one of those big issues that lurk in the background like a silent demon about which no one will talk.

Chapter Thirty-Seven

Teri

The one good thing after Victoria's little explosion was that she spent less time at my flat. She made excuses that she was away with friends, going off somewhere with her mother, or simply chilling at home. It hurt Dan and he spent a lot of time on the phone with her trying to suggest things they could do together. He arranged to take her and some of her little school friends bowling.

'Do you want to come?' he asked.

'Not really,' I replied. 'I've got better things to do than spend the evening with a load of seventeen-year-olds.'

Dan looked hurt, but I noticed when he arranged to take the same little pack to see a new teen movie, I wasn't invited.

'I didn't think you'd be interested,' Dan reasoned later. 'I know there is an atmosphere between you and Victoria, so I thought it would be easier to see her on my own.'

To be honest, I was losing respect for Dan. Why should a man his age spend so much time with a needy daughter? I never understood this father-daughter business. Hell, I hardly saw my father when I was growing up – and I survived. Dad was always at the mill, working from early in the morning until late at night and often at weekends too. Yes, the mill was very busy then, he had a huge workforce and he had endless business meetings. But, secretly, I thought he stayed away because he couldn't stand being with

129

my mother, and she couldn't stand being on her own with me and Charlie so she hit the sherry bottle. Charlie and I were left to our own devices, and that was okay with me. It made me independent; it made me realise if I was going to do anything with my life, I would have to sort it out myself.

Lee once asked me if I'd had a happy childhood; if I'd been loved. Odd question, but we'd been out for a drink or two and were having a girly chat about all sorts of things. I didn't quite know how to reply; I'd never thought about whether I'd been happy or loved.

'We never went without' was the best I could come up with at short notice. 'Dad always made sure we had enough money.'

Thinking about Dan's relationship with his daughter and how different it was to mine with Dad, I worried Dan was demeaning himself, so, one evening, I suggested he man-up, stop making a fool of himself and leave her to stew. He looked up from the letter he was reading and his eyes were cold. It might have been the effect of readjusting from the printed type on the letter to my face, but I'd have been kidding myself to believe the refocusing process involved a look of such intense distaste. For someone as nice and kind as Dan – someone who'd do anything for anyone – that look was as painful as anything I'd experienced. Momentarily it made me sway, doubtful about how solid was my argument, but I gathered myself together, put my hands on my hips and snapped at him. 'Don't you dare look at me like that.'

'Like what?' he asked.

'Like you hate me,' I shouted. 'I'm your WIFE. The people you should look at like that are those ridiculous television types you hang around with, and your damn ex-wife and kid. It's them you should be looking at like that.'

'Why?' he asked.

'Because they're all leeches,' I screamed. 'They take advantage of your good nature and they sponge off you – and you're too nice to see what's happening. You won't say no to anyone even if it interferes with something we're doing. Even at the expense of our marriage.'

Dan wiped a hand across his eyes and used a finger to rub into the corner of one of them. 'Oh. Teri…this dismays me so much,' he said, shaking his head. 'I hate it when you're like this.'

I slammed my hand down on the table. 'Like what?'

'Like this, Teri. Seeing fault in everyone…the people I work with…my family. I don't know why you can't accept that I had a life before I met you, and I still have that life. You have to accept that I love my job and I love my daughter, and I'm not giving up either of them to make you happy.'

'Right,' I shouted. 'That's all I need to hear.'

'No, it's not,' he insisted, standing up quickly and moving round the table towards me. 'I can love you – and love other people. I wish I could get that through to you, but you seem insistent that I can love only you. What do you want me to do – give up my job, stop seeing Victoria, spend every waking moment with just you?'

I thought one of those propositions out of the three would work, but I was too wound up to care what he was trying to say. My mind was racing: why had I never had anyone's exclusive love? Why had I always had to fight for what I had? Why did no one understand what I wanted? Why had I always been so lonely?

He moved as if to take me in his arms, but I shrugged him away.

'Forget it,' I snarled, heading for the door. 'Ring your fucking daughter and offer to buy her something nice. That'll get her attention.'

Chapter Thirty-Eight

Teri

I thought it would've all blown over. Dan would realise how unreasonable he'd been, beg my forgiveness and reassure me everything would be all right. After the row, I'd stormed into the bedroom, kicking over my antique French Angelique chair. But kicking it was a stupid thing to do as it jarred my foot. I did a quick check to make sure the chair was all right, but left it on its side and threw myself across the bed so the scene Dan would confront when he came in to apologise would be a dramatic one.

But he didn't come in to comfort me. Instead, I heard him go up the hallway, collect his keys from the glass dish on the side table and head out the door.

He came home later that night but went straight into the spare room.

The next morning, he was up and gone before I woke, so I assumed he was reading the early breakfast bulletin. I felt dull and weakened by the row – and I certainly didn't feel like going into university. The students hadn't started back, but Peter Heron liked us to be in and doing things before the semester started proper, although goodness knows what 'things' we were supposed to be doing as timetabling hadn't been finalised, so no one knew where they would be teaching, on which days and at what time. In the first couple of weeks of October when the little darlings arrived, we'd give them what we laughingly called their Lecture and Seminar Planners, which were supposed to tell them which lectures and tutorials they were having where and when, and which lecturers would be teaching them. But the planners were more an indication that Chrissie and the rest of the admin team had been swanning around. They were supposed to work through the summer vacation while the lecturers took a well-earned rest, but, rather than actually doing the job – filling in the teaching grids – they spent their time Facebooking, Tweeting and eating chocolate eclairs. The resulting planners were always a shambolic mess.

Peter had called a staff meeting for 10am, but I thought, bugger that, and took my time with a long, hot bath and, having calmed down, sent Dan a text: 'I'm sorry…x.' I left it at that, got in the car and headed for the campus.

From the buzz coming from the senior common room, I guessed correctly that Peter Heron's meeting was going on in there. Sure enough, when I pushed open the door, about twenty faces turned to look and Peter, who was at the head of the room facing the crowd, nodded at me. 'Thank you for coming, Teri,' he said. Sarcastically.

'Sorry, I'm late,' I said, squeezing in, and passed the back row to join Lee who was gesticulating to show she'd saved me a seat.

She put a hand over her mouth, leaned towards me and hissed, 'You're late.'

'Only half an hour,' I replied. 'Have I missed much?'

It turns out I'd missed all of it. Peter had been announcing new appointments, our latest research status (which was bugger all) and plans to re-examine academic provision for the next academic year.

'What does that mean?' I asked Lee later.

'He's looking very closely at what each of us is doing in terms of academic integrity and relevancy. If it doesn't fit his new model, it's out.'

'When has academia been relevant to anything?' I asked. I loved winding Lee up especially about the importance or otherwise of young people today studying for degrees which will stand them in no good stead whatsoever. 'Why don't they just learn a trade?' I generally asked her. But the last time we had this 'discussion' she'd turned to me quite seriously and said, 'You know, Teri, you need to think about your subject. For instance, I'm really not sure your Moral and Monarchical Panics of the 1600s will survive this new wind of change.'

'Oh, my rakes and libertines are totally relevant,' I argued. 'My naughty boys will survive.' She'd tutted at me in a friendly enough way but with a hint of sympathy thrown in.

The staff meeting had also included the announcement of another of Peter Heron's personal little pets: he was going to hold another of his wretched soirees and in the interests of inclusivity had invited the whole department to come along for a spot of warm white wine and cheesy nibbles, which is how, a week later, I came to be standing with Lee, Chrissie and Mrs Mimms (dressed in her black and white combo as she does for all these 'formal' occasions) in front of the buffet-laden counter top.

Despite it being a 'media' event, the only people from the *actual* media were the spotty, bog-brush-haired youth from the local commercial radio station who I remembered from last year, and a young girl of about eighteen, with long brown hair parted in the middle, who turned out to be a junior reporter at the Evening Leader called Cassie and who wasn't entirely sure why she was there as there didn't seem to be any story to report. Other guests dribbled in, including a chap who told us he did something called 'digital storytelling', which meant taking video on his smartphone of everything he did and uploading it on to Twitter.

'What? Everything?' I asked.

'Yeah, especially visits to my gran's,' he said. 'That goes down a storm – my gran's very popular on Twitter.'

There was also a 'data journalist' who spent all day interpreting masses and masses of data from whatever Freedom of Information request he'd successfully made, to offer analysis on the latest crime figures for a suburb of the town in a six-week period three years ago. 'Very topical and relevant,' I muttered.

Dan had been invited, but Victoria was appearing in a school dance show being staged to launch the new term and for which she'd been rehearsing all summer, so he chose to spend the evening watching his daughter perform, rather than supporting his wife.

Peter Heron had made a point of being nice to me ever since I married Dan, hoping, perhaps, that I would put in a good word for him apropos the book programme that, so far, hadn't made it onto the Ridings Today schedule. Peter lived in hope. He had also been very excited announcing that

Richard Walker, MD of Ridings Today, *might* be coming to the soiree. Something stirred when I heard this. A shiver of – not alarm exactly – apprehension more like. What had I said to Duck's Arse that night at the RTS dinner? Oh, for goodness' sake. It was months ago. Duck's Arse would've forgotten and, anyway, we were all very drunk.

Chapter Thirty-Nine

Lee

As a manager, Peter Heron had a very clear idea of what he wanted to achieve and what he needed to do to reach his goals. Having joined the university from a traditional red brick, he was determined to drag us upwards and onwards and if that meant ruffling a few feathers – actually, quite a lot of feathers – he didn't much care.

To be fair, I had a lot of sympathy with his determination to change the somewhat laissez-faire attitude that previously prevailed, and whilst his targets were ambitious – some faculty staff thought they were unrealistic – I shared his belief that if we wanted to survive in a rapidly changing higher education landscape, we needed a root and branch overhaul. His words not mine.

Unfortunately, despite his best endeavours, he wasn't entirely successful in carrying the team with him. His management style, as he told us, frequently, was collegiate. This meant he held regular departmental meetings where he shared his visions for the future, and brought staff up-to-date with progress and upcoming initiatives. He put a lot of emphasis on consultation and claimed to listen and respond to feedback. I'm not sure those on the receiving end always felt they'd been adequately heard or that his responses were all they desired but, hey ho, the man was trying.

Very trying, said those who found their faces didn't quite fit the style and focus of the new regime, and who found themselves at the sharp end of his all-out war against 'the lazy arses' who, he said, 'were holding us back'.

Teri, in his view, definitely fell into that category.

She did little to convince him otherwise. In fact, her maverick attitude to rules and regulations and attempts to improve delivery and raise standards drove him to distraction. 'Nit picking,' she'd say, feeding the latest edition of his assessment review regulations into the paper shredder. 'Pointless, time-wasting,' she'd rage, deleting another email asking her to fill in a time allocation survey. 'Too busy,' she'd respond to an invitation to attend a workshop on the utilisation of effective learning spaces.

I don't know if it was simply a knee-jerk reaction to conformity or if she genuinely thought she was striking a blow for academic freedom. Either way, she was never going to figure as Peter Heron's poster girl.

I tried to give her a hint or two. It was some time since Mike warned me Peter's 'efficiencies' would inevitably lead to redundancies, but the threat hadn't gone away. And Teri, who had more enemies than friends, would be an easy target. But she could be every bit as stubborn as Peter. In particular, she thought Peter's frequent meetings were little more than 'talking shops' in which he talked and we listened. She had a point – but that's not the point as I tried to explain when she declared her intention to skip the first departmental meeting of the new academic semester. 'Nobody will even notice I'm not there,' she said. 'And you can fill me in with anything important.

'Not that there will be anything important,' she added.

I despaired.

Chapter Forty

Lee

I'd made a big effort to keep Chrissie at arm's length ever since she blabbed to Mike's wife about our short-lived relationship. I knew she was quite pally with Mrs Orme, and, it was understandable that Chrissie should've shared her suspicions with her friend, but she was my pal too – goodness, we'd worked together long enough – and she might've kept her gob shut. And then there was the question of her disloyalty to Mike, who was, first and foremost, her boss. No, we might have been out of order in having an affair, but it was none of Chrissie's business. It was silly of her to get involved too. Mike, who was chair of the department's remuneration committee, had vetoed her spring performance bonus on the basis she'd been performing below par. He'd been overruled by other members of the committee, and she got her bonus, but it was half what it might have been.

Serve her right, Teri would've said. I thought it did, too. Treacherous snake.

It was impossible, unfortunately, to completely avoid Chrissie – she was fairly integral to the smooth running of the department, but I kept things as business-like as possible, exchanging the time of day when we passed in the corridor, or met at meetings, or if I called into the admin office. But there were no more lunchtime natters in the senior common room and certainly no more after-work happy hour drinks in town. Inevitably, this meant missing out on a lot of work-related gossip. I hadn't realised until I stopped hobnobbing with Chrissie just how much 'news' she spread. But, on the whole, it was a price worth paying.

I wasn't, therefore, best pleased when she cornered me at Peter's first soiree of the new academic year.

'Lee,' she said, apparently with pleasure, 'it's been ages since we've had a chance for a proper catch-up.'

Well, it was nice she'd noticed.

'Tell me your news,' she invited.

Not bloody likely! If, and when, I needed the services of a town crier, I'd hire one.

'Pardon?' she asked.

I must've sworn aloud.

'Nothing,' I mumbled, taking a huge slurp of wine. 'What have you been up to over the summer?' Not that I cared, but I might as well try to be polite.

She didn't answer. Instead, she stared intently across the room where Teri was flirting outrageously with Declan.

'Excuse me,' I murmured, looking for somewhere to place my empty glass. 'I need to go and talk to someone.' Fucking Declan!

'He's a shit, isn't he?'

Had I spoken aloud again? This was getting to be a really bad habit. But no, Chrissie was blinking rapidly and agitatedly.

'He was all over me at last year's pre-Christmas soiree.'

Yes, and she'd been rather obviously all over him too.

'Dumped me like a ton of bricks afterwards.' More rapid blinking.

Good Lord – were those tears in her eyes?

'He'll find Miss High-and-Mighty-Meyer a different kettle of fish,' Chrissie said, rather nastily, I thought.

'Excuse me,' I repeated. 'I need to...'

'You're wasting your time,' Chrissie said.

Let me be the judge of that.

'I know his type,' she continued. Huh! If you *had* known his type, you wouldn't have been daft enough to get stuck in the broom cupboard with him.

'They think they can have any woman they want.'

Well, Declan couldn't be stupid enough to think that – or had he forgotten the leaver's disco at English Martyrs High School? Proms they call them nowadays, and spend a small fortune on fancy venues, live bands and professional DJs – we had to make do with the church hall and Mr O'Brien and his record deck. It had been good fun though – we were sixteen and euphoric that our GCSEs were finally over, the summer stretched ahead and sixth-form college and a grown-up life beckoned. Declan, as ever, was the best-looking bloke in the room, and was surrounded by a score of adoring girls – a bunch that – Ha! Ha! – did not include me. Instead, I was making a diet coke last a phenomenally long time as I chatted with Kelvin Turvey – a geeky lad, who'd been my best friend ever since he'd moved next door to us in the Alderwoods. It was a lucky coincidence his family was also Catholic and he ended up in my class: first, at primary school and, later, at high school too. He was clever and shy and good-looking in a long-legged, clumsy sort of way. He was my first love. and I think he had a little crush on me too. We hadn't yet got as far as kissing, but I was hopeful that evening might seal the deal. It did – and all thanks to Declan. He sauntered over to our table, swooning hand maidens in tow, and tried to pull me to my feet.

'Come on, Lee. Let's dance.'

No, thanks. It had taken only one painful session at Primley School of Dance to teach me I had two left feet, and I had no intention of displaying them to Declan. He was nonplussed and so were his harem. Kooky Kelvin? Dreamy Declan? No competition. They were right. I pulled my hand from Declan's grasp and sat back down.

'No thanks,' I repeated.

Declan shrugged. 'Your loss,' he said.

I'm not sure it was – Kooky Kelvin did kiss me on the way home. Just a little brush of his lips against mine, and it was lovely.

'I knew you were mine,' he whispered, 'when you said you'd rather chat with me than dance with Declan.'

Eeek! When had I said that? Who wouldn't rather dance with Declan? He was gorgeous. But I was a crap dancer, and I had no intention of making myself a laughing stock. Besides, I really did like Kelvin and, I thought virtuously, it wouldn't do Declan any harm to know that not every girl was prepared to worship at his feet. Secretly, I wondered if playing hard to get mightn't be a good tactic. Fool! Declan didn't waste time hankering after

140

what he couldn't have. Especially, when there was plenty of other fish in the sea. Much better-looking fish too.

But *je ne regrette rien*. Kelvin and I had a sweet, chaste lovey-dovey summer before his family moved again, this time to London, and we lost touch.

So Chrissie was deluding herself if she thought Declan always got what he wanted – and he wasn't going to get Teri now if I could help it. I raised my empty glass and signalled to her to join me for a refill.

She shook her head slightly – and frowned reprovingly. 'Go away' those expensively shaped and tinted eyebrows signalled as clearly as if she'd shouted it across the room.

'Don't!' I mouthed back. She stuck her tongue out.

Serve you bloody well right if you get your heart broken, I thought. Didn't she remember anything I'd told her about Declan when they'd been briefly introduced after Christmas Mass last year? Clearly not. She might have no scruples about getting tangled with a married man, but had she learned nothing from my sorry affair? And come to that – she was married herself. How could she even contemplate being unfaithful to nice, kind Dan? Because she most definitely was contemplating it – it was obvious from the way her body language mirrored his. She might as well have screamed from the bloody roof tops 'I'm having you!'

Not if I can help it, I decided, and thrusting my glass into Chrissie's unwilling hand, I went to head them off.

Damn Peter Heron. I might've caught the pair before they left the room, but he collared me before I even got within spitting distance. 'Lee,' he said, 'there's someone I'd like you to meet.'

No help for it; manners dictated I stop and exchange handshakes with a smart-suited gent with a strangely gelled 'up front' hair-do. Richard Walker, managing director of Ridings Today.

'Nothing happened,' Teri said when I finally ran her to ground the next morning. 'Declan just wanted to have a chat about featuring Dad in an autumn business supplement.'

And she believed him? I could've slapped her.

'I've told you about Declan,' I said. 'He's got enough baggage to fill a mini-bus.'

She didn't care. 'He's unlike any man I've ever known,' she cooed.

A weak excuse, I said, to justify the unjustifiable.

She disagreed, and, besides, she added, I was a fine one to cast aspersions.

True. If I could be stupid enough to get involved with a married man, there was precious little hope for Teri.

But I'm not a quitter. 'You haven't forgotten he's married?' I asked. No point reminding her that she too was also married.

No, she hadn't forgotten. And, to be fair, Declan hadn't tried to pretend otherwise either.

'He'll break your heart,' I warned.

'You don't need to worry about me,' she said.

'But...'

It was a waste of time. The bloody idiot. I knew what she was thinking – that Marnie was no match and that...what? Repressing a sigh, I realised I really didn't know what she was thinking – but it didn't augur well for Dan. Poor sod!

Chapter Forty-One

Teri

Another day, another row with Dan. Generally we managed to be polite with each other, but each time he mentioned his daughter I'd freeze, and it got so that he hardly dared mention her at all and simply said 'I'm going out on Monday night...' or something like that, and I would know he was meeting her or taking her somewhere. Never mind me. I only live here; I'm only your wife.

He tried occasionally to say something along the lines of 'Look, Teri, we're not leaving you out of things. You are more than welcome to come with us.' But I told him I'd married him and not his fucking daughter, and as far as I was concerned he could go and play happy families; I had better things to do. He'd sigh as though I was missing some point or making a big mistake. And life got more icily polite.

It nearly blew up a couple of months before when I wanted to go on holiday, but Dan said he couldn't get away from work. I rang D'reen and (innocently) asked her to look at Dan's work diary on the pretext I wanted to find a week when I could spring a surprise holiday on him. The daft cluck believed me and said, yes, he did have a week marked off in June. Idiotically, I thought for a minute he'd marked the week off to surprise me, but no. When I asked him about it he was first annoyed I'd gone behind his back to D'reen, and then sheepish because he had to confess he wanted to take Victoria away somewhere as she was apparently 'growing up' and probably wouldn't want to go on holiday with the 'old man' in future years. He tried to say he had hoped I would go with them, but for goodness' sake, why on earth would I want to go anywhere with this man who became cloyingly doting and boring when he was with his insufferable daughter? So off they went for a week in Lanzarote (hah! wonder if they bumped into my drunken mother), and I stayed at home, neglected, resentful and alone.

I saw Lee from time to time, but often when I rang she was just about to go to the gym or she'd just come back from the gym. What was it with that girl? I couldn't see any noticeable difference for all this gym business. But, I needed to talk to her, and on the rare occasions we did get together, I would tell her chapter and verse about what was happening or not happening with me and Dan – and Victoria. She tried to give me advice about 'seeing the other person's point of view' and I asked, what about my point of view? She said, maybe I was being a bit unreasonable expecting everyone to fall in line and do whatever it was I wanted. 'I don't think it's unreasonable for a wife to want to spend time with her husband,' I said.

'But you do spend time with him,' Lee said.

'But he has so many other commitments. I'm fed up of sharing him.'

'No one can have another person exclusively,' she responded.

'It's so bloody unfair,' I moaned.

'Life's unfair,' she said, taking a sip of her white wine, 'and I'm afraid you have to make compromises.'

So the next row was about Peter Heron's media soiree and whether Dan would accept the invitation to come and be a telly type and thus provide me with some Brownie points as it would put me in Peter's good books. But, no. Darling Victoria had been rehearsing some dance routine all summer and was taking part in school show, and going to see that was more important than helping me.

The row was short, sharp and explosive. Dan stormed out, got into his BMW and accelerated away while I reached down, grabbed the coffee table with both hands and pulled upwards, overturning it and sending coffee cups and magazines flying off. Shit, one of the mugs still had coffee in it, and as it hit the floor, the mug, forced under its own centrifugal force, spun round in a tight circle spilling the cold, brown liquid over my oak flooring.

So I went to the soiree on my own and had probably drunk a little too much because I was actually having fun. I took the piss out of these ridiculous 'media' types who took themselves and their 'digital first', 'crowd sourcing apps' and 'live update threads' so seriously. Especially entertaining was Cassie who, intermittently flicking her long, lank hair back from her face, was responding well to my teasing that she must meet a lot of interesting people in her job (as if interviewing Diamond Wedding couples and moaning council tenants could possibly be interesting). She was just expounding on the fact that the most interesting people were not celebrities and royalty but 'ordinary people with extraordinary stories' when a startlingly good-looking man came up behind her, put his finger to his lips to indicate 'shush' to me, then put his hands over her eyes and went 'Boo!' Cassie squealed, ducked down and, under his hands, spun round and giggled. 'Oh…Declan…you daft sod.' She'd turned pink with delight.

Declan? I knew him from somewhere. That's it: Christmas at Lee's church. He'd been sitting in the pew in front of us.

Declan grinned at me. 'Cassie,' he said, 'you're needed. There's a fire at the tyre warehouse on Wellington Road, can you nip down there and join Jon. A photographer's on the way too.'

'Are you not coming?' Cassie asked, buttoning up her jacket.

'No, I've got things to do here,' he said, looking at me and winking.

Cassie broke into a run and headed for the exit. 'Ah, these young cubs,' Declan sighed, half turning away from me to watch her skip through the door.

I studied the back of his head: the light brown hair, longish and floppy, cutely curling over the top of his collar, and I remembered he'd also been at last year's Peter Heron soiree (only that time he'd been cosying up to Chrissie in quite a purposeful way).

'Don't you want to go with her?' I asked.

He turned back to me. 'Nah. Not much of a fire really, and it'll be out by the time she gets there.'

I looked round the room and saw Lee, standing with Chrissie, looking our way. Chrissie was sending daggers. Tough, I thought; you had your chance. Lee had that concerned look on her face and was making some sort of gesture with her hands. Should I beckon her over? I knew she knew this guy, and they'd been in intense conversation last time he was here. She'd have told me, surely, if they had history. On the other hand, this guy was seriously gorgeous and was looking at me in a way that made me feel as though I was the most fascinating object in the room. He introduced himself, and when I told him who I was, he said, 'I know.' Ridiculously and girlishly flattered, I asked him if he wanted a drink, indicating Mrs Mimms' less than well-stocked supply of bottles.

'Yes, but not here,' he said. 'Look, I'm a good friend of Lee's so you know you can trust me, and I know who you are and there's something I'd like to talk about. So can we go somewhere quieter and have a chat?'

It was never meant to happen. But, to be honest, after the time I'd been having with the Dan situation, it had to happen. I needed some happiness in my life, and here it was being offered to me by this gorgeous man.

I knew nothing about Declan other than he was some boss at the local paper and, although he was 'media' he wasn't screechy telly. He seemed more down-to-earth than these theatrical TV bods with their video scripts and autocue dramas. And he was seriously interested in me. I could tell by the way he propelled me out of the soiree room. I looked back over my shoulder to indicate to Lee I was going, and I could see her mouth opening as if to shout after me, but I flapped my arm in the hope she'd understand the semaphore for 'everything's okay, I know what I'm doing'. She started to move towards us, but I spotted Peter Heron heading her way with Richard Walker – Duck's Arse – in tow. 'Good old Peter,' I thought.

I left my car at the university, because even I recognised I'd had too much to drink and travelled with Declan in his rather battered, silver grey VW Golf. As I was climbing in I noticed a sticker on the windscreen: 'Evening Leader Leads'.

'Leads where?' I joked.

'Huh, very funny,' he said, obviously having heard that one before.

We headed up Wellington Road where black smoke pumped out of the roof of a warehouse, and I spotted young Cassie, notebook and pen poised, standing on the pavement talking to one of the firemen. 'Atta girl,' Declan said, grinning.

He knew a little basement bistro on Parker Place and we ducked down some stone steps into the bar where he ordered a bottle of white wine, and we settled into a corner on some not very comfortable cushions dotted along a bench placed uncomfortably low beside an old wine barrel doing service as a table.

'Well,' I said, taking a drink. 'Was this just a ruse to get me here, or do you really need to talk to me about something?'

'Would I lie to you?' he joked. 'What it is, is that I wanted to meet your old man.'

Part of me was disappointed; I thought it was me he'd wanted to get to know. The other part was shocked. Why did he want to meet my father?

Declan read the look on my face and said, 'We've started a new business supplement in the Leader, and we're featuring some of the county's most important industrialists. I know your dad is more or less retired, but he'd make a really interesting profile.'

I felt used and let down; my anger rose. 'Oh for God's sake, why couldn't you just ring the factory?'

'Because,' he said, 'I wanted to get to know you, and this seemed a good way of getting you on your own.' I started to stand, but he put a hand on my arm and pulled me gently back down. 'Honestly, believe me. I did ring the factory, but the bugger in charge wouldn't tell me anything but by then I'd seen you – at that last do at the uni – and I wanted to get to know you. I have to say it was our friend Lee who stopped me.'

'You were more than happy with one of the admin girls at that event, if I remember rightly,' I reminded him, thinking of the way he had Chrissie pinned up against a wall.

He grinned again. 'Yes, but I'd rather have been with you.'

Why should I believe him? He was a journalist, for goodness' sake. He'd sell his granny for a good story.

'Look,' I said, relenting a little. 'Dad has very little to do with the factory now; he's semi-retired and perfectly happy living in deepest France where he doesn't like to be disturbed. And he certainly wouldn't appreciate any publicity. In fact, if you spoke to him, he'd probably tell you to shove off in not very polite terms.'

Declan looked a little crestfallen but not altogether surprised. 'Gotta confess,' he said. 'I did speak to him.'

'What...?'

'I'm a journalist, I have my sources,' he said. 'I found out where your old man was living and went to see him.'

'You actually went down there?'

'It has been heard of for people to go to France,' he laughed.

'What did he say?'

'Ah, he told me to shove off and not in very polite terms.'

'So you did get me here under false pretences,' I said.

'I did,' he laughed and then he leaned forward and kissed me.

I pursed my lips tightly and pushed him back. 'What are you doing?' I demanded.

'Something I've been wanting to do for months,' he said, pulling me towards him and kissing me again.

This time I didn't push him away but, in between kisses, I managed to tell him I was married.

'I know,' he said.

I told him we shouldn't be doing this.

'I know,' he said.

I explained I couldn't take him back to my flat.

'I know,' he said, clearly disappointed. 'And we can't go back to my place,' he said and, stupidly, I knew better than to question why not. 'We could get a room…?' he suggested.

'At this time of night,' I said, looking at my watch. It was gone eleven thirty. 'They'd know we were only after one thing,' I said.

'I know. We are,' Declan replied.

'No,' I said. 'This is ridiculous. I'm going to call a taxi and go home.'

He looked at me like a little boy lost, but then he nodded, gave me one last, quick kiss on the forehead and stood up, pulling me to my feet. 'You're right. I'll wait with you till the taxi comes.'

I have to confess, I was surprised he gave up so easily but, true to his word, he waited with me on the pavement outside the bistro until the cab arrived, saw me into it and waved me off cheerily.

As we pulled away up Wellington Road, the smoke still drifted heavenwards from the warehouse and the stench of burning rubber hung in the air. But there was no sign of Cassie who'd probably Tweeted everything she'd seen and heard, and long since filled in the Leader's website templates with a story that captured the whole drama of hundreds of tyres going up in flames.

My mobile beeped. I looked down and saw a missed call, a voicemail and two texts. The missed call and the voicemail were from Lee. 'What are you doing? Are you mad? Ring me the instant you get this message.' The first text was also from Lee. 'Ring me NOW.' The second text was from an unknown number: 'Safe journey home. I think I'm in love.'

My phone popped a request: 'Save this number to your contacts?' I pressed the 'yes' button and keyed in Declan's name.

Lee was incandescent when I saw her at uni the next day. She hadn't dared ring me at home in case Dan answered and had been on tenterhooks all night.

'You don't want to get involved with Declan,' she said. 'You're married to Dan, Teri. What are you thinking?'

'Look, Lee. It was all innocent. He wanted to talk about my father for some business supplement. I told him Dad would never do it, and he accepted that and he was the perfect gentleman, and we had a drink, and I got a taxi home.'

Lee looked at me as though she didn't believe a word. I didn't tell her about the kissing or the mobile phone message or the fact Declan had sent twelve further texts during the night along the lines of 'Yup, definitely in love...'

Chapter Forty-Two

Lee

One unexpected consequence of my relationship with David was his increasing frustration with life as a personal trainer. 'You're a very inspiring person, Lee,' he said once over drinks in a chic wine bar. I was only half-listening – too busy scanning the clientele to check there was nobody I knew. It was still early days, and I wasn't quite ready to go public with our relationship. He leaned in closer. 'You make me feel I'm capable of achieving anything I want.'

Eek! I love a compliment as much as the next woman, but hold your horses, buddy. What exactly did he want to achieve?

It seemed he'd been giving it some thought and concluded his current career progression was limited and, while he hadn't entirely ruled out the prospect of bagging a wealthy and high-profile client, whose fitness makeover would propel David into the stratosphere, he felt it was somewhat unlikely.

His logic was impeccable.

'So...?'

He needed a change of direction, he said.

'Okay.' But what?

A First Class Honours degree, no less.

What on earth had given him that idea?

'You, Lee,' he laughed.

Had I? How?

'You make is sound so interesting.'

Really? At what point had my most recent grumbles about the drudgery of marking thirty-six essays comparing and contrasting the novels of African and African-American women writers become an inspiration?

He struggled to explain. 'I don't really know...except I've never read any African-American writers – couldn't even name one. Or African writers...and, I don't know...I just wanted to...'

But you don't have to go to university to read Alice Walker. Or Toni Morrison. Or Maya Angelou. Or even Buchi Emcheta.

No, he knew. 'But...'

And, I thought, why am I trying to dissuade you? Why shouldn't you go to university? Except, unlike Cinderella's fairy godmother, I couldn't magic the necessary entry qualifications.

Turns out I didn't need to – he'd got the right number of UCAS points so he applied, sailed through his interview and accepted a place on our undergraduate programme, and joined us in the first week of October as a (slightly) mature student. To help pay his way, and his fees – student loans don't go as far as some would think – he carried on working at the gym but couldn't afford the flat he'd been renting and moved instead into something cheaper in the 'student area' of town.

By this time, of course, we had more-or-less by mutual agreement called time on the relationship. It might've lasted a little longer if he'd gone to another university or even picked a course from another UCY faculty, but probably not. Instead, we agreed we'd keep our relationship professional – at the gym we were workout buddies and at university we were polite strangers. It helped I didn't teach any of his first-year modules, so on those rare occasions when we bumped into each other on campus, David simply winked knowingly in a (successful) bid to make me blush.

The name Gorgeous Greenspan started as a joke. Induction week is always a bit of a grind, and David was part of a fairly large cohort of eighty-two students. En masse there was little to tell one from another – the girls all seemed to patronise the same hairdresser and shop in the same high street chains, and the boys all looked as if they hadn't yet grown into their feet. David, of course, was the exception that proved the rule. He stood out right

151

from the start – largely because he strolled into the freshers' week induction lecture ten minutes late, waved airily at Peter Heron, who paused pointedly at the interruption, and parked himself in an empty aisle seat near the front of the auditorium.

No apology, no blush of embarrassment, no self-conscious attempt to assume an interested, listening expression. He simply sat down, crossed his legs, right ankle resting comfortably on left knee, and leant back in his seat, hands clasped behind his head. A picture of raw, young, fresh sexuality.

Teri and I exchanged glances. 'Gorgeous,' she mouthed. I blushed. It was so odd to see David here. So out of context.

And Teri was right. Looked at objectively – and I could be objective now that I'd got any desire to bed him out of my system – he was just the sort of male Adonis that no reasonable woman would kick out of bed for eating biscuits.

Not that I seriously thought Teri had any serious ambitions in that direction. But there was a certain delicious irony in Teri eyeing up young Greenspan – she wouldn't have been at all pleased if she'd known I'd already been there, done that and instigated the break-up. It would have been a first though – Teri dating one of my cast-offs.

Chapter Forty-Three

Teri

The dozen or so texts Declan left on my mobile had to be wiped off, even though I was reluctant to do so. The poor boy was obviously smitten and it was flattering. But, although Dan wasn't the sort of man to go checking my phone, I didn't want him to see the messages. There was the argument that, yes, he deserved to know someone else fancied me and wanted to be with me, which might bring him to his senses and realise I was not to be messed with. But the counter argument was that I didn't want to hurt Dan by him thinking I was being unfaithful. After all, I wasn't being unfaithful. Quite the opposite. I had always been loyal to Dan despite the various temptations that offered themselves.

Take for instance, David Greenspan, a student in my Level 1 English in the Time of Charles II. Older than the usual student, he'd just arrived at uni – totally gorgeous. Shaggy blond hair, six pack in a tight t-shirt, and long, lean limbs in designer-ripped jeans. And quick and clever as well. Who wouldn't be tempted? I was, but I had to consider Dan.

And now Declan was on the scene.

Was I planning to be unfaithful with him? I knew I shouldn't, but he was an extremely gorgeous man, and, what made him even more gorgeous was the fact he found me gorgeous too.

I didn't respond to any of the texts, thinking Declan would get the message, go away and leave me to mend whatever was left of my broken marriage. Dan and I hardly spoke now. I was cold and frosty most of the time, and he was out and about most of the time, either with his daughter or, more often, with his television mates working in programme proposals. He did manage to tell me, over one particularly polite Monday night dinner where we found ourselves at home together at the same time, heating up a Marks & Spencer ready meal for two, that he was working on a documentary that would mean him going away for a week's filming in Scotland. He'd be meeting and interviewing former Yorkshire folk who'd moved north of the border on what their plans were should Scotland declare independence on top of it already having been awarded devolutionary concessions.

With something of an effort that I saw, and appreciated, Dan suggested I go with him. 'We'll be filming all over the place, including the Western Isles – it's beautiful up there – and you could go exploring, walking…'

It was a good try and typical of nice, old Dan. But surely he knew me better than to think I could bear to spend my spare time up in the Highlands eating haggis and battling midges. I was civil in my reply. 'It's good of you, but I'd be bored rigid. No, you go off with your mates and have a good time filming.'

'It won't be a holiday, Teri,' he said, 'it's work.'

'Even more reason why I shouldn't go with you,' I said. 'That way you don't need to worry about me and what I'm doing when you're supposed to be working.'

Dan tried to interest me further by showing me a map of Scotland with places highlighted in red he'd be visiting, but other than noting the names and numbers of the various hotels in which they'd be staying, I left it at that. 'I can ring you on your mobile if I need to get in touch,' I told him.

'We'll be in places where there's no mobile signal,' he said.

'Phew.' I managed a weak laugh. 'In that case, I'm glad I'm not coming.'

We left it at that, and he set off for Scotland a couple of weeks later in a large, white estate car with Bill, the cameraman, Patsy, the researcher-producer, and a boot-load of television recording equipment.

The large, white estate car had probably barely reached Newcastle on the A1 when I texted Declan.

Chapter Forty-Four

Teri

I knew I shouldn't be doing this, but he continued to text me although the number of messages dropped to one at a time (rather than a dozen) and the frequency to just once a day. His last one read: 'Not giving up' and my message back simply said: 'Good.'

We met for a drink that night after he'd 'put the paper to bed'.

'Do people really say that on a newspaper?' I asked him as we sat in the Parker Place basement bistro, considering it to be 'our' place, no doubt.

'No, not really. Now everything's digital and on websites, the news is never safely tucked up and done with for the night,' he said. 'If something happened now – say this bistro burnt down – I'd be able to get a story on the website within seconds whatever time of the day or night.'

'Well, let's hope it doesn't burn down then, and you can have another drink,' I said.

'It might not be burning down,' Declan said, 'but it sure is hot in here. It must be you.'

I'd never been called hot stuff before, well, not to my face, and, talking of bed – while the newspaper wasn't safely tucked up – we eventually were. We'd hardly had time to down the first glass of wine before Declan was kissing me, running his hands lightly over my silk shirt and suggesting we get a room.

'We don't need to,' I said, thinking how Dan would, by now, be safely over the border and considering kilt patterns in the Edinburgh evening mist.

I shouldn't, I knew that, especially after talking again to Lee about Declan. She half believed my story about his only wanting to talk to me about my father, but I couldn't resist questioning her some more about him. Turns out they'd been at school together and she knew – or semi-knew – his wife.

'Oh,' I said, feeling momentarily deflated, 'he's married?'

'Yes, Teri,' she said. 'You must have realised that?'

'No, he seems such a happy type – young, free and single – not the married sort at all. I mean, look at the way he was sniffing and licking Chrissie.'

'Ugh, you're disgusting, Teri,' she said. 'And another thing: he's got kids.'

That should have been the red alert. But... There was something about Declan I couldn't resist. Surely it would do no harm to have a drink with him.

But once I saw him again, sitting in the basement bistro in the semi darkness, waiting for me to arrive, thoughts of wives and kids went out of my head.

We drove back separately to my duplex, me getting there first so I was able to check my hair and make-up, undo a few buttons of my shirt, and be standing, welcoming, in the hallway when he rang the buzzer. He came in and, without taking his eyes off me, gently nudged the door closed behind him with his foot while reaching for me and pulling me into his chest, nuzzling his face down into the side of my neck. I've read in cheap novels how women melt into their men's arms, but, honestly, I melted. There was nothing I could do; I wanted this man. I've known lust before – hell, I've known love before – but nothing like this. I wanted to consume him; lap up every part of him; be part of him. Quite simply, I couldn't keep my hands off. He pulled me down onto the white oak floorboards and with an urgency that had us both scrabbling, pulling and tearing clothes off each other, we were kissing, pulling and rubbing, sighing, snarling, and then came together right there in the hallway. At one point, he kicked out with his foot against the reclaimed wood hall dresser, but I was too distracted, too happy, to say 'Be careful. That's antique.'

When we finished and lay there, half naked and panting, neither of us spoke for a few minutes. I lay in Declan's arms and we both stared at the ceiling.

'Nice place you have here,' he said eventually, laughing. 'Er, does it have a bedroom or should we stay here?'

We spent that night together – well, we spent the rest of that night and the early morning hours together, making love three times more, before Declan finally said he had to go. He pulled on his clothes, and as he fastened his watch, I looked at the bedside clock: 3.30am. I wasn't going to ask where he was going, who he was going back to, what he would say when he got back. I didn't want to know. He leaned over to kiss me goodbye. 'I'll let myself out,' he said. 'You need your rest, you've been a busy girl.' That twinkly-eyed look again. 'Tell you what,' he added. 'Take tomorrow off – let's go somewhere.'

I should've been in uni the next morning, but what the hell? It was only Level 1 tutorials. They could catch up, and, having composed a general 'send to all' text to the students saying I was ill, I waited for Declan to return.

The rest of the week followed a pattern. Declan said he'd taken some much-owed time off work, and I rang Chrissie to say I was really ill and wouldn't be coming in for a few days, and could she look at my timetable and let all my students know to save me the bother of having to get out of my sick bed to text them every day? She grumpily agreed.

Declan came to the flat each morning and, surprisingly, we didn't fall back into bed. Instead, we went off: for a walk round the park, for a picnic by a lake, to visit a local stately home, to have lunch in a museum café. We drove up into the Dales, and I took photos on my camera of the limestone pavements at Malham. Declan wouldn't have his picture taken. 'Can't stand having my photo taken, so don't even try,' he warned me, and got quite cross when I tried to take a surreptitious selfie of the two of us.

Wherever we went, we wandered hand in hand or arm in arm, stopping at gates to kiss, leaning over coffee pots to kiss, buying gallery tickets only to walk away from the booth to kiss, looking at paintings in an exhibition and kissing; constantly stroking, rubbing and pulling at each other. 'I can't keep my hands off you,' he said.

'Don't even try,' I told him.

We bought food and returned to my duplex to cook dinner, which we ate together sitting listening to CDs Declan had in his car – unusual choices given they were classical rather than pop. They included Elgar's Cello Concerto and Faure's Requiem, which made me sad and surprisingly tearful.

'Hey…hey,' he said, when he realised I was crying. 'What's wrong?'

'It's the music. It's just so beautiful,' I told him. 'And I'm so happy. I don't want this to end.'

And then, only then, when we'd had dinner, listened to music, did we go to bed and make love – sometimes gentle and soft, sometimes passionate and wild. And Declan stayed with me all night.

It was probably Day 3 when I told myself again that I shouldn't be doing this – at least, not without having some questions answered. I could hardly believe it myself that I managed not to ask until then, but a huge part of me didn't want to know or accept what the answers would be.

Declan said, yes, he'd been married to Marnie for nearly twenty-five years.

'What…?' I was genuinely stunned he'd been married for so long.

'We were sixteen,' he said. 'First boyfriend and girlfriend and, of course, she got pregnant – and everyone was saying we were too young and that it would never work, so we got married to prove 'em all wrong.'

'And the baby?'

'Ah,' Declan said. 'She had a miscarriage when we got back from honeymoon. But by then we were married, and I could hardly bugger off and leave her; I thought it was the right thing to do to stand by her. I'd just started at the paper as a junior reporter, so I was busy and time went on and well… suddenly twenty-five years go by.'

'But you've got other kids?' I said.

'Yeah. We thought, after the miscarriage, that she couldn't get pregnant and she didn't for years 'n' years. She turned thirty and God knows what happened, but, pow! She started pushing them out like peas. Well, not peas exactly, but a lad, who's now fourteen, and two girls, one ten and the other eight months.'

'Well, you can't be an unhappily married man if you're still having kids together?' I said.

'That's the point,' Declan said, looking at me seriously. 'I'm not an unhappily married man. I won't lie to you, Teri, there was nothing wrong with my marriage; I wasn't looking to leave. I wasn't looking to find anyone else. But then I met you.'

And it was a good line. The only problem was, I believed it. Oh, I knew I shouldn't be doing this, but it had been a glorious week of long lunches, relaxed walks and days that drifted. Normally November would be misty, wet and miserable, but that week was full of late autumnal colours. Declan talked some more about his family. He told his wife he was away on a week's assignment for the paper. Strangely, he didn't seem to feel guilty about this. He didn't exactly say what she didn't know wouldn't hurt her, but he was almost casual in the knowledge he was getting away with being unfaithful to his wife of twenty-five years as if, by some gross self-delusion, after that length of time, he deserved an affair.

'I love her,' he insisted. 'But I love you.' And that was his excuse and his reasoning.

I felt incredibly sad as we made love on the final night, the night before Dan was due back and the night before Declan was supposed to return from his 'work trip'.

I cried as Declan lay over me as though this was the last time we'd ever be together.

'Hey,' he said, pausing and looking down at me, lying on the bed beneath him. 'What's up?'

'Oh, I don't know…it's just that…well, life's going to go back to normal again, isn't it?'

'Afraid so,' he said matter-of-factly.

Only for me, it didn't go back to quite the normal I'd known.

Chapter Forty-Five

Lee

Sometimes it felt as if my primary purpose in life was to provide relationship counselling for all and sundry.

Chrissie, having confessed to her dalliance with Declan, cornered me at every available opportunity to moan about his ungentlemanly conduct. A harder-hearted woman than me – Teri, for instance – would've told her he was out of her league, and she should be grateful for the smidgeon of attention he'd given her. But, brutal hard-truths are more Teri's style than mine, and, having finally just about forgiven her for dropping me in the shit with Mrs Orme, I responded more circumspectly and sympathetically and resisted the temptation to tell her to 'woman-up'.

Mrs Orme too seemed to have decided I was sympathy queen and had taken to popping into the senior common room at least once a week, sometimes twice, to share confidences about bedroom matters chez Orme. Mike, it seemed, had become very attentive, but Mrs Orme ('call me, Judy') was suspicious. Did I think he was having another affair? How the hell should I know? And what did she think I could do if he was? The suggestion she should start divorce proceedings went down like a lead balloon.

Teri was annoyed on my behalf. 'What makes either of them think you care a fig for their problems?' she demanded.

Don't ask me. And I checked the mirror just to make sure the word 'sucker' wasn't lipsticked across my forehead.

'Tell them to push off,' she said. 'You don't have time to waste on their self-centred obsessing.'

Too right, I didn't. She'd already earmarked my listening time for her own use, anguishing ad nauseum about Declan.

'I know I shouldn't be falling in love with him,' she said.

'Don't,' I said.

'You can't just *not* fall in love with someone,' she said.

'Yes, you can, especially when the "someone" is already married.'

'It didn't stop you,' she said, glaring at me.

'I wasn't in love,' I said.

'That's even worse,' she said.

She was right. But, I pointed out Mike had hit on me at Granddaddy's funeral when I was vulnerable.

'I'm vulnerable,' Teri said, pulling her mouth down in a pathetic attempt to look sad.

'Nobody's died,' I said.

'My marriage is dead.'

Bloody drama queen. 'The ink's barely dry on your marriage certificate. It hasn't had time to die.'

'Lee,' she said, 'you're turning into a sour old maid.'

Well! There was no way of answering that one. Not politely anyway.

About the only person who didn't have a broken heart was David. His brief experience of courting an older woman seemed to have set him on the straight and narrow. After various one-night stands with girls nearer his own age – which was quite a revelation, I hadn't realised casual sex was so commonplace – he became smitten with a hairdresser called Becky. 'It's love,' he confided as I plodded on the treadmill. How sweet. Sickeningly so, because, whereas initially I'd found David's accounts of his nights on the town and the girls he pulled mildly interesting, post-Becky the conversation became a monotonous round of 'Becky this...' and 'Becky that...' Once he even pulled out his mobile and made me scroll through some photographs taken during a weekend break in Scarborough. Why? What possible interest did he think I might have in seeing his holiday snaps? I never showed him mine. Why would I? The temptation to point out that boring his clients to death was a sure way to kill business was almost impossible to resist. But I bit my tongue and even made the right sort of interested noises at appropriate intervals. And said nice things about the Scarborough pics.

They certainly made an attractive-looking pair: David, long and lean, and Becky, petite and blonde (albeit of the peroxide variety). Yes, she was a very fetching accessory, but, having been introduced to her when we bumped into each other at the supermarket, it was also clear she was several curlers short of a perm. And, though, Becky-mania seemed to have temporarily anaesthetised his brain cells, I couldn't see David settling long-term for such an airhead.

However, as it turned out, it was Becky who decided not to settle – she dumped him in favour of one of the other gym trainers. A guy with better-defined pecs and a bright red mini Cooper with a Union Jack roof. How shallow.

And that's when David and I finally ended up in bed.

Chapter Forty-Six

Teri

Dan arrived home full of tales about the Yorkshire folk managing to survive in deepest Scotland – running fish and chip shops, selling whittled walking sticks and rebuilding dry stone walls. He'd found it all fascinating. But his cheery persona only irritated me. He was too nice; he saw good and interest in everyone while I could only be cynical about them.

Over the next few weeks Declan and I managed sneaky lunches together and we sometimes met for a drink after I finished work, but he could never stay long. He had to either get back to the paper or go home to his wife, and we certainly had no chance to get a room and make love.

And that was really frustrating. I never knew how much I missed sex until I wasn't having any with Declan. Dan tried once or twice to get amorous, but I brushed him off. I couldn't stand his wretched fumbling. If I couldn't have Declan, I didn't want anyone.

Dan withdrew into his cool, polite shell and we had a final, glorious row as Christmas approached.

I remembered the argument this time last year and now, my first Christmas as Dan's wife, and what does he want to do? Spend the fucking festive season with his fucking daughter. Again.

'But you had her last year,' I said. 'I thought it was your ex-wife's turn to have the precious child.'

He sighed in exasperation. His reasoning was that, as I'd been so hostile lately and clearly didn't want to be with him, he might as well spend Christmas with Victoria. 'And where exactly will you go?' I asked, telling him he needn't think about having jolly crackers and fun and games in *my* flat. He blew the wind out of me: he was going to his former marital home (for which he was still paying the mortgage, obviously). Sara was going away with a new boyfriend to some tropical island, leaving Victoria on her own. Made sense for Dan to bunk down over there. I told him if that was what he was going to do, he could pack his things and move over there permanently. So he packed his things and, because Sara didn't want him moving in there and then, he moved into a hotel until he could find a flat, which he then moved into. And I started divorce proceedings.

And told Declan I was free.

Chapter Forty-Seven

Teri

I thought Declan would want to celebrate, and certainly the night after Dan moved out, Declan came round to the duplex and we made riotous love, laughing and yelping in delight, right there in the hallway minutes after he stepped over the threshold.

'God, I've missed you,' I said as we both struggled to our feet.

'Me too,' he said, pulling on his jeans and flattening his hair down with his hands. We were still in the hallway, and I pulled at his arm to lead him into the living room. 'Ah,' he said. 'I can't stop. Sorry, love. There's a big story on, and I've got to get back to the office.'

'But I thought...' But whatever I thought, he didn't want to know, and with a quick peck on the cheek and a friendly slap on my behind, he was gone.

We saw each other when we could; I appreciated Declan had a senior post at the paper, and he was a busy man and on-call much of the time – and he also had a family – so he couldn't just drop everything and come when I wanted him to, and when we were together he'd often have to dash off to cope with something at the office or at home. But being the 'other woman' took some getting used to, and the full realisation of it hit me at Christmas.

Declan and I were having a meal together at my flat one evening after he'd told the office he was leaving early and persuaded Marnie he was working late, and he suddenly looked up and around, and said, 'This is a fabulous place you have here,' as though he was seeing it for the first time. 'I mean, how great to have a place like this – and the freedom.'

I took it as a hint that his marriage, his wife and his kids were oppressing him and said, 'Well, you know you're welcome to move in.'

He looked thoughtful for a moment, considering, as though the idea of moving in with me had never occurred to him, and then he shook his head. 'No, I mean the freedom to move, without anyone else around telling you what to do,' he said. 'I'd love a place where I could just be on my own, to do whatever I wanted to do, whenever I wanted to do it. I've never had that.' He looked wistful.

I refused to feel deflated and persisted; it made sense. He could leave his wife and move in with me. We loved each other; we were good together.

Even I could see I was pressurising him and was annoyed at having to do it. What was wrong with the man? It was bad enough my having to persuade Lee that what Declan and I had was wonderful – in the face of her continuing and strong disapproval – without my having to persuade Declan too.

'Look, Declan,' I said. 'I don't like being the other woman. I'm not willing to play second fiddle. I love you, and you love me. You've got to decide what you want to do.' I wasn't exactly saying it's Marnie or me. But that's what I meant.

It took a few days. I nagged him. I pleaded with him. I even cried. And eventually he said, 'Okay. Okay. I'll leave. But I'm not moving in with you – yet. Do it gradually; let Marnie get used to the idea. I'll get a flat – how will that be?'

That will be just fine, I thought. But then he said he wouldn't do anything about it until after Christmas. He wanted to spend Christmas with his wife and kids.

Chapter Forty-Eight

Teri

The flat was on the top floor of a three-storey Victorian terrace in a not-all-that-smart part of town.

Leyland Road could've looked better if the residents had bothered about the peeling paintwork on the doors and window frames, or the general neglect in the front gardens, or the number of cars that had seen better days parked on the road. But they didn't and the overall effect was of a tired and run-down place. It was probably because of the students; they'd commandeered the area – not just Leyland Road but all the terraces around there. Owners of what had once been smart, large Victorian houses had rented the odd room to a student and then, finding there was money to be made, either let off the whole house or sold up to a landlord. The net effect was the same: elegant, old, stone houses taken over by as many students as could be safely – and sometimes not so safely – squeezed in between health and safety regulations and crammed into poky little bedsits.

I shouldn't grumble given that most of the students attended the university where I taught. They had to live somewhere. But I hated the idea when Declan decided to move there.

'It's cheap,' he said. And when your wife throws you out – and demands maintenance for her and the kids – cheap is good.

'Look on it as shabby chic,' he laughed.

He had, as he'd wanted, spent Christmas with Marnie and the kids but, as

167

he told me later, they'd had a furious row the day after Boxing Day. Marnie had been cleaning up after the festivities and found Declan's mobile under the bed (where he left it having used it to send me a night-time text before we both went to sleep). Of course, she'd turned it on (she knew his password: 0000. The daft boy never changed it from the factory setting). She found dozens and dozens of texts to and from me. At least I'd had the sense to delete my messages, although once Dan left there was no need and I treasured the little bings and beeps that came through announcing another missive about how much Declan loved/missed/needed me.

Declan told me the row and resultant 'talking' went on for days. The kids were sent to stay with their grandmother, Declan's mother, away from the raised voices, accusations and tears, while he and Marnie thrashed amongst the dying embers of their marriage wondering if they could or should throw something on the mess to reignite it. In the end, Marnie, from what Declan told me, said Declan 'must give up that whore' and Declan defended my honour and said he couldn't, so Marnie said he'd have to leave, and he packed a bag and went off to stay with one of his walking mates. Within a couple of days he'd seen the flat in Leyland Road and signed the lease.

He hadn't let me help him move in, and I'm rather glad. It would hardly have been the right thing to be sitting in the removal van as he loaded whatever his wife had allowed him to take from the marital home. Nor did I much want to see the reaction of his children. It would've been messy, noisy and sad. Even someone like me wouldn't want to see that.

He said I could go round later that evening, once he'd got sorted. As it turned out, he hadn't needed a particularly large removal van and there was very little to sort. Marnie hadn't allowed him to leave with much other than a single bed, some sheets, a duvet and towels, a CD player – for the collection of CDs he kept in his car, a portable TV, one badly beaten, brown leather chair – which must've once partnered an elegant Chesterfield sofa, two suitcases full of clothes, a cardboard box containing an assortment of mismatched crockery, cutlery and pans, a pile of books and maps, a rucksack, and his walking boots.

'Welcome to the happy home,' he said as he waved me in.

All the depressing features of a rented attic flat were there. Any ideas I might've had that it could be a romantic hideaway gave way in the face of

168

the white Artexing on the walls, the frayed carpet and the general air of gloom. 'I bet the bath is yellow plastic,' I said.

'Mustard,' he yelped. 'It'll be all right – for now,' he said, holding out his arms, pulling me to him.

'Let's go back to my flat,' I suggested.

'No,' he said, nibbling my ear, pulling me closer. 'I've made the bed. Let's christen this place.'

Chapter Forty-Nine

Teri

There'd been moments during the night when I honestly believed I could get used to sleeping with him in a single bed. We made love riotously and passionately – he, almost angrily, trying to drown out the hurt and anger of what had just happened to him, I suppose.

But by morning, after we woke and had sleepy sex, hardly able to speak to each other, I longed to have space to move.

'You'll have to get a double bed,' I said.

'Why,' he replied, leaning over, holding himself above me, but close, so his bare chest just hovered over my breasts. 'Don't you like being so close to me?'

'Go get me some breakfast.'

'I'll have to go to the corner shop – it means leaving you,' he said.

'Go then,' I said.

I listened as his feet thumped down the stairs and then his mobile rang. Where was it? His jacket was slung over the back of the leather chair in the room; the mobile was in one of the pockets. I answered it without thinking. It was Marnie.

'Is he there?' she asked. No 'hello' or 'may I speak to Declan, please?' Just 'is he there?'

'No, he's er…' I said and before I could finish, she put the phone down.

What had I expected? Did I expect her to be cheery and make polite conversation? I stole her husband. He left her for me. She wasn't going to ring up and pretend we were friends, was she? She wasn't going to waste her time being nice. But nor did she waste her time being nasty. She didn't scream at me on the phone accusing me of being a scheming, conniving cow who couldn't give a damn about a man's wife or his children; she didn't ask me if I was satisfied now I'd played my little tricks. She didn't ask if I realised what I'd done, and how I could live with myself. She didn't ask so much as a How Dare You? Hey, I felt like saying, play the game. I'm waiting for you to make me feel even more guilt than I do now so I can have a good wallow in it. But Marnie wasn't playing the game. Was she being subtle? Was she making me wait? Would there come a time when she wouldn't be able to resist shouting at me, telling me how much she hated me? I hoped so. The 'you're a thieving, lying bitch' approach would be easier than this short, sharp 'Is he there?' routine.

Chapter Fifty

Lee

It was after midnight when the phone rang. I was in bed, although sleep was proving elusive. No need to check the caller ID to know it was Teri – at this time of night, it always was. No doubt there'd been another altercation between Teri and Marnie, and Teri needed confirmation she was the good witch and Marnie wasn't.

I slugged the last drop from the glass of wine I'd been cuddling, dug deep into the 'we were so in love, we couldn't help ourselves' sympathy reservoir, and picked up the phone. There was barely time to say 'hello' before Teri launched into her spiel...the passionate sex...the narrow bed...the craving for space...and finally Marnie.

Phone plugged to one ear, I picked up the empty glass and headed downstairs where, with a dexterity born of long practice, I hunched the receiver into my shoulder and opened a fresh bottle of wine and took a long, fortifying draught. Refilling the glass, bottle in hand, phone still precariously perched, I returned to bed.

By now, Teri was at the Scarlett O'Hara tremulously brave and beautiful stage – little half sobs, punctuated by the merest hint of a decorous sniff. 'I know I've hurt her, and I'd understand if she screamed and shouted at me but...' and 'it would be so much easier if we could just get all the anger out into the open...' and 'what does she think she's achieving by ignoring me like this?'

She had, it soon became clear, spent the whole day mulling over all possible permutations of the significance of Marnie's telephone silence. On the one hand, Marnie wasn't facing reality, she couldn't accept that Teri and Declan were now a couple and she hoped that ignoring Teri would make her go away. Alternatively, Marnie thought Teri was little more than a despicable floosie, and the whole thing was just a temporary blip – hence, her refusal to recognise Teri or even speak to her. Or, perhaps, Marnie was playing a long drawn-out psychological game and, by refusing to conform to the stereotype of the hysterical, abandoned wife and mother, thought she could guilt-trip Teri into renouncing Declan. Or, was she trying to provoke Teri into some overreaction that would turn Declan against her?

What to answer? All of the above? Marnie, it was clear, was fighting tooth and nail to save her marriage though why she wanted to hang on to a love rat like Declan was beyond me. She'd have done herself a big favour if she'd just let go.

And me too – these late night phone calls were terribly draining.

'Am I a bad person?'

'No.' What else could I say?

'Is it so wrong to love Declan?'

'Nobody chooses to fall in love.' I know – pass the sick bucket, but I'd given up trying to make her see sense.

'Things will work out in the end, won't they?'

How the hell should I know? Hadn't she learned anything from Dan? First marriages and kids can't be wiped off the face of the earth simply by wishing them away. I told her so and added, 'Not unless you fancy a long stretch for what American cop shows describe as first-degree murder.'

There was a long, almost thoughtful pause and I knew, without a shadow of doubt, she was indulging in a mental picture of herself in the dock – the beautiful, passionate woman driven to extremes by the Machiavellian machinations of her embittered and, of course, terribly plain rival. I punctured her bubble. 'Incarceration at her Majesty's pleasure might just prove a touch tedious.'

Another pause, followed by a sigh. 'What does she want from me? I can't give him up, I can't, I can't.'

'Well, I only ever see Marnie at church and we never really speak. So I can't be sure, but I'd guess she's achieved exactly what she wanted, which was to get you well and truly rattled.'

Teri gasped and then laughed: a hearty belly laugh. 'Oh, Lee, do you think so?'

I wish it had ended there. I was tired. Teri, however, was wide awake and ready for a good old chinwag.

'Lee…?'

I must've dropped off.

'I'm sorry,' she was saying. 'I'm a selfish cow? Especially when you've got other things on your mind.'

Oh. She'd remembered it was this time last year I'd had the abortion. No, my mistake. 'Your research paper is due in at the end of the month, isn't it?'

Yes, it was and, it was sweet of her to think of it, but it wasn't the most pressing thing on my mind.

'I'm okay,' I lied, 'but I'm teaching in the morning.' In other words, get off the bloody phone, and let me go back to crying myself to sleep.

'We'll chat tomorrow,' I said, hung up and poured another glass of wine. Perhaps if I drank enough, it wouldn't hurt quite so much. Some hope.

Chapter Fifty-One

Teri

Declan is unlike any other man I've ever met.

Lee's always said I can twist men around my little finger and to an extent, she's right. But with Declan, well, that wasn't the case. I couldn't take him for granted. He was definitely his own man, liked his own space (especially now he was living in a flat on his own), didn't suffer fools gladly, was matter-of-fact to the point of being almost blunt, and if he didn't want to do something, he wouldn't do it.

For instance, many's the time I suggested we go out for a drink or meet for a meal and he was tied up at work and, rather than passing the job on to a deputy or someone like young Cassie, he stayed at the office to do it himself. 'Sorry, big story on…' was the most common excuse I heard.

Having thought when he moved into Leyland Road I'd be seeing him practically every day, almost the opposite was true. We saw each other probably twice a week. It was even difficult to see him at weekends when I'd have expected we could spend the whole of Saturday and Sunday, plus nights, together. 'Stories still have to be written on a weekend, love,' he'd say if on duty at the paper or, 'I've got to have my own life,' he'd say if planning to go up into the Dales or to the Lakes with his walking pals, or, 'I've got to see the kids,' if Marnie allowed him visiting rights to take them to the park or whatever. I didn't offer to go with them. Been there and done the kid-sitting business.

So, all in all, there was precious little time left for me.

He still texted me but the messages were never quite as frequent or, frankly, as loving as they had been.

Then, one Friday evening leaving work, I was feeling particularly sorry for myself as I knew I'd be going back to my empty flat, and there was no chance of Declan coming round because this was his weekend to see the kids. What was the point of having gone through my split from Dan and played the 'other woman' with Declan if I was still on my own? Wasn't I supposed to be getting more out of this? So I rang Declan.

'Oh, I'm glad you called,' he said, which cheered me up because I reckoned it meant he'd cancelled his babysitting duties for a night of lovemaking with me. 'Can you email me over a recipe for a casserole?'

What…?

'Yeah, I'm doing a casserole…for the kids' tea…got most of the ingredients, but don't know exactly how to put it all together…'

'Do you want me to come over and make it for you?' I asked.

'No, no. The kids have been horribly fractious today. Wouldn't want to inflict them on you.'

'Today? You mean you've had them all day?'

'Yeah, I took the day off and they bunked off school. We've been up to Malham. Great day for it but they're not great walkers.' He laughed. I didn't. He could take days off for his kids, but not for me. I was about to tell him what I thought of his child-bonding antics, but he interrupted me to say he was rushing. 'Just wing the recipe over as soon as poss please, love. See you.'

I kept the recipe simple. We don't want the poor darlings choking on tough meat, do we? I was too angry to cook for myself so opened a bottle of white wine and poured a generous glass. It must've been about 9pm, and several glasses later, when I rang Declan to hope the casserole worked out and he was having a lovely evening. His phone was switched off, which was unusual given he had the kids with him, and Marnie was in the habit of ringing every couple of hours to make sure he hadn't poisoned them or something.

Then I did something bad. I don't know what it was that made me do it, but some niggling little doubt was scratching away at my wine-fuddled brain.

I rang Marnie's number.

She answered and I said, 'Er, hello, Marnie. It's Teri. Sorry to bother you, but I've got some of your son's books here – Declan must have accidentally left them – and I wondered if he would need them for school on Monday?' Where had that come from?

'Oh…er…' said Marnie, obviously considering whether to slam down the phone without speaking as part of the silent treatment she'd given me before. But, because this was about her precious firstborn, she obviously thought better of it. 'Hang on,' she said and I heard her ask someone: 'Do you need the books that your dad left at Teri's?' and that someone replied: 'No, I've got all my stuff in my bag.'

'Oh, is he there – your son, I mean? I thought the kids were with Declan tonight?'

'No,' said Marnie. 'They're all here.' Her tone suddenly took a snidely cheerful note as she added, 'So he's told you he's with *our* children tonight, has he? Well, well.' And it was me who slammed the phone down.

Clearly, I had to challenge Declan, and when he came round to my flat the following Monday evening I was ready with the lie that I'd popped out to Tesco and bumped into Marnie, and she had the children with her, and I thought they were with him, and Marnie insinuated that Declan had lied to me. Hearing all this, Declan laughed and said Marnie was a devious woman, and I wasn't to read anything into anything she said or did, and that she should've told me a big story had broken and he'd had to hand the kids back and return to the newsroom.

Which was a good excuse and well executed given that Declan had to think fast on his feet, but by then he was pulling me to him, nibbling my cheek, my ear, stroking my back and asking how I could ever doubt him and his love for me, and he was kissing me and, well, one thing led to another and what could I do but give in to him?

Chapter Fifty-Two

Teri

Why did I do it? Have I no self-respect?

Declan had been remote the last few days – last few days? He'd been remote for weeks. I put it down to his missing his children. Well, he should've thought about that before taking up with me. I know that sounds harsh, but it takes two to tango and I genuinely wouldn't have been interested in a married man if he hadn't been so interested in me.

Declan was having problems with his son who, after Declan left home three months ago, had adopted the role of head of household and resented his father's visits, which he saw as an intrusion. In truth, the kid was probably badly hurt. He sounded a bright boy, academic from what I made out from the very little Declan told me when he was in the mood to talk about such things – which he often wasn't. 'Can't be doing with all that emoting shit,' he'd say.

His eldest daughter, though, was a different matter. She Loves Her Daddy and Her Daddy Loves Her. Declan called her his Little Miss Mouse, for goodness' sake! Coming back from having taken her out one day, he'd stared dreamily at the hoodie he'd let her borrow during a sudden downpour. It hung, drying over the bath in his mustard-coloured bathroom. I'd tried to console myself with the thought that the child was probably an overweight, spoilt brat.

Declan had been happily married for twenty-five years until I 'came along and started playing my little tricks' as he so cruelly told me during one of our rows. I get the guilt; I get the blame. I wasn't aware of playing any tricks. I thought I was just going along with what he wanted.

Anyway, I thought, if he can be remote, so can I. As it happened I'd planned a trip to Oxfordshire to look at Spelsbury Church that weekend. Originally, I'd asked Declan if he wanted to come too.

'What on earth for?' he asked.

'Well it's where Rochester is buried,' I said.

'Don't tell me,' Declan said, 'you're going to look at his grave and get all earnest about your research again.'

'Well, yes and no. I've been stuck for ages and not done any serious stuff on it for years. It might do me good to wander round places where he had connections.'

'But what good will it do? He's been dead and buried for over three hundred years. Why go this weekend? Stay and connect with me.' I think he almost leered.

'No, if you're not coming, I'm going on my own.'

'Please yourself,' he said, and added, 'and bloody Rochester.'

I'd booked into a B&B, taken my overnight bag with me to university so I could get straight off on Friday afternoon, and treated myself to a new spiral-bound notebook. At the top of the first page I wrote: 'John Wilmot, the second Earl of Rochester, buried under a plain stone in the graveyard...'

And then I changed my mind. Declan was right. Why was I going on what could amount to nothing more than a wild goose chase in the Oxfordshire countryside when I could be with him? I decided to surprise him. I'd nip to the supermarket and buy a decent bottle of wine and some food, take it round to his flat and we'd have a fabulous picnic in bed. I'd show him remote.

I was late leaving university, thanks to Mike Orme wanting to discuss student support. He could see I was in a hurry to be off, but our associate dean is not one for picking up on hints that his colleagues have a life outside work. And, I suspected, any life he might've had outside work had been severely curtailed by his wife following that very peculiar affair with Lee. I say peculiar because I just can't see him doing anything as daring and exciting as making love in one of the university store cupboards. But then, I

179

was surprised to hear he had – and with Lee! No, Mike's a quiet, scholarly man – totally out of place at our university where, apart from the odd feeble stab at historical research, like my half-hearted dabbling into the roistering Rochester, nothing of note gets studied in any great detail. Knowing this, and that his colleagues are on the whole well-meaning but lazy, Mike tries to make our lives as miserable as possible by imposing on us as many student mentoring-type activities – outside of actual lectures and tutorials – as he can manage.

Part of me thinks he's quite a sad person, given that he wears a uniform that always consists of grey trousers and white shirts, with a variety of tank tops to ring the changes. The other part reckons he's a sadist, given his love of administration, much of which he does for Peter Heron.

'Mike, put me down for whatever. I've got to dash,' I said. 'See you Monday.'

I half ran into the car park, but as I approached my car, saw it had a flat tyre.

'Shit.' I ran back to the gym where I knew Frank would be clearing up after the early evening staff Shanghai Yoga session. He was still a bit off with me over the Stella Lastings rumour I put about. For goodness' sake, I thought, can't the man take a joke? Anyway, bless him, after much muttering he lolloped down to the car park like an obedient Labrador and changed the tyre for me.

By the time I got to the supermarket it was really busy with those Friday-night-family-goes-shopping-together groups where one kid sits in the trolley – which is always parked to block as much of the aisle as possible – grabbing everything in sight and mewling when its mother tells it to put things back, while dad and the other kid just dawdle looking bored and getting in the way.

By the time I'd dashed home, had a quick shower and got back to Leyland Road, it was nearly eight and Declan's flat was in darkness. I rang the doorbell, but there was no reply. I rang his mobile, but the voicemail kicked in. I didn't leave a message.

I reasoned with myself that he must've gone for a drink after work and would be back later, and so I would return later too, find him relaxed and happily surprised to find me on his doorstep.

I left it until about ten, then drove back round to Leyland Road. What a surprise he's going to get, I told myself.

There was a light on in the bedroom of his flat. I pulled in behind a battered looking red VW Polo parked right behind Declan's car. I walked towards the door of Number 12 and took a reassuring look back at Declan's silver Golf, with the 'Evening Leader Leads' sticker in the windscreen. Looking at the Polo parked behind his, I noticed it too had a poster in the windscreen. And it too read 'Evening Leader Leads'.

I rang the bell marked 'O'Brien'.

And now, after tying myself up in knots about being the other woman, I found myself standing on Declan's doorstep while, presumably, another other woman was inside possibly enjoying the double bed I made Declan buy during one of our few domesticated outings, this one to Ikea. Declan and I rarely did those domestic things other couples do. We went to the cinema now and then, but he hated the theatre as being 'too much arsing about in make-up' and only listened to opera on his car CD player because he could never sit still long enough to hear the fat lady sing. We occasionally went wandering around a local park, but he preferred to go off for a day's walking on his own. He'd only ever come to the two Peter Heron soirees under protest, and I never got invited to anything going on at the Evening Leader. It might 'lead' somewhere but it certainly wasn't to any form of social life. Having got the paper out this Friday night, however, Declan had clearly found time to socialise, probably with some tarty little tramp from telesales.

Oh come on, I told myself. He's been out with a mate – a male mate who owns the Polo – and they've come back for a beer. But why were there no lights on other than in the bedroom? And why, having heard the bell, hadn't Declan stuck his head out of the window as he sometimes did to toss me the keys and save him the bother of coming down three flights of stairs?

Perhaps the car belonged to someone from the Leader who just happened to live in Leyland Road? Perhaps Declan was in there on his own. In the bath. In bed, asleep.

I debated ringing the doorbell again. No. If he's in the bath, he won't want to be bothered. Likewise if he's asleep. I'll just go and call him in the morning. I won't disturb him.

As I walked back past the Polo, I tried hard not to look in the windows. I wished I hadn't seen what looked like a green silk scarf on the front passenger seat, or the lipstick case, or the half-empty bottle of mineral water.

Oh come on, I told myself again. Okay, it was a woman's car, and obviously someone who worked for the Leader, but there was no reason to assume she wasn't someone who lived on Leyland Road. She was probably a mousy little person who worked in something incredibly dull like quality assessment control, and probably had no idea there was someone else from the Leader who lived on her street. That, or she didn't work for the Leader but had just bought the car from someone who did and hadn't had time to peel off the 'Evening Leader Leads' sticker. Feeling better, I drove home.

Chapter Fifty-Three

Lee

David was devastated when Becky chucked him. He pretended he was okay about it, but the bags under his eyes told a different story. I worried about him but there didn't seem to be much I could do. The 'other fish in the sea' speech had bombed, and for the first time he started hanging out with the other kids in his year group. A mistake; he lacked their experience, and tolerance, of alcohol and other banned substances. He started coming in late to lectures and seminars and had the attention span of a gnat – his teetotal lifestyle hadn't equipped him to deal with the mother of all hangovers.

The inevitable rude awakening came one Saturday evening after he joined a gang of students on a St Patrick's night bar crawl. After just a couple of pints David was pretty much hammered and puking up on the doorstep of a high street wine bar, whilst being rather roughly manhandled by the bouncer who'd ejected him from the premises. It was lucky I happened to be driving past on my way home after a late-night babysitting gig with Ritchie and baby Fee – otherwise, he'd have almost certainly ended up in the back of one of the police vans parked at strategic intervals around the city centre.

On impulse, I pulled up and negotiated with the bouncer and the two coppers about to arrest him for being drunk and disorderly. They agreed to release him into my custody, which was pretty decent of them, although perhaps they were simply trying to reduce the next day's paperwork burden.

I may have given them the impression he was my son.

Together, the bouncer and I got him into the passenger seat and, with a final warning from the police to 'keep a better eye on the boy', I headed...where? I had no idea what to do with the drunken lump, spewing dribbles of vomit out of the car window. Taking him home was not an option – no one would ever describe me as house proud, but there was no way on God's earth he was going to kip on my sofa. And definitely not in the spare room. Bad enough the car would need hosing down and de-fumigating in the morning without having to start on the house as well.

'Take me home, Lee,' he mumbled. 'Take me home.'

Home, it turned out, was a dinky, first-floor flat a couple of doors down from Declan's attic pad on Leyland Road. I knew this because Teri had given me a guided tour a few weeks previously. She was dropping off some knick-knacks she said would make the place more homely. It was asking rather a lot of a pair of scented candles, some brightly coloured cushions and a couple of pretty vases of dried flowers.

'Of course, Declan still needs to do a bit of work on the place,' she said.

Only a bit?

'And he needs to get some new furniture.'

You said it.

'But, for now, we're happy to do shabby chic.'

Which any sane person would define as cheap and nasty.

Poor Teri.

As I pulled into Leyland Road, Declan's car with its distinctive yellow and blue Evening Leader sticker was parked outside David's front door. The capital 'E' was partially peeling – Teri had attacked it with her fingernails in an attempt to remove it. 'It's so common,' she'd grumbled to him. 'And you're not a bleeding ad rep.' But Declan put his foot down. 'No, I'm the news editor and the Leader puts food on my table and a roof over my head.'

Some bloody roof, she might've argued, but didn't.

A rather battered red Polo, also sporting a Leader sticker, was kissing-close to Declan's back bumper. There was a small-ish gap behind it that, with a bit of adroitness, left just enough room for me to squeeze in – except I lacked that all important bit of adroitness. Parallel parking had never been a strong point and, after a couple of abortive efforts, I decided to look for a space further up the road. There weren't any and I ended up on the next street but one, which was less than ideal. First, because Leyland Road was not the greatest of neighbourhoods, and I would've preferred to have the car where I could keep an eye on it; and, second, there was the slight problem of how to get David out of the car and into the house. Which was achieved at last with a lot of pushing and pulling and a bit of bad language. Well, even a saint would've lost patience with him. He'd managed to get vomit down the front of his shirt and his jeans and he stank to high heaven. The car suffered a bit too – both inside and out. And, though he wasn't deliberately uncooperative, he seemed to have little control over his arms and legs. There's a good reason why the Good Samaritan is an endangered species – it's too much bloody effort.

However, we got there in the end and, with a lot more cussing, as well as some more unsympathetic manhandling, I stripped his clothes off and got him into bed – where he promptly burst into great, heart-stopping tears, followed by shuddering little sobs and half-sniffs. It was completely unexpected, and he reminded me so much of baby Fee that I cradled him in my arms, shushing and stroking his hair which – ugh! – was now matted and rank and dirty. Gradually, just like Fee, he quietened down and gently drifted off to sleep, with his head on my chest and his arms wrapped tight around me. And, again just like Fee, he stirred into wakefulness every time I tried to wriggle free. So, I stayed put and slept as best I could – which wasn't terribly well. Teri might extol the virtues of a narrow bed and a handsome bloke, but I prefer a bit more room and someone who isn't snoring loud enough to wake the dead. Somewhere nearby I heard a car's engine revving noisily and impatiently and, once, I heard someone hammering loudly at a door. Bloody students, I thought. Why can't they keep normal hours like the rest of us?

Eventually – not soon enough – morning came and David loosened his grip, but my plan to slip away backfired. As I eased myself out of bed, he gave an extra loud snore – like a pig having its throat cut – and woke himself up. To cut a long story short, he was horrendously hungover – turned out he'd consumed considerably more than a couple of pints. Surprise. Surprise. I offered to make coffee but the cupboard was bare. 'I've been staying over at Becky's a lot,' he said, 'so didn't bother getting anything in.' He wasn't kidding. There was no tea or milk or bread or anything to provide even a modicum of sustenance. So, while he groaned and closed his eyes and whined – I wanted to slap him – I shuttled off to the local mini-mart and bought some store cupboard essentials. Then I made breakfast, force fed him some toast and a couple of Paracetamol tablets, and, because the stench was almost overpowering, shoved his vomit-ridden clothes into the washing machine. And went to the mini-mart again to buy a packet of washing powder.

By the time I got back he was sitting up and, although still seriously hungover, said he fancied a shower. Except – wouldn't you know it? – there was no shampoo or shower gel in the bathroom. The boy was a complete and utter slob. So, back to the mini-mart – again. The checkout assistant was becoming my new best friend.

'Here again?' she said.

No, it's my doppelganger.

She kept up the flow of conversation as she scanned the toiletries – I'd added toothpaste and a toothbrush. I hadn't planned on sleeping out and didn't have my brush with me and didn't place any great dependency on David having either in his bathroom cabinet.

'You'd forget your head if it wasn't screwed on,' the assistant said.

Honestly, what a way to talk to customers?

It was mid-afternoon when I eventually headed home. Funny, but, though I went in and out of David's door three or four times, neither Declan's car nor the Polo behind moved an inch. Both cars remained within kissing distance all night and a large part of the next day.

Funniest of all though, I didn't see Teri, who I later discovered, had practically camped on the doorstep, and she didn't see me either. Wonder what would've happened if our paths had crossed that day? Would I have told her I recognised the Polo and that it belonged to Marnie? And what would she have done if I had?

Chapter Fifty-Four

Teri

'So what did you do?' Lee asked, putting her tea cup down on a table in the senior common room the following Monday morning.

'Well, I just drove home,' I told her.

'But if it was as innocent as you're now suggesting, why didn't you ring his doorbell again and why, for that matter, are you so upset about it?'

The thing I like about Lee is I can tell her anything and she usually understands. What I don't like is when she starts asking me questions like this, which are full of common sense, but to which there is no answer.

'Did you ring him the next day?'

'Yes.'

'And?'

'There was no reply.'

'When did you ring? He could've popped out for some milk or something.'

'I rang at 7am, 7.30am, 8am, 8.15am, 9am...'

'I get the picture.' She looked as though she was about to laugh but, seeing my pale face and the dark circles under my eyes, thought better of it. 'Did you speak to him at all over the weekend?'

'Not until last night.'

'And then what?'

'Well, he sounded pleased to hear from me.'

'Did you tell him you'd been round on Friday…that you'd been trying to get hold of him?'

'Er…'

'You didn't, did you?' She looked aghast. 'Oh, Teri. You should've said something.'

'I know. But I don't want him to think I'm spying on him.'

'You aren't spying on him. You want to know who the nasty little trollop in his bedroom was on Friday night.'

'Oh, I really don't think that…'

'Then why not ask him what he was doing?'

'Oh, Lee. For goodness' sake!' I said crossly, snapping my arms against my sides in frustration.

But I knew she was right. Why hadn't I told Declan I'd been standing on his doorstep, unable to get an answer on Friday night, and that I'd been ringing him every half hour all day Saturday and most of Sunday too? When he finally picked up the phone on Sunday night, he was cheerful.

'Hey. How'd the weekend go?' he asked.

'Brilliant,' I lied. Why did I do that?

'How was Rochester?'

'Still dead,' I laughed. 'What have you been up to?' I tried to keep my voice light.

'Oh, not much. Had a couple of bevies after work on Friday, came home, early night. Went up to the Lakes on Saturday – on my own – did a bit of climbing. Weather was good, so stayed up there – camped. Just this minute got back.'

I would've believed him, I honestly would, except that to go climbing and camping in the Lakes, Declan would've taken his car. And his car was parked outside his flat in Leyland Road every time I went round there during the weekend. And I went round at regular two-hourly intervals. I parked at the end of the road so I couldn't be seen from Number 12, and I swear that car never moved. And nor did the red Polo parked behind it.

I didn't tell Lee that.

Chapter Fifty-Five

Lee

I worried endlessly about that blasted Polo. While I was prepared to believe Declan was perfectly capable of cheating on Teri, it seemed inconceivable he'd do so with Marnie. And could betraying your mistress by sleeping with your estranged wife really be classed as cheating? Because though Teri liked to describe him as her significant other, Declan's frequently cavalier trampling over her feelings indicated as far as he was concerned she remained nothing more than a nice bit on the side.

In my more optimistic moments it was possible to pretend I'd made a mistake, and the car belonged to someone else who worked at the Leader and who just happened to live on the same street. Probably a flash-suited advertising rep – a *male* flash-suited rep. But mostly I remained pretty certain it was Marnie's car, which I'd seen her park in the church car park Sunday after Sunday. And seen Declan, who was still nominally Catholic, getting out of it too. Their little girl was an altar server so they always arrived early for Mass – as did Mammy, who liked to light a bonfire of candles in memory of long-dead relations. And even when Declan moved out and took up with Teri he still showed up for Mass from time to time and always arrived with Marnie and their children in the red Polo. The boy, who must've been in his early teens, was a sulky, moody-looking kid – probably resented Dad playing fast and loose – but the girl always held his hand tightly as she skipped up the church path. Clearly, Daddy's Little Girl was in

189

seventh heaven. The baby, of course, showed no preferences whatsoever.

Even so, it seemed a particularly callous carry on and, though Teri had a poor opinion of her, Marnie couldn't possibly be so...what? Needy? In love? Trying to save her family? Because she must've known church tongues would be wagging – we're Catholic and holier-than-thou, but we're human too. So, as she knelt, head bent in prayer, one hundred-and-more heads were also bowed and wondering 'Are they getting back together?' And, more importantly, 'Did he stay the night?' And now I was also getting all churned up about the stationary Polo with the tell-tale Leader Leads sticker necking the bumper of Declan's car. Had its owner spent the weekend kissing Declan? And, if Marnie had spent the weekend in the dingy top-floor flat, what had she made of Teri's homely little fixtures and fittings? And what had she done with the children? They were too young to be left home alone. With Declan's mother, perhaps? Mammy, who was one of her oldest friends, would know, but I didn't dare ask, in case I didn't like the answer. Aagh! My head was in a spin.

And that was without even considering the BIG question: how much should I tell Teri? There were times when I really, really hated Marnie.

Here's the thing: as a good Catholic girl I'd been brought up to believe in the sanctity of marriage – let's just ignore my own brief stint as the 'other woman' for a moment – and, as a result, conscience and upbringing, were all on the side of Marnie and the kids and their desire to preserve their family intact. Well, perhaps not the boy, who clearly wished his father would rot in hell. But, at the same time, as a paid-up former member of the mistress club, I also thought a marriage that wasn't broken wouldn't have acquired a significant other and my instincts, as ever, were 'if it's broke, chuck it'. And I was definitely with the boy in thinking Declan deserved all that hell fire and damnation could throw at him – this wasn't the first time his philandering had provided food for gossip for the church biddies. And probably wouldn't be the last either. Bottom line, though, I was batting for Teri: while I had nothing against Marnie per se, I didn't want her happiness to be bought at the expense of my friend, who, this time, seemed to be head over heels in love. Oh, Teri...

So, after endless prevarications, the perfect solution presented itself: do nothing. And hang around to pick up the pieces as and when necessary.

Chapter Fifty-Six

Teri

Monday went by in a blur of misery. Why hadn't I been honest with Declan? He would've had a perfectly reasonable explanation. Perhaps he went up to the Lakes with a friend in the friend's car – although he'd said he went on his own. He'd sounded pleased to hear from me on Sunday night, but when I suggested he come round to my house, had said he was knackered and on an early shift at the paper the next day. I offered to cook him a meal after work. He said he was doing a late shift.

'But you're on earlies,' I reminded him.

'Yeah. I'm doing back-to-back shifts. There's a big story on – double murder over the weekend and there are police press conferences and re-enactments – and we need everyone in the newsroom. Sorry, love. I'll ring you…'

Level 2 got less than their tuition fees' worth during my lecture on the Moral and Monarchical Panics of the 1600s, and in the tutorial that followed it was easier to let them body swerve any suggestion we discuss puritanical stances in favour of the sex, scandal and hedonistic pleasures of our own dear twenty-first century royal family.

'Life still bloody?' Lee asked when we bumped into each other later in the day.

'Bloodier,' I said.

'Come for a drink after work,' she suggested.

191

'No, I'm going to catch up on some sleep,' I told her. 'I didn't get much last night.' What with driving round to Leyland Road every couple of hours, I didn't get any sleep at all.

I had an early night, and the following day felt better, went into uni, did a couple of tutorials but otherwise, wasn't too busy. I texted Declan offering to make him a meal, but he texted back saying he had to go to a press conference.

'What??? !!! In the evning???!!!' I texted.

'Dble murder...' he texted back. Funny, I hadn't seen anything about a murder over the weekend on the news, but then, I hardly watch the local news nowadays. I can't risk seeing Dan.

'2morrow, then??' I texted.

'Can't.'

'Thurs???'

'OK, c u at yours.'

Why did I feel as though I was just getting crumbs in this relationship? I had to have it out with Declan. There was no way I was letting a man treat me like this. But, I love him. I love him. I love him. And that was the bloody problem. For the first time in my life I'd found a man who meant more to me than I obviously did to him.

And I didn't trust him. All his excuses. All his lies. He was obviously up to something, and that something was seeing other women. What else could it be? He could only spend so much time at work or with his kids. There were far too many nights now when he claimed to be 'too tired' to come round or busy 'seeing someone about a story'.

On the Thursday, I'd cooked cassoulet and opened a bottle of expensive red wine, and before the poor boy had a chance to swallow the first mouthful I started.

'Look, Declan, I'm not nagging...'

'Which means you're about to,' he said, adding, 'Women always do that. I'm not nagging but... Okay, what do you want?' His tone was harsh and it startled me.

'I was only going to say that I love you and want to spend more time with you...'

He sighed and shook his head. 'For God's sake, Teri. I'm busy at work,

192

I've got three fucking kids to feed, I've got an ex-wife who's constantly on my back for one thing or another, and now I've got a girlfriend who wants to have me at her beck and call all the time. Don't any of you fucking well see – I need some space.'

'I'm sorry, Declan,' I said as softly as I could. 'Look, I promise not to keep on at you. It's just I want to see you…'

'You're seeing me now and you're ruining it with your bloody nagging.' He slammed his glass down on the coffee table, allowing some of the red wine to splash on the white wood, and stood up. I stood up too and reached out to try and hold his arms, but he shrugged me off, reached for his jacket and stormed out.

I cried. I really cried. What on earth was wrong with me? Why did I feel like this? Angrily I walked into the kitchen, saw the cassoulet dish and scraped the food into the bin with bad tempered, heavy strokes. I threw the dish into a bowl of soapy water so that suds flicked up and around the sink, spattering the lazulite blue and yellow tiles. I went back into the living room where I picked up my glass of wine and downed it in one. For a moment I felt breathless and dizzy, and then the doorbell buzzed. I went into the hallway and opened the door ready to tell whoever it was to 'fuck off'. Declan stood there with a sheepish look on his face, his eyes twinkling behind an ever so slightly mischievous smile.

'Oh, hell, Teri. I'm so sorry.' And he stepped forward, took hold of my arms and pulled me to him and then onto the floor.

Again we found ourselves having urgent, breathless sex, which ended with us giggling as we lay in each other's arms looking up at the ceiling.

'Nice place you've got here,' Declan said. 'Can I have something to eat now?'

'Afraid not, I just chucked it out,' I told him.

'Ah well, we'll have to live on love tonight. One thing, not as many calories.'

Oh, how I love him.

He stayed all night and I revelled in having him with me. I was careful with everything I said; I didn't want to annoy him again. I asked what he was doing at the weekend.

'Off to the Lakes,' he said.

'Can I come?' I asked.

'What...? Teri, you've never walked further than round the local park. You couldn't get up one of those fells.'

'I can if you take me,' I said, imagining the two of us hand in hand, climbing a remote hill and making love on the summit as the sun went down.

He was thoughtful for a moment. Then he said, 'Right, lass. We're taking you up a mountain.'

Chapter Fifty-Seven

Teri

I was beginning to regret my insistence on going for a 'day's walking' with Declan. But he'd been so incredulous and, I have to say, mocking, when I asked him to take me to the Lakes, I thought I'd better put my request into action.

Declan had laughed as he sought reassurance. 'Are you absolutely, positively, completely sure you want to come?'

'Yes.'

'It'll be cold, wet and hard work – they're hills, you know, not pedestrianised shopping areas.'

It was just so good to see him in such a good mood, and he was obviously looking forward to spending time with me on the Lakeland Fells.

He'd even come to the camping and clothing shop with me to buy boots and a waterproof jacket – a nasty plastic thing with toggles and zips and a hood with an elasticated edge to keep it tight against my face if it rained. What a sight. He said I could borrow one of his old rucksacks to stop me buying a lovely soft leather version in tan. 'One drop of rain and that thing'll be ruined,' he said, spluttering over the £250 price tag, and I had to agree his breathable nylon version was probably more cost-effective and serviceable. I drew the line at buying a zip-up fleece, which came in either bottle green or the most peculiar shade of orangey-red. I'd seen too many pensioners wearing those shapeless things to think of ever wearing one myself. I told

Declan I'd take one of my old cashmere sweaters for if it got cold.

I've met many men in my life and, although it might sound conceited, I've never had to do the chasing. Men have always been keen to take me out for dinner, join me at the theatre, come on holiday with me, cancel something else they'd planned so they could be with me, laugh at my jokes…Declan was different. I didn't repeat my stalking exercise because I had my pride, but I was gradually beginning to realise that while this was a relationship of mutual lust for both of us, it was not one of mutual love and longing – it was only me doing the loving and longing, and that's an unusual place for me to be. But the more Declan seemed to push me away, the more I wanted him. Oh God. What happened to the girl who could love 'em and leave 'em?

I thought this trip to the Lake District would seal something between us.

Chapter Fifty-Eight

Lee

The Daily Mail is an oft-maligned publication. But, credit where it's due, I owe a debt of gratitude to the paper's travel writer who penned a piece on a cooking and walking holiday in Tuscany. Whoever she was, she made it sound good fun – much more entertaining than Fliss's suggestion that I join her and the family in a rented cottage in North Wales. I've nothing against either the Principality or its people but it's undeniably wetter and colder than Italy, so I lied and said I couldn't get annual leave on the scheduled dates and booked the walking and cooking trip instead. God knows why the write up stuck in my memory, but the holiday was well-priced, the single room supplement was reasonable, and I'd never been to Italy before.

Teri hooted with laughter. 'Cooking. You?'

It would've been insulting if her incredulity hadn't been one hundred per cent well-deserved. And she was far less rude than either Charles or Felicity. 'The walking will kill you,' Charles said, conveniently ignoring the fact he'd said something very similar when Ritchie and I proposed hiring bikes last year. Which might've been excusable then but was a little unfair now. Clearly Teri wasn't the only one who hadn't noticed the new, fitter me.

Ritchie was equally sceptical. 'Do people have to eat the food?'

Of course.

'Glad I'm not staying in your hotel.'

Also less than encouraging, but I'd done my homework – the walks were all moderately graded; we'd do no more than eight to ten kilometres a day; and we'd cook on just three afternoons. Plus, we'd get a day off midweek to explore nearby Florence. It all seemed eminently do-able.

Except as departure day approached, I began to share some of their reservations – in particular, Teri's disdain for organised tours with total strangers.

'You won't have anything in common,' she said. 'They'll all be energetic, outdoor types with weather-beaten complexions and hand-knitted socks and woollies.'

Talk about stereotyping.

'And they'll all be teetotal and drink green tea and be tucked up in bed by half past nine.'

Oh Lord! But drinking alone had never bothered me before, so why should it bother me now?

'Or else, they'll be sad little spinsters who'll stop every two minutes to admire the view and take photographs of obscure alpine plants.'

'I'm not going to the Alps.'

'Whatever – you get the picture.'

And I did, horribly. And I'd have cancelled and forfeited the deposit if Teri hadn't already suggested it; I didn't want to give her the satisfaction.

So, I was not a happy bunny when she dropped me off at Leeds-Bradford airport for a connecting flight to Heathrow.

'Chill,' she said as we kissed goodbye.

Chill? Where had she got that from? It was the sort of thing Declan might say, but, to be honest, she didn't seem to mention him much these days, and I didn't like to ask because the last time I had (innocently) enquired, how's Declan? she turned a bit icy, so I was playing it safe and not mentioning him either.

'You'll enjoy it once you get there,' she promised. 'I know you will – and don't forget to look out for Dan.'

Dan?

'I hear he's holidaying in Tuscany this year. It's very popular with media types.'

Just what I needed to cheer me up – a gaggle of luvvies.

At Heathrow, things began to look up, thanks to a funny little chap, who accosted me as we queued to go through passport control.

'You're Rambling, aren't you?'

Eh?

'Rambling – walking and cooking in Tuscany.'

He didn't wait for an answer. 'This will be my twenty-fifth Rambling holiday,' he said, 'and I've loved every single one of them.'

And for the next hour or so as we waited for our flight to be called, Maurice Entwhistle-Moody told me all about his holidays. He was like a real-life *Carry On* character – think Charles Hawtry or Kenneth Connor – and absolutely charming. If he was typical of the sort of people to be found on Rambling holidays I was in for a whale of a time.

'I like to play a little game,' he confided.

A game? Here?

'I try and spot other Ramblings,' he said.

Pardon?

'Look, that lady over there.' He pointed to a grey-haired woman, wearing a waterproof anorak and matching trousers. 'The boots are the give-away.' True enough, while most of the other travellers wore ordinary footwear, Maurice's lady was sporting a pair of well-worn and well-polished hiking boots.

'All experienced Ramblings travel in their walking boots – makes a huge saving on the luggage allowance.'

Heavens, why hadn't I thought of that? We both looked at my strappy sandals.

He laughed. 'Clearly, a Ramblings virgin.'

So, until we were herded into our seats, one at the front and one at the back of the aircraft, we spotted other Ramblings and, at the other end, collected our baggage and headed for the arrivals hall, scanning the crowds for the holiday rep-cum-tour and walking guide. Myrtle was a tall, very English, jolly-hockey-sticks gel. I'd bet even money she'd been head girl or captain of games at her own expensive boarding school. Maurice winked at me as we surveyed the rest of our little group – we'd done pretty well at spotting the Ramblings.

One person was missing: a gentleman Myrtle said, who'd booked too late to secure a seat on the scheduled British Airways plane. Instead, he'd taken an alternative flight from Gatwick, which was due in just twenty minutes. So, we waited and gossiped, sizing each other up. It was a pretty mixed bunch: a handful of husband and wife couples, or singles, like myself and Maurice – although there was no one quite like Maurice – plus a mother and daughter pairing and a couple of others travelling with either a relative or friend. Twenty of us in total – well, nineteen. We were still waiting for the Gatwick gent.

You don't, surely, need me to tell you the identity of the missing traveller?

Chapter Fifty-Nine

Teri

Rather than clearing as the weather forecast promised, the mist had grown thicker by the time we got to the Lake District. Seen just a short time ago from the approach road two thousand feet below, the fluffy white clouds appeared like cotton, lightly suspended above the fell top; wispy things.

'It'll shift,' Declan said, hardly looking up at the mist in his haste to lace his boots. I could only take his word for it. I shoved my feet into my new walking boots and bent down to lace the damn things up. They were so stiff.

'You should've broken them in,' Declan said.

Broken them in? They're boots. I'd had dozens of pairs of boots that hadn't needed breaking in. Mind you, they were generally made of the softest leather and felt more like slippers. These were great hulking things like over-sized, clompy trainers.

Declan's rucksack felt uneven and bulky on my back even though I hadn't put much in it apart from a bottle of sparkling spring water and a prawn sandwich I'd grabbed from M&S. Oh and a dinky little beret in case my hair got wet, and some lip salve, a tube of hand cream and my moisturiser.

We set off. Or rather Declan leapt off, and I trailed behind. We were on an incline immediately, and all I could see was uphill.

'Are we going right up there?' I asked.

'Yup. Right to the top,' Declan said with a slightly impatient tone. His mood had chilled since our shopping expedition, and he'd been quiet on the drive up to the Lakes, turning the radio on so we could listen to music rather than talk. 'Look, you can stay in the car and read the paper if you don't want to come,' he said as I looked at the looming hillside.

'No. I'm coming,' I said.

I couldn't see the top because of the mist. So that wasn't terribly reassuring.

Oddly, I got into my stride. Thanks to a bit of power walking round the park I *was* semi-fit, but I couldn't catch up with Declan; he took off like a bat out of hell. Walking in the hills was something he liked to do alone – or with his climbing buddies – and he'd warned I'd slow him down and if I did, he wouldn't wait for me. I hesitated to admit that despite the earlier jokes when I'd asked if I could come with him, he didn't particularly want to be with me today.

Declan was moving faster up ahead and there was now a fair distance between us. I was soon aware the only sounds were the bleating of sheep back down the hill, behind and below, and my own heavy breathing.

The rough grass gave way in parts to chewed mud and then occasional stretches of snow where I had to kick my toes in to stop slithering. Snow! In April. But then we were climbing quite high and, I realised, the mist was getting thicker and wetter.

I stopped and yanked the rucksack off my back, found my natty little beret and put it on, and then took the bottle and had a swig of water, which exploded in my mouth. Fizzy water was a mistake; it felt dry and powdery on my tongue. I rammed the bottle back in the rucksack and looked up expecting to see Declan, hands on hips, waiting impatiently for me. But he'd disappeared into the mist.

Uneasy that he'd got so far ahead, I tried to move faster, but my boots, which had been rubbing, were now making my heels and toes feel quite sore. The hillside was getting steeper and the mist thicker, and soon I could see just a couple of yards in front. I was aware of white cobwebs of damp mist forming on the sleeve of my jacket. I placed my feet heavily, trudging slower and slower, aware of how cold and tired I was getting. I hooked my thumbs through the shoulder straps of the rucksack to ease it off my back as though that would somehow lighten the load and make walking easier.

Suddenly the ground levelled off and I guessed I'd reached the top, although I couldn't really see given the mist was now like a thick, white blanket. Well, I'd got there but I didn't have a clue as to how I was going to get down. Suddenly scared, I looked around wildly, hoping for the reassuring bulk of another human figure. But everywhere I looked was whiteness and all was quiet and still.

'DECLAN!' I shouted. Over two thousand feet up a mountain and, as far as I knew, completely alone, but the noise felt embarrassingly loud, and if I hadn't been so frightened, I would've felt stupid. What does one do, stranded in a white-out on top of a mountain? I didn't want to walk on as I wasn't sure where I was going. If I turned round, could I retrace my steps well enough to find a path going back down? Declan warned me about people wandering off the wrong side of a mountain and descending into a completely different valley to the one in which they'd started. 'If you did that,' Declan said, 'you'd have a long walk back – there aren't any buses in these hills.'

It was too cold and wet to sit and simply wait in the hope the selfish bastard would return and find me. Maybe other walkers would appear and help me down? But what other idiots would there be climbing misty, mud-sodden mountains in this weather? My feet hurt. My hands were cold. The cashmere sweater was useless. I'd have given anything for a warm, comfy fleece right then. Against my better judgment, I sank down on the wet grass and hugged my knees, more for comfort than anything else. Perhaps I'd get hypothermia and die, and the search and rescue party would eventually find my body and put up a plaque: 'She came to the hills and the hills spat at her....'

'What on earth did you do?' Lee asked, wide eyed in astonishment when we met for coffee in the senior common room. 'Well, I yelled for Declan again – but no reply, again. Then I had a brainwave. I had my mobile with me, so I got it out, although my hands were so cold I could hardly key in his number.'

'But you wouldn't have got a signal up a mountain,' Lee said.

'You're absolutely right,' I agreed. 'So I just started screaming. Really loudly.'

'And Declan appeared?'

'No. A rather nice couple from Lytham St Anne's emerged, coming up out of the mist like a pair of shining angels. God, who are these people who enjoy labouring up mountains in the mist? Anyway, Eric and Diane – that's the couple – realised I was in a bad way and abandoned their summit attempt to help guide me down. It seems I'd not reached the top but something they called a false summit. There were bags more to go, which was presumably where Declan had gone. Anyway, they had maps and compasses and, best of all, some Kendal Mint Cake and a flask of coffee, so they gave me something to eat and drink, and it was all very jolly and we got down safe and sound, and they left me in a nice little tea shop near where we'd left the car.'

'Yes, but what about Declan?'

'Well, Diane wanted Eric to go back up the mountain to see if he could find Declan coming down. I think Diane wanted to stay with me having a cup of tea in the warm, but Eric persuaded her to go with him and, bless them, they found Declan about half way up, going frantic, looking for me. They told him where I was, and all three of them came down together. I thought we'd all have some nice toasted teacakes, but Declan was in a bloody foul mood and demanded – demanded – we head off home straight away.'

'Is he still mad with you?' asked Lee.

'Mad with me? Why on earth should he be mad with me? I'm the one who was abandoned and left to die a miserable death on a sodden hillside in the middle of bloody nowhere. If Diane and Eric – love them – hadn't come along, I'd still be up there – probably dead.'

I told Lee Declan hardly spoke on the way home. He dropped me at my flat and said he wouldn't come in. I didn't hear from him the following day – Sunday – and nor did I bother texting or ringing him. 'I thought I'd make him suffer,' I said.

Lee gave me one of her funny, close scrutiny looks.

Chapter Sixty

Lee

The missing traveller's flight was delayed so we spent nearly an hour hanging around the concourse of Pisa airport before he finally showed up. He was apologetic and grateful.

'I thought you'd go without me and I'd have to take a taxi,' he said, shaking hands with Myrtle.

'Oh no,' she said. 'Nobody minded.'

Well, I did. I was tired and grumpy – Teri had picked me up at 4am to make the check-in at Leeds-Bradford and I was annoyed with Myrtle who, having herded us together, wouldn't allow us to leave the group for a cup of coffee (or tea) and a sit down. So, we'd stood listlessly and, with the exception of Maurice, mostly silent having run out of polite inanities. Maurice talked virtually non-stop – he was playing another game: guessing the occupation, which he claimed he could do by studying faces. He couldn't – he thought I must be a care home worker and the chap who he identified with certainty as a medic was a forklift truck driver in a meat factory. And, his wife 'definitely a maths teacher' was a checkout assistant in a discount supermarket. Only a couple of hours into the holiday, and I wanted to wring his neck.

The missing traveller, however, breezed in completely oblivious to the gathering ill-humour.

Myrtle clapped her hands. 'Everybody, I'd like you to meet the final member of our group. This is...' and she turned to the gentleman and gestured to him to introduce himself. Except, he didn't need any introductions.

'Dan,' I said. 'What the bloody hell are you doing here?'

Dumb question: walking and cooking obviously.

'Lee,' he said. 'What a lovely surprise.'

Hmmm – when Teri said 'look out for Dan' I didn't think she actually meant it literally.

At last, Myrtle led us to the coach waiting to transfer us to our hotel in San Marcello. Suitcases and backpacks stored in the baggage hold, we boarded. I'd assumed Dan would sit with me – he didn't. Maurice didn't sit next to me either. Instead, they both sat alone – like me. And, thus, I was introduced to one of the golden rules of Ramblings – couples sit together, singles on their own. It's acceptable to sit behind or in front of another walker and conduct an over-the-shoulder conversation, but sit together? Definitely not. Why? God only knows.

So, I stared morosely out of the window, feeling just a little sorry for myself. The almost-but-not-quite a crush I'd had on Dan when he first started dating Teri had long since evaporated – actually, it hadn't survived Teri's 'fluffer' anecdote, which I thought indicated a rather coarse side to Dan that the Catholic prude found rather unappealing. But still...he might've been a bit more sociable.

We didn't even sit next to each other at the evening meal; the hotel's owners Cinzia and Rudy had set aside a couple of long tables – think school dinners – for the Ramblings group, and we ended up pretty much at opposite ends of the room. Actually, that was no bad thing because it forced me to break the ice with a couple of other members of the group. But, I'm jumping ahead here; dinner was preceded by a group briefing that included an outline of the next day's programme and an invitation to join Myrtle on a little after-dinner tour of the town – high spot a visit to the cemetery to admire the dragonflies and the gravestone lanterns that local custom dictated were lit every evening to commemorate the dead.

Count me out – but no, it was less an invitation and more a command appearance. A no-show was not permitted. Teri's dire predictions seemed to be coming true. All I wanted to do was go to bed, with a large glass of Pinot

Grigio – the bloody Italians didn't stock Muscadet – and a book. Instead, I was dragged around in the dark while Myrtle gave us a running commentary on the history of the place.

'Here's the town hall – it was built in the mid-fifteenth century and extensively renovated in the 1960s,' she said, indicating a nondescript stone-built mausoleum. 'And this little shop has a good range of postcards and some nice regional gifts.' Oh, pleeease – as if I care. 'And this lovely little square is home to the village market on Tuesday and Fridays. But you have to get up early,' she warned, 'because the market opens at 7am and everything is all packed up by noon.' Count me out then. There was no way I was dragging myself out of bed at some God-awful hour to wander round half a dozen flea-bitten stalls.

Maurice, of course, lapped it up. 'Oh my,' he said. 'Oh my, isn't it lovely?'

No! It's a very ordinary town square not dissimilar to umpteen thousand other squares scattered all over the Mediterranean and beyond. I was in a minority of one though because everyone else seemed to think the place was delightful. Holy Cow! I thought Maurice was going to have an orgasm when we got to the church. Pre-Renaissance, naturally.

Dan wasn't much better; for the first time I was reminded of how sceptical, disapproving even, I'd been when Teri grumbled about his endless good nature. Now I could see what she meant – someone who always looked on the bright side could be a real pain in the backside.

And so, not soon enough, to bed.

Chapter Sixty-One

Teri

Declan's behaviour got me thinking. I didn't want to repeat that awful night in March, but I did take to popping round to Leyland Road on certain nights when Declan said he was either working late or taking his kids out somewhere. And on those nights when you might not expect to see his car parked near his flat, it generally was. Even I found it too tiring to organise reasons and excuses as to why this might be. Nor could I explain the blonde-haired woman who parked her Mercedes SLK outside Number 12 and walked up to the door to ring the buzzer. I could only watch as Declan stuck his head out of the top-floor window, wave and throw his keys down to her so she could let herself in and save him having to come down several flights of stairs. It wasn't so much the blonde hair or the flash car, it was the way Declan seemed so relaxed and pleased to see the woman. He chucked down the keys in that familiar, trusting, loving way he used to do for me.

That woman was clearly not his mother, aunt or sister – not that I'd ever met any of his relatives apart from sitting behind his mother in church at the Christmas before last, but I was on a champagne-fuelled giggly high then and hadn't taken much notice of either her or Declan sitting beside her.

I very much doubted the blonde was a work mate. You don't lean out of a window and laugh unless the person below is someone with whom you have done this before. It's just…well…too familiar. I wasn't handling the Declan situation very well; I was too scared to face the truth.

Chapter Sixty-Two

Teri

I wasn't handling the Declan situation very well, and I don't think I handled the David Greenspan business very well either.

It was supposed to be harmless enough. The second semester was coming to an end and, as usual, the students had planned a May Ball. It was a chance for the boys to dress up in their rented tux and the girls to spend Mummy and Daddy's money on ludicrous, skin-tight, bosom-revealing ball gowns. They arrived at the university's Thomas Packenham Hall in their stretch limos, giggly with all the booze they'd drunk beforehand.

A few lecturers went, in fact, Lee and I were planning to go together until she decided to go on her madcap holiday instead. Declan refused to go – typical – so I found myself climbing the steps up to the grand hall entrance on my own in a rather stunning hot-pink gown with a be-jewelled peplum and mermaid skirt. Entering the foyer I could see a mass of colourful gowns ahead of me in the grand hall. But amongst the wave of bobbing heads and coiffed hair, one person with a shaggy, blond head and long, lean limbs stood out: Gorgeous Greenspan. I'd only ever seen him in scruffy jeans and t-shirts and here he was in a slim-fitting, contemporary one-button dinner jacket with a black bow tie and looking every inch the sharp hero of a James Bond movie. He looked a knock-out.

'Well, hiya David,' I said, running my hand up and down an expensive sleeve. 'Don't you look the part?'

'You look pretty amazing yourself,' he said, eyeing my breasts rounding over the top of the hot-pink bodice, before collecting himself and adding, 'Shall I get you a drink?'

I said a white wine would be great, and off he loped in the direction of the bar leaving me wondering what the heck I was doing.

The hall became crowded as more and more people arrived. I was nudged and bustled by those coming in behind me, so I moved over to the wall on the right-hand side and hoped David would find me. I must've waited about ten minutes, nodding hello to various people who looked my way. Then, horrors, I saw Mike Orme bearing down. Of course the old tight fist wasn't wearing a dinner jacket but a dark blue jacket with trousers that didn't quite match, with a white shirt and university tie. 'No tank top tonight, Mike?' I said. He looked at me oddly as though he had no idea what I was talking about.

'Are you here on your own?' he asked, leaning slightly towards me, his glass of red wine slopping dangerously at the edge of the glass.

'No, I'm waiting for someone...'

'Lucky man,' he leered. 'My wife won't come to these dos so I'm here on my own,' he added.

'As I said, Mike, I'm waiting for someone, so please don't let me hold you up.'

Mike looked crestfallen but shambled off, and I stood on tiptoe to try and see over the heads of the crowd for signs of David returning with my now much-needed drink. No sign. I headed off in the direction of the bar, bought myself a bottle of white wine and found an empty table at the edge of the hall and sat down. I needed a couple of glasses to fortify me before I went in search of the arrogant boy.

Heartened after drinking, fairly quickly, nearly the whole bottle of Pinot Grigio, I edged my way through the crowd and back to the bar for another. With the new bottle in one hand and two glasses in the other, I spotted him. I'd recognise that trim back view anywhere. 'Hi, David.'

He turned and as he did so, I noticed the girl he'd been talking to. He quickly turned back to her and said something I couldn't hear. She looked at me and laughed, then nodded and David turned back and walked towards me.

'Sorry…I was meant to get you a drink, wasn't I, but I see you managed…' he said, looking at the bottle.

Something about his lazy insolence annoyed me. You don't offer to buy me a drink and then leave me waiting, I thought, but swallowed my pride and said, 'Look, come and help me finish this bottle and then we'll get another.'

'I've got a beer, thanks,' he said, raising a half-pint glass.

'Well, come anyway,' I said rather more harshly than I meant to.

Poor lamb, off to the slaughter. We found a table. We chatted, I can't remember what about. I was just so happy to be with someone who clearly liked me and who wasn't Declan. Before I knew it, I'd drunk about half the bottle; David was still sipping at his beer.

'Look, Teri,' he said. 'Don't you think you've had enough?'

Cheeky little snot.

'Oh, I've hardly started. Come on, David. Have another drink.'

'I don't drink much,' he said. 'I had a bad experience with booze and…'

'Oh for God's sake, David, lighten up,' I snapped, slopping more wine into my glass. I took a huge slug, placed it back down carefully on the table then reached over and took one of his hands. I raised it to my lips and kissed it or rather (I hate to think about it) it was probably more of a slobber.

'Wha…?' he said, snatching his hand back.

'Oh, come on, David…We're both adults. What's wrong with you?' I stood up and in one fluid movement swung round the edge of the table and into his lap, which is not easy to do when you're wearing six-inch heels. I put both arms around his neck and nudged my face into his and kissed him firmly on the lips. At this stage his arms should've gone round my waist, all the better to pull me in and closer to him, but instead, he put two large hands on either side of my hips and pushed me away. It was only my holding on to the back of his neck that stopped me from slithering to the floor, albeit I was balancing precariously on the edge of his knees. I yanked myself back into his lap and tried again. This time he stood up, and I did slither to the floor. Not a good look whether in hot pink or not.

'You're drunk, Teri,' he said. He reached down and pulled me to my feet. One of my shoes had come off so I stood there doing a sort of dance as I balanced first on one high-heeled foot and then the other shoeless one. A small knot of people had witnessed the whole thing including the daft, little girl David had been speaking to earlier.

Suddenly, little miss found a voice. 'David,' she yelled. 'Are you coming with us?'

'Will you be all right?' he asked, looking doubtfully at me.

'Oh, fuck off, David,' I said.

Chapter Sixty-Three

Lee

My mood wasn't much improved the next morning. I awoke, just after seven, feeling only marginally more cheerful. The walk was scheduled to start at nine, and I had to shower, breakfast and sort out a packed lunch first. And though that might not seem a tall order, last night I discovered a) the water pressure was so poor that the shower amounted to little more than a trickle and b) the water pressure was so poor it took fifteen minutes for enough water to dribble through the taps to cover the bottom of the bath. It was going to be a long week.

Eventually, I made it down to breakfast, hair tied loosely in a dripping ponytail – my travel adaptor wasn't compatible with the ancient electrical system and, therefore, my hairdryer was redundant. More worryingly, I couldn't recharge my mobile phone. Catastrophe.

Dan was already tucking into yoghurt and muesli – Greenspan would've been proud of him, but he'd have disowned me because I piled my plate with pastries and fruit. 'Never eat fruit at breakfast,' he'd say. 'Interferes with the digestion.'

Huh! I preferred indigestion to constipation.

And, I leave you to guess what he says about pastries.

Things perked up a little after breakfast. I walked the short distance into town with Jean, a Cockney lady there with her husband, Sidney. He'd gone upstairs to finish getting ready – a euphemism for going to the loo – while she bought their lunch. We found a nice little grocery – which, to be fair, Myrtle pointed out the previous evening – where we bought focaccia rolls filled with thinly sliced prosciutto, tomatoes, fresh fruit and some dried figs. I couldn't wait for lunch.

And then we set off walking: here, I need to make it clear that if you're expecting a blow-by-blow account of each day's tramp, or even cooking, forget it. You'll get highlights and nothing more – and be thankful. Anything else would be an utter bore. Besides, I don't do scenery – although the scenery and the views from the mountains were pretty spectacular.

Each day followed a similar pattern: a couple of times we set off from the hotel (always at 9am); other times we travelled by coach and walked back to the hotel or to an agreed coach rendezvous. Always we walked for about ninety minutes before stopping for a short break – in a coffee shop or bar if the walk happened to take us through a village or small town, or, if not, we plonked down on the grass and quenched our thirst from our water bottles. The same at lunchtime; we'd stop about 1pm and spread ourselves out and tuck in. I've some lovely photos Dan took of me trying to catch fish in a rock pool. Once, when we took a cable car for a high altitude walk, we bought a simple hot lunch in a climbers' retreat. The toilets were a bit basic – you can't be a female Rambling without becoming a loo connoisseur – but the food was good, and both Dan and I tucked in to a hearty stew. And, when the proprietor's elderly Labrador came sniffing and I started getting twitchy – dogs scare the living daylights out of me – Dan calmly shooed him away and provided an escort to the loo because the dog decided to take a post-lunch snooze on the welcome mat.

About those toilets: try as I might, I couldn't overcome my squeamishness about squatting behind a bush and emptying my bladder outdoors. Stopping for a drink in a bar was a mixed blessing, because even if you dashed for the lavatory as soon as you entered – and I did – you couldn't escape the obligation to buy a drink. Which meant drinking it – and topping up the bladder all over again. And even if I went to the loo a second time before we set off again, it was never long before the whole wee cycle was in train.

Most days we covered about ten kilometres and got back to the hotel between 4 and 4.30pm. Group debrief always took place at 6.30pm and dinner half an hour later. Most nights I was in bed and asleep by 9.30pm – almost as Teri predicted. On cooking days we had fewer and shorter stops and headed for the kitchen for 3pm where, among other things, we learned to make fresh pasta and chicken liver pâté and Tuscan bread salad – none of which I've been able to reproduce successfully back home. But the chopping and stirring and tasting were huge fun and there was a lot of good-humoured banter – my toilet obsession was a bit of a running joke. And the others really took the mickey out of me. The others? Well, not the whole group, of course, but the little coterie that became 'our' gang – Maurice, Dan, me and Christian, a blond, bearded Scandinavian, originally from Copenhagen but who now taught modern languages at a very good sixth-form college in Huddersfield. Maurice called us the Three Tykes and a half-pint Cockney – except he wasn't a Cockney. Far too posh. But he couldn't think of an appropriate moniker for a civil servant from Battersea. To be honest, I'd never thought of Battersea as being posh – but he assured us his bit was 'very nice'. He was half-pint sized though. (And actually I was the only true Tyke – although Maurice ruled that the other two qualified on the grounds of residency.)

Now about Christian: I would've said Christian didn't really stand out amongst the group gathered at the airport waiting with varying degrees of impatience for Dan – except he was so tall that Christian stood out wherever he stood. He wasn't flamboyant or quirky like Maurice, or affable and amiable like Dan; instead he was shy and quiet and, on that first day, spoke when he was spoken to, answering questions with careful precision but otherwise remaining quietly watchful.

Frankly, he seemed rather dull.

Day two though revealed a droll sense of humour. He was at the grocery deli counter when Jean and I arrived to order our sandwiches and, in a gentlemanly gesture, which he must have regretted, stepped aside to allow us to go first. My order was pretty straightforward – well, when the choice is bread filled with cheese or bread filled with ham, and you don't like cheese, there's not much to procrastinate about – but Jean couldn't decide whether Sidney would prefer Parma ham or prosciutto and would he want Dutch Edam or a hard local cheese or…? And then there was the question of bread: plain foccacia or tomato and rosemary or, perhaps, cheese and onion bread?

And should she buy a small tub of green olives? Or black? Or would figs be nicer? Talk about indecisive.

'I'm so sorry,' she apologised. 'I'm holding you up.'

'Not at all,' Christian said. 'It's important that you consider all the options.'

I glanced at him, unsure whether to take his words at face value – or what? Jean had no such inhibitions and promptly asked his opinion of the various breads on offer. They'd tried continental black bread yesterday, and Sid had been none too keen on it. 'Didn't agree with him at all,' she said. Christian raised his eyebrows. 'Had a bit of a funny effect on his digestive system,' Jean elaborated, gesturing generally in the direction of the lower tummy region. 'He was up-and-down all night.' Christian nodded sympathetically, which was all the encouragement Jean needed to expand on the subject of poor Sid and his dodgy belly. 'Went through him like a dose of salts...' she started.

Heavens woman, I thought, at this rate we'll be here all day.

Oops! A startled guffaw from Christian and a quick intake of breath from Jean indicated that, not for the first time, I'd spoken aloud thoughts that would've been better kept to myself.

Useless to try and apologise or pretend the words had come out wrong when clearly they shouldn't have come out at all. Jean, though, bless her, didn't take offence. 'Too right,' she said, 'I need to get a move on.' And she briskly bought one ham and one cheese sandwich on large flat ciabatta bread, a couple of loose tomatoes and a small bunch of black grapes, together with a bar of milk chocolate, which melted into a disgusting mess long before lunchtime.

'I'll have to come shopping with you again,' she said as the three of us walked back to the hotel. 'No time for dithering when I'm with you pair.'

You pair – I liked the sound of that.

I'm not quite sure at what point we became a proper pair or realised that was the direction in which we were heading. But from that first morning we gravitated towards each other – walking together, eating our sandwiches together and sitting opposite each other at dinner. And because Dan and I were already acquainted, and because Maurice had decided, on no grounds whatsoever, he and I were buddies, the four of us became a group within the group. Sure, we made friends with the others, and most mornings Christian and I walked down to the shop with Jean, but our little foursome always brought up the ramblings tail and, when we eventually had our day off in Florence, we separated from the rest and together ambled across the Ponte Vecchio and along the banks of the river Arno.

Maurice was already lamenting the end of the holiday and the dispersal of 'our gang'. He carried a large, old-fashioned manual camera on a strap around his neck and kept stopping to take pictures. It was an elaborate process that frequently required one or all of us to pose stiffly in front of whichever view he happened to be snapping.

'I do NOT snap,' he grumbled when we teased him.

Dead right, he didn't. Where Dan snatched quick pics on his smart phone, and Christian captured more studied views on his digital camera, Maurice took almost a month of Sundays just to unpack his camera from its carrying case and unravel it from the several layers of bubble wrap with which he protected it. And then he had to check the light and frame the shot. And pose us. 'People add depth and context,' he said as he pushed and pulled us into place.

Dan became his photographic assistant. 'I hate having my picture taken,' the TV presenter said without a trace of irony. He had a good eye for detail. Once Maurice had Christian and I roughly in the frame, Dan would adjust the positioning – draping Christian's arm around my shoulders, snuggling my head into his chest, ordering the pair of us to look at each other. 'Not the camera!'

'This is silly,' Christian complained, embarrassed by the fuss and the grins from passing holidaymakers.

'No, it isn't. It will make a lovely snap.'

'I do NOT take snaps,' Maurice said.

Dan raised his eyes to heaven. 'And, for God's sake, Lee, smile. Look as if you're enjoying yourself.'

And, bizarrely, I was.

Florence marked a turning point – cuddling Christian for the camera, I knew Mike was well and truly behind me. And the next time I 'fell' in love it would be with someone who was his own man and not somebody else's.

217

Chapter Sixty-Four

Teri

I never thought I'd say it, but I was not looking forward to that summer's vacation. For a start, I hadn't any money apart from my salary. Dad hadn't sent a cheque – again. I'll have to ring him, I thought, and chase it up. And so I couldn't really afford to go anywhere; Declan didn't seem interested in any of the long weekends or days out I suggested, in fact, since our trip to the Lakes, he'd been distinctly chilly and only been round to the flat once or twice for a bit of hot sex, which, given the mood he was in, was still surprisingly good. We could lose ourselves in our passion, I suppose. But he rarely stayed overnight and never arranged when we were going to meet again. I'd just get a text saying something like 'U free 2nite?' and, as there was very little else going on in my life, I texted back 'Yes.'

I'm not proud of that either.

And another thing, there was no one about. Most of the lecturers had buggered off to their cottages in Cornwall or some rustic gîte in rural France, and there was nothing to do. God, I was so bored. And angry, if you want to know. Usually, I'd been able to rely on Lee, but she let me down big time and I didn't know what she was playing at.

It's not that she wasn't around to meet for lunch or do a spot of shopping – it's that she'd been going off on ludicrous holidays with my ex-husband. I mean, for goodness' sake. Where does she get off? And what the hell was either of them doing on a damn cookery holiday?

Because Dan and I still texted each other every now and then, I knew he was going to Tuscany, but he hadn't elaborated so I imagined it would be for the galleries and architecture. For a nano second I thought about offering to go with him, but that was when I still thought I could persuade Declan to take a holiday with me, and decided Dan would be better off on his own.

I couldn't believe it when Lee told me she was off to Tuscany too but on a walking and cooking holiday. 'Cooking. You?' I said. 'You'd be far better off meeting some gorgeous Spanish chef and getting him to teach you how to light your grill.'

'Ah,' Lee replied, 'that didn't work out so well for you, did it? If I remember rightly, didn't his wife show up once cuddly Carlos taught you all you needed to be a galley slave?'

'Hah,' I laughed. 'I'd got bored of him by then.' It had been after I dumped Jazz, the rock singer, and left the tediously boring teacher training college that I met Carlos. I'd been staying in Greece on the island of Paxos and met up with Vasillis, the son of a tavern owner. He spent so much time showing me the delights of the Ionian islands when he should have been working in Papa's place, that Mama – finding us brushing up Anglo-Greco relations in an olive grove – turned nasty. I caught the first boat taxi back to Corfu where, instead of hopping on the first flight out of there, I met up with some yachties in a bar on the waterfront looking for crew.

'Can you cook?' one of them asked.

'Cook? Me? Sure,' I lied. How difficult could it be?

Every two weeks we picked up a new set of clients from the northern tip of Cephalonia for a fortnight's sailing, swimming and snorkelling. I stayed with the crew for six months and learned to cook along the way thanks to the chef, Carlos, whose body was tanned and taut, and who taught me a hundred and one things to do with eggs in the galley and some nifty tricks in the cabin bunk too.

It was only as we sailed back into Corfu to drop off some clients that Carlos revealed he hadn't been entirely straight with me. His wife was flying in to join him on the next voyage. She flew in. I flew out. And found myself in London with no job, no home, no anything except a suntan and a book full of meal ideas for the high seas.

I enrolled on a short catering course, did some cheffing here and there, but really, I was drifting. It's amazing how long you can drift so it was several years before I got a grip and headed back to my old home town.

And now Lee was telling me about her plans for a cooking and walking holiday. I tried to put her off. Heavens, she wouldn't be able to keep up with all those hairy ramblers, and hadn't my little adventure up one of the highest mountains in England put her off?

But, no. She was going.

Very magnanimously I offered to take her to the airport for her flight to Heathrow and nearly changed my mind when I realised she needed picking up at 4am. I was going to tell her about Declan's latest shenanigans but, to be honest, I didn't really want to talk to her about him. I wasn't sure what was happening and I knew she disapproved. so it was sometimes better to cut her off if she mentioned the subject. Besides which, we were both so tired at that time in the morning, we hardly spoke at all.

'Chill,' I said, 'and look out for Dan.'

She seemed genuinely puzzled. 'Dan?'

'Yes, he's holidaying in Tuscany – it's very popular with these media types,' I said. It was a joke. I never for a minute imagined Lee and Dan would meet up, far less end up on the same holiday. Far less become best buddies.

It's typical of both of them: bugger off and enjoy themselves while I'm having such a rotten time.

Right, I thought. I'm going to enjoy myself. It was nearly midday and I'd spent the morning loafing around feeling miserable. I'll go check out the new John Lewis store on the outskirts of town and have a wonderful afternoon shopping. Would my credit card stand it? Oh blow it, a girl's got to enjoy herself. I called in at a garage to fill up with diesel and started driving towards the ring road when I realised I was passing the dull grey concrete block that contained the throbbing news-gathering offices of the Evening Leader. I'd never been inside; Declan always warned me off.

'It's a miserable, soul-destroying place with no windows. The newsroom is a vast, open-plan arrangement, like an aircraft hangar, where sad-looking gits spend their days staring at their computer screens.'

'You make it sound so welcoming,' I said.

'Let me tell you, it's not,' he said.

There's a small visitors' car park at the front of the building and, on what instinct I don't know, I pulled in and parked up. I turned off the engine and sat, looking at the double glass doors with 'Evening Leader' etched in large lettering on the front. Through the glass I made out a long counter behind which stood a couple of women serving, presumably, readers who'd gone in to place an ad. I'd been surprised when Declan told me the Leader still operated a 'front door' policy for the public when a lot of newspapers handled ads digitally. 'We like to see the whites of their eyes,' he said.

One of the glass doors swung open inwards and an elderly woman, holding her long, tweed coat tightly closed at the front, stepped out having, presumably, just placed an appeal for her lost cat. Right behind her came a young girl with long hair, which she flicked back from her face as she stepped, laughing, into the paved area between the doors and the car park. Now, who did she remind me of? Cassie! Yes, it was definitely her – last seen at the tyre factory fire. Behind her came a youngish looking man, someone I assumed was another reporter. And then Declan. I gasped in surprise. Why was I surprised? It was lunchtime. They were off for lunch. But then the youngish man waved and strode off, and Declan reached out and put his arm around Cassie's shoulders and steered her away in the opposite direction. I watched as they walked up the road, away from the car park and disappeared around the corner. Oh for goodness' sake, I told myself. You are not going to start this again. You are not going to follow them. You are not going to do this sort of thing. Besides which, it's all perfectly innocent. She's a junior reporter; he's her boss. They are probably working on a story together.

Even so, I got out of my car, locked it, and marched quickly, following them. When I got to the corner, I could see the road stretching ahead but no sign of the two of them. There was a pub, The Old Duke, on the left, and I strode up to the first window and looked in. Declan leant on the bar with Cassie beside him. It was a lunchtime drink for two colleagues. A working lunch. Innocent. So why did Declan still have his arm around her, and why was she giggling so much?

When Lee got back from her holiday, I decided not to tell her about the illicit lunchtime drink incident because I didn't want her thinking I was spying on Declan. But she asked how the May Ball had gone, and I explained how David and I had both got drunk and been a bit silly before I sent him packing.

'David doesn't drink,' she said. It crossed my mind to ask her how she knew that, but I had more to say.

'Anyway, off David goes with his friends and then Mike Orme came to my rescue.' Lee looked interested and quizzical at the same time.

I didn't go into detail with her, but it's true. Mike had seen the whole thing and came over, marched me to the foyer from where he called a taxi to take me home. My knight in a shiny blue jacket and ill-matching trousers.

Nor did I tell Lee that the following Monday I had to go into uni to deliver some mark sheets. She would have tutted that I'd left it late. While we do all the marking and inputting of results online via a slow-moving and electronically-clanking system called MarkItIn, for some reason the mark sheets themselves had to be signed by individual lecturers and handed in personally. So much for the paperless society. Admittedly, the mark sheets should've been in earlier to give the admin team time to collate them and let the undergrads know their final scores, but I'd been so miserable I hadn't had the energy to mark anything. I must say, when I logged into the system and realised how many essays there were, I panicked. I whizzed through each one, adding the odd comment here and there to make it look as though someone had read the stuff and gave each one a mark I felt roughly suited whichever student the work belonged to. When it came to David Greenspan's essay I hovered between a good First and a poor Third and ended up giving him a decent 2:1.

I went up the carpeted corridor that contained Peter Heron and Mike Orme's offices and the admin department. There were four girls working in admin with Chrissie, and they all looked in my direction as I entered. I noticed a plastic container of chocolate and cream eclairs open on one of the desks, pointed at them and laughed. 'Forever on the hips, girls,' I said, but their expressions were icy. I tried again with a cheerful 'Here you go...' and waved the mark sheets.

Chrissie stood up, and unsmiling, walked over and took them. 'We've been waiting for these,' she said. I love a person who feels they have been wronged; they adopt this self-righteous tone of tolerance.

'Well they're here now,' I said.

'Yes, but we've collated all the other marks – apart from yours – and we're going to have to stay late tonight redoing everything.' I remember now. Didn't she try to get off with Declan at some soiree or other? She obviously knew about Declan and me and she was jealous.

'Good luck,' I said, leaving the office, relieved that all my academic responsibilities had been dealt with until September – and bumped straight into David Greenspan. 'Hi, David,' I said. 'I'm glad I've bumped into you. Can we have a little chat?' He shrugged and nodded and, before he had a chance to retract, I grabbed his hand and pulled him along to the far end of the corridor where there was a leather couch and coffee table at which visitors sat while waiting for their appointment with Peter or Mike, and where Chrissie and her mates sometimes sat to have their sandwiches and, no doubt, eclairs.

I sat down and pulled David down beside me. 'I'm so sorry about the other night...' I began.

'Look, Teri, it's okay,' he said. 'You'd had a bit too much to drink...it happens...'

'No, listen,' I said. 'I've been going through it since my divorce and everything and, well, I've been feeling down, and you cheer me up. I know you like me, and I'm not that much older than you and...'

'Teri,' he interrupted. 'I do like you, honest. Who wouldn't? But you're not my type. I have a girlfriend...Let's just leave it at that.'

'What do you mean, leave it at that? David,' I said, bristling, 'I'm sitting here telling you I *like* you, and I think we could be good for each other...'

He stood. I looked up and, seeing the exasperated expression on his face, something inside me broke. I rose to face him and said rather more loudly than I had intended, 'David, I have to warn you that I've just marked one of your final Level 1 essays, but the mark can be changed. It could be a fail...' Even I knew as I said it that I'd gone too far.

'Oh, do your worst,' he said. 'You're pathetic.'

And as he strode off back down the corridor to the admin office, there was Chrissie, standing in the open admin doorway looking at me with a knowing smile on her face.

Chapter Sixty-Five

Lee

The last night of the holiday was a little sad – after dinner the whole group, plus Myrtle, congregated around a couple of tables in the hotel garden and reminisced about our adventures. One or two people pulled out diaries and address books and made empty promises to keep in touch. Not Jean. 'I've had a lovely time, dear,' she said, 'and I've enjoyed getting to know you, but there's no point exchanging addresses. Holiday friendships are like holiday romances. Best packed away with the suntan lotion.'

I wondered if this was an oblique reference to me and Christian. I hoped not.

Maurice, unsurprisingly, was determined to keep in touch with all and sundry. He went methodically around the group and painstakingly collected home addresses, phone numbers, mobile and landline, and email addresses (work and home) too.

Dan simply handed me his mobile and told me to add my number to his contacts book.

'Do you want Christian's number too?' I asked.

He gave me an odd little look. 'I doubt we'll see much of him back home,' he said.

I looked surprised. 'But we've had such fun together.'

He sipped his glass of wine and grinned. 'There's fun and there's fun,' he said.

Whatever did he mean?

The flight home was strange. We boarded the aircraft as a coherent group and alighted as individuals. Passport control was a bit rushed – I got separated from Christian, Maurice and Dan in the queue, and though I managed to say a quick goodbye to Jean and Sid, my connecting flight was already being called, and I didn't have time to wait for the others who all had train connections. I felt a bit sad, but even as I was fastening my seatbelt on the next leg of the journey a text message from Dan pinged into my inbox. 'Bon voyage,' it said. Two other texts, one from Maurice and one from Christian followed swiftly. 'See you soon,' Maurice said. 'Fancy a night at the opera?' Christian asked.

Well, no, I didn't. But I did want to see him again. 'Sure,' I texted back. Silly Dan, he'd got Christian all wrong.

Teri was waiting for me at the other end. I'd been dying to tell her all my news, but it was clear she was in no mood for idle gossip. No need to ask 'What's wrong?' That long face could mean only one thing: Declan, and the path of true love, was not running to plan. Oh dear.

Chapter Sixty-Six

Teri

'Look, sweetheart,œ Declan said, stretching the word 'sweetheart' into a lazy drawl. Very patronising. 'We are both single people; we're not married; we don't own each other.'

'Yes, but,' I replied, 'we are in a relationship – or so I thought.'

'Hardly a relationship, is it,' he snapped back, 'if you're forever following me, checking up on me?'

'So why do I feel I have to do that?' I demanded. 'You never tell me what you're doing – or who you're doing it with. How can I trust you?'

'Oh sorry,' he said. 'I didn't realise I had to check in with you every day.'

'Don't be so ludicrous.' I rounded on him. 'You don't. But it would help if you were honest with me.'

'Honest? What do you mean?'

'Well, all these other women you're seeing. You tell me you're not seeing anyone else, but you are! Just tell me the truth, Declan, that's all I'm asking.'

'Tell you what? What other women?' He sounded genuinely offended, but for once, his little boy lost look, his defensive reasoning, had no effect on me.

It was a couple of weeks after I'd seen the woman parking up outside his flat in her Mercedes. As I looked at Declan a sudden thought of Dan came

226

into my head, and I felt a tinge of sadness. Dan would never have treated me the way Declan was doing now. Why hadn't I gone on that Christmas holiday with him, even if it had meant taking the wretched daughter along? I would've been with Dan, looked after and cared for. I certainly wouldn't be sitting here now, in my flat on a rare visit from Declan, demanding to know who all these other bloody women were, especially the blonde who, I very much doubted was a work mate. You don't lean out of a window and laugh as you chuck your keys down unless the person below is someone with whom you've done this before.

I'd steeled myself for this visit – demanded he came to see me – and was determined to either sort things out between us or finish it completely. I reeled off facts and dates starting with the awful weekend in March when I kept going back to his flat, filling in with the night of the blighted casserole and his illicit lunchtime soiree with Cassie, and finishing in triumph with the blonde and her bloody Merc.

He just glared at me. Gone was the sorrowful, pity-me-I'm-only-an-innocent-puppy look and in its place, a look, not of anger at having been caught out, but of rebellious determination. Triumph, almost. He didn't even try to reach out and touch me, and I was glad, because what I didn't want to do was listen to his pathetic excuses, forgive him and melt into his arms. Lee thinks I'm completely clueless sometimes, but on this occasion, I knew exactly what I had to do, and, I thought, Lee is going to be proud of me. Although what it had to do with her, I wasn't sure, given she hardly had any time for me. Last time we spoke she was crowing about finally getting over Mike – getting over Mike! God. She should never have got into bed with that idiot in the first place. But now it's all Christian, Christian, Christian. I must say, though, she's pulled a stunner there. He's not half bad and, if I hadn't been so wrapped up in the Declan situation – and, of course, if Lee hadn't been going out with him – I could've quite fancied Christian myself.

Perhaps if things didn't work out between him and Lee…?

But no, I had the Declan situation to sort out, and while I was trying to be articulate and reasonable, Declan shook his head in a sorrowfully pitying way as though I was the one at fault and he was trying to be patient with me. That made me see red. He was trying to say he'd already explained about the March weekend and the night of the casserole; the drink with Cassie had been just that – a drink; and the blonde – well, she was a secretary at the Leader who'd been delivering something…

It was pathetic. He was pathetic. Did he honestly think I was going to believe this crap?

'Oh, for God's sake, Declan,' I shouted. 'Do you think I'm absolutely stupid?' And then I had some sort of out-of-body experience and wasn't really there saying what I was saying as I leapt to my feet to look down on him sitting on the sofa, staring up at me intently, defiantly. I shouted a lot of things mainly to do with him being a two-timing, lying bastard who took what he wanted and used people, then just threw them away. The defiance bled from his face and he tried to interject, but I hammered on, shouting and swearing, tossing my head in rage, throwing my arms in the air until finally my heart pounded. Light-headed, my whole body burned, and if I didn't do something soon, I would slump on to the sofa, crying. So with one almighty effort I screamed at him, 'FUCKING well get out of my FUCKING life you FUCKING moronic bastard.' And I stretched out my left arm to indicate the door, Declan rose wearily from the sofa and, with head low, he walked slowly, quietly – and, I like to think, shame-facedly – out of the room, out of my flat and out of my life.

Well, that last bit was a bit dramatic, but that's how I felt. Only when I heard the flat door close, did I reel round and drop on to the sofa. But I didn't cry. I just sat there, shaking with anger and hurt, and staring at my knees.

Chapter Sixty-Seven

Lee

Perhaps inevitably like all holiday romances, my little thing with Christian didn't survive our homecoming. In theory, it might've worked – Huddersfield, after all, isn't a million miles from Leeds, but, in practice, it might as well have been. We went on a couple of dates – but it quickly became clear that, apart from walking, we had very little in common. I'm sure it was very kind and thoughtful of him to buy surprise tickets for a gala performance by Calderwood Choral Society, but if he'd asked first he might've saved himself a lot of money. And I'd have been spared one of the most ear-shatteringly awful evenings of my life. Definitely not my cup of tea.

I wasn't over-keen on our night at the opera either. I've nothing against Northern Dales Opera per se – but my God! They do make a dreadful racket.

And the best thing about our evening watching the last avant-garde offering from the Ptarmigan Ballet Company was Teri's surprised appreciation of my new beau. 'Ey up, lass,' she drawled in a mock Yorkshire accent when we bumped into her in the foyer. 'What have we here?' And she gave me a knowing little wink as if to say 'You're batting above your weight with this one.'

No, Christian was aesthetically pleasing – not on a par with David Greenspan perhaps, although close – but on his home turf the dry humour that had been so amusing in Tuscany turned out to be little more than

Scandinavian pedantry. And I didn't think I could take very many more nights at the opera. Or anywhere else even remotely highbrow for that matter. I might be an academic with a string of erudite papers to my name, but that didn't mean I was a cultural snob. In fact, quite the reverse. Give me *Spiderman the Movie* over *Die Fledermaus* any day.

So, more or less by mutual consent, we downgraded our relationship – in other words, we made a couple of half-hearted efforts to arrange to see a film or visit to the theatre but, sadly, our diaries were incompatible, and gradually we became just friends. In fact, the last time we spoke, Maurice had come up to stay with Dan for a long weekend, and we'd invited Christian to join the three of us for a walk on Ilkley Moor. He declined, which was a shame, but we didn't really miss him – turned out the real chemistry had been between the three of us. We had a lovely walk and talked almost non-stop – Maurice was so droll and funny – and afterwards we had dinner at a little Italian trattoria that Dan said had been a favourite of his and Teri's. He looked a little sad when he said that.

'Do you miss her?'

He sighed deeply. 'Not as much now.'

Poor Dan. I'd never really experienced the sort of passion he and Teri shared.

He tried to explain. 'She's so like...' His voice trailed off and he appeared lost in thought. 'Quicksilver,' he said eventually.

Quicksilver?

'Mmm – sort of. Captivating, I suppose, and fascinating and ethereal and....'

Ethereal? I stifled a giggle. I'd heard Teri called many things in her life and, granted, she was slim and graceful, and, at a pinch, might be described as delicate and light. But other-wordly? No, definitely not. I've never met anyone more grounded in the here and now. But, he was so serious and trying so hard to find the right words, I just felt unbearably sorry for him. He must've really loved her.

'Damned hard work, though!'

What?

'Oh, I know you two are still good friends, and you wouldn't hear a word against her. But, don't you sometimes think she can be a little self-centred?'

A little self-centred? Are we talking about the same woman here?

He was definitely in a reminiscing mood. 'And she could be very sharp tongued.'

Had to agree with that.

'And very intolerant.'

She could, indeed.

'Not to say downright nasty if she didn't get her own way.'

This conversation wasn't going the way I'd expected at all.

Maurice interrupted. 'She doesn't sound like a very nice person.' I jumped in surprise – I'd forgotten he was there. Neither of us said anything. I thought Dan ought to be the one to contradict Maurice, and I suppose he thought it was up to me.

'Actually,' Dan said, 'the first time we met, it was Lee I had my eye on.'

What!

He smiled at me. 'You had such a lovely sense of humour, and I thought it was really kind, and smart, of you to make a joke to save your friend embarrassment.'

Maurice looked puzzled. 'So why on earth did you end up with the other woman?'

'Dunno.' Dan shrugged. 'You tell me. I suppose I was flattered. I thought Teri was way out of my league.'

And I wasn't, of course. Thanks for the compliment. It's okay me knowing Teri is ten times more attractive than I'll ever be, but don't rub my nose in it.

'I couldn't believe my luck at first,' Dan said.

'Lucky escape,' I interjected.

'Eh? Pardon?' Dan asked.

'If Teri hadn't lured you away, you might have ended up with me. Wouldn't that have been terrible?'

Yes, you're right. I was feeling hurt. And, why shouldn't I be? Okay, at the time I wasn't in the market for romance, but there was no need for him to make it so clear he thought he'd struck gold.

Thank God for Maurice. 'I don't see how it was a lucky escape,' he said. 'Sounds like the most awful bad luck.'

'You're right,' Dan said. 'I think I began to suspect even before the wedding that we weren't quite right for each other.'

So, why the hell did you marry her? Poor Teri – she'd really been given a bum's rush. 'It wasn't really very kind or smart of you to go ahead and get married if you were having doubts.' I deliberately echoed his earlier words.

'I know,' he acknowledged. 'But Teri can be quite overwhelming, and I suppose I just allowed myself to be carried along. It was quite exciting at the time. And Teri can be quite forceful when she sets her mind on something.'

Not so forceful after all – she'd had to give up her dream wedding for a run-of-the-mill register office do.

'It sounds clichéd,' he said. 'But she swept me off my feet.'

He was right – it did sound clichéd.

'Dumb too,' Maurice said, who'd been following the conversation with interest.

Absolutely, I thought. Good old Maurice.

'know,' Dan agreed. 'But it wasn't until after the wedding that I really began to wonder if I'd done the right thing. She wasn't very nice to Victoria, you know?'

Well, I did, of course, but Maurice didn't – though he wasn't surprised, he said.

'I'm sure she dropped the idea of a tropical beach wedding because she didn't want Victoria to come on honeymoon.'

'Can hardly blame her for that,' Maurice butted in.

He'd taken the words right out of my mouth.

Dan ignored him. 'I've always rather liked the idea of getting married somewhere sunny and exotic. A simple ceremony, surrounded by family and friends. Golden sands. A cooling sea breeze. The sun setting over a pale turquoise sky. Waves lapping.'

Goodness, the man was an old-fashioned romantic.

'Sounds like a load of twaddle to me,' Maurice said. 'There'd be sand everywhere, and I bet the wind would be blowing a gale. And, when you got home, all the nearest and dearest who weren't invited would have your guts for garters.'

Couldn't have put it better myself.

Dan looked a little pained. 'Well, I definitely didn't want a repeat of my first wedding. It was the most elaborate and costly shindig it's ever been my misfortune to attend. And I picked up the tab for most of it because neither my parents nor Sara's had two ha'pennies to rub together.'

He gave a theatrical shudder. 'And two of the twelve white doves Sara insisted should be released as we emerged from the church got themselves electrocuted. One of them nearly knocked the best man for six as it dropped to the ground.'

'You don't seem to have had much luck with the marrying lark,' I said.

An understatement.

'Next time, I'm going to do it differently,' he promised. And looked at me.

Now, whatever was that all about?

Chapter Sixty-Eight

Teri

I blame Dan. If he'd listened to me and tried to understand what I was saying, we'd never have got divorced. But he wouldn't listen, would he? If he'd only opened his eyes to what that little vixen of a daughter of his was doing, he'd have seen the light. That little she-devil broke up our marriage. Well, I hope she's satisfied. If it hadn't been for her, Dan and I would still be together. And if Dan had only considered me – his wife – and not treated me so inconsiderately, I wouldn't have felt the need to go off with Declan.

And I blame Declan. If he'd behaved responsibly instead of going off with every other woman he saw, we could've made a go of it. But, no. Any lips on sticks in a skirt and whoosh. Can't keep his prick in his pants. I wouldn't mind, but he's the one who started it all. 'I love you, Teri...I can't live without you, Teri...' If he felt like that why the hell did he feel the need to go off? Typical bloody man. And if Declan'd come to the May Ball with me, like I asked, the business with Greenspan wouldn't have happened. And what was wrong with that little creep? Immature pseudo-intellectual little dickhead who couldn't see a good thing when it happened.

And why the hell did Lee go swanning off on her ridiculous cooking holiday? When she got back she couldn't stop wittering about her new friends, and Dan, of course. Dan this...Christian that...Maurice the other...blah, blah, blah. She should've been here. God! Talk about selfish bastards. I don't know why I wasted my time with the lot of them.

Chapter Sixty-Nine

Lee

I met up again with Dan and Maurice for Sunday lunch. L'homme-vert. Very expensive. Silver service. And waiters with faux French accents.

'Didn't you used to take Teri here?' I asked.

'No,' Dan said. 'I booked a table once, but we had to cry off.'

He caught my eye – and I remembered. Oh, yes, Teri hadn't been best pleased.

'I'm sure you took her somewhere equally nice,' I said.

'Most definitely – she talked about it for ages afterwards.' And we both roared with laughter.

Maurice looked puzzled. 'What's the joke?'

'Nothing, nothing. It's not really funny at all.' Dan frowned. 'Water under the bridge.'

Okay – if you say so.

Maurice was studying the menu. 'What's the difference between chicken liver parfait and chicken pâté?'

I looked at Dan. 'You're the gourmet.'

'About five quid,' he quipped. 'You'd get pâté in a cheap and cheerful bistro and parfait in a banged-up-to-the-nines brasserie.'

'And potted meat in a greasy spoon,' I added. And we both roared with laughter again. Why? I don't know – the joke wasn't especially funny, but somehow I felt in a giggly mood.

Maurice was not amused. 'You two are being silly.'

'All right,' Dan said. 'I'll be serious. Lee, do you like ten-pin bowling?'

Maurice gave him a dirty look. 'How's that being serious?'

We ignored him. 'No,' I said. 'I don't like *like* ten-pin bowling...'

'Now you're not even making sense,' Maurice interrupted.

'But I do like ten-pin bowling with my nephew Ritchie. I love his excited little face when he scores a strike.'

'And I bet you don't mind burger and chips in the cafe afterwards.'

'Actually, I'd rather not. But Ritchie does – so we usually do.'

'Exactly,' Dan said as if he'd proved a point.

'Still not making sense,' Maurice said.

Oh, but I think he was. For possibly the first time in my life I was being compared to Teri – and coming out on top. I could get to like this.

Afterwards, Dan suggested driving across to Westchester. Maurice should see the new internationally acclaimed museum and sculpture gallery, he said. But Maurice, who'd rambled all over Europe, had barely ventured north of Watford Gap and was nervous about leaving the comparative safety of our metropolis. 'Isn't it a bit rough there?' he asked.

Whatever gave him that idea?

'I'm sure there was something on your programme last night about an illegal dog fight near Westchester.'

'That was in East Grimley,' Dan said. 'Different class of people altogether in Westchester.'

I'd seen the same news item too – and decided against pointing out that two of the three pit bull breeders who'd been arrested were Westchester born and bred. Although I did suggest the sort of people who went in for dog fighting tended not to be arty types and were most unlikely to be counted among the million or so visitors who'd visited the museum since it opened.

But Maurice said he got car sick after a big lunch – the wimp – and instead we made the short journey to the nearby ancestral home of the local gentry and strolled around the rhododendron gardens for a couple of hours until it was time for his train back to London.

'Be careful,' Dan warned him as we waved goodbye at the ticket barrier.

'Careful? Why?'

'The first stop is Westchester.'

Maurice texted when he got back to London. He'd had a terrible journey, he said. Having secured a front-facing corner seat with a table, he was looking forward to a quiet couple of hours working on the Sunday Telegraph crossword when a group of postal workers boarded the train at Doncaster. They were heading for the England vs India test match at Lord's the next day and, having spent the afternoon in the pub, were in party mood. Maurice, it appeared, did not share their good cheer and several times declined their hospitable offer of a can of lager from one of the several carrier bags now piled on their shared table.

'They kept calling me cock,' he texted.

'It's a term of endearment,' I texted back.

'No, it isn't,' he replied. 'It's a very rude word. And I didn't get to finish my crossword.'

Clearly, the north was a foreign country.

I showed Dan the message – he'd suggested a drink after we'd seen Maurice on his way and, more than two and a half hours later, we were still sharing a communal table and bench in the low ceiling, floor-boarded basement of a wonderful bar and charcuterie round the corner from the railway station. It's one of the city's lesser known gems, although, these days, since a critic in one of the Sunday supplements gave it a big thumbs up, it's not quite such a well-kept secret. Tonight the place was heaving, and the noise and banter from the other punters was so loud it was almost impossible to hear oneself think – let alone whatever it was Dan had just said.

'Pardon?' I leaned closer. 'I can't hear you.'

He leaned closer too and, brushing my hair aside, almost bellowed in my ear. 'Fancy ten-pin bowling?'

And the chatter, which had been rising and falling all evening, did what chatter always does at such moments and dropped several decibels.

The silence was deafening and the old fellow nursing a Belgian beer bottle on the bench opposite winked. 'Great chat up line, mate.'

Dan blushed and looked away.

'I thought it might be fun – if you're free next Saturday.'

Damn! 'I can't,' I said. 'I'm looking after my niece and nephew – their mum and dad are going to York races. I've got the kids all day and

237

overnight as well.'

'Bring them along,' Dan said. 'It'll be fun.'

Fun? He hadn't met Fee, who was toddling around now and turning into a little terror. 'I don't know...'

'I like small children,' he insisted.

You do? Even ones you've never met before? You're mad.

'Go on, love.' The old fellow raised his bottle in Dan's direction. 'Can't you see he's smitten?'

Who's mad now?

I demurred at first – the combination of me, the region's premier autocue-reading media tart (his words, not mine), a ten-year-old and a nearly two-year-old seemed a recipe made in hell.

But both Dan and the Belgian beer bloke were adamant.

'Give him a break,' the beer bloke insisted.

'I was a little boy once,' Dan said.

What's that got to do with it?

In the end, I capitulated. It was the peck on the cheek as we left the bar that did it. And the warm hand that grasped mine as we stepped in the street.

'I'd better hold your hand,' Dan said.

Why?

'The Sunday supplement critic who recommended this place said this street was only used by those trying to leave town or locate someone to mug.'

'When did he say that?'

'Didn't you read his review? It was mostly complimentary. But he was a bit rude about this part of the city.'

'Oh,' I said. And I didn't need to tell Dan that 'Oh' meant, yes, hold my hand, and yes, meet me at the bowling alley.

Of course, I'd forgotten about Teri.

Chapter Seventy

Teri

There's some software on the university central computer system called LookItUp that allows lecturers and admin staff to gain access to individual student's personal details – home addresses, next-of-kin, medical history, that sort of thing. If you were a personal tutor – and we were each allocated a certain number of Level 1 students to whom we had to act in this capacity; for instance, helping them to settle into university and cope with homesickness – you were automatically given two passwords. One was to gain entry to LookItUp, and the second was specific to a particular student. We all had the initial password to access LookItUp but, under the Data Protection Act, University Rule Securities or some privacy nonsense like that, you weren't allowed the second password unless that individual student was one of your personal tutees. David Greenspan hadn't been on my personal tutee list and, as a reasonably mature student, I'm not entirely sure he would've needed a personal tutor to help him cope anyway. I did, however, have his mobile phone number because he was in one of my tutorial groups, and one way of keeping in touch with those I taught directly was to text them. So, shortly after my carpeted corridor debacle with him in May, I texted David, ostensibly to apologise. I'm not sure if I had any ulterior motives at the time, but there is something about being snubbed by a man that doesn't sit easy with me, and I was determined to get back on to – if nothing else – a level footing with him.

'Hi. Just wantd 2 apolgse. How u doing?' I texted. But he didn't reply. So I rang him. And the phone went on to voicemail. So I left a message. 'Hi, David. Hope you got my text okay. I just wanted to apologise for being such a prat. Can I buy you a drink to show there are no hard feelings? Ring me back.' He didn't ring back.

I left it a few weeks, but then popped into uni. Universities are a bit like the Marie Celeste during the summer vacation given there are no students other than those attending summer schools, and very few staff other than those in admin.

It was lunchtime, and I hovered at the end of the carpeted corridor in the hope Chrissie and her admin mates weren't going to assemble their fat little bums on the sofas to eat their carefully prepared home-packed plastic tubs of salad preferring instead to head off into town where they could have some proper food by way of a long lunch at the local pizza place. And as luck would have it, all was quiet and I was able to nip into the office without having to think up an excuse as to why I was there. The only person on guard was a little work experience girl who looked up nervously as I entered.

'Oh, hi,' I said. 'I need to get in touch with one of my students and my computer's packed up at home. Can I use one of yours? Oh, by the way, save me looking it up, have you the password for LookItUp as I've left my address book behind?'

'Er,' she said. 'I'm not sure I can...'

'Oh, don't worry, I'll use this one,' I said, plonking myself down at Chrissie's desk, switching the machine on and logging in as quickly as the very slow, antiquated system would allow. 'Now, the password?' I said, looking up expectantly. The little love pulled a file from her drawer, opened it and read out the main password. I entered the system. 'Ah, damn,' I said, thinking how convincing an actress I would make. 'I've forgotten David's password. Have you got the one for Greenspan D?'

'Oh, I'm not supposed to...'

'It's okay, love,' I reassured her. 'I just need something quickly and then I'll be gone.' She wilted in the face of my authority and read out the password to David's personal file. I keyed it in and up popped everything I needed to know. Would you believe it? There was an address on Leyland

Road – Number 22, Flat 4. He lived just a few doors down from Declan. All those times I was round there, and I'd never known Gorgeous Greenspan lived just a few yards away. I made a note of the address, exited LookItUp, and then remembered to log off and shut down the computer. That was clever of me: I didn't fancy Chrissie coming back and discovering I'd been using her PC.

It wasn't an entirely proud moment when I realised I was driving slowly up and down Leyland Road once again. The last time had been trying to find out what Declan was up to. This time I was looking for an altogether younger model. I parked the car, walked up to the front door of Number 22, looked at a list of names with separate buttons against each of them, saw Greenspan, and pressed. It was one of those intercom systems and shortly after my buzz, I heard David's voice saying 'Hello?'

'Hi, David. It's me. Teri. Can I have a word?' He should've responded by saying something like 'Oh, hi. Yes, come on up' and pressing the buzzer that would let me in, but he didn't say anything at all and he clearly didn't press the entry buzzer. 'David?' I queried.

Then he spoke. 'Look Teri, whatever it is you want, can you please just forget it.'

'But I only wanted to apologise.'

'I don't want or need your apology. Just, please, leave me alone.'

'Oh come on, David. I only want to talk.'

'I'm sorry, Teri…' Just then the front door swung open and a resident emerged. I stepped forward, through the door and into the foyer. Ahead of me was a flight of stairs, and I assumed, rightly, that Flat 4 was on the first floor. Sure enough, at the top of the first flight was a battered-looking brown door with the number '4' roughly scrawled in white paint. I knocked. If a door can open angrily, this one did.

'What the fuck?' David glared at me.

'Like I said,' I said, 'I've come to apologise. You weren't answering my messages, so I thought I'd better come to check you were all right.'

'I did get your messages,' he retorted. 'But I chose to ignore them. Teri, can't you get the picture? How can I put this? I'm not interested. I don't fancy you. I don't want us to be friends. I wish you would just fuck off and leave me alone.' And he slammed the door in my face.

241

Chapter Seventy-One

Lee

The days leading up to what I hardly dared think of as my 'date' with Dan were fraught with tension. Logically, there was no reason why Teri should object – she was the one who'd filed for divorce after all. Who was I trying to kid? Teri would blow a gasket. Just because she'd dumped Dan didn't mean she'd look kindly on me muscling in. Besides, I was breaking the cardinal rule of friendship: hands off a mate's ex. So I cravenly spent the entire week actively avoiding her – which was easy enough since we were now in the close season, waiting for the new academic year to begin. Technically, I was on annual leave, which removed the possibility of bumping into Teri at work, and I carefully screened phone calls, not picking up when she rang.

She left a couple of voicemails, but they were inconsequential, gossipy messages. She was clearly at a bit of a loose end and though, under normal circumstances, I would've enjoyed a long, wine-fuelled lunch while she let off steam, but not right now. Once, when I popped to the supermarket for a few essentials, I spotted her browsing through a copy of Harper's Bazaar in the periodicals aisle. I dumped my basket and fled. Which was a bit of a nuisance, because I then had to drive to the Sainsbury's Local at the petrol station near the university, and they were clean out of Muscadet so I had to settle for Pinot Grigio. And, yes, I know it serves me right – and it's a hard life when you have to make do with Pinot Grigio – but what would you have done? She'd have been bound to ask about my plans for the weekend – one of her voicemails had suggested lunch at Romilee's in Harrogate – and, even if I fudged and said I was looking after Ritchie and Fee, she'd probably guess I was hiding something. She always does. She can read me like a book.

Damn her!

When I got home, another voicemail was waiting. Teri again.

'Lee, sorry. Change of plans. Can't do Romilee's after all. Something's come up. Can't tell you now, but watch this space.'

Phew! That was me off the hook. But the ambiguous message could mean only one thing – another man was on the horizon.

Felicity and Charles dropped the children off at my house just before noon. We had a light lunch, then Fee had a nap and Ritchie settled himself at my PC and spent a couple of hours saving the world from prehistoric monsters, vampires and extra-terrestrials with two heads and multiple arms. He wasn't best pleased when I told him a friend of mine was planning to join us at the bowling alley.

'It's bad enough having to bring Fee,' he said with one eye still on his computer game. And he wasn't over-impressed when I played what I thought would be a trump card.

'He's off the telly.' No, the only acceptable him-off-the-telly in Ritchie's eyes was either a soccer presenter or a motor racing commentator. And, once it was clear Dan was neither, his status dive-bombed. Still, Ritchie accepted the inevitable and went back to saving the world. And I attempted to while away the time with a book. I might as well have tried to fly to the moon; I could barely keep my eyes off the clock. What time should we leave? Should I wake Fee?

'Don't,' advised Ritchie. 'She's grumpy as hell if you wake her up before she's ready.'

'Don't swear,' I said.

And Fee carried on snoring in her buggy in the hallway – Ritchie had pushed her out there because, he said, she was disturbing his concentration – and I carried on trying to read and the clock crept slow as a snail and the butterflies in my tummy danced a clog dance.

At last – long, long last – Fee, who'd been grizzly earlier, woke sunny and refreshed, so, once I'd changed her nappy and cleaned her up – ugh! – the three of us got into the car and headed for the bowling alley.

I suppose parents take the packhorse element of travelling even very short distances with small children for granted. But, for me, it was a bit like a poorly-executed military operation – I struggled to get Fee's car seat fastened properly and, then, once it was secure-ish, I struggled to manhandle Fee into it and, in the end, almost drove off with her baby bag, change of clothes and emergency toys and rations still sitting on the roof. Thank God for Ritchie! After several pantomime

minutes, he elbowed me aside and, clunk-click, the seat was safely secured, and, another clunk-click, and Fee was also securely stowed. And, just as I turned the ignition, he remembered the baby paraphernalia. Shame he forgot about the baby buggy, which we'd left sitting in the hallway. But never mind, we'd only gone a couple of miles when he reminded me, and if we hadn't then got stuck behind a funeral procession we might've arrived at the bowling alley promptly at 4pm as arranged. He wasn't there. Obviously he'd got fed-up with waiting; we were twenty-five minutes late, after all. I could've cried. I hadn't realised until that moment just how much I'd been looking forward to it.

'Where's your friend?' Ritchie asked.

I shrugged, determined not to spoil his afternoon as well as mine. 'I expect something else cropped up and when we weren't here on time, he had to go.'

'We're not that late,' Ritchie said, looking at his watch and doing some mental arithmetic. I smiled – Ritchie had a somewhat elastic sense of time. 'You'd have waited at least half an hour for him, wouldn't you?' Actually, I'd probably have waited a lot more than half an hour – in fact, if I was being strictly honest, I'd been waiting several years for a nice man like Dan to take me on a date. Even a date with a couple of kids in tow.

But, never mind, we could still enjoy the bowling. Well, Ritchie could enjoy it, I'd go through the motions and Fee would come along for the ride. She was already mesmerised by the flashing lights and blinking noises from the gallery of soft machines banked against the side walls of the entrance lobby.

'Let's pay and get our shoes,' I said, hunting for my purse.

'Lee, I'm so sorry we're late.'

We're late? Who? I looked and standing behind Dan was a young, blonde woman – Victoria.

'It's my fault,' she apologised. 'I missed the bus to Dad's house, and he had to come and pick me up. And then we got stuck behind a funeral procession and Dad, stupidly, followed it all the way to the cemetery, instead of turning off towards the bowling alley.'

'Who are you?' Ritchie asked. He looked at me accusingly. 'You didn't say he was bringing a girl.'

'I wasn't,' Dan said. 'But Victoria wants to be a children's nurse, so she offered to come and help look after Fee.'

'And my friends call me Tory. Nobody calls me Victoria,' she said, giving Dan a filthy look.

'I do,' he protested.

'And I wish you wouldn't.'

'I know what you mean,' Ritchie said. 'My nana always calls me Richard – it's such a sissy name. I pretend not to hear her. But she told my mum I needed to get my hearing tested, and when Mum said there was nothing wrong with my hearing, she dragged me out of footy practice and took me to the doctor's herself.'

Yes, she had. Fliss had been furious. And so had Mammy. The doctor diagnosed a severe case of selective deafness.

'I'd been going to pretend to the doctor I was deaf too,' said Ritchie. 'But then I thought if I did that, there'd be more tests and more tests, and if Dad had to pay for an expensive hearing aid that I didn't really need, he'd be furious.

'And I was really worried that our footy coach would drop me from the squad if he thought I couldn't hear him shouting from the sideline.'

Dan looked at him in awe. 'And does your nana call you Ritchie now?'

'Naw. She still calls me Richard.'

'And, do you still pretend not to hear her?'

'No.' Ritchie's shoulders drooped. 'Dad said I had to stop being rude or he'd ban me from footy.'

'Well, I think he's mean,' Victoria said. 'Parents can be such a pain in the backside.'

'Victoria!'

She gave Dan a cheeky grin, and she and Ritchie swaggered off together towards bowling lane number thirteen.

'Mine's a diet coke,' she said over her shoulder.

'And so's mine,' Ritchie said.

Chapter Seventy-Two

Lee

Until the bowling alley trip, I'd met Victoria perhaps a handful of times, and my view of her had been very much coloured by Teri's one-sided, somewhat biased, opinions. I'd never quite believed she was the devil child of Teri's imaginings but, even if only half the things Teri said about her were true, she was undoubtedly a remarkably spoiled and self-centred young person. How wrong can you be? She was, perhaps, a little young for her age, but she and Ritchie hit it off straight away and Fee, who doesn't take easily to strangers, fell passionately in love, climbing onto her lap and sharing her post-bowling plate of nuggets and chips. Dan watched the pair of them feeding each other fries with a funny look on his face. He looked wishful and pleased at the same time.

'Penny for them?' I asked.

He took my hand and shook his head. 'It's nothing.'

He dropped my hand abruptly as the waitress arrived with another round of drinks. Fizzy stuff for Dan and the kids, and mineral water for me.

'Nice kids, you've got there,' the woman said. 'Makes a change to see a family what likes each other.'

And she was wiping down the next table before we could put her straight.

I *did* like Victoria though, and when Dan said he had to work the following weekend – a regional business conference – and Victoria pouted and said, 'But what about me? Mummy's at a spa all day Saturday,' it seemed perfectly natural to suggest she spend the day with us instead.

'It'll be boring,' I warned, 'but you'll be very welcome.' And when Ritchie added his voice to mine, and Fee slapped a whopping great kiss on her forehead, she accepted gratefully.

She mucked in as if she'd known us forever, elbowing me aside at the supermarket checkout to repack my shopping. 'Lee,' she said, 'put the fridge stuff in one bag and the veg in another. And don't mix store cupboard stuff and toiletries.'

Fliss, who was doing her Saturday big shop with me, raised her eyebrows. 'Bossy boots,' she mouthed. But I noticed she was quite happy to let Victoria play peek-a-boo with Fee, who was holding court in her buggy, while she packed her own shopping. And she didn't mix store cupboard and toiletries or fridge and veg stuff either.

Afterwards we went for ice cream – well, Ritchie and Fee had big chocolate fudge sundaes and Fliss and I sipped polystyrene mugs of tea while Victoria 'helped' Fee with her sundae. Helped is a deliberate euphemism. 'One for you,' she said in a sing-song voice as the spoon followed an aeroplane trail through the air into Fee's open mouth. 'And one for me,' she said as she popped a scoop into her own mouth. Fee giggled delightedly. 'Again, again...'

'Sorry,' Victoria said. 'I'm eating rather a lot of her ice cream.'

'No worries,' Fliss said. 'You need the calories more than this little fatty.' And she tickled Fee's chubby pink feet.

Victoria blushed. 'I'm much better at eating now than I was.'

Startled, Fliss and I exchanged a look of surprise.

'Last week I put on a whole pound,' she said it as if this was something to celebrate.

'And Lee lost another two pounds at her Slimmer's Nation weigh-in,' chipped in Ritchie.

'Slimmer's Nation!'

'Shush, everyone can hear you.' I glared at Ritchie and the family at the neighbouring table, who'd momentarily stopped shovelling fries into their mouths.

'You never told me,' Fliss accused. 'And how do *you* know?' She turned

248

on her son.

'Because I thought he could keep a secret,' I answered.

'I can. I can,' he protested. 'I didn't tell when Tory sicked up her chips. Or when Mummy was sick before breakfast.'

'Ritchie!' It seemed to be his day for letting cats out of bags.

'More drinks all round,' I said. 'Tory come and help me – give Fliss the ice cream. Sounds like she's the one in need of extra sustenance.' And I gave my little sister a meaningful glance.

We joined the counter queue, behind a gaggle of young teens who'd clearly just been released from the matinee performance of the season's mini-blockbuster at the nearby multiplex.

'Don't tell Dad,' Victoria pleaded. 'I hardly ever do it now. And I was on my period, and I had a really, really bad belly ache.' She sniffed. 'I've been trying so hard and Dad...'

'Here.' I held out a paper tissue.

She dabbed at her eyes. The queue inched forward. Every one of the blasted kids was ordering separately and paying with pennies and tuppences from their piggy banks. I dug out my own purse and started counting coins. I needed time to think. 'I can't *not* tell your dad,' I said at last. 'He needs to know.'

'No. No. He doesn't.' She sounded desperate. 'It would just be worrying him when there's nothing to worry about.' The tissue was now a mangled sausage, twisted around her twitching fingers.

'Isn't there?'

'No! I'm cured now.'

'How do I know that?' I felt quite desperate myself. This was the first time the spectre of anorexia had raised its head, and I felt out of my depth. And just a little angry Dan had never mentioned anything. It was like struggling to put the lid back on a can of worms I'd never wanted to open in the first place.

'What do you mean by cured?'

'I keep a photo of Teri next to my bedroom mirror.' Her tone sounded as if she was stating the bleeding obvious when it was about as clear as mud to me. 'It was sort of Dad's idea,' she explained and then stopped – we'd reached the front of the queue. I ordered the drinks and, Slimmer's Nation be damned, some muffins too. I needed a sugar hit if no one else did.

Ritchie grabbed one as if he hadn't seen food in a month of Sundays. 'Yum,' he said, spitting crumbs across the table. 'Thanks Auntie Lee, you're the best,' and he gave a thumbs-up.

Whatever Fliss said to him while we queued didn't seem to have dampened his spirits.

'You and I need to talk,' I said.

'No, we don't,' he replied, 'me and Mum have already talked.'

'Yes, and I need to talk to your mum too.' I looked at Fliss.

'And you and me need to talk,' Victoria said.

'We all need to talk,' Ritchie said. He started to sing in a high-pitched Pidgin Falsetto, 'Happy talk, keep talking happy talk. Talk about things you'd like to do.'

I should never have taken him to see *South Pacific* last Christmas.

Later as we ambled back to the cars, Victoria tucked an arm through mine. 'I wouldn't lie to you, Lee. I am better.'

Fliss, who was pushing the baby buggy on my other side, looked across at her and shoved the buggy in her direction. 'Tory, darling, be a love and strap Fee into her car seat.' She fumbled in her pocket and zapped the keys in the direction of the car. There was a satisfying click. 'It's open,' she said and pulled me back as Ritchie and Victoria raced ahead.

'Take her out for a drive,' she whispered.

Eh?

'Anywhere. Doesn't matter. Just go somewhere this afternoon that involves a long-ish drive. She'll open up in the car. Kids always do.'

I grasped on to the one bit of this statement that made any kind of sense. 'But she's not a kid.'

Fliss harrumphed. 'She's the youngest nineteen-year-old I've ever met.'

True. It was one of the things that struck me last weekend. It was partly why I struggled to understand why Teri had been so intolerant of the child. But perhaps that was it – Teri saw a burgeoning young woman and expected her to behave accordingly. And when she didn't...my musings were interrupted by Victoria. 'What are you two muttering about?' she asked.

'I was just asking Fliss if she fancied a mooch around the new John Lewis store.' Gosh. That was a brilliant piece of improvisation.

'But, I can't,' Fliss said. 'The kids would hate it, and Charles is playing golf this afternoon, so I can't dump them and run.' She smiled affectionately at her son, who looked distinctly unimpressed at the prospect of an afternoon being dragged around the shops. Then his face brightened.

'It's okay,' he said. 'You can go – Dad's not...Ouch!' He squealed. 'Mum, what did you do that for?' He rubbed at the bright red pinch mark where Fliss had grabbed his arm.

'Because Dad *is* playing golf this afternoon,' she said with heavy emphasis and frowned at Ritchie. 'Why don't you go instead, Tory? I'm sure Lee would enjoy the company.'

This was my cue – but I'm afraid I missed it.

Instead, Victoria, who clearly didn't quite buy into the golf charade, gave us both a sceptical look. 'You're plotting something,' she said. 'What?'

Thank God for Ritchie. 'I know,' he shouted. 'Mum probably wants Auntie Lee out of the way this afternoon so she can bake her birthday cake. She's trying to be subtle.' Birthday cake? Since when had Fliss baked birthday cakes for me? 'It's for her surprise party next weekend.' Trust Ritchie to spill all the beans.

Fliss laughed and pushed Victoria in the direction of my car. 'Tory. Lee. Go.'

So we went.

For a Saturday, the traffic was relatively light. However, Fliss and her confident prediction 'she'll open up in the car' proved misplaced.

'I wish I had a sister to plan a surprise birthday party for me,' she said as we eased out of the car park, and didn't say another word until we reached the outskirts of town.

I tried a couple of times to start a conversation, but it was like trying to get blood out of a stone. Her responses were monosyllabic and almost sulky. I gave up in the end and switched on the radio and caught the tail end of Jonathan Dimbleby and 'Any Questions'?

Victoria folded her arms and glared out of the window. Hmm – was this Teri's devil child?

Eventually, with a theatrical sigh, she closed her eyes and pretended to nap. I might've been fooled, except, a couple of times I caught her eyeing me speculatively. I said nothing. Whatever Fliss might say, there would be no 'happy talk' on this car ride.

We got lost. My fault. You'd think I could find a brand new retail park on the outskirts of town, but I got confused on the ring road and we started going round in circles. 'This isn't right,' I muttered as I made a second circuit. Victoria, who'd dozed off, jerked awake as I did an emergency stop at a pelican crossing. Bloody pedestrians.

'Are we there?' Victoria tried to get her bearings. Me too. I recognised the railway station – I ought to, I'd passed it twice already. 'Pull into the car park,' Victoria ordered. 'Okay, don't,' she said as I sailed past the entrance, unable to envisage indicating, braking and turning into what looked like a narrow entrance in the nano second available. 'Just keep driving, and I'll get some directions.'

How? Where? I was beginning to feel stressed. I'd already taken a wrong turn down a one-way street – fortunately Victoria was still asleep at that point, although the beeping horns from oncoming drivers and my own panicked expletives as I executed a hasty three-point turn were loud enough to wake the dead.

Thank God for Victoria. She pulled out her mobile phone, Googled a sat nav app and, in almost no time at all, had us heading back out of the city and in the right direction.

As it happened, the new shopping centre was well-signposted – once we were on the right road – and busy. We weren't the only ones to fancy a Saturday afternoon potter around the shops. Victoria's nap seemed to have done her a power of good though. Nice Tory was back.

'What's so special about John Lewis?' she asked as we strolled across the car park. 'I liked their Christmas ad but it didn't make me want to rush to the store and start spending money.'

I agreed. The last time I really enjoyed shopping I'd been perhaps seven or eight. I spent most Saturday afternoons with Mammy and Fliss exploring the delights of the old Victorian indoor market in town. Even then, the big attraction wasn't the shopping but the old-fashioned sweet stall we visited for cola cubes or pear drops. We'd get the bus home, and if the conductress knew Mammy she'd take our fares but give lots of change in coppers and small silver. My mother got off the bus with exactly the same sum as when she'd boarded. The conductress said she was 'looking after her own'.

But, here we were at the new, giant retail park, looking for John Lewis because, whatever Victoria's phone app said, we couldn't see it. 'It's over there somewhere,' she said, pointing vaguely. Phone app two provided much better directions than number one. A couple of minutes brisk walking and we entered the hallowed portals of the newest temple to retail therapy. It was a bit of a disappointment if I'm honest, although I did pick up a tunic I'd had my eye on for a while but hadn't been able to find in my size and, which was reduced in the sale too.

Victoria, though, had the shopping attention span of a gnat – clearly a girl after my own heart – and made a beeline for the first-floor cafeteria. 'I'm starving.'

Starving? It was barely a couple of hours since she'd last eaten. And didn't she have an eating disorder? You wouldn't have thought it judging by the speed with which she polished off her share of our cream tea. She was right. She was cured – or, if not completely cured, well on the mend. And I followed her to the ladies loo afterwards and listened carefully for any puking noises.

She pulled a face at me in the washroom mirror. 'You're dying to ask, aren't you?'

Ask what? I had so many questions I didn't know where to start.

'Teri and the picture on my bedroom mirror?'

It seemed as good a place to start as any. So we headed back to the car and, on the drive home Victoria talked, just as Fliss had predicted she would.

'Dad suggested I put her photo on the mirror. He said it would be a daily reminder.'

It sounded bloody bizarre to me.

'He has this theory about Teri.'

Oh, yes?

'I suppose, I shouldn't tell you this...you're her friend after all.'

Don't let that stop you. I'm agog.

'Dad reckons Teri is a bitch because she's always starving hungry.'

Pardon?

'Have you ever seen her eat a proper meal?'

Actually, no, come to think of it, I hadn't. Not recently anyway.

'She picks at things and pushes them around her plate.'

Yes, that's right, she did. Does. In fact, the only thing I'd ever seen her eat with any degree of enthusiasm was a rocket salad. And she always eschewed the dressing. Oh God. Had she been ill all these years and I'd never noticed? What sort of a friend was I?

'Dad doesn't think she's anorexic or bulimic.'

Huh! When did he qualify in medicine?

'Because she never gets any thinner. Her weight stays more-or-less stable.'

Thank God, yes, that's true.

'But proper anorexics, like me, do. Get thinner and thinner, I mean.'

You know something? I was really beginning to wish I'd never taken Victoria to the supermarket with me that morning. If I hadn't chivvied her into coming, if I'd just left her slumped in front of reality show repeats on the TV, I wouldn't now be confronting unpleasant truths that, quite frankly, I preferred not to know.

Slowly, I pieced the whole story together. Victoria had become anorexic and bulimic shortly after she moved from her safe, non-threatening primary school to high school. Dan, despite his status as a high-profile television presenter, was a firm believer in comprehensive education, so he'd insisted Victoria attend the local academy, as I suppose we should now call it, rather than the expensive, exclusive private girl's school preferred by his wife. Almost inevitably, Victoria had been bullied and, in an effort to make herself invisible, had stopped eating.

'I managed to keep it hidden for a couple of years,' she said almost proudly.

How? Didn't her parents notice the shrinking schoolgirl hunched over the dinner table? Apparently not. Dan was busy at work, and her mother, who sounded like she could have been Teri's secret twin, was too busy being a lady who lunched. Hell's bells! She even went to my gym. How many times had I heard women like her moaning about their selfish husbands and stroppy teenagers? Poor little Tory. Obviously, I'm paraphrasing a bit here. Victoria insisted her parents were blameless. 'I got really good at skipping meals and pretending I'd eaten before they got home.' She used to rustle up healthy-ish suppers, like beans on toast. She'd cook the beans and butter some toast and dish it up on a plate and dirty a knife and fork. And then flush the whole plate of food, untouched, down the toilet and load the dishwasher with the 'used' saucepan, crockery and cutlery.

'I once nearly blocked the loo. I didn't know to cut the toast into chunks so it would flush away more easily. The toilet pan almost flooded.' She chuckled. I'm afraid I didn't see the funny side.

'And beans float horribly,' she said. 'I used to pour tonnes of bleach down the loo trying to get rid of them.'

Eventually, of course, Dan and his wife realised what was happening, and so began an endless round of quarrels and recriminations and trips to the doctor and long spells in therapy and special care.

'It was awful,' Victoria said.

At some point, the marriage broke up. Her mother, apparently, went to the hairdresser one day and, as well as a new cut and blonde highlights, acquired a boyfriend and packed a suitcase for Dan and booked him into the Herriot Hotel in the city centre. And there he stayed until D'Reen from work sorted him out with a two bedroom apartment in town.

Victoria, of course, blamed herself. 'They wouldn't have been arguing if it wasn't for me,' she said.

Possibly? More likely there would've been another catalyst. Chez Caine didn't sound a very happy ship even at the best of times.

And Sara, her mother, behaved badly. Despite the fact she'd instigated the break up and subsequent divorce, she wasn't very happy when Dan started getting his life back together. And drip, drip, drip, she fed Victoria little bits of nastiness.

'Your father has always been unfaithful...he never wanted children...this isn't the first time he's walked out on us...he was too mean to send you to a decent school...I told him you were ill, but he said you were a spoilt brat...I've begged him to come back, but he says he hates us both...'

And Victoria, who was battling the demon of being a teenager alongside the twin evils of anorexia and bulimia, was a mess.

The Dan she saw on his weekend and mid-week access visits was just as he had always been – genial and loving and indulgent. And the Dan her mother described was a penny-pinching monster who couldn't wait for her to grow up and get out of his life. Throw in puberty and her periods starting and her body changing shape and it was no wonder she was confused. Teri, of course, didn't help.

'I don't think I was very nice to her,' Victoria said. 'But she made me feel as if I was really greedy and always wanting Dad to buy new things. And she treated me as if I was a naughty child who kept getting in the way.'

Which was exactly what Sara was telling her.

But none of this really explained the photograph of Teri on her bedroom mirror. Dan, it appeared, had fairly quickly realised the marriage was a mistake.

'On the rebound,' Victoria said unnecessarily.

It didn't take a genius to work out he'd jumped from the frying pan into the fire. So, he wasn't quite as heartbroken as Teri had thought when they too divorced, but had employed a very effective bit of cod psychology to help Victoria manage her eating disorders.

'He said to take a good hard look at Teri every morning. He said people who don't eat have no heart.' So she started eating again and, though she still had bad days when she gave in to the temptation to sick up her supper, these were becoming rarer and rarer.

I guess you could say Teri cured her. She'd have been thrilled.

Chapter Seventy-Three

Teri

'You did what?' I could hardly believe what Lee was telling me.

'I've been ten-pin bowling,' she repeated.

'Yes, so you said. But you went with Dan?'

'Well, yes. We're friends…he suggested it might be fun. We took the kids, you know, my niece and nephew – and Victoria.'

'I can't believe this,' I said. 'Honestly, Lee, I can't believe you did that. Going with Dan behind my back. It's ridiculous.'

'Why is it ridiculous?' Lee was indignant. 'And we're not doing anything behind your back. You and Dan are divorced. He's a free agent to do what he likes.'

'Yes,' I stormed at her. 'But not with YOU.'

I wish now I hadn't managed to get through to her. God knew I'd been ringing and ringing but she never picked up. I needed to talk to her about the David Greenspan business, but I kept getting her voicemail, and there was no way I could tell her the ins and outs of it all in a message, so I kept it light and chatty – suggesting lunch instead – and she still didn't call me back. Then I had a brainwave and left a message suggesting we go to Romilee's for afternoon tea at the weekend. It's a fabulous little place that does every blend of herbal tea and exquisite little iced cakes. Just the sort of thing Lee goes in for. That would get her talking to me. But no, still no reply. So I rang back and left another message saying I couldn't do afternoon tea now, something had come up. She wouldn't be able to resist ringing me now to find out what was going on. Unfortunately, nothing was going on.

There was one odd thing, though. I was in the local supermarket, having a quick scan at the expensive magazines and, out of the corner of my eye, I thought I spotted her, but by the time I turned to have a proper look, she'd scarpered. Can't have been her, but it was certainly someone who looked just like her from the back.

It'd been an odd few weeks. I suppose the David Greenspan situation had taken my mind off the Declan situation. Maybe what I thought I'd felt about David was a reaction to what had happened with Declan: was I on the rebound or was it some sort of love transference? Anyway, even I could see I hadn't behaved particularly well with regards to David but, although I thought about trying again to apologise to him, I decided against it. He'd made himself fairly clear. So David was off the list then. Lee broke up with Christian some while back, and when I jokingly suggested he'd be free to go out with me now, she hadn't thrown a wobbly as I thought she would, but laughed instead. 'He'd bore even you to death,' she said. *Even* me? I didn't ask for clarification; she can be so sarcastic sometimes but generally she means well. Lee seemed a lot happier now she'd finally got Mike out of her system and, while I thought she'd have clung on to Christian, she didn't seem that bothered they'd split up. But this business about her and Dan 'walking' each other really got up my nose; who the hell did she think she was?

Lee finally deigned to ring me.

'Where the hell have you been?' I demanded. 'I've been trying to get hold of you for days.' She wittered on about this and that and how busy she'd been and then, finally, she told me about her little family outing with my ex and his wretched daughter – to the bowling alley of all places. God, I was furious. I'd told her about the time Dan and I went bowling, and she'd obviously decided this was the sort of thing she had to do as well. Scheming little cow.

Chapter Seventy-Four

Lee

I know, I know...you're wondering about Slimmer's Nation. Fliss was wondering too. And, unlike you, who have to wait patiently for me to provide enlightenment, Fliss didn't believe in hanging about.

In fact, and this is a measure of how sneaky she can be, she cornered me after Mass – which was very annoying because I'd given Mammy a lift there and was waiting to run her back home while she sorted out some finer points with Mrs O'Brien relating to Tuesday's UCM meeting. I hovered nearby hoping Mrs O' Brien might know something about Teri and Declan that I didn't. For one reason or another I hadn't seen much of Teri lately but, from the various messages she'd left on my voicemail, it was evident the path of true love was not running smoothly.

Damn Fliss. She swanned over just as Mammy, business finally concluded, leaned towards Declan's mother and said, 'I hear there's another little one on the way?'

What? If that meant what I thought it meant...

In fact – pause for thought here. Perhaps there were things I needed to find out on my own doorstep before I concerned myself with someone else's affairs? I looked at Fliss, who had the grace to look slightly embarrassed.

I grabbed her arm. 'Mammy,' I said over my shoulder as I pulled Fliss in the direction of the church hall, where the St Vincent de Paul ladies served after-Mass tea and biscuits. 'Fliss and I are going for a cuppa.'

'My treat,' I said, throwing a couple of pound coins into the collection box. Sister Mary, who was in charge of the tea-cups, tutted. 'The proceeds go to helping the poor and needy, Lee. You could be a little more generous with the pennies from your fat university income.'

What? Generous? I'd just paid two quid for two cups of stewed tea. If that wasn't generous, what was? I was about to answer back, when Fliss took out her purse and dropped a two pound coin in the box. 'Will that do?' Sister Mary, who seemed to have forgotten she was supposed to be a sister of charity, sniffed most uncharitably. 'Biscuits are extra,' she said.

Keep your bloody biscuits, I thought – but said nothing and smiled politely instead.

'Pardon?' she asked.

Oh my God. I'd done it again and spoken aloud when I should've kept my mouth shut. Giggling, Fliss hustled me away.

'She'll tell, Mammy,' she said. 'You wait and see.'

We elbowed our way through the crowd – Declan and Marnie, who as usual had come to Mass together, sipped tea at a window table. Their son stared moodily at his mobile phone while their little girl, now divested of her altar garments, sat on Declan's knee, twiddling the hair at the back of his collar. I almost choked. I remembered Teri telling me how much she liked to curl up on his lap and nuzzle his neck and twirl her fingers through his hair – which, I have to admit looked temptingly lush and twirl-able.

I looked around, hoping to see a vacant table nearby. I hadn't given up all hope of getting some inside information. But Fliss now waved from the other side of the room. Oh well, perhaps later.

'Me first,' Fliss said as I sat down. 'What's this about Slimmer's Nation? And Victoria – come on,' she crooked her finger and waggled it, 'tell your little sister…'

Hang on a minute. I've got some questions of my own.

But Fliss was having none of it. 'You tell first.' She always was a bossy little bugger.

She listened with sympathy as I told her about Victoria. 'Poor little thing,' she said when I finished. 'But she's not cured, you know. Not yet. It's not that simple.'

That's what Dan had said last night. He wanted to tell me, he said, but it was Victoria's secret (Ha! Ha!), and he felt it had to be her decision about what and when and if she told me. Okay, I got that – it was early days and we were all still getting to know each other, but I still felt just a little hurt he hadn't trusted me enough.

Fliss patted my hand reassuringly. 'It's a control thing. It always is with eating disorders. Sufferers feel helpless about the big things in life, so food becomes a way of getting some power back – even if it's just over what they do and don't put in their mouth.'

Hell's bells. This was getting profound. 'So Dan...?'

'...was absolutely right to leave it to Victoria to tell you herself. And it's a big compliment that she felt able to tell you so early in the relationship.'

Okay, I got that. But he might have given me a hint – he'd left her in my care for a day, and it was a big responsibility.

Fliss was exasperated. 'She's not a child, even if she might seem like one. And don't be so bloody self-centred. You're beginning to sound just like Miss-the-whole-world-revolves-around-me-Meyer.'

Fliss! She's not that bad.

'Oh yes, she is,' Fliss said. 'You can't see it – you never have. But even a baby like Fee shows more consideration for other people.'

That was a bit of an exaggeration. Fee could be pretty single-minded when she wanted something. But, on the other hand, she was still in nappies, and Teri...well, Teri wasn't. But talking of babies. 'Your turn now.'

'There's nothing much to tell.'

Stop being so coy.

'You mustn't tell anyone,' she said. 'Especially not Mammy. Ritchie hasn't even put two and two together yet. Charles and I want to keep it a secret a little bit longer. At least, until I've had my first scan.'

'But you're having another baby?'

'Yes.'

Wow. Another niece or nephew. I stifled a little twinge of jealousy.

'I'll tell you more later,' Fliss said. Mammy stood in the doorway of the parish hall, having a word with Sister Mary, who – Holy Cow! – had abandoned her teapot and was clearly tittle-tattling. Fliss nodded in their direction. 'Quick, Slimmer's Nation?'

Nothing much to tell. Why does anyone join an organisation whose raison d'être is helping people lose weight, get active and eat healthily? Same reason as most other people – I wanted to get into a posh frock for a special engagement, of course. Don't jump ahead – this particular engagement was about Victoria not me.

'It was David's idea – I've told you about Gorgeous Greenspan?' Fliss nodded. Yes, David, who sometimes seemed to forget I was the grown up one in our relationship and who constantly nagged about what he described as my 'unhealthy' diet. Sometimes he could be very patronising. 'A healthy diet is more than just eating five fruit and veg a day,' he preached. 'It's a way of life.'

Huh! I'd seen his idea of a healthy diet – boiled eggs and nutrition shakes for breakfast, dinner and tea. Practice what you preach, mate. But, blow me down, the little sod signed me up at a Slimmer's Nation group run by his Auntie Joyce. I was initially furious with him. 'I ought to smack you good and hard,' I said. But he just grinned and – do you know what? – he turned up on the night of the first meeting and frog-marched me to my first group. 'You've lost weight,' he said as he deposited me at the door. 'You're active.'

'And,' he added, pushing me into the room, 'now you need to square the final side of the triangle and learn to eat healthily, and, this is as good a place to learn as any.'

Don't even get me started on the ridiculousness of his mixed metaphor.

But, hey-ho. He was right. I did have a lot to learn about healthy eating and, though I still enjoyed French fries and greasy burgers as much as the next woman, I cut out a lot of the crap that previously characterised my diet – although I hadn't yet had the willpower to completely give up on the dry white wine. And I'm not sure I ever will.

Glasses of Muscadet withstanding, I'd almost finished the transformation that started with Ritchie and our bike rides on the Île de Ré.

Chapter Seventy-Five

Lee

Frankly, Teri lied about her encounter with David – I know, because when he eventually told me his version of events it had a far more convincing ring of truth to it. More importantly his account tallied with the one Chrissie said she'd been reluctant to draw to my attention because she didn't want to cause trouble but...

There was no bloody 'but' about it. She loved every minute. And made a meal of spitting out the facts.

'...as deputy head of teaching and learning I think you need to know that Ms Meyer is guilty of professional misconduct.'

I groaned. It sounded like she too had heard about Teri and David's drunken fumble – there was, I suspected, a bit more to it than Teri had implied when she confessed he'd made a drunken pass at her. A drunken David? I'd like to have seen that. But, nevertheless, it sounded like nothing more serious than a consensual bit of misplaced drunken fumbling.

'I wouldn't say it was quite as serious as that,' I said.

'Wouldn't you?' Chrissie was surprised.

'It's not as if he was just out of school,' I said. 'Technically, he's a mature student – old enough to look after himself.'

'What's his age got to do with anything?' Chrissie asked.

God! The woman was a moron. 'Because he's not a kid. He's been around the block a few times. Kissed a few princesses and his share of

263

witches too.'

Phut! Chrissie made a rude noise. 'I don't care who he's been kissing. Although if he's been snogging Ms Meyer he's dafter than he looks.'

How unkind.

'But I do care that Ms Meyer threatened him with a fail grade if he didn't respond to her sexual advances. And her module marks were days late. And, contrary to what she might think, it does matter. And they very nearly weren't ready in time for the award board. I'd bet my bottom dollar too that none of her scripts had been second marked or internally moderated either,' she ended.

Good God!

'Sit down,' I said, pulling out a chair. 'Tell me about it.' And I felt my stomach twist in a cold knot of fear as she did – at length and in damning detail.

She really hadn't wanted to cause trouble, she said, again. She was just a little more convincing this time – perhaps trying to justify the long delay between overhearing Teri's foolish outburst and finally coming to someone in authority about it.

Why me though?

'You know what it's like over the summer, Lee. Can't find an academic on the premises for love nor money.'

I knew I should've stayed away, but, it was the first day of Clearing and duty had called. Damn. Damn. Damn. But Mike and Peter were both in today – I'd seen them. So, again, why me?

'I really didn't want to cause trouble,' she repeated.

Heavens. She was like a broken record.

'I've worried about it all summer, and I thought at first when the module marks seemed broadly in line with what students were getting on other modules that maybe I should let it go.'

Well, why hadn't she?

'It just seemed wrong. If a male lecturer had propositioned a female student...'

The sentence trailed off. She didn't really need to finish it.

And she'd come to me because she thought I'd be sympathetic and, basically, she was kicking the ball into my court. She'd raised her concerns with 'someone in authority' and, if I did nothing, it would be my neck on the line if the whole thing blew up. Huh. I wasn't having that.

'Hang on,' I said. 'You need to speak to Mike.' Chrissie wasn't the only one who could pass the buck. But God help Teri though.

Predictably, Mike wanted to call David in and interrogate him then and there. With difficulty, I persuaded him to hold fire. Let me talk to David off the record, I said. No point launching a full scale inquiry, with all the ramifications that were involved, until we were sure of the facts. 'Okay,' Mike said, 'no need to involve Peter Heron, and Human Resources, just yet.'

It was a breathing space.

Chapter Seventy-Six

Lee

If I'm honest, I'd hoped I could persuade David to let sleeping dogs lie – which, yes, was unprofessional of me. But old habits die hard, and protecting Teri's back was almost a reflex action.

I decided against speaking to David on university premises, instead I thought I'd raise the matter, casually, at the gym. I didn't get a chance. David had been mulling things over and, before I could say a word, he dropped his own bombshell.

We were running side by side on neighbouring treadmills. 'More companionable,' he said and, in deference to the fact our relationship had irrevocably changed after the miserable evening when he spewed up all over my car, he no longer charged me personal trainer rates either. 'We're gym buddies now,' he said. 'You're almost my second mother. I can't take money off you.' Thanks, I thought. I'm now officially old.

I knew what was coming as soon as he started to speak. 'I don't want to bother you,' he said, 'but...'

'But...?' I asked.

'I need advice,' he said. 'Tutor to student.'

Aagh! Why did he have to say that? If I'd been able to keep things off the record I might've been able to keep a lid on this. Now, though, I hadn't a hope in hell. Without an official complaint from David, it was Chrissie's word against Teri's – and Teri was the best liar I knew. But those three little words, *three little words!* – tutor to student – made the whole damn thing official. F***! F***! F***!

I'd suspected Teri wasn't being completely honest when she said she and David had been 'a bit silly'. Teri never stopped at being 'a bit silly' and, that one time aside, when David got drunk as a skunk over his silly little hairdresser, I didn't think he'd ever been 'silly' in his entire life. He was too damn earnest – and romantic. He had some very old-fashioned ideas about how to treat a girl, and taking advantage of a drunken woman just wasn't in his DNA. And it went without saying that Teri would've been drunk. In the old days she had a rule: she didn't drink until the sun dipped below the yardarm – these days the sun seemed to go down earlier and earlier. 'It's half past six somewhere in the world,' she would say when she telephoned at 4.30pm, already ever so slightly the worse for wear, and banged on about her many real and imagined grievances. It was impossible, and I tried, believe me, to distract her. I never thought I'd say this about Teri, but she was becoming a complete and utter bore.

I stopped the treadmill. 'I think we'd better find somewhere a bit quieter,' I said. So we went and sat in the coffee lounge – which wasn't terribly private but it was almost deserted and would have to suffice.

David was prepared to overlook her drunken advances at the May Ball. 'It was the booze talking,' he said, which was generous because he must've been embarrassed. He wasn't even concerned about her little overture outside the admin office or her attempted apology at his flat. 'I'd rather forget about it,' he said. But he couldn't ignore her threat to amend his essay mark if he didn't comply. 'That's the bit that's nasty,' he said. 'And isn't it against the rules? Aren't we supposed to be marked on academic merit? Not favouritism.'

He'd got it in one – David might want to forget about propositions one, two and three, and, at a pinch, the university could overlook them too. But demanding sexual favours in return for a good mark, for that's what it amounted to, was practically a hanging matter. Good God, Chrissie was dead right; if a male tutor had made a similar suggestion to a female student, he'd have been hung out to dry with his professional reputation in tatters. And, for the life of me, I couldn't see how Teri could escape the same fate.

I felt a little shaky and trembly – it was precisely to avoid this sort of conflict of interest that I'd ended my own burgeoning relationship with David. And I'd made sure both Mike and Peter Heron were aware I knew him socially outside the university and – just to be doubly careful – when he signed up for my semester two first-year module, always invited one or other of them to double mark any assessed work he completed for me. Teri, damn her, had mocked. 'What are you afraid of?' Fool! I was covering my back. If only she'd had the sense to do the same.

'What should I do?' David asked.

I sighed. 'It's out of both our hands now.'

'What do you mean? I don't want a big fuss.'

'It's not really up to you,' I said. 'It's not up to me either.'

Chrissie, I told him, had already raised the matter with me, and with Mike. Chrissie hadn't filed a formal complaint yet but Mike, I felt sure, would insist she did so. He liked things to be neat and tidy. There would have to be an investigation – it was a very serious accusation and, if true, would have serious consequences for Teri.

'Oh Lee.' He patted my shoulder. 'I'm so sorry – I know Teri's a good friend.'

Huh! With good friends like her, I was rapidly running out of the need for enemies.

Without corroboration, I told him, it would've been a simple case of Teri's word against Chrissie – impossible to prove either way. But now that we'd spoken, and he'd confirmed Chrissie's version of events, the case was cut and dried.

'Can't you pretend I never said anything?'

No! I wished I could – but, no! 'Things don't work that way.'

'I'm sorry,' he mumbled. 'I'm so, so sorry.'

I gave him a hug. 'It's not your fault,' I reassured him. 'You're the innocent party here.'

'What happens next?'

I explained: once a formal complaint was received, he'd be invited in to speak to Mike and, probably Peter Heron too.

'The dean?' David asked. 'It's that serious?'

'Yes,' I said, 'but don't worry.' I hugged him again. 'I'm sure Teri will wriggle out of trouble. She usually does.'

Who was I trying to kid? Peter Heron would have a field day when Chrissie's complaint landed on his desk. Talk about fastening your own noose and sticking your neck in it. Teri couldn't have done a better job if she'd tried.

Chapter Seventy-Seven

Teri

It was bad enough when I found out Lee was going off playing happy families with Dan, but now she tells me how well she and Victoria were getting on. They'd been shopping together and not just to the supermarket, but to the new John Lewis store. She never thought to ask me if I'd go with her, oh no, she had to go with a bloody selfish, spoilt teenager.

'What on earth did you take her for?' I asked. For a start, Lee is no good at shopping unless I'm with her. She never wants to try anything on even when I've picked out lovely things that would suit her figure (or lack of it), and she gets bored after only a couple of hours and starts demanding that we go and sit down somewhere and have lunch. Second, who wants to drag a stroppy kid round the sort of shops where only stroppy kids go?

'Lee, you must have the patience of a saint,' I told her. 'What did you do with her? What did you talk about?' The idea of having a conversation with Victoria left me puzzled; she could never string two sentences together when she'd been with me.

'Well actually,' Lee said, 'the girl's had to put up with an awful lot – and she's not had an easy time of it…'

'Oh, play me the violins,' I said.

Lee suddenly snapped. 'Look Teri, you don't know anything about her situation and frankly, you never bothered to find out when you had the chance. But take it from me, the kid has problems, and I thought a trip out shopping would be just the thing for her.'

'Very noble,' I snapped back. 'But I don't remember her ever being short of shopping trips when I knew her – and Dan usually gave her thousands of pounds to do it with, *if* you remember?'

Lee shook her head in that way she has when she can't think of anything fast, funny or clever to say.

We were talking at her house. Because she'd been playing silly buggers and not answering her phone, I'd gone round to surprise her one evening with a bottle of her favourite Pinot Grigio (I prefer Sauvignon myself, but you can't account for other people's tastes). Previously, she'd have smiled in delight at seeing me on her doorstep waving a bottle of wine, and she'd drag me inside, grab the bottle opener and two large glasses and we'd plonk down on her sofa to gossip. But this evening she seemed distracted and not entirely delighted to see me. I thought for a moment she wasn't going to invite me in, and I stood on the doorstep feeling slightly foolish, but then she relented, stood aside, and I strode past her into the kitchen to uncork the wine.

'What are you up to?' I asked, trying to lighten what seemed to be a tense mood as I leaned back against the kitchen sink and raised my glass towards her. 'Oh, before you tell me,' I continued, 'did I tell you I went to the new John Lewis retail park, you know, the one on the outskirts of town, and guess what I found? The most wonderful Georgia Le Riska skirt. It's the most heavenly shade of...'

'Yes,' Lee interrupted, 'I've been there.'

'Where?'

'The new John Lewis...'

'When did you go?' Frankly, I was surprised. Lee doesn't go shopping on her own and she'd be too nervous to go to a big new store like that without me.

And then she told me how she'd been quite recently – with Victoria – and went into a spiel about how Victoria had been having it tough and needed help sorting her problems out. When I tried to remind Lee about how spoilt that child was, she started doing her disappointed-shaking-of-head at me and I just said, 'Oh fuck it. It's nothing to me what that wretched girl does. I'm just sorry you've been sucked into it, Lee.'

I wasn't sure, but Lee looked as though she was about to cry. I took a quick swig of my wine hoping to encourage her to do the same. I had so many problems of my own, I wasn't in the mood to start hearing any more of Lee's sob stories. Yes, she'd been through a lot, but was over all that now: the abortion, Mike, Christian and everything. I'd tried to be supportive, but, hell's bells, she shouldn't still be filling up all the time.

'Come on, Lee. What's up?'

'Nothing...' But it really didn't sound like nothing.

'Well, okay,' I tried again. 'What have you been up to?'

'Oh, this and that,' she said.

'What is it, Lee?' I said in as concerned a way as I could muster. 'I know something's wrong. You're not answering my calls; I hardly ever see you.'

Lee looked at me as if considering something. Then she said, 'It's nothing, or, rather, I've got a lot on my mind, and I can't talk to you about it at the moment.'

Now I was intrigued. 'That's ridiculous. What can't you talk about?'

Then she shrugged and pulled her shoulders back.

'Oh, Teri,' she sighed, exasperated. 'If you must know, it's about the David Greenspan business.'

'What about it?'

'Well...' She checked herself and then added, 'Have you thought about what would happen if David makes an official complaint?'

'Oh, for goodness' sake, Lee. He's not going to do that. I told you, it was all very innocent. We got drunk, and one thing led to another...'

She held up a hand to shut me up. 'Teri, can we please not talk about it? It's putting me in a very bad position.'

I couldn't quite see why what happened at the May Ball would put Lee in a bad position and I told her so. I also added that whatever had gone on between David and me was my business and nothing to do with her. And anyway, it was all months ago, nothing happened, nothing was going to happen. But when she started shaking her head and looking pityingly at me in the way she does, I saw red. How dare she look at me like that? It wasn't bad enough that she had cosy meals out with my ex-husband, but she tried to muscle her way in further by taking his darling daughter off shopping, and now she was interfering in my relationship with David or rather, my non-relationship with David. I slammed my glass down on the draining board, told her I couldn't be doing with her superior attitude – especially not after the way she was behaving – and stormed out.

Chapter Seventy-Eight

Teri

I was so cross with Lee I drove home perhaps a little too fast. One of those dratted speed cameras on the A615 got me as I was aware of a sudden flash. But I was angry and couldn't be bothered. Let them fine me. Just try it. Who cares?

I got to the flat, still angry and shaking and went straight inside to open another bottle. After the first glass, I felt a bit calmer and picked up my mobile to call Lee. I wasn't going to apologise. Why should I? But I shouldn't have stormed out. She was only trying to help. But as I tapped the contacts button to get her number on screen, the phone beeped with a message. Hah! I thought. Lee, texting to apologise. But it was Declan, texting to ask if he could come in.

Obviously, I texted back 'No', but he came straight back, saying he was sitting outside and needed to see me. 'No,' I texted again.

'Please, please, please,' he texted again.

'No.'

Then my doorbell rang.

Why did I answer it? Why did that lost-puppy-look cause me to crumple? Why did that lopsided grin make me smile? Why did I let him reach out for me, pull me into his chest, kiss the top of my head, push me against the wall running his hands up and down the sides of my body and, then, pull me gently to the floor? Why?

'I've missed you so much,' he breathed into my ear as we lay, later, on the bleached hallway floorboards. 'And I've missed this,' he laughed waving an arm to take in the reclaimed wood hall dresser and soft vanilla surroundings.

I got up and reached down to pull him to his feet. 'Declan, what are you doing here?'

He looked serious. 'I've missed you. Pure and simple. It's been a bloody awful couple of months; I can't live without you. I had to see you. I've been so lonely. I love you, Teri, and I only realised just how much when I could no longer see you.'

'But what about all the other women?'

'Oh, come on, Teri. You know all that was innocent stuff. I explained, but you wouldn't believe me.'

We went through into the lounge, and he picked up the bottle of wine I'd left on the coffee table, poured some into my empty glass and took a drink. 'Make yourself at home.' I smiled and went into the kitchen to get another glass.

As conversationally as I could, I added, 'Talking of home, are you still at Leyland Road?'

He looked sheepish. 'Ah, no,' he said. 'Got a bit expensive what with paying the rent and the mortgage on the old house. So I…er…had to move back in with Marnie.'

'You're back living with your ex-wife?'

'Well, technically, she's not my ex as we never got divorced. But it's not what you think. I sleep in the spare room. We live in the same house but separately. It's just the cheapest option. Cheaper all round until the divorce comes through and we can sell the house. Plus I get to see the kids.'

'It can't be very pleasant, having to dodge round your wife all the time.'

'Oh, it's not that bad. Anyway, I don't want to talk about her when I've got you…come here and tell your uncle Declan what you've been up to.'

Reason, experience, logic – all those – should have told me to stop it right there. But I was still angry and emotional from my row with Lee – and hurt, to be honest. I needed some love and affection in my life. But, honestly, what could I have been thinking taking up with Declan again when he'd not only been unfaithful to me with several other women but clearly lied to me on numerous occasions? And now he wanted us to get back together again even though he still lived with his wife in the marital home.

I could just hear Lee's voice in the background telling me what an idiot I was. But I knew how happy Declan could make me. He told me how much he'd missed me; he even admitted he'd taken me for granted before and now realised what a fool he'd been. He never wanted to let me out of his sight, out of his arms, out of his life. We were meant to be together – didn't I realise that? – and he would do anything to prove to me he was a changed man. He was getting a divorce – didn't that tell me how serious he was?

And idiot I am, I believed him.

He didn't stay that first night although we made love again – in the bedroom this time – and we met for lunch the next day. Over the next two weeks, he would dash round to the flat during the day when he was supposed to be out on a job; I went to meet him when he finished work; he spent his time off with me. If he couldn't see me, he rang and texted, even sending late night messages on his mobile like he used to do.

'I love you,' he said.

'I love you too – and I can't live without you,' I replied.

It was a glorious couple of weeks.

Chapter Seventy-Nine

Teri

And then the doorbell rang.

I didn't recognise the woman standing there. She was small, plump-faced and despite not wearing much make-up, fairly pretty. Her hair was a nondescript brown in an equally nondescript style. But what I noticed immediately was how enormous she was and how her belly stuck out in a most unattractive way from between an unbuttoned brown, boiled wool coat. She breathed heavily, as though she'd run up the stairs to my flat, and leaned towards me with one hand on the doorsill as if to prop herself up and the other laid on top of the bulge in that odd way pregnant women do as they absentmindedly rub their bump. I wondered if she was one of the other residents in my block and perhaps the baby was on its way and she needed help. I stared at the bulge, praying that no waters were about to break. Hell, I didn't want her having her bloody baby on my hall floorboards.

'Yes,' she said, still rubbing her stomach, 'you might well look surprised.'

And there was something about the voice that jolted me. I'd heard that voice, that slight accent, once before on the phone. Marnie. And she was heavily pregnant.

I'm no judge when it comes to guessing how many months gone women are and, to be honest, the sight of them heavily pregnant in close-fitting puma cotton tops, leggings and cheap, gaping coats makes my stomach

277

churn. She must've seen the quizzical look on my face because she said, 'Six months – and it's twins.'

'Oh, my God,' was all I could manage.

'And you might want to know – they're Declan's.'

'Yes, but…'

'While you were playing your fancy games with him, you obviously didn't know that Declan and I were attempting a reconciliation?'

She made it sound like a question, but didn't give me time to answer. Instead she went on. 'You might also want to know that we had a fairly romantic weekend of our own at his flat – and that's when this happened.' She pointed at the frankly obscene bulge. 'And we didn't take kindly to you coming round and continually ringing the bell. But from what Declan tells me, you're a bit of a stalker. I wanted to call the police then, but he wouldn't let me.'

I was speechless. She barged past me into the lounge, still breathing heavily with the effort, went to the sofa, turned slowly and, like a rather large walrus, lowered herself down, one hand on the armrest, the other still laid over her stomach, which from that position, looked fit to burst.

'So you two…?' was all I could manage.

'Yes, despite your little games, we're still very much together,' Marnie said, looking me in the eye as I sat opposite her on the matching chair.

'But what about all the other…?'

'All the other what? Women?' Marnie said, finishing my sentence. 'Oh, I've always known about women who throw themselves at him, and I know he can't resist the odd shenanigans. I've been married to him for long enough. He goes off and does his thing and gets it out of his system, but he always – always – comes back to me and the kids.'

I wanted to say something about how demeaning this must be for her, but something about the determined look on her face stopped me.

'You probably think I'm a naïve, stupid little wife who lets her husband get away with murder,' she said as if reading my thoughts.

Well, yes, I was going to say, but thought better of it.

'But what you don't understand, pet,' she said, 'is that when two people love and understand each other, their relationship can stand the odd indiscretion.'

I must say, I thought the poor woman was deceiving herself, and I suddenly wanted her out of the flat. God, what if her waters broke? But she had more to say.

'You might think that Declan loves you but he doesn't. I know he's been seeing you over the last couple of weeks.' She held up her hand to stop my denial. 'Don't worry,' she said. 'He told me. He told me about your attempted suicide and how he had to come round to look after you...'

'What...?'

'Yes, another of your tricks. I don't suppose you had any intention of killing yourself – more's the pity,' she snapped. 'You just wanted him here on whatever pretences you could find. Frankly, pet, I find that a pretty low thing to do. You worried the life out of him, ringing him like that and saying you'd taken all those pills. You should be ashamed.'

'But, I never...'

'He's told me how you manipulate him, how you threaten him by saying you'll make a complaint against him to his editor. Well, lady, do it; do your worst. He wants rid of you once and for all, so we don't care what you do. But I'm asking you – no, I'm telling you – get out of our lives and stay out. If you ever come near my husband, me or our children ever again I shall call the police and have you arrested.'

The drama of her final statement was lost to some extent by the effort it took her to drag her fat body off of my sofa and waddle across the room. But I'd got the message so didn't argue, and neither of us said anything as she struggled down the hallway to the door. There she turned, probably to get her breath, but so as not to waste the moment, she added, 'I mean it.'

'But I never tried to...'

'I don't want to hear it,' she said as she pulled on the handle, opened the door and lurched out as tidily as all that extra weight she was carrying allowed.

She headed towards the stairs, thought better of it and walked towards the lift as I watched, speechless. When I heard the familiar 'ping' of the lift announcing its imminent arrival, I woke from my stunned silence and shouted, 'Declan's told you a complete pack of lies; he's done nothing but lie to you, me and every other woman he's met throughout his whole sad little life. He's a womaniser, a total bastard who just uses women – and

279

you're stupid and gullible if you believe any of his crap. If I were you – pet – I'd get the hell out of it before you have those bastard twins of his.' And I slammed the door shut.

I strode up the hall, into the lounge and over to the window. I don't know why, but I wanted to make sure Marnie was off the premises. Confronting and rowing with me was enough to induce labour, and I didn't want any bloody O'Brien offspring being born in my block of flats.

I pulled up the white wooden slatted blinds and looked down into the car park and saw Declan's silver grey Golf, and Declan leaning against the closed, driver's side door. He was looking intently at the mobile phone in his hand as if he had some important call to make but then he looked round at the entrance to the flats and the beached whale that was his wife waddled out and across towards him. He rushed round to open the passenger door, and I could see by the way Marnie angrily wagged her finger at him he wasn't going to be able to make that call.

Chapter Eighty

Lee

The first few weeks of the academic year are always stressful, and this year was no different. Getting back into the swing of teaching is straightforward enough, but there is always an endless round of minor problems: timetable anomalies, new staff – who haven't been set up on the email system (despite filling in the required forms in triplicate) – and umpteen departmental meetings – some of which are useful and some of which, frankly, aren't. Unfortunately, it's hard to know which you can miss (without missing out on something vital) and which are desperately important (and not to be missed at any cost). As a result, I end up attending them all and, more often than not, find myself doodling on the back of the minutes and wishing I was somewhere else.

It all settles down eventually but, usually, not before I've begun to think about a career change. Digging coal sometimes seems a preferable alternative.

This year was worse than usual because always in the background was the pending complaint investigation. Nothing happens quickly at a university – they're like bloody oil tankers and movement requires careful consideration and planning and always happens at the pace of a geriatric snail. And so it was with the complaint against Teri. The relevant authorities had been notified and due process had begun, although, God only knew when a decision might be expected. My nerves were wrecked – at best I thought Teri might escape with a severe rebuke and, at worst... suspension? A downgrade from senior to junior lecturer level? Transfer to another department? I don't know why I was worrying – Teri certainly wasn't.

'Pah!' she said. 'Who's going to take a silly complaint like that seriously?'

Quite a lot of people.

'Pah!' she said again.

And that was it. She flatly refused to cooperate with the investigation, and I couldn't decide whether she was burying her head in the sand because she was too scared to contemplate the implications, or, because she genuinely thought there was no case to answer. Either way, it wasn't comfortable.

No, she preferred to blether on about me and Dan and not to raise my hopes in that direction. Raise my hopes? How old did she think I was?

I tried pointing out he was a free agent and could choose his own friends, but she wouldn't listen. Instead, she started moaning about Victoria and, while I know the poor kid's no saint, and, yes, had sometimes behaved like a spoilt brat, there were, I thought, extenuating circumstances. Not in Teri's book. 'Play me the violins,' she sneered. So, I simply downed my glass of Pinot Grigio – and wished for the millionth time she'd stop trying to educate my palate and simply stick to Muscadet – and changed the subject. Which was a waste of time since she was clearly spoiling for a fight and, since I was fed up with listening to her moans, I obliged.

Cheers, I thought, as she slammed the door behind her. And good riddance too.

Afterwards, I wished I'd been a little more tolerant. Let's face it, I'd spent donkey's years not letting Teri wind me up, what was so different now? Dan, of course. It's the golden rule of friendship, isn't it? Except not dating Teri's exes would seriously restrict the pool of available men in our neck of the woods. So, feeling thoroughly guilty, I resolved to offer an olive branch at the first available opportunity – as it turned out, the following morning in the ladies' loo at work where she caught me doing my hair and make-up, and offered advice on the benefits of a good blow-dry.

'I've just been to the gym,' I said.

She wasn't listening – instead she picked up the mini tube of face cream, which I'd left by the side of the wash basin, and squeezed a pinch onto her finger. She sniffed it. 'It doesn't smell too bad,' she conceded, 'although it's really not a good idea to use hand cream on your face.'

It's not bloody hand cream! It's a handbag-sized tube of the not inexpensive super-concentrate paraben-free face cream I use night and day because it doesn't bring me out in hives – unlike the heavily-perfumed fungi-stuff she'd gifted me last Christmas.

'But, why don't you use that lovely truffle serum I bought you for Christmas?' she continued.

Because I'm allergic to it, and if I'd told her once, I'd told her a thousand times. But did she listen? Of course she didn't.

She didn't wait for an answer now either – she poked around in my make-up bag instead. She held up my eyeliner and inspected it. 'Have you ever tried...?'

'No,' I snapped, snatching the eyeliner out of her hand and bundling the make-up bag back into my handbag. Today, of all days, I had neither the time nor inclination to engage in a discussion about my sartorial shortcomings.

Yes, it's true I can't blow dry my hair like the girl at the hairdresser – but who can? And, I know I'm never going to be Teri-svelte and streamlined because I'm not about to half-starve myself like she does.

And it's been months too since I wore a pair of jeggings.

But none of this mattered, because if Teri wasn't worried sick about the Greenspan business, I was. And, it was far more important to tactfully let her know that she really ought to be on her best behaviour and not give people additional ammunition to fire at her, because if *I'd* noticed she was idling away her time in the powder room at nine forty-five on a Monday morning when she should be mid-lecture with her Level 2 Renaissance literature group, it was a safe bet that other folk had too.

A dead safe bet – a toilet flushed and Chrissie, from admin, emerged from the cubicle.

She nodded at me but ignored Teri until she'd finished washing her hands. She gave them a hasty wipe on a paper towel and, as she dropped it into the waste bin, asked in a disinterested voice, 'Lecture finished early, Teri?'

She didn't wait for a reply and, as the door slammed behind her, Teri launched into a tirade about 'pen-pushing Chrissie' who, it seemed, had the temerity to 'invite' Teri to a 9am meeting with Peter on Wednesday. And, further, had refused to tell her a) why she needed to meet Heron at such an early hour, and b) why she needed to meet with him in the first place.

'Do you know what he wants, Lee?'

Oh for goodness' sake! It didn't take a genius to work out the Greenspan powder keg might be on the agenda. Not to mention the departmental restructure that had been on the cards for a month of Sundays.

'Perhaps it's a promotion?' she suggested and got quite cross with me when I pointed out the little matter of David Greenspan had still to be resolved.

'That's a storm in a teacup,' she said. 'The boy's got the mark he deserves, and I'm not going back on it just because he's got an inflated sense of his own intelligence.'

I couldn't agree – and this storm in a teacup had all the makings of a full-blown hurricane.

'I really think there was no need for you to get involved, Lee,' Teri said.

At that point, I lost patience with her. It was her funeral after all, and, if she chose to go around with her head in the clouds, there was no point in wasting time and energy trying to offer unwanted advice. And, for almost the first time in our long friendship, I stomped off in a huff.

And, just like yesterday when we rowed over the Pinot Grigio, almost instantly regretted it. But, there was no chance to apologise and offer another olive branch because the rest of the day was pretty full-on with teaching and meetings and other stuff. It wasn't until I finally got home that I had five minutes to myself and, of course, started fretting. Poor Teri; lately she seemed to have lurched from one mess to another. I knew I wasn't responsible but felt guilty I hadn't been more supportive.

But what to do? Especially as whatever Peter Heron planned to discuss with her on Wednesday, it was a dead cert today's missed lecture would come up – along with so many others she'd missed or cancelled.

Should I ring her? Would she listen to some advice? And then there was the little matter of my own piece of news which she needed to know sooner rather than later.

My news? Oh yes, something rather wonderful happened. Three nights ago, over dinner at L'homme-vert, Dan pulled a little gift box out of his pocket. He'd just got back from Ireland where he'd been filming a series of packages about James Joyce's Dublin to kick-start a new Ridings Today late night book programme. He had a little present for me, he said, when he called from the airport taxi to tell me to meet him at the restaurant at 7pm.

I'd grumbled a bit – I was tired and didn't feel like getting all tarted up to go somewhere posh. L'homme-vert is not a baggy jeans and t-shirt sort of establishment. But Dan insisted and, after a glass of wine and a sharing platter of charcuterie and figs and crusty French bread, I was in a much better frame of mind.

That's when he produced the gift box. It was clumsily wrapped. 'Christmas paper?' I queried.

'Couldn't find anything else. Open it,' he urged. Easier said than done. Dan belongs to the 'you can never have too much sealing tape' school-of-wrapping. 'Here,' he said, snatching the box as I fumbled with the tape. He pulled at the wrappings with his teeth. 'There,' he said, handing me the mangled package again.

I pulled at the paper and stroked the velvety box.

'What is it?' I looked at him. 'Not the pearl earrings I was looking at last weekend?' I felt touched by his kindness. The earrings had been outrageously expensive, and I'd balked at shelling out the asking price. 'You darling,' I said, leaning across the table and kissing him.

'Open it. Open it,' he said again.

I lifted the lid and gasped at the gold, bejewelled Claddagh ring nestling inside.

'Do you like it?' he asked.

I was lost for words. When Mammy and Daddy married they exchanged the traditional Irish ring, representing love, loyalty and friendship. 'It's lovely,' I said, unsure if he understood the symbolism.

'Try it on. Does it fit?'

I slipped it on the third finger of my right hand, the heart facing inward. 'You've captured my heart,' I told him.

'No,' he said. And, taking my hand, he pulled the ring from my finger, and slid it gently onto the third finger of my left hand, heart facing outward.

'Have I got it right?' he asked. 'This way round, it means you're engaged?'

Me? Engaged? To Dan? I wanted to cry. I *was* crying.

'I'm sorry, I'm sorry,' he said, wiping away my tears. 'Don't cry. I didn't mean to upset you. It's too soon, I know, but I love you so much...' He looked miserable. 'I'm sorry,' he repeated. 'I don't know why I thought you might want to marry me. I know I'm second-hand goods.'

'Third-hand,' I corrected.

He groaned. 'How could I be so stupid?'

'You're not stupid,' I said. 'I'd love to marry you. I can't think of anything nicer.'

I'll draw a veil over the rest of the evening – some things should not be shared with third parties.

Reality, of course, kicked in the next morning. Teri. It didn't take a rocket scientist to work out we could expect explosions. If she didn't take happily to us being 'good friends' she'd be apoplectic at the notion of a replacement Mrs Caine. Especially as I had a feeling she still held a candle for Dan. She'd hinted as much a few times. 'Don't get too attached to him,' she warned. 'I've only got to lift a finger and he'll come running back.' She hugged me. 'We've got unfinished business, Dan and I. He's on the rebound at the moment but it won't last, and I don't want you to be hurt.'

How kind. Deluded too.

Nevertheless, she was definitely a fly in our happy little ointment.

Chapter Eighty-One

Teri

I looked at the pile of essays waiting to be marked in my office and decided it could wait. I was going home. It had been a bad day from the start. First, I slept through the alarm. Had one or two glasses of wine last night to cheer myself up, and they must've knocked me out because I slept like a baby for the first time in months. I'd had an awful time of it since my marriage broke up, and Declan started playing his tricks again, and that damned student, David Greenspan…well, let's not go there right now.

Anyway, it all seemed to be swirling round in my head. No one understood the pressure I'd been under. I was late getting into uni, and, of course, today was the day I was supposed to give a lecture at 9am – Rochester: The Enlightened Poetical Hero of the 1600s. But by the time I got there, half the students had buggered off. Level 2 students, for God's sake. They pay all that money in tuition fees and then don't bother turning up for lectures.

Then I got a message from Peter Heron – and what a prick he was. Anyway, the message, sent via Chrissie in admin, said could I see him on Wednesday at 9am. Why can't he tell me himself, I asked Chrissie. He's away on a conference, she said. Conferences. That's all these academics here do – go to conferences to talk about Deep Seated Learning Environments in the Digital Age.

I'd no idea what plonker-Heron wanted, so, thank you, because I would now be worrying about that.

Then, Lee was in a mood about something that morning. All I did was try to give her some advice about her make-up, and she got uppity when I looked in her bag to see what she slathered on her face nowadays.

You know, I spent eighty-five pounds on that truffle serum I gave her, and she didn't even use it. I sometimes wondered if she cared about her looks. She went to the gym for a while, but I couldn't tell if it did much good. I thought I detected a bit of weight loss, but she wore those baggy tunics so you couldn't really tell what was underneath. No, she didn't make the best of herself. I told her that, for someone like her who's carrying a bit of extra flab, it could be disguised with a well-cut dress rather than those awful jeggings and shapeless tops.

I tried to talk to her about what Peter Heron might want me for, but she went all evasive and huffed off.

What a relief to get back to my flat. I love to shut the door and unwind. My style is minimal; I don't over-furnish or fill the place with objects. Everything is pale and subtle. I can relax here; it's calm and restful – monastically aesthetic.

I plonked the tote on the sofa, eased off my shoes and walked into the kitchen, opened the fridge door, took out a two-thirds empty bottle of white wine and poured the remnants into a wine glass plucked off the drainer. I went into the sitting room, sat down wearily, reached for the zapper and pressed the TV button.

Ah! A shopping channel and a prancing, over-made-up girl having orgasms about a handbag as she opened the flap to point out the 'mechanics' of the zipped section inside.

Flick to another channel and…oh! It was Dan staring back at me. Well, not so much staring at me as reading the latest news on Ridings Today.

Seeing my ex-husband. That's all I needed.

Chapter Eighty-Two

Lee

My phone had been red-hot all evening. First, Fliss warning me to expect a call from Mammy. 'Act surprised,' she ordered. And hung up.

The phone was hardly back on its hook when it rang again. Mammy herself, cooing over the prospect of a new baby and delighted to be the first to tell me the good news.

'And you really didn't guess?' she asked.

I told a little white lie. 'No, hadn't a clue.'

No need though to act surprised, or anything else for that matter, because I could barely get a word in edgeways. 'Due date blah, blah, blah...first scan blah, blah, blah...don't mind if it's a boy or a girl blah, blah, blah.' I was only half-listening, feeling just a little sad. But, no point dwelling on might have-beens.

She rang off eventually, and two minutes later Fliss was back on the line again.

'I've been trying to get through for ages. What did Mammy have to say?'

Do you want the short or the long answer? 'A lot.'

'Such as?'

Oh, Fliss. What do you think she said? 'She's thrilled to bits, of course. Expect lots of fussing,' I warned.

I could almost hear her grimacing.

'It's your own fault,' I said. 'I thought you weren't going to say anything

289

just yet?'

Seems she'd seriously underestimated Ritchie and his ability to put two and two together. He'd blabbed when Mammy did her usual Tuesday tea-time school pick-up, utterly delighted at the prospect of a little brother. 'Because God couldn't be so mean as to give me another sister.' Oh, the innocence of youth. God could, and might well, do just that.

Fliss was on the phone, talking babies, even longer than Mammy.

Next to call was Declan, also grumbling about my line being engaged. 'I tried your mobile too,' he said.

Yes, I'd seen the missed call but could only hold one phone conversation at a time.

'Don't be sarcastic,' he said.

Feeling a bit touchy, Declan? 'What do you want?' I really couldn't be bothered with the pleasantries. Nor could he.

'Have you spoken to Teri recently?'

Daft question. 'We work together,' I said. 'We're best friends. What do you think?'

'Okay. Okay. You're joined at the hip...I get it.'

Now who's being sarcastic? But I held my tongue. No point in quarrelling.

There was a short silence. 'How's she taking things?'

What to say? She's a mess? You broke her heart? She's barely coping?

'Couldn't be better,' I lied. 'In fact, I think she's got her sights set on someone new.' Well, if she hadn't, it wouldn't be long before she did. 'You know Teri, she doesn't let the grass grow under her feet.'

Another silence. 'Declan?'

'I wanted to call...tell her I was sorry...try to explain...'

'Why didn't you?'

Silence again. 'I daren't.'

For God's sake. Why ever not? She won't bite you.

'Marnie,' he said. 'I know she's checking my phone – that's how she found out about Teri in the first place.'

I sighed. Teri and her 'cheeky' text messages. It made sense.

'Marnie said she'd kill herself, and the babies, if I didn't come back.'

What? That wasn't what Teri told me.

290

'She's crazy, Lee. It's the pregnancy – hormones or something. I don't know.'

Huh. Trust a man to blame a woman's hormones. 'And who got her pregnant?'

'She said she was on the pill,' he wailed.

Idiot. You wouldn't think he'd be stupid enough to fall for that one.

'Call her bluff,' I said. Sorry, but he wasn't getting any sympathy from me.

'Would you risk it?'

'It's not my call.'

'You're a cow, Lee.' he growled. 'I only called because I was concerned about Teri and wanted you to pass on a message.'

'Don't believe you. And, no, I won't.' No sense in beating about the bush. 'She's well shut of you, and if you think I'm going to pave the way for reconciliation so you can break her heart again...'

'Break whose heart?' he asked.

'It doesn't matter. Do your own dirty work. Ring Teri yourself – if you dare. And,' I added, 'I don't bloody believe you about Marnie.' I slammed the phone down so hard it practically bounced back off the hook.

The liar. Serve him right if Marnie did commit suicide. Oh, how horrible of me? I crossed myself and muttered Mammy's favourite prayer: 'God forgive, my body spoke not I.'

But Declan's call left me feeling thoroughly churned up and fretting even more about Teri than I had been earlier. I knew I should ring her but, at the same time, it was getting late and I was tired and didn't know if I could face another long drawn-out conversation listening to someone else let off steam. It was about time someone listened to me for a change.

Fat chance. The phone rang again. Dan. What did he want? Sighing, I picked up the receiver.

'Can I come round?'

I knew what that meant. He was still running shy about coming clean with Teri. I sympathised, but he was her ex-husband and it wasn't fair to expect someone else – me! – to do his dirty work. He was supposed to break the news that afternoon – he texted earlier to say he'd decided not to put things off any longer. And I'd texted back, 'YOU'D BETTER!!!' And I

291

knew damn well, because Teri was just about the only person who hadn't telephoned tonight, he'd chickened out again.

'You bloody coward,' I said as he walked in, his face still shiny from scrubbing off his studio make-up.

'I know, I know.' He held up his hands in a gesture of surrender. 'Don't shout. I didn't dare.'

Men! First, Declan, now Dan. The pair of them could do with a balls transplant.

'Man up,' I said.

He said nothing, just poured himself a glass of lime cordial.

'What do you want to do?'

He shook his head. 'Don't know.' He screwed the bottle top back on. 'I wish you wouldn't leave the top off,' he said as he returned the bottle to the soft drinks cupboard. I smiled, remembering Teri's grumbles about his untidy little ways. Should have listened to me. There's more than one way to skin a cat, Teri.

Mentally, I slapped myself. Don't be unkind, I thought. Or smug. Doesn't suit you.

And I remembered that when the chips were down, Teri had been there for me. Okay – I opened the fridge and extracted a bottle of Muscadet. Dan had already got the glasses. I filled them both almost to the brim.

'I'll speak to her tomorrow,' I said.

'Promise?' he asked.

'Promise,' I said.

Chapter Eighty-Three

Teri

I stared out into a lecture theatre full of students; most offered blank, bored faces. True, there were some expectant looks but these were from the handful of 'mature' students treating their Eng Lit BA as a lucky dip in which they got to read books they should've read when they were younger. In the main though, the students were dull-looking; not interested and not bothered. Some even had their heads down, staring at their laps. 'Could you turn your mobiles off,' I instructed. Do they think I was born yesterday and didn't realise half of them were Tweeting or Facebooking?

'Rochester,' I said as authoritatively as I could. 'He's a fallen lyric poet, obsessed with the poignancy of absence, loss and fear.'

I'd said those words many times before (hell, why rewrite your lectures year after year?) There is no better way of describing Rochester. Love, for him, is linked with pain. For him and for his lovers. But now, standing in front of Level 2 and repeating the well-worn themes of love, despair and wantonness, I shivered. I was describing the libertine, the rake, the masochistic poet for whom sexual activity and conquering the woman was the only way of coming to terms with morality. 'Rochester is tortured by the increasing gap between the love that he believes is divine and human love which he finds impossible to achieve,' I said.

Something snapped in my brain. Hang on, I thought. What am I talking about? A man who needs to put flesh on flesh like no one else; a man who treats women as his personal playthings and whores. Why does this remind me so much of Declan? Surely, I thought, I must've seen this before. Declan, the womaniser, the libertine, the rake. What irony. The man I'd been researching all my academic life and the man I'd had as my lover were one and the same. Rochester, the poet and libertine; Declan, the writer and rake.

I felt dizzy with the sudden awareness. Bastards. Both of them. I must've looked spaced out for a moment because there was a general rustling of anticipation as Level 2 realised I wasn't speaking but staring into the ether.

David Greenspan broke the spell. He was leaning back – comfortably – in his seat and ever so lazily, raised an arm. It would be him. Damn him. 'Yes, David?'

'Aren't you over-egging this idea?' the impudent little sod asked. 'Wasn't he just one of those blokes who liked a good time?'

Who, I thought, confused for the moment: Declan or Rochester?

Half a dozen faces lit up. There were some nudges as some of the more half-asleep students realised something had happened and they wanted to know what. Another half dozen looked up from their texting to see what all the fuss was about. Suddenly, I had everyone's attention.

'If blokes behave the way he does then they're not very nice people,' I said. 'For Rochester, sexual activity is a momentary act of need; something that offers instant gratification.'

'Yes, but it's not just men who are like that, is it?' Greenspan suggested. 'Can't women be just as predatory?'

'I'm not saying Rochester was predatory. In fact, I don't believe he needed to be. He was wanton and he made no secret of his pleasure-seeking.' (Hah, Declan, again.)

'Oh, so you think it's wrong to make a secret of pleasure-seeking. Rather like stalking?' Greenspan put much emphasis on that word stalking.

'I don't know how we got to talking about stalking,' I stammered. 'Rochester was debauched but he never stalked anyone...'

'Unlike some modern day heroes – and heroines?' Greenspan said.

My brain churned. How was I going to get this back on track? I had everyone's attention now. They didn't realise what was going on, but they were delighted something was.

'I mean,' Greenspan said, 'what would you say about a woman, ooh in her forties, being a bit of a libertine with her students?'

That certainly sparked a few bums to wriggle in their seats.

My head became suddenly hot. I could feel tiny globs of perspiration breaking out on my top lip and, worse, running between my breasts. Oh hell. I can't get damp patches on this silk shirt.

'But we're not talking about a female libertine, David,' I offered as reasonably as I could. 'We're talking about a Restoration man who wrote pornography – often about his king – and managed to not just satirise a licentious seventeenth century court but roister neck deep in it as well. Here was a man for whom relationships with women amounted to as much sex as he could get but with non-permanence as the overriding feature.'

The full force of it hit me. It was Declan. I was talking about Declan. How that bastard had used me. The only man I'd ever loved…how had it got to this? Self-pity slathered over me like hot oil from an overhead cauldron. It knocked the breath out of me and my whole body weakened.

I reached for the front of the desk on which my notes and bottle of water stood. The room span as I leaned forward. Oh, God, no. Don't let me faint in front of Level 2. I grabbed the bottle, twisted the top off and took a swig. The room settled. The students were silent. Watching. What sport, they must be thinking. One of the mature women students shifted forwards in her seat as if ready to lunge in my direction to catch me should I fall.

I needed to say something, but I couldn't get my breath. Was I having a heart attack? I tried to drag some air into my lungs. No. Couldn't breathe. I clenched my fist and thumped it against my chest, trying to make the action seem as natural as possible but, in fact, hoping that some self-administered chest compressions would restart my heart. Which was ludicrous as my heart was thumping so loudly I was surprised the daft little twerp with the Mohican haircut at the back of the hall couldn't hear it drumming.

'Basically, David Greenspan,' I managed to say at last. 'Men like that are bastards. Fucking evil, selfish, time-wasting bastards. And you,' I added, glaring at him with all the venom I could muster, 'are the male equivalent of a prick tease – a pretty boy who's trying to play with the big boys. Only you picked the wrong woman, didn't you?'

'Very literary,' I heard him say before I turned from the lectern and ran out of the room.

Chapter Eighty-Four

Teri

It's not like me to have panic attacks, and I can only assume that's what it was. I certainly wasn't having a heart attack and I didn't pass out, but all I'd been able to think about was getting out of that lecture theatre and away from those inquisitive little faces, enlivened by the idea that something pretty catastrophic was happening to their English lecturer.

I was supposed to be running a couple of seminar groups later in the day, but there was no way once I got out into the staff car park and into my car I was going back into that university.

I drove straight home, parked the car, went into the flat and poured myself the remnants of a bottle of white wine I'd left in the fridge the night before. As I sloshed it into a glass and knocked it back there was a satisfying warm glow starting somewhere in the gut I always get when I have a drink. So what that it was just after 11am; so what that I'd not had breakfast; so what if I was going to open another bottle; so what if it meant I would probably spend the rest of the day lying on the sofa, slightly drunk and watching mind-numbing programmes on daytime television. So what? Who cared?

Dan would care, I told myself later having polished off a couple of glasses from the next bottle of wine. He was the only one who ever cared for me – at least, he was the only one who ever cared enough to marry me. Why didn't I realise earlier what a lovely, kind, patient man he was. I mean, look how nice he was being to Lee. He realised how lonely she was and, to be honest, she'd had a bit of a bad time of it what with that creep Mike Orme and the abortion and then the love affair – or whatever it was – with Christian going belly up. It was nice of Dan to be so concerned; he was such a softy. I just hoped Lee wouldn't get the wrong idea and think Dan fancied her or something.

Dan and I had some good times, didn't we? We were good together, weren't we? Why did I let him go? He'd be round like a shot if he knew how bad I was feeling; he'd want to come and take care of me. He'd look at me lying here on the sofa, my eyes red from crying, and he would take me in his arms. 'Darling Teri,' he would say, softly kissing away my tears. 'You were the only one for me. Take me back.'

Oh, get a grip, girl, I told myself. You're sounding like a Mills and Boon novel. But it would be nice to talk to Dan. I rang his mobile.

'Hi, Teri,' he said. (Bless him, I was still in his mobile contacts list.)

'Oh, Dan, I'm so glad to get you.' The relief at hearing his voice turned my words to sobs. 'Please help me, Dan. You're the only one who can.'

'God, Teri. What's happened? What's the matter?' He sounded alarmed.

'Something awful happened today…'

'Are you all right? Have you had an accident?'

'No, no, nothing like that. It's just that things have got out of control. I need to talk to you, Dan. I need you.'

'Oh, Teri. I'm just about to go into a pre-record for tonight's programme…'

Of course, once again, the programme took precedence; that was how it was throughout our marriage. I resisted the desire to tell him to forget it and instead said weakly, 'Oh, of course, you must do the programme. I'm sorry, I'd forgotten how busy you are. Don't you worry about me, I'll be all right.' And I clicked my mobile off and left it switched off.

It worked. Thirty minutes later, the doorbell rang and I walked gingerly to open the door and let Dan in. He took one look at me and slipping an arm around my waist he gently guided me back to the sofa. 'God, you look awful,' he said.

'I feel awful,' I told him.

'Listen, I got someone else to do the pre-record, and I'm here now. Tell me what's wrong.'

'I just realise what a fool I've been,' I said between breathy sobs. 'I behaved really badly towards you, and I forced you away, and I'm really, really sorry. Ever since we split up life has just got worse. It's all crap; shit.'

I told him in short, sharp sentences how Declan had let me down; how I made a fool of myself over David Greenspan, and how, he, Dan, had been the only man to ever truly love me. 'I need you, Dan. I want you back.'

I looked at him appealingly, probably aware that my mascara was running down my cheeks and making me look ridiculously pathetic, but not caring – for once – about how I looked. There would be plenty of time for looking more like myself again once Dan was back in my life.

But Dan shook his head reluctantly. 'Teri, I'm sorry,' he said.

'Why are you sorry?' I asked, reaching a hand up towards him, aware that he was still standing over me instead of nestling down where I lay slumped and panda-eyed on the sofa.

He took an intake of breath. 'Teri, I did have enormous feelings for you, but come on, you've got to admit it, it didn't work out between us. We wanted different things; different lives. We simply couldn't live together; we rowed constantly.'

'I could change,' I pleaded. 'I will change. We'll do things together; we'll work it out. I'll be different…'

'No, Teri,' he said.

'Please, Dan. I'll do anything…'

'No,' he repeated, wiping his brow with the back of his fingers. 'I'm sorry, love, but it's too late. After Sara and then you, I felt as though I was never going to have a relationship that worked. But I've found someone else and we're really good together…'

'Who?' I demanded, pulling myself upright.

'Well…er…look, who she is isn't the point. The point is it's never going to work between you and me. Even you've got to see that. I think you're just feeling sorry for yourself at the moment but, hey, this is Teri Meyer we're talking about, and what does she do best? She pulls herself up and gets back on with it, and this is exactly what you'll do. In a couple of weeks' time, you'll be laughing at the idea that you and I could ever get back together. That's how you are, Teri. You want instant gratification but when you get it, you're still not satisfied. You always want something else; something more. If I agreed to come back now, it would be good for a day or two and then – pow! It would be all over again. I'm right, aren't I?' He smiled down at me. 'I'm going to make you a cup of strong, black coffee,' he said. 'Then I will leave you to drink it while I hotfoot it back to the studios. When I've gone, I want you to have a shower, scrub that make-up off that gorgeous face of yours because it doesn't need all the slap you put on it, slip into something comfortable that isn't silk, short or tight-fitting, put the wine bottle away and give yourself a night off from stressing about your life. Will you do that?'

I nodded sadly. 'I might even watch your programme and look out for skateboarding ducks,' I told him. 'Will you make some sign to acknowledge me – you know: use your right arm to scratch your left ear.' I smiled at Dan and he laughed, remembering how I'd asked him to do that once before.

He ruffled my hair with his right hand. 'I'll just gaze out at you via the camera,' he said. 'If that's all right with you.'

Chapter Eighty-Five

Lee

But I didn't call tomorrow – because before I could, Dan texted to say he'd had a call from Teri. She was frantic, and he was nipping out of work to check on her. He promised to call as soon as he got a chance. I texted back, 'YOU TELL HER!!!' And I knew damn well, he wouldn't.

Later, he apologised. 'You bloody coward,' I told him again. I was getting really fed up with the whole situation. It wasn't fair on Teri, and it wasn't fair on me – or Dan either, I supposed.

'Don't shout,' he said. 'She was almost hysterical – I just couldn't kick her when she was already down.'

No, but you bloody well expect me to.

Sometimes, Dan, I thought, I really don't like you.

But I was angry with myself too – because, I could've rung her that morning instead of making excuses and putting things off until the afternoon. And then, when I got Dan's text message, I thought I might as well wait so he could talk to her instead. I was a bloody coward too.

'I'll ring her now,' I said.

'Don't,' Dan said. 'I've had enough for one day. Leave it until tomorrow.'

And, once again, I took the easy way out.

Chapter Eighty-Six

Teri

'Ah, come in Miss Meyer.' Peter Heron looked suave in a pale blue, heavy linen jacket with darker blue trousers and a crisp, white t-shirt. I thought, nice combo, but at the same time wondering, why *Miss Meyer* and not simply Teri?

Oh, the prat is playing at being formal; we're going to get lots of Heron-buzz-speak.

He'd come to the door when I knocked and now stood on the threshold holding it open for me, which surprised me as normally he likes to stay seated behind his great desk and call 'Come' in the way senior managers do when they think they're above saying 'Come in'.

I stepped into the office and saw someone else in the room, sitting at the very boardroom table where two years previously I'd sat for the interview for my job. The someone else was also the someone else who'd been sitting at the boardroom table then: Tim, the rather good-looking and only bloke in Human Resources, the rest of them being simpering girlies who did nothing but ask staff to fill out forms demanding to know which training courses they'd been on – although why Man Handling and Understanding Fire Extinguishers was on the list of training courses is beyond me. Tim looked up and didn't return my smile. He appeared a bit glum.

'Oh,' I said, turning to Peter Heron. 'Shall I wait outside while you finish with Tim?'

'No,' Peter said. 'Tim is in on the meeting. I thought it advisable that someone from Human Resources was here. Have you not brought anyone with you?'

Ah, this was either going to be a promotion or something else, and I remembered with not inconsiderable alarm something Lee suggested when I told her I had a meeting with Peter. She'd adopted that concerned look and said, 'You know, Teri, it might be something and nothing, but, whatever, why don't you take along someone from the union?'

'Why on earth would I want a union rep with me?'

'Well...' She hesitated. 'It's always useful to have another pair of eyes and ears in any sort of meeting, whether it's about something good or bad.'

'What do you think it could be about?' I asked her, rattled now.

Again, she hesitated. Then she said 'I don't know' in that resigned tone she reserves for people who aren't thinking sensibly.

'Well, anyway,' I retorted, suddenly angry with her, 'I'm not in the union. I never joined; didn't see the point. They're always spouting a lot of hot air and taking days off on strike, and I just can't be doing with them. So I doubt very much any of the reps will want to sit with me *if* I'm going to have my hands slapped.'

For a nano second I wondered about asking Lee if she'd come with me, but then dismissed the idea. Ever since that bloody Tuscan holiday she and Dan went on, she'd been insufferable. They'd become best buddies, for goodness' sake. They saw themselves as each other's 'walker', all very palsy and platonic and friendly. I mean, what the hell were they playing at? Dan would never fancy Lee in a million years. And, anyway, from what he'd told me last night, he'd met someone else and, although he wanted to keep it hush-hush, it sounded serious. Lee was in for a surprise when she found out. She obviously thought she was in the running with Dan. Hah! Well, it served her right for being so treacherous; anyone who pals up with their best friend's ex is frankly asking for trouble. Dan would have to drop her like a tonne of the proverbial when this new woman was made public. She wouldn't want pally Lee around.

So I wouldn't give Lee the satisfaction of asking her for any help. But what could Peter Heron be planning that required armed back up? Okay, so I'd missed a few lectures, and my research had ground to a halt, and the ungrateful undergraduates were giving up on my Moral and Monarchical Panics of the 1600s in droves, but what's the worst he could do to me?

'Ah, sit down, Miss Meyer,' Peter said using the formal tone again and indicating a seat on the other side of the boardroom table to Tim, who now looked closely through a pile of papers stacked in an open green file. Peter sat down next to him, opposite me, with a similarly sized stack of papers in a similarly open green file.

'Looks ominous,' I joked.

'This is a serious matter,' Peter said, taking a sheet of paper from the top of the file and examining it. 'Let's start here. Cancelled and missed lectures…'

Ah, I could see where this was going so I leaned forward and started to say something about how there were reasons…and everyone cancelled or missed…but Heron ignored me, raising a hand with his palm flat out in my direction in the way of a bored dictator who wants to silence a rebellious insubordinate before he has him taken out for execution.

He read off a list of dates starting with one in December 2012 and ending with yesterday's. My mind whirred. December 2012? Oh yes. That was the day of the RTS awards dinner, and I'd taken time off to get ready. The other dates went on…and on. Heron took his time, enunciating clearly and crisply. When he got to yesterday, I interjected, 'I was ill…'

'I'm sorry, Miss Meyer,' Heron said, again dismissing me. 'There are too many dates on this list to warrant any kind of excuse: missed and cancelled lectures; group seminars where you started late or finished early or simply did not turn up; individual tutorials – similarly. While I accept that illness, traffic delays and urgent meetings can affect delivery of some lectures, seminars and tutorials, there are, quite simply, far too many dates on this list in which you failed to turn up, failed to offer a reasonable excuse for your absence, and abdicated your responsibilities to your students who, I might add, pay a high price for attending this university and expect to be treated with a larger degree of respect than you seem able to offer.'

'Ah, but…' I tried to say, but he went on.

'Next, we turn to mark sheets.' He lifted another sheet of paper from the pile. 'Mark sheets never handed in on time, and you do not need me to tell you how inconvenient this is to not only the admin staff who have to collate

303

hundreds of marks from across the Faculty at one of the busiest times of the whole academic year, but to the entire teaching cohort on whom final marks are crucial to the awarding of overall student results.'

'Oh, it was just…' I tried to say, but he went on.

'And, even more seriously, on examining the marks on the mark sheets that you *eventually* handed in in May, this year, for example, we find huge inconsistencies in the comments you make and the results you award.'

'The marks were all…' I tried to say, but he went on.

'And when we had the marks that you awarded subjected to second marking and external scrutiny, we found – interestingly – that while the second marker and the external examiner both agreed their marks, the results were vastly at odds with the marks that you, yourself had awarded.'

'Well, no two examiners always agree entirely…'

'You're right, they don't, but the inconsistencies between the marks of the second and external examiners and your own are of such variance that we've had to come to the conclusion that your judgment in these particular results was highly – how can I say? – suspect.'

'Are you accusing me of…'

'We are not accusing you, Miss Meyer, we are telling you: if you award a student a mark of seventy-five, which equates to a good First, yet both a second marker and a respected external examiner award that same piece of work a fifty-one, which equates to a low 2:2, what are we supposed to deduce?'

I decided not to deduce anything. I looked down at my hands, neatly folded in my lap. It was a fair cop. Of course I remembered rushing through the marking I had to do back in May, but how many lecturers haven't done the same? Who hasn't skimmed the surface from time to time?

But Heron had more to say. 'And now we come to an even more serious matter,' he said, leaning forward with yet another piece of paper from the pile. Tim hardly dared look at me. 'We have received a serious complaint from a student…'

'What…?'

'…from a student who alleges that you made a quite specific threat to him regarding his mark…'

Gorgeous Greenspan!

'It wasn't a serious threat…I just…'

'Miss Meyer, the allegation is that you made a serious threat regarding a student and one of his end-of-year marks. You threatened the student that if he didn't behave in a particular way – and I won't go into the details here because I think we all know what we're talking about – you would reduce his mark from what would have been deemed a Pass to what would then be deemed a Fail. We consider this to be totally unacceptable as well as unprofessional and, frankly, outrageous behaviour from a member of staff.'

'I really don't think…' I stammered, wondering how Gorgeous Greenspan could possibly have taken me seriously, but Heron cut me off again.

'You might be relieved to hear that the student in question was extremely reluctant to make a complaint against you, but your threat was overhead by a member of staff who felt under a professional obligation to report the matter albeit after a period of time while the said member of staff considered the implications of her doing so.'

Fucking Chrissie. Trust her to open her big mouth.

'Now look…' I began, but I wasn't sure where I was going, which was not a problem as Heron had even more to say and cut me off.

'I come to another matter which, while it was something that occurred outside of the university campus and outside the usual university hours, is still of grave concern given that it involved the same student – who is the subject of the existing complaint – and yourself at an event in which dozens of other undergraduates were present and who, I am sorry to say, witnessed what happened.'

The May Ball!

'We take an extremely dim view of any member of staff behaving in a drunken, lewd manner whether it's on university property, in university time, or not. We do not expect our members of staff to do other than behave professionally at all times and set a good example to the young people studying at our institution and, on this occasion, what they witnessed in your behaviour, Miss Meyer, did not attain the highest standards that we endeavour to achieve in our professional capacity as capable and responsible examples to, and leaders of, young people.' He went on. 'As dean of the Faculty of English and Media, I need to be quality focused and while I have

305

parked various of your indiscretions during the two years you have been with us…'

'Parked indiscretions?' I asked, genuinely surprised.

'Yes,' he replied. 'Let me explain. Your research, for example. You were awarded a place at this university partly on the strength of a research bursary of thirty thousand pounds that you gave every impression was expected to be awarded to you by the Association of English Educators. But it transpires that it was several months *after* that bursary was awarded to *another* academic at *another* university – in fact, a competitor of ours – that you chose to reveal you had failed in your application and that, in fact, you had not attained the bursary. Keeping this knowledge to yourself, as you did, you continued, nonetheless, to give every impression that the AEE had not made the award and that you, yourself, were still being considered for it.'

'Ah, there was a reason…'

'Whatever the reason, Miss Meyer, we offered you employment partly based on the understanding you would be enriching our research facility with a major piece of academic work and it was your responsibility to inform us the minute the wherewithal for said same research was withdrawn. As I said, this was one of those indiscretions that we chose to park, giving you the benefit of the doubt. But, may I ask, what has happened to your research?'

'I…'

'I'll tell you,' he went on. 'Nothing.

'Miss Meyer,' he said, verbally changing tack. 'As I said, I need to be quality focused, have clarity of purpose to empower everyone on my team, and while I have parked various indiscretions of yours on the cloud…'

Oh no. He wasn't going to go on – not using Heron-speak. 'Oh for goodness' sake, Peter,' I said, brittle and stern. 'You don't need to go on. I know and you know that you've parked your so-called indiscretions because I was married to Dan Caine and you thought you had to keep me sweet so I would put in a good word for you and your hopes of being a television star. And now that Dan and I are divorced you don't need me anymore, so I guess what's happening here is that you're trying to get rid of me – how's that for professional behaviour from a dean?' I looked at Tim for support, but he suddenly found his notes extremely interesting and wouldn't look up.

306

'Well, *Mister* Heron, I'm afraid your chances of being on the telly are extremely dim…'

'We're not here to talk about my future, Miss Meyer. We are here to talk about yours. And you are right, although your phraseology is somewhat amiss. I am going to offer you the chance to resign – rather than be dismissed for gross misconduct – and, although your contract of employment allows you two months' notice of termination, I am willing to let you go right away. Frank, the porter, is waiting outside, and he will escort you to your office so that you can collect any items of a personal nature and then he will accompany you to Human Resources where I would ask you to hand over your staff badge and security swipe card, and then Frank will escort you to your car – and off the premises. Unless you need any further clarity, or have any further questions, I shall expect a letter of resignation from you delivered by Recorded Delivery on my desk tomorrow morning. Thank you, Miss Meyer.'

I'm sure there should have been a thousand and one things I could've said. But rather than appeal, apologise, explain or simply sob, I stood up – Tim and arsehole Heron stood too – and I made for the door and tried not to wobble too much in my six-inch heels that I'd chosen for the occasion.

Bugger me, but Frank was standing outside with pure satisfaction stamped on his face. He was just about to follow me as I set off down the corridor when I realised Heron had snuck up behind.

'Er, one moment, Teri,' he said, gripping my arm, pulling me to a stop and offering me a sickly smile. 'You'll be delighted to know that Richard Walker – you know, the MD of Ridings Today – came to see me yesterday to tell me that the idea for a Friday night books programme, which had been shelved, is back on again and – despite the very kind reference you gave him about me – he offered me the role of presenter. Thought you'd want to know.'

Frank stood in the doorway of my office as I opened and shut drawers and ran my hand along shelves looking for any items of what Peter Heron described as of a personal nature that I needed to remove. Someone had left a clear Perspex box on my desk in readiness for the haul and, like Frank waiting outside Heron's office to escort me, I could see my leaving had been an anticipated and probably foregone conclusion to which there would be no appeal and for which I had been the only one not to have seen coming.

Odd, that after two years, there was very little accumulation of items of a personal nature. Certainly no photographs – I don't have kids, but, anyway, I wouldn't have been one of those women who needed pictures of their precious little darlings glued to the wall above their computers in the unlikely event of their forgetting what the progeny looked like. Nor did I have pictures of meaningful partners – I'd torn up all my wedding photos when Dan left, and Declan was always reluctant to have his picture taken (fearful, no doubt, they could be used in evidence should his daft little wife or his latest mistress find them).

My books? There was a limited demand for tomes majoring on the restoration period, and I didn't have the energy to sell them on the second-hand book market. My research? It was all there: the libertine lying in wait in a big, black box file. I picked it up and dumped it in the waste bin with a loud clatter which made Frank look across in my direction. 'You must be loving this,' I said to him.

'Actually, I'm not,' he said. 'I thought, earlier, outside Mr. Heron's office, that you'd got your comeuppance, but when it comes down to it, I feel sorry for you.'

'Well, that's hunky dory of you,'' I snapped. 'But I don't need your sympathy. I'm well shot of this place.' Frank shrugged. I reached into the bin and retrieved the box file and put it in the Perspex box. Might come in useful at some later date, I told myself.

Once the humiliating trip to Human Remains and the formal handing-in of my staff badge and swipe card was over, my Perspex box containing my life's research and I walked out to the car park. 'I know my way from here,' I said to Frank, but he shook his head.

'Got to see you off the premises,' he said. I placed the Perspex box on the roof of my car while I fumbled around in my handbag for the keys and saw that my mobile phone was flashing a message. I'd check it later once I was away from here. I put the box in the boot of the car, climbed into the driving seat and closed the door, winding down the window. 'Bye, Frank. No hard feelings?'

He had the grace to smile. 'No hard feelings, Teri.'

I accelerated away perhaps a little too quickly and had to break sharply to avoid someone stepping out into my path from between a row of parked cars. I recognised the plump and dumpy figure of Stella Lastings and cursed myself for stopping so suddenly. Better to hit and squash her to a pulp. She looked up, realised it was me and inhaled a sharp breath. Oh yes, she knew, damn her. 'Yes, Stella,' I said through the open window. 'It's me – and I'm off.' She looked about to say something, but I beat her to it. 'Some advice for you, Stella. Try a diet, you fat cow!' Not the most erudite of farewells, but who knows, she might be glad of the advice.

As I pulled out of the main university entrance my legs shook. My mind reeled. What just happened? Had I really been sacked? I checked in the mirror to make sure neither Frank nor Stella were watching, then pulled over into the layby on the other side of the gates and laid my head on the steering wheel to get my breath. I reached into my bag on the passenger seat for a small bottle of water I always keep at the ready.

I took a pull of water and breathed deeply once or twice until I felt calmer. Taking the phone, I saw the message was a text from Dad.

'Ring urgently.'

I scrolled down my contacts until 'Dad' featured on the screen, and I pressed the green 'talk' button, eventually hearing the long tone that meant the battered old dial phone Dad preferred to a modern device was ringing somewhere inside an old, stone cottage whose walls were covered in a mix of wisteria and knot weed in deepest rural France. I imagined him putting his book down on the ground beside him, pulling himself out of his wicker sun lounger on the back patch of grass and shuffling along the stone flooring of the kitchen to the old, wooden plant stand where the phone sat with its cord curled in tight corkscrews.

'Bonjour?' he said.

'Dad, it's me. What's up?' He never contacts me so I guessed this was some emergency to do with him, Mum or Charlie. As it happened, it was to do with all of them – and me.

'Bad news, love,' he said. 'We've gone bust.'

It turns out finances at the factory had been on the downward slide for months. Dad was saying something about being shafted by 'that bastard' and explaining something to do with a bad investment in new machinery at a time when orders were dwindling thanks to competition from cheap foreign imports, but I couldn't take it in. 'What are you saying, Dad? Who's shafted us and is this something we can recover from?' I couldn't imagine life without the factory in the background turning out its sheets of metal and, more importantly, the money that kept this family going.

'Pranks has shafted us – and I'm saying that it's the end of the line,' he replied. 'There's nothing left.'

Dad said he'd assumed I realised something was wrong when my allowance had become more erratic; some months it was late and other months it didn't arrive at all. Well, of course I'd noticed, but what with all I'd had to put up with over the last couple of years, I hadn't chased it up as I might've done.

'I should have warned you,' Dad said. 'Pranks started laying people off to save costs and then, of course, when a big order came in, he didn't have enough people to process it so we lost that too. The order book has been empty since then – so everyone's been given the boot – and there's no money to pay any redundancy so you can imagine how the workforce is feeling about that.'

'But surely there's some money left? What about the factory itself – can that be sold?'

'Pranks sold it off two years ago,' Dad said, sighing. 'The idea was to capitalise on the property by releasing equity to put into the business and then lease the building back, but it seems Pranks didn't put any of the capital into the factory – and nor did he pay any rent or rates for the last eighteen months.'

'Didn't he discuss any of this with you?'

'Well, yes – and no,' Dad said. 'He'd discussed selling the building, and I thought it was the right idea at the time so I left it all to him – gave him the power; signed everything over to him to take full control. I was an idiot, but stupidly, I trusted him.'

'And where is Pranks now?'

'Ah,' Dad said. 'That's the thing. He's done a bunk.'

'Done a bunk?'

'Yes, he's buggered off somewhere – with all the money from the sale of the factory, plus what he should've been paying in rent and rates – and the entire company pension fund. He had full financial control over everything,

310

you see.'

'And can't we find him? Stop his bank account? Do something?'

'Sorry, darling. I've been trying everything for the last couple of weeks since I realised what was going on. Pranks has been planning his getaway for years. The police said he's probably gone abroad somewhere, created a new identity for himself, and opened accounts under a new name. They doubt we'll ever find him. Meanwhile, the creditors are circling, and I'm going to be made bankrupt.'

'So what does it mean for us?'

'It means there is no money left.'

'But Dad,' I wailed. 'I've just been sacked. How am I going to manage?'

'I'm sorry, darling, but you're on your own.'

I switched off my mobile and sat, blindly staring at nothing at all, trying to take it all in. I hadn't been able to think; to move; to do anything. A sudden knocking on my driver's window made me jump and I looked to the right. A figure was bending down looking into the car. Stella fucking Lastings was tap-tap-tapping on the window. 'Teri...' she mouthed. I wound down the window so I could hear what she was saying.

'Are you all right?' she asked. 'You've been sitting here for ages. We were getting worried about you.' I noticed Frank behind her, shifting his weight from one leg to the other.

I couldn't speak; I wanted to yell, to scream, to cry, even to laugh. To do anything other than sit here while Stella and Frank took in the sight of me, pathetic and broken; a sad fool who'd clearly had some sort of breakdown and was now unable to move or say anything.

Stella reached into the car with her podgy arm and gently stroked my shoulder. 'You've had a shock. Why don't you come back into uni with me, and I'll get you a cup of tea or something.'

I stared in her direction but couldn't focus. 'I can't...' I said. 'Not allowed...'

'Oh, I'm sure it would be all right.' I looked more intently and took in her pretty, plump face, the rose red lips formed in a compressed heart shape, which I read as being her concerned look. She smiled ever so weakly in the face of my suddenly focused scrutiny.

'Oh, God, Stella. Why are you being so nice to me?'

'Because you're upset, and I'm worried about you.' With sudden clarity I realised she was being honest and genuine, and it shook me. I felt something give way – the iron grip around my middle that normally held me so tightly suddenly released. I took a deep breath and as I let the breath out, the tightness round my stomach slackened even more. My shoulders dropped, my clenched fists loosened, and I slumped forward slightly and, for the first time for what seemed like years, I relaxed into my own body. Someone was worried about me, and it happened to be the one person I'd been so awful to over the last two years. I'd even shouted a totally offensive instruction at her after narrowly failing to run her down just minutes ago.

'Why? I mean, why are you worried about me?'

She looked nonplussed for a moment, and said, 'Because I think you need help.'

'Stella,' I said, 'thank you…' I was going to add something cutting along the lines that I didn't need help, and I certainly didn't need help from an oversized do-gooder like her, but in this new-found sense of grace that overwhelmed me, I couldn't. I felt she had been kind – more kind than I deserved – and I should try to reciprocate the feeling even if it meant giving her the satisfaction of knowing she had done her good deed for the day. 'Look, I've just had some bad news – no, nothing for anyone to worry about,' I added, seeing her look of increased concern. 'No death or destruction. But I'm okay now. I'm on top of it. I know what I'm doing. I'm off now – but thanks again.' I pressed down on the clutch, switched on the engine and pushed the car into gear. Stella withdrew from the window and stood back.

'Take care,' she said as I accelerated away.

Chapter Eighty-Seven

Lee

I didn't call in the morning because I knew Teri had her meeting with Peter Heron. I was nervous. He and Mike had been very tight-lipped and Chrissie, who clearly knew something I didn't, had been irritatingly discreet. Which was not like her. Normally she was very quick to share gossip, especially when it was bad news. So, when I telephoned yesterday afternoon and asked if I'd be needed, I took it as a good sign that she had nothing untoward to pass on. But, still I didn't feel comfortable. Turned out I was right to fear the worst. Later in the morning, I got a call from Stella Lastings. She was very distressed and shocked too. Like me, she'd known trouble was brewing, but neither of us anticipated such a swift and brutal outcome.

'There must be something we can do,' she said.

What? I wished I knew.

Finally, I managed to get her off the phone and immediately keyed Teri's number. No answer. I left a message and, to kill time while I waited for her to get back to me, went to the supermarket. Fliss and Charles and the family were supposed to be coming to dinner at the weekend, and I figured I might as well stock up.

I was loading the shopping into the boot of the car when my phone finally rang. Heart in mouth, I answered.

Chapter Eighty-Eight

Teri

I was probably driving too fast as that bloody camera on the A615 flashed again as I went past, but I didn't care. I just needed to get home. If I could get home before anything else happened I would be all right. As Dan said, I'd pull myself up and get back on with it. I just needed to think things through. Like what am I going to do for money? Will I get redundancy from the university? Probably won't get a reference. Besides which, do I want another academic job? Look where it's got me so far: nowhere.

I thought about Rochester lying in his big, black box file in the boot of my car – the lying libertine, the randy, old rake. Then it dawned on me. I could write a book about him; I'd done enough research, I'd got enough material. I would explore Rochester's libertine philosophy, one of non-permanence, the breakdown of life's norms, and the dedicating of oneself to the moment – no matter how debauched that moment might be. It would be the ultimate story of a lyric writer constantly poised between a longing for Eden and a knowledge of its impossibility, writing poems of fallen sexual activity that remind us not of love, but of the world we have lost. A Falling Friend I'd call it.

I raced home, gathered Rochester into my arms and slipped into the flat with a sense of overwhelming relief that, like Dan had predicted, I'd got myself together, had purpose again. I could hardly wait to start writing.

I switched my mobile back on. Three missed calls: one from my mother, who'd obviously surfaced long enough from her drunken reveries to digest the latest news from Dad; one from Charlie, same – although he'd have emerged from tending his goats; and one from Lee. She'd obviously heard about the great sacking and ejecting, no doubt from Frank or Stella – or from Peter Heron himself – so I listened to hers and ignored the other two.

'Oh, God. Teri. I'm so sorry. Why didn't you call me? Please ring me now.'

I rang. It took a few moments for her to answer, and when she did I could hear traffic noise and a sort of clanking in the background.

'I'm just at the supermarket, loading stuff into my car,' she said and added hastily, 'But I need to talk to you.'

'Well, let's talk now,' I said.

'Wouldn't you rather…?'

'No, I've got things to do tonight,' I said. 'Lots to digest. It's been quite a day.'

I gave her a potted, breathless version of my meeting with Peter Heron, launched into the dramatic saga of Edward Pranks and the missing millions, and finished off with my Stella-inspired epiphany.

Then I told her about Dan having rushed round to see me yesterday and how supportive he'd been. I didn't tell her he'd met someone else, in fact, thinking about it, I questioned how serious he could be about this other woman, whoever she was. He'd been so nice to me, so understanding. I told Lee I was sure he still had strong feelings for me, and what did she think? Was there a chance he and I could get back together?

She hardly said a word, but I could hear rustling at the other end as she shifted the phone from ear to ear and packed bags into the boot of her car. 'Are you listening to me?'

'Yes, but Teri,' she said, 'there's something else you need to know.' Then what she said next was blurted out as though she'd been wanting to say this all along but been too nervous. 'I've just got engaged.'

'What?'

'Engaged. To be married.'

'Who to? Not that Christian chap? I thought that was all over.'

'No. Not Christian.'

'Who? For God's sake, Lee. Don't keep a poor girl in suspense.'

TO BE CONTINUED...

Acknowledgements

There are lots of people, miscellaneous friends and family, who have offered us support and encouragement during the long gestation of this book. It's impossible to name you all individually but we're grateful more than we can say.

We must, however, say a special thank you to a small number of people who kept us going. Particular thanks then to Geoff and Kevin, Meg, Annie and Dandy.

Thank you too to Jackie, Edie and Kay for their feedback on work in progress and Debbie for providing the inspiration for the frog fishing incident.

We're grateful too to the wonderful team at Lakewater Press, especially our editor Kate Foster, who has been a star, and to E.L. Wicker for her breathtaking cover design.

And, of course, thank you, Lord Rochester.

More from Lakewater Press

Poor Boy Road
James L. Weaver

As a mob enforcer, Jake Caldwell is in the dark business of breaking kneecaps and snapping bones. But each job sends him one step closer to turning into the man he swore he'd never become – his violent and abusive father. Leaving the mob is easier said than done. When his boss offers a bloody way out, Jake has no choice but to take it, even if it means confronting ghosts of old.

Arriving in his Lake of the Ozarks hometown, Jake has two things on his mind: kill ruthless drug lord Shane Langston and bury his dying father. What he doesn't expect is to fall in love all over again and team up with his best friend Bear, the Sheriff of Benton County, to take Langston down. Racing through the countryside searching for Langston, the web of murder, meth and kidnapping widens, all pointing toward a past Jake can't escape and a place he never wanted to return – Poor Boy Road.

In The Blood
R.L. Martinez

The Warrior

The war may have ended, but a new battle begins for disgraced prisoner-of-war, Ottilde Dominax. Dreams of her witchbreed twin are visions of death and betrayal. Driven by their grim
warning, she escapes her captors and races across nations to save her sister.

But she may arrive too late…

The Witch

Lady Oriabel Dominax has kept her healing magic secret while she cares for her family's struggling estate. But the arrival of a new lord hiding secrets of his own, the discovery of a dark and addictive magic and threats from a cruel blackmailer push her closer to disaster.

Through it all, the Witch's Tree calls…